# THE KINGMAKER'S DAUGHTER

Few historical figures provoke such passions and debates as Richard the Third – few have such charisma. Enigmatic, ambitious, ruthless, single-minded in his pursuit of power, Richard Plantagenet none the less remained loyal and true to those he loved.

Through the life and times of Anne, daughter to the great Warwick the Kingmaker, Richard is seen as the youngest of eight sons, his mother's favourite; as a determined lover and doting father. Anne was caught between the warring Houses of York and Lancaster, between the thorns of the white rose and the red. Wedded at sixteen to a Lancastrian Prince of Wales; rescued by Richard from the Duke of Clarence's kitchens, she subsequently became Queen of England – and mother to a Yorkist Prince of Wales.

A satisfying novel, *The Kingmaker's Daughter* asks a lot of questions and gives as many answers. Meticulously researched, its characterizations are brilliantly drawn and wholly convincing.

PHILIPPA WIAT

# *The Kingmaker's Daughter*

ROBERT HALE · LONDON

ISBN 0 7090 3746 5

Robert Hale Limited
Clerkenwell House
Clerkenwell Green
London EC1R 0HT

Photoset in North Wales by
Derek Doyle & Associates, Mold, Clwyd.
Printed in Great Britain by
St Edmundsbury Press Ltd, Bury St Edmunds, Suffolk.
Bound by WBC Bookbinders Limited.

# Contents

# THE HOUSES OF YORK AND LANCASTER

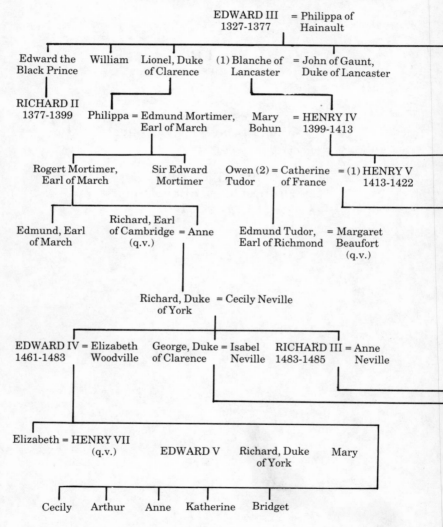

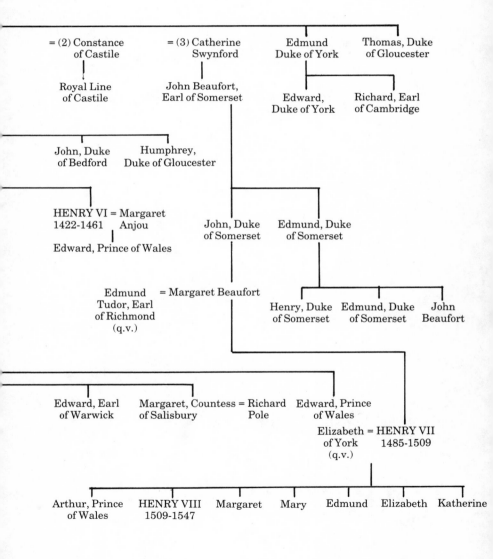

To Paul Turpin, my grandson

# PART ONE

*Anne, Princess of Wales*

# One

It was love at first sight. It had all begun, the chroniclers insisted, when the lady Anne had been presented to the prince in Paris.

Certainly Edward Prince of Wales, renowned as one of the most accomplished young princes in Europe, had afterwards made no secret of the fact that he was enamoured of the lady Anne Neville.

Not a word had been exchanged between the couple at that introduction, save the customary 'my lord,' 'my lady,' as each had made a formal obeisance to the other within the thronging court.

The gallant springing young Plantagenet, as some called him, was handsome, well-liked and of fine presence. Anne, though considered less beautiful than her sister Isabel, had delicate features, large dreamy blue eyes and a wealth of long fair hair. These attributes, enhanced by a gentle and pleasing manner, held much appeal.

But Anne's eyes as they met those of the prince had no longer looked dreamy – they shone with such brilliance as suggested that the sun had of a sudden taken over the moon.

The glance the couple exchanged was brief – but infinitely haunting – for each in that magical moment had given their heart to the other. Nothing, neither distance nor adversity – nor even death itself – could truly separate them then. Each possessed the heart of the other for all eternity.

It was a year before they met again; an eventful year for Edward, only son of Henry the Sixth, King of England, as well as for Anne, daughter of Richard Neville, Earl of Warwick – he who was dubbed The Kingmaker –a year in which each cherished a secret, dreamed dreams and yearned for another sight of the beloved.

At the end of that year, love found its own reward. The bud blossomed, basked in a season's flowering and glory, came to fruition and then fell ...

The summer idyll was over. The long winter followed; that bleak winter that looks not to the spring and renewal.

Love alone survived.

# Two

The young couple met again in the following summer at Angers. The prince having gained the support of Louis King of France, his kinsman, the Countess of Warwick and her daughter were presented by Louis to Margaret Queen of England.

Fifteen years of age, Anne was great-great-granddaughter to John of Gaunt, the patriarchal stem of the royal line of Lancaster. She was thus distantly related to the prince – and rather less distantly related to his enemies of the House of York. Co-heiress with her sister to mighty possessions, their father having no other offspring, Anne's wealth and position made her a not unsuitable bride for the heir to the English throne.

Margaret, her son at her side, received mother and daughter graciously enough – yet there was a hauteur in her manner and a coldness in her gaze that was not lost on the seventeen-year-old prince her son. His mother, Edward was unhappily aware, regarded the Earl of Warwick as the author of the misfortunes that had beset herself and her lord and husband, King Henry.

'The Earl of Warwick,' she had been heard to say, 'has pierced my heart with wounds which can never be healed: they will bleed till the day of judgement when I shall appeal to the justice of God for vengeance against him. His pride and insolence first broke the peace of England, and stirred up those future wars which desolated the realm. Through him, I and the prince my son, have been attainted, proscribed and driven out to beg our bread in foreign lands. Alas, not only has this person injured me as a queen, but defamed my reputation as a woman by divers false and malicious slanders, as if I had been false to my royal lord and imposed a spurious prince on the people of England – which things I never could forgive.'

Edward waited with some trepidation therefore as Louis broached the subject of an alliance. None but Louis, his mother's kinsman, would have ventured such a proposal. Outwardly calm but inwardly agitated, his hopes of making Anne his bride hanging by a thread, Edward carefully denied himself so much as a glance at the subject of his devotion who was standing demurely beside her mother.

He heard as in a dream his advocate's voice. Fearful of the outcome, he stifled an urge to place his hands over his ears.

'It is a project of my own devising, dear lady,' Louis was saying, without batting a royal eyelid. 'Is not it eminently suitable that you should make your peace with the Earl of Warwick – affiancing your son to his daughter as an earnest of that peace? Would not such a match be advantageous in every respect?'

There was a long silence in the audience chamber. With the exception of Louis himself, all waited with some degree of tension for Margaret's reaction to the royal audacity. Edward held his breath – and wondered how Anne was reacting to the proposal.

'What!' exclaimed Margaret then – so suddenly that the Countess gave a start. 'Will Warwick indeed give his daughter to my son, whom he has ofttimes branded as the offspring of adultery or fraud!'

\* \* \*

Louis had never been one to take no for an answer – and had no intention of doing so from one who had more than once fled to him for protection from her royal husband's enemies.

Some days later therefore, he again broached the subject of her son's marriage – and again found himself on the receiving end of Margaret's wrath.

'I see neither honour nor profit in such an alliance –' she responded haughtily '– not for myself, nor for my son the prince.'

One week later, Louis again raised the matter – choosing a time when he judged his formidable kinswoman to be in a particularly amiable frame of mind. She seems pleased about something, Louis thought. Perchance she has recognized after all the advantages of such an alliance …

She received the proposal this time with an air of triumph.

'All praise to Your Grace for perseverance!' she said lightly. 'Yet still the answer is nay, sir.'

'Dear lady!' sighed Louis. 'I fear you know not what is best for you and yours. It grieves me deeply …'

But Margaret was handing him a letter.

'I would – and I should – find a more profitable party, and of more advantage, with the King of England,' she told him.

'The King of England, madam?' frowned Louis. 'What has the king your husband, being at present a prisoner in the Tower of London, to do with the matter?'

'I refer to King Edward.'

'The Yorkist usurper? *Par Dieu*, why speak you thus?' demanded Louis. 'Is not your captive lord the rightful King of England!'

'As many at this time would have it, nay,' Margaret said with a sigh. 'I but referred to Edward of York – King Edward the Fourth as some call him – and his eldest daughter, Elizabeth of York. The letter, as you will see, was sent to me out of England this last week, by the which is offered to my son my lady princess.'

'If that be your desire, madam, then far be it from Louis of France to seek to dissuade you,' Louis said in a resigned tone, convinced she would not seriously consider an alliance with her husband's enemy. 'Indeed, it might be wise to accept the offer.'

'Wise?' demanded Margaret, in the manner of one on the receiving end of a gross insult. 'Wise! Your Grace believes I shall accept?'

'I doubt not you will act as you deem best, madam,' shrugged Louis – as if the matter were of little concern one way or another.

'Then you would lend your support to such a …'

'Only give thought to it,' interposed Louis benignly, showing signs of a hasty departure. 'I doubt not that, with God's help, your decision will be the right one. Give thought to it, madam.'

# Three

Margaret of Anjou was a remarkable woman, one to whom life in recent years had been less than kind.

Born some forty years earlier, daughter to René King of Anjou, gifted and privileged, her misfortunes had begun when, at the age of fifteen, she had been married by proxy at Nancy to King Henry. Crowned at Westminster Abbey that same year, she had thereafter devoted her life to assisting her husband retain his crown.

Latterly, with the deposed Henry a prisoner in the Tower of London, Margaret and her son had sought refuge in France, where she had worked unceasingly for the restoration of the House of Lancaster. Having recently sent Jasper Tudor, Earl of Pembroke, to raise an insurrection in Wales, she planned to muster an army sufficient to return to England, release her husband from captivity and return him to the throne. But there were many complications, not least among them the arrival in France of her old enemy, the Earl of Warwick. A hero to the English people, Warwick had broken with Edward the Fourth after the new king's marriage with Elizabeth Woodville. Resentful of having to negotiate foreign alliances to suit the queen's acquisitive relatives, he had withdrawn from court, married his elder daughter to George Duke of Clarence, King Edward's brother, and accompanied by Clarence, retired to France.

Margaret's ambitions lay solely with her only child, the Prince of Wales. Despite her protestations to Louis, she was in truth deeply perturbed by the question of an alliance between the prince and the lady Anne. As she saw it, the proposed alliance had less to do with the marriage of her son to Warwick's daughter, than to a device for making peace with her old enemy – that was to say her deposed husband's old enemy.

She knew that Edward was said to be enamoured of the lady Anne, and her own brief meeting with Anne had shown her a maiden of grace and charm. She seems docile enough, said Margaret to herself, one who could be manipulated by a determined mother-in-law, yet it would be foolish to ignore the fact that she is, when all is said and done, daughter to the great Warwick, maker and breaker of kings. Warwick himself can on occasion be gracious and amiable – when he judges it as to his advantage.

Her son's happiness and well-being meant everything to Margaret. Whilst ostensibly she had fought tirelessly for the restoration of her husband, in fact it had all been for her son's sake – that he might one day take his rightful place in the succession.

From the time of his birth, eight long years after her marriage, Edward had been the mainspring of Margaret's existence. Now, at seventeen, he was personable and chivalrous – a youth without blemish, as many said – one born, reared and ready for kingship.

Seated alone in her solar following her interview with Louis, Margaret's thoughts winged back to the months that had preceded her son's birth. She tried always to keep the past firmly in its place, banishing the painful memories from her mind. But this time they would not be banished.

The past was, after all, the cause of her sitting there alone, dispirited and uncertain, a woman born to high estate, gifted and handsome – one much sought-after in her youth, but whom love, true love and all it implied, had none the less passed by.

Henry, her lord and husband, was a great Christian but a weak king. Proclaimed at Westminster at the age of nine months, he had fulfilled the adage, *Woe to that nation whose prince is a child*! As a monarch, he showed mercy where he should have shown ruthlessness, forgiveness where he should have sought vengeance, humility where he should have displayed pride in his sovereignty. He possessed many virtues: he was humane, temperate, abhorred cruelty and injustice.

Chaste to a degree, Henry's lack of interest in the

pleasures of the flesh had prevented his siring a brood of lusty sons which might well have saved his throne – and spared his subjects the ravages of thirty years of civil war.

Margaret sighed – as she always did at that point in her reverie. How right is the saying, she thought, *Many are fit for good subjects but very few for good kings*! A princess of Anjou, her marriage to the King of England had seemed eminently suitable. Renowned even then for his goodness and piety, such attributes allied to a fine physique, youth and good looks, had merely enhanced the romantic dreams of the fifteen-year-old Margaret.

Meeting her new husband for the first time at her coronation, enchanted by his handsome appearance and gentle courtesy, she had fallen in love with him. She had told herself then that she was the luckiest maiden in the world – and a maiden she was to remain for a long time!

For over eight years the marriage had remained unconsummated. Frustrated and unhappy, aware that her lord's subjects blamed her for failing to produce an heir, she had prayed over and over again that she would somehow become fruitful.

Then had come that night, eagerly awaited and yet so shocking in the event, when the marriage had at last been completed. Even now, some eighteen years after, Margaret's heart pounded and her limbs trembled as she recalled the horror of that night.

Accustomed to the ascetic man who had occasionally for appearance's sake, shared her bed in the early days of their marriage, only to fall immediately into a deep slumber, she had been totally unprepared for that assault upon her person.

She had awakened to find herself struggling in the clutches of a powerful monster – some night creature, she had imagined, which had invaded her darkened chamber. Struggling? Shocked by the onslaught, she had indeed struggled. But then, realizing the truth, that her assailant was none other than her chaste and pious husband, she had submitted.

It was as if the pent-up emotions of a lifetime had been released in Henry that night. Despite the mixture of shock and pain that beset her then – even a modicum of pleasure, as she was afterwards to realize, for she herself was a woman of passion – she had known a sense of triumph.

Again and again he had taken her, without caress or endearment – or a word exchanged between them. Telling herself ruefully that this must be the answer to her prayers, recognizing the urgency of those moments if she were to conceive a child, Margaret had given herself up to his lust.

When at last he had climbed from the bed, still without a word, he had made his way unsteadily from the chamber.

On the day following, Henry's violence had found a new impetus. Turned this time against himself, it became necessary that he be forcibly restrained.

It was the first appearance of the tragic illness which was to dog his remaining years, rendering him unfit for government whilst the bout lasted – and prompting his Yorkist relatives to make a bid for his crown. Henry's grandfather, Charles the Sixth of France, had been similarly afflicted with an inflammation of the brain aggravated by the pressures of statecraft. In Henry's case, the hereditary malady affected both mind and body, to the extent that at the onset the court physician had held out little hope of his retaining his life, let alone his reason.

Margaret thereafter was called upon to carry a double burden: the reins of government had fallen into her hands just as, for the first time, she found herself with child.

Edward had been born at Westminster Palace on the fifteenth day of the October following. Unable to consult the wishes of the infant's still-stricken sire, and seeing his arrival on St. Edward's day as auspicious, she had bestowed on him that name most favoured by the English people.

For the next eighteen months Henry's illness had continued and he had been confined night and day to his apartments. Then suddenly and for no apparent reason, he had recovered and become his normal kindly self.

He had regained his health and his senses. He had also, inexplicably as far as he was concerned, gained a son.

Margaret recalled only too well the day when her husband had first seen his son. New Year's Day it was, but

Henry, in full possession of his faculties, had none the less been sunk in melancholy.

The Duke of Buckingham, in accordance with the age-old custom, had taken the little prince in his arms and presented him to his father.

'Sire,' he said, 'pray grant me the honour of presenting to Your Grace your son the prince.'

If Henry heard the words, he had given no sign.

'Sire, I beseech you to give the prince your blessing,' persisted Buckingham, after a suitable interval.

His chin on his hands, Henry appeared lost in apathy.

'Sire, you were unwell, alas, at the time of the infant's birth,' pointed out Buckingham, breaching the uneasy silence. 'Is not he a lusty babe – a child to gladden any father's heart? I beg Your Grace to give him a father's blessing.'

But still there had been no response.

Margaret had been close to tears. It was something she had not envisaged. She had heard rumours, the dreadful slanders that her little Edward was not the king's child – but so wild and fanciful were they, that she had consoled herself with the thought that no right-thinking person would take them seriously.

The most prevalent stories suggested either that the child had been the fruit of an amorous liaison with her principal but generally unpopular minister, the Duke of Somerset, or that her own infant had been stillborn and replaced by that of a beggar-woman.

Both in England and France, it had long been the custom for the sovereign, on the birth of his first-born son, publicly to acknowledge the child's paternity by taking him in his arms and blessing him, before presenting him to his nobles. Margaret had therefore promised herself that as soon as Henry was restored to health, he would follow the custom and formally acknowledge the child to his subjects – thus quelling the rumours once and for all.

As Henry still made no move, Margaret's spirits had sunk. *He too has heard the lies,* she told herself – *and, in his melancholic state, believes what he has heard. But nay, it cannot be so. It is out of the question. Henry could be in no doubt of the truth – he of all people is able to refute the* slander and still those evil tongues!

She had taken the child from Buckingham then, and herself held him out for Henry's inspection.

'My lord King, look upon your son, I beseech you, and give him a father's blessing,' she pleaded.

Henry's gaze was stern – and unaccountably cold.

'My son, you say?' he asked. 'Why speak you so, my lady? Long years ago I took a vow of chastity and have known none carnally.'

Margaret had been aghast. An icy chill had pervaded her being – it was as if, unbeknown to herself, she had indeed committed the sin of which she stood accused. Is it possible? she asked herself ... Mary have pity! Could it be I was mistaken, that it was not my lord who took me in the darkness? If so, then who in God's name was it? Did some hellish demon invade first my chamber and then my body that night? Nay, nay, I must put such thoughts from me – I must be calm, resolute ...

'My lord, he is your son,' she had said quietly. 'Do not you recall the night of his conception – how, out of a sovereign's need to beget an heir, you took me many times? Surely, my dear lord ...'

He had silenced her with a gesture.

'Desist from such loose talk, madam!' he commanded her. 'Sully not mine ears with lies. We have known none carnally – nor ever will. Did not our blessed Lord remain always chaste!'

It was too much.

'Our Lord had no need to beget heirs to secure his kingdom, sire,' she had retorted.

Henry had looked at her for a few moments in silence, registering with obvious surprise her tears and her pallor.

'Margaret,' he had said gently then, 'we have known you always to be a loyal and faithful spouse as devoted to the cause of chastity as we ourself. If you conceived a child without our assistance, it cannot then be a sin – but a gift from God.'

'I fail to understand your meaning, my lord.'

'It is surely a child begotten of the Holy Ghost, madam.'

Merciful heavens! Margaret had thought. Some ghost it was took me that night! A ghost as weighty and virile as any crude soldier violating a virgin during the sacking of a town!

She had started to protest further, but to no purpose. Her protestations had fallen on deaf ears. For Henry had picked up a book, a small leather-bound volume of meditations, and started to read.

It seemed to her and the uneasy Buckingham then that Henry was no longer aware of their presence – and not so much as a glance had he given the prince.

Inevitably, the rumours that the infant was not Henry's child increased alarmingly after this distressing episode. Had not the king denied all knowledge of the child's begetting? his subjects asked themselves and each other. Was not Somerset over-attentive to the queen?

The rumours and the doubts had done nothing to improve Henry's standing with his nobles – or to strengthen allegiance to his son.

Thenceforth the prince had been all in all to Margaret. And when in the year following, rumour and doubt had abated sufficiently for the nine-month-old child to be created Prince of Wales, her pride and joy had been great. She had ridden the storm, she told herself, and could look to fair weather ahead!

The prince's life, and therefore her own, had been checkered indeed in the years that followed. When he was six, she had fled with him to the comparative safety of Harlech Castle, he having been disinherited by parliament. At eight, he had been present at the battle of St. Albans, when he had been knighted by his father. He was nine when his mother had been forced to flee with him, first to Scotland and then to Brittany and France. Ultimately, mother and son had taken refuge in Lorraine where their cause had been taken up by King Louis and the prince's grandfather, King René.

Now Louis and René were actively supporting the Earl of Warwick's proposed invasion of England – a project which, if successful, would restore the deposed Henry.

Edward was in his eighteenth year and it seemed to his mother that she had of a sudden grown old and cantakerous in the pursuit of a lost cause. For his sake, if ostensibly for Henry's, she had ridden interminable miles, leading Lancastrian supporters into battles that had gone this way and that – one time a victory for the Yorkists and the next for themselves. She had crossed the seas time and again in order to muster troops in her native Anjou and beg for money for her campaigns from the King of France.

Yet is the cause truly lost? she asked herself, gazing at the leaping flames in the hearth as if for inspiration. Edward is gallant and courageous – and has found favour with many. One day, like Henry the Fifth his grandfather, he will be a great king. The blood of doughty warriors runs in his veins – he is a Plantagenet through and through. Given the chance, he too will win renown.

Given the chance? Margaret was prey to misgiving. Courageous though Edward was, he was inexperienced in statecraft, and would therefore be easy prey to the fawning and flattering of time-serving rogues. He needed a man of experience, a warrior, one who could be relied upon to serve the prince's best interests; and powerful enough – even ruthless enough – to command his armies and teach him how best to attain his goal.

The Earl of Warwick was just such a man. As Richard Neville, he had been heir in right of his mother to the vast inheritance of the Earls of Salisbury. He had increased his wealth and status still further by marrying Ann, sister of the Beauchamp Earl of Warwick and sole heiress of that line. He had soon after been created Earl of Warwick in right of his lady. Above all he was a brilliant soldier and strategist. At once the most feared and admired man of his age, brave and heroic, he was regarded by the commonalty as England's uncrowned king.

Like it or not – and Margaret told herself she did not like it at all – for her son's sake, she needed Warwick. As was well known, Warwick doted on his two daughters, co-heirs to the Lancastrian fortune. As husband to one of those daughters, Edward would be Warwick's son-in-law – and the earl first and foremost looked after his own.

Margaret's antipathy to Warwick was well-founded. She held him responsible for, amongst other things, the calumny concerning her son's paternity. Having first played the traitor to Henry, she told herself, displeased

latterly by the usurper's marriage with Elizabeth Wood-
ville, Warwick married his elder daughter to the Duke of
Clarence, with a view to crowning Clarence in place of the
usurper and thereby making his daughter queen. But
Warwick has another daughter, and my son is Prince of
Wales ...

Margaret sighed again. What of Edward himself? she
wondered. I noticed his expression that day when the
Countess of Warwick and her daughter were presented to
me. His eyes lit up at the mere sight of the lady Anne.

She had heard it said that her son was deeply
enamoured of the maiden, she having been presented to
him in Paris. A passing interest, she had told herself at the
time – but registering his expression at that second
meeting, she had not been so sure. The lady Anne had met
his gaze, fleetingly but intimately – blushing most
becomingly before she lowered her gaze. 'Twas as if they
shared some joyous secret, she thought.

Her mother's heart was touched. She would take a
chance on Warwick. She would bury her pride, entrust
him with that she held most dear – the future of her son in
whom was vested the survival of the red-rose House of
Lancaster.

\* \* \*

It had taken Margaret fifteen days and the persuasions of
King René's emissaries to reach a decision.

On the day following, as if to commend her decision,
came the news that Louis's queen, Charlotte of Savoy, had
given birth to a son at Amboise; and that Edward had been
singled out to be godfather to the infant dauphin.

Margaret was delighted – not as much for the first
happening as the second. She and the French queen had
been ever at loggerheads, but the unlooked-for honour
indicated that Louis had high hopes of the prince's future.

Margaret, her mind already made up, responded
whole-heartedly. If it were agreeable to all parties, she told
Louis, the Prince of Wales would plight his troth to the
lady Anne Neville by proxy immediately after the baptism
of the dauphin.

Thus, an agreement having been drawn up between the parties in the interim, a brief betrothal ceremony took place at Amboise in the presence of the King of France – though in the absence of the Prince of Wales and his bride-to-be. The ceremony itself however was overshadowed by the solemn declarations which preceded it.

Warwick swore upon the Cross that without change he would always support King Henry, and serve him, the queen and prince as a true and faithful subject to a sovereign lord. Louis of France, together with his brother, the Duke of Guienne, clothed in crimson robes, swore to support to the utmost of their ability the Earl of Warwick in the quarrel of King Henry.

Then it was Margaret's turn. Her hesitation was momentary. Kneeling, she swore as Queen of England to treat the earl as true and faithful to King Henry and her son – and never to reproach him with past deeds.

# Four

It had been agreed between Margaret and the Earl of Warwick that, prior to the finalizing of the wedding arrangements, the bridal couple be permitted to discuss the matter alone.

'Alone?' had frowned Warwick when the suggestion was put to him. 'I am not sure, dear madam, that ...'

'By the Prince of Wales's express wish, my lord,' Margaret had interposed. 'He seeks to assure himself that the alliance is to the lady Anne's liking.'

Warwick would have liked to reply that his daughters did as they were bid and married in accordance with his wishes. He did not so do. His daughters were his pride and joy, his most dear children ... The lad is right – good for him, he said to himself. His heart is in the right place and far be it from me to wish it otherwise!

'To my daughter's liking, you say, madam?' He nodded. 'Yea – why not? But alone is a different matter.'

'Alone only in a manner of speaking. In the long gallery – what else are long galleries for, my lord?' Margaret had asked with a smile. 'There they could converse privately and get to know each other a little – the lady Anne's chaperon waiting out of earshot at the far end of the chamber?'

'Excellent, dear madam,' declared Warwick whole-heartedly. 'Excellent – could not have planned the manoeuvre better myself!'

\* \* \*

Thus Edward and Anne found themselves alone – almost alone, that is – for the first time. Each was determined to make the most of the precious half-hour allotted them – all the while aware of the undercurrent which suggested that, had they been really and truly alone, they would have made even better use of that highly-charged thirty minutes.

At first Anne seemed tongue-tied. She was beset by shyness – a sense of disbelief almost at finding herself alone with the young nobleman for whom she had long nursed a secret passion.

'It is nigh on a twelve-month since we met in Paris, my lady,' Edward reminded her. 'Ofttimes since then have you occupied my thoughts.'

'Indeed, my lord?'

'Alas that you cannot in truth say the same!' Edward's air of sorrow was carefully calculated. 'Alas, alas!'

'Oh, but I can …!' she said quickly. 'Ofttimes I have – ever so often in fact!'

'You would have me believe you did indeed give thought to our meeting? Nay, my lady, it is surely not so – but rather that out of your gentleness, you wish to spare my wounded pride.'

'Would I lie about such a matter?' she demanded. 'Always I speak the truth. I have naught to fear. How could it be otherwise – am not I the great Warwick's daughter!'

Edward smiled. Her nervousness had disappeared, it seemed. How enchanting she is! he thought. Simply and becomingly gowned in white silk, she wore a single row of pearls; while her fair hair, gracefully flowing, was drawn back from her forehead by a gold band.

'And you thought kindly of me?' he asked.

'Very kindly.' She blushed then, afraid she had given away too much. 'That is to say I – I suppose – well, yea, very kindly, as I said!'

'I am glad,' Edward said simply. 'Very glad.'

'I wished for many things, my lord – to see you, to speak with you, be always with you. I prayed for many things – even those of which a maiden may not speak!'

'Then the marriage will be to your liking, God be thanked!' said Edward. 'I had to know, you understand – I would not have agreed else. My parents, you see …' His expression clouded and she guessed he was thinking of his parents' unhappy marriage. 'I had resolved to wed only out of deep mutual regard. And that day in Paris, though we spoke scarcely at all and in the company of many, I knew that you were the bride for me.'

'The bridal is a mere four weeks hence – there is much to be done in a small space of time,' she reminded him. 'I said as much to papa. "My bridal gown, papa –" I said, "– what of my bridal gown?" "If you are willing to let a gown come betwixt you and him you love, you're no daughter of mine!" he said – and he laughed as only papa knows how.'

'He knew of our regard for each other even then?' asked Edward in surprise.

Anne dimpled. 'He knew. I know not how he knew – but papa knows everything.'

Edward suddenly looked serious. 'Alas there is a difficulty regarding our alliance. I wonder if the earl your father has spoken of it.'

'A difficulty, you say? Nay, papa has said naught of that, my lord.'

'Our marriage was promised for us following the dauphin's baptism at Amboise, as you surely know.'

'I was told of it, my lord – needless to say, I was not there.'

'I was there,' Edward told her quietly. 'I insisted on being present – if unofficially so. I remained there after the christening. Should a bond of such importance be forged without the presence of the chief parties?'

'It was a formal agreement only, my lord. Our really-and-truly bridal has yet to take place.' Anne smiled. 'I promise I shall be there then.'

'But that formal agreement could be important, my lady – to you and me.'

She nodded. 'Yea, papa told me how King Louis and his brother swore to support his endeavour in restoring the crown to King Henry and his heirs. That is certainly of importance to you and me, my lord.'

'And is that all the earl your father told you of the agreement, pray?'

'He also told me that, after the recovery of the kingdom, you would become regent of the realm of England – and that the Duke of Clarence, my brother-in-law, would have his own lands restored to him together with those of the usurper.'

'And what besides?' asked Edward soberly.

'That was all, my lord – methinks my brother-in-law should be well satisfied!'

There is that in her tone which suggests she has small liking for Clarence, Edward thought – and he her own sister's husband!

'I was asking just then, my lady, not of the duke's estates – but as to whether the earl your father had informed you of another matter.'

'Truth to tell, my lord, the question of possessions and to whom restored estates should be apportioned, concerns me little – papa doubtless decided therefore to leave it at that.'

'Then you are unaware of the next part of the agreement – the section which most concerns ourselves –' Edward had a shrewd suspicion that Warwick had deliberately withheld the information. '– whereby, were the political scene to change, our alliance would likely be annulled.'

'The political scene?' Anne sighed. 'I confess I am little concerned with politics, my lord. I recall how, at Warwick Castle as a child, papa then being guardian to Richard of Gloucester, it seemed to me that my Yorkist cousins had but two interests – the joust and politics!'

'My lady –' Edward's voice was low and caressing – and she watched him wonderingly. '– hearken to me, I pray you. The clause in the agreement which follows those you mentioned, concerns you and me personally.'

'Then I would hear it, my lord.'

Edward unrolled the parchment he had brought with him.

'This is a copy of the agreement,' he told her. 'I insisted on retaining a transcript. With your permission, my lady, I shall read the aforementioned item.'

'Pray continue, my lord.'

'*From that time forth,* it says – the time referred to being the successful recovery of the kingdom – *the daughter of the Earl of Warwick shall be put and remain in the hands and the keeping of the queen Margaret; but the said marriage not to be perfected till the Earl of Warwick had been with an army over into England, and recovered the realm in the most part thereof for King Henry.'*

As he finished reading, Edward rolled up the parchment and placed it on a nearby table before meeting Anne's gaze.

Her eyes were wide and met his unblinkingly – though the colour in her cheeks had deepened. She looked a little shocked, he thought – but whether from a natural delicacy or a sense of outrage there was no knowing.

Dismayed by that section of the agreement which, included without the knowledge and consent of the betrothed couple, could render them indefinitely committed to a marriage that was not a marriage, Edward had already expressed his resentment in no uncertain terms to his harassed mother.

'Then we should not be ...' Anne started to say. But then, uncertain how to express herself, she fell silent and gazed helplessly at Edward.

'We would be wed only contractually,' he told her practically. 'For as long as it takes to secure the king my father's kingdom – never maybe, if Fortune be unkind! – we would be man and wife in name only. Neither of us could wed another if we so desired, for a contract of marriage is lawfully binding and may not be set aside.'

'So that is how it is,' Anne said softly. 'You are telling me we could not company together maybe for years.'

Edward nodded. 'We could not, as you say, company together. In other words, our marriage will not be completed until it suits the political interests of our elders.'

'But that is monstrous!' cried Anne, her eyes shining with tears of anger – thereby revealing her own unpolitical interests. 'God have pity, it cannot be so! We must not let it be so.'

He took her hand and kissed it formally, and then – with a passing glance at her chaperon who seemed to be gazing tactfully out of a far window – he gently turned it over and implanted a warm lingering kiss on the palm.

She gave an almost imperceptible shiver at that, an involuntary sensual movement – but did not withdraw her hand.

'We shall not let it be so,' he assured her then, meeting her gaze. 'Have no fear – we shall thwart their design. It was needful, dear heart, to discover if we were of one mind ere I concocted a plan.'

'You have my assurance on that, my lord. Ever since our meeting in Paris, I have had my dreams – and they had naught to do with a marriage that was not a marriage, I promise you!'

'Then certes, lady, we know for truth what must be done. I shall devise a plan – a secret plan. I know not yet how our design may best be accomplished – but accomplished it shall be. After the bridal, hold yourself ready, I pray you, to act in accordance with the message I shall send you.'

'My lord, what if – if afterwards ...'

'If our secret were discovered, do you mean?' Edward smiled wickedly. 'By sweet St. George! It would be no more than they deserve. And what matter once the deed is accomplished? There is no remedy, 'tis commonly said, for a broken ...'

He paused significantly.

'Pray continue, my lord,' Anne prompted in a still, small voice.

'... for a completed marriage,' he said coolly. 'Our elders would have to make the best of it – just as shall we ourselves!'

# Five

At the beginning of August in the year 1470, there took place at Angers one of the most popular and romantic weddings seen by King René's court for many a long day.

The nuptial Mass was celebrated in the presence of Queen Margaret, King Louis, King René and his consort Jeanne de Laval, the Duke and Duchess of Clarence, the Earl and Countess of Warwick, and many members of the exiled Lancastrian court. Banquets, entertainments and much rejoicing followed.

Three days later, accompanied by Clarence and a large following, Warwick set out for England, leaving his countess, Queen Margaret and the newly-weds to enjoy René's liberal hospitality until such time as he was in a position to send for them.

Anne had enjoyed every moment of the wedding celebrations. She had been reminded of earlier days, of the all too brief visits to Warwick Court, her father's London mansion.

Much of her early childhood had been spent at her father's estates at Calais, well away from the bitter feuds which had racked England as the Houses of York and Lancaster, symbolized by the white rose and the red, had fought for supremacy.

But occasionally, when Warwick had judged a lull in the proceedings as of sufficient duration to permit a visit from his family, he had summoned them to London.

Warwick Court was renowned for its lavish, even ostentatious, hospitality. It was staffed by six hundred retainers, all in a livery of red jackets embroidered back and front with Warwick's bear and ragged staff emblems. Six oxen were roasted each day for breakfast – the uneaten beef being left for the tavern-keepers of the area, each of whom, sticking a long dagger into the meat, was permitted to carry away as much as his dagger would hold.

Those visits to Warwick Court had been to Anne the outstanding events of an idyllically happy childhood. She thought of England with affection and nostalgia, recalling a time when the sun had always shone, save for those equally delightful days when snow, crisp and sparkling, had lain thick upon the ground.

Now, she told herself, she must look to the future – those happy childhood days were of the past. The future would be just as idyllic. She was bride to the most handsome and chivalrous prince in Christendom and one day, if God were kind – and God had always been kind to Anne – she would be queen of England and her children would be princes and princesses ...

She had reached that point in her reverie, without realizing where it had been leading. Seated alone in her new apartments in Queen Margaret's household, dwelling on the past and appraising the future, she felt of a sudden a trifle forlorn, a stranger in unaccustomed surroundings.

She drew from her bodice the crumpled message that Edward had given her and read it to herself for the fourth time.

'Two nights hence, my lady, we shall be together,' it said. 'Sooner could well awaken suspicion, as some might be on guard for such an undertaking! When that hour arrives, we shall become truly man and wife – alas that two nights and days can seem as a lifetime! God bless you and keep you ever in his loving protection.
'From your own
'EDWARD'

He had managed to convey it to her just before they had parted following the nuptial repast. Bowing formally, he had presented to her a superb red rose – the emblem of his House.

'To my lady –' he said, '– my own perfect rose!'

She had taken the rose and thanked him most graciously – and as he bent to kiss her hand, she had caught his words.

'Look to the heart of the rose,' he had murmured – and that had been all. Had any of the guests overheard, it would not have mattered – the language of courtly love, they would have told themselves.

\* \* \*

Anne saw no more of her bridegroom during the next two days, and there were no more secret messages. She sought to fill the empty hours with needlework and in writing affectionate letters to her family – but all the while her mind was a-flutter with uncertainty.

When the second evening arrived, her agitation had grown. What time might she expect her new-wedded lord? she wondered. He will wait till he judges the coast clear, till I have dismissed my servants and the household has settled down for the night.

Will he arrive like a thief in the night? Will it seem like our bridal night, or a clandestine meeting between lovers? What if I wait and wait, even as I am doing now, and go on waiting till morning or slumber releases me from my vigil? Supposing something detains him – or his plan be discovered and comes to naught? What if I should hear not from him – and weeks pass and I am still here like a prisoner in Queen Margaret's house?

But of course I am not a prisoner. I may stroll in the gardens in the daytime whensoever I wish, invite members of my family to dine or sup with me – but always in the company of the chaperon appointed by Queen Margaret.

I am not a prisoner in the way that poor King Henry is a prisoner – yet it seems to me that I have to a large extent lost my freedom. And why? As bride to the Prince of Wales, I must be guarded and protected, as Queen Margaret told me, with a smile of course, when I came here with her after the wedding? Protected from whom? I wanted to ask her. From Yorkist supporters perchance? Or George of Clarence – my sister's lecherous spouse? From the usurper Edward himself – or any of the minions of the white rose?

I did not ask. Already I knew the answer. As Queen Margaret sees it, I need protection from none of those –

but from her own son, the Prince of Wales. How could that be? I have had plenty of time for meditating these past two days – and I know the answer to that also. As long as the marriage is incomplete, should papa for some reason fail to restore King Henry to his throne, I could be dispensed with. The marriage could be dissolved and Edward forced to wed another. Forced? By my faith, that word is hard to associate with my new-wedded lord!

Why did papa, who loves me and wants what is best for me, put his name to such an agreement? Simply because he could not envisage failure. He will lead an army to England, do battle and vanquish the Yorkists, and free King Henry – and in due course his daughter Anne will become queen of England. Dear papa – how greatly I love him! I doubt not it will be as he plans. It always is.

Something has detained my lord prince, she thought then. He will surely be here anon. He wished it as much as did I myself. Something has delayed him. Or prevented his coming here tonight at all? Nay, he would permit naught save fire, flood or earthquake to keep us apart tonight ...

Made drowsy by the heat from the fire, she almost fell asleep. She loosened her fur-trimmed robe and then, looking at the clock, saw with dismay that it was an hour past midnight.

Disappointment overcame her then. In a fit of pique, telling herself she had not really wanted to see her bridegroom that evening anyway, the sixteen-year-old bride flung off her robe, extinguished all but two of the candles and climbed into the lofty bed.

But perhaps, after all, she *had* wanted to see him – for tears welled from her eyes and fell upon the virginal white nightgown ...

She awoke with a start to find a tall figure standing beside the bed. At first, she was unable to recall where she was – she had been dreaming that she was in her chamber at Warwick Court far away across the sea in London. As to how long she had been asleep, she had no idea.

'Pray forgive me,' said her bridegroom. 'I was unavoidably detained. I was on the point of departure, when my lady mother came to my chamber. She wished to reveal the secret plan for the restoration of the king my

father. What could I say, my lady? *Maman*, my bride awaits
– my father's crown must wait a little longer"?'

Anne smiled at that. 'You are here now, my lord –
naught else matters.'

'I rehearsed what I would say to you.' His expression
was rueful. 'I practised an especially elegant obeisance,
had a nosegay prepared and hid it away in my closet – and
told myself we would sit by the fire at first, getting to know
each other.'

'But what happened to that especially elegant obeisance,
my lord?' dimpled Anne.

'It was intended for a wide awake maiden – not one
sleeping fast in her bed!'

'And the nosegay?'

Edward shrugged. 'Alas, 'twas abandoned along with
the rest! The fine words are forgotten, relegated to
wherever it is that forgotten words go – though I did go
back for the nosegay, creeping through unlit galleries like
a marauding Yorkist!'

'And?'

'It had withered, alas!'

Anne glanced at the hearth. 'No fine words, obeisance
or nosegay – and now not even a fire to sit by and get to
know each other, alas, alas!' she said, her eyes twinkling.

Edward sighed ostentatiously. 'Then there is no help for
it than to return whence I came …'

'Return? But …'

'… unless there is room for me in that fine bed.'

'The bed is spacious, my prince,' she said softly. 'And
your bride is willing.'

And then she was in his arms, her nightgown seeming of
a sudden reduced to the size of a cobweb and her
bridegroom's naked body close to hers.

'You are so beautiful,' he said, raining kisses on her. 'So
beautiful.'

'Beautiful? Some might say I was wicked!'

'Wicked? To lie with your lord and husband? To wait
two whole days to be bedded – and then round almost to
another day! We are married – or had you forgotten
already?'

'I do not *feel* married.'

'You will very soon, I promise you!'

'But what if ...?'

He kissed her passionately on the lips, cutting her short.

'But what if ...?' she started again.

'You said that before,' he interposed. 'And now is no time for words, fair lady.'

'All the same, my lord, what if ...?'

He took her then, stopping her words, holding her close, his caresses sending ripples of pleasure through her body. Held captive in his embrace, she was lost in wonder and sensation; conscious only of warmth and excitement, of her lover's heart beating against her breasts, and then an inexplicable throbbing in her belly ...

After he had withdrawn from her, he leaned on one elbow, looking down at her.

'I love you,' he said quietly. 'I love you very much.'

'And I you, my sweet prince,' she said dreamily.

She felt tired, drowsy, as if the lateness – or perhaps the earliness – of the hour had of a sudden caught up with her. She wanted to sleep and sleep. She wanted to wake later and find her lover still there by her side – as with any ordinary bridegroom.

'To answer your question –' he said coolly.

'What question was that, my lord?' she asked, not remembering.

The question was before – this was after. That was her former life, when she had been a maid: now she was a bride, a princess – and above all a wife, truly a wife.

'You asked me, "What if ..." '

'Oh, that question!' she said dismissively.

'It would be a love-child,' he told her. 'Edward Prince of Wales would have sired a love-child – would not that be romantic!'

'About the question,' she said, turning to meet his gaze. 'How did you know ...?'

# *Six*

The Earl of Warwick and his company landed at Dartmouth, where he raised his standard and proclaimed his intention of delivering King Henry from captivity.

As word of the proclamation spread through the countryside and the populace recalled the reign of the gentle Henry with approval and affection, Warwick and his supporters were given a rapturous reception. Nobles raised their banners in the Lancastrian cause to cries of, 'A Harry – a Harry! A Warwick – a Warwick!' and Warwick very soon found himself at the head of an army of sixty thousand men.

The great concourse set out for London, men continuing *en route* to flock to Warwick's standard in their thousands. As news spread of a huge army advancing to do battle with King Edward, the Yorkist usurper, realizing he was heavily outnumbered, embarked hurriedly for Holland.

Warwick thus found himself virtually in command of the realm, his enterprise having succeeded without a blow being struck. His followers were cock-a-hoop about the bloodless victory and marched in record time to Winchester, where Warwick held a meeting with the bishop of that city to plan his next move.

As a result, the Bishop of Winchester set out a few days later for the Tower of London, where he secured the release of King Henry.

Henry, it was discovered, was in poor shape, having been woefully neglected by his gaolers. Ill-clad and under-nourished, he was conducted secretly to Warwick Court where tailors were engaged to fit out the king in attire befitting his station.

Three days later, richly apparelled and looking every inch a king, Henry headed a procession through the streets of the city, Warwick and the Bishop of Winchester riding a few paces behind him. Scenes of rejoicing and jubilation greeted him all along the route and there could be no doubt where the hearts of the English people lay. Citizens lined the streets from the Tower to Westminster Palace, some kneeling by the roadway, calling out to Henry to bless them, to intercede with the Almighty for a cure for themselves or their families of some fatal disease or malady.

To the latter, Henry nodded benignly, making the Sign of the Cross over them and continuing on his way with a prayer on his lips. Now more than ever did he resemble a monk rather than a monarch: the commonalty loved him for it, while the nobility was alarmed by it. The years of privation, it seemed, had served to strengthen his asceticism and, despite the fine raiment so hastily made ready for him, still he was a saintly figure.

Warwick next despatched messengers to Angers, to convey the good tidings to those who were waiting anxiously for news: Margaret for her son's sake, the Prince of Wales for his father's sake, the Countess of Warwick – who had been prey to forebodings regarding her lord's safety – for her husband's sake, the Princess of Wales for her bridegroom's sake, and the Duchess of Clarence – who believed her father would crown her husband king of England, and herself queen – for her own sake.

None was disappointed when the news arrived. All rejoiced, looking to a rosy future, to an end of the Wars of the Roses as they were popularly called, and to new prosperity and lasting peace in the realm of England.

A *Te Deum* was sung in Paris in thanksgiving for King Henry's deliverance from his foes and a three-day festival was proclaimed by order of King Louis.

In the November, Margaret and her court in exile set out for Paris on the first stage of their journey to England. Margaret was attended by an impressive group of French nobles which Louis had appointed as his cousin's guard of honour. On reaching Paris, they were given a welcome no less enthusiastic than that which had greeted Henry's recent triumphal procession through the streets of London.

Margaret and her entourage remained in Paris whilst plans were made for the embarkation of the great company. By the February following, René's coffers having financed the purveyances for the voyage, all was ready. Everything had gone without a hitch and an air of enthusiasm and optimism pervaded the whole company.

Only the weather refused to play its part. The wind was not in their favour – and was to continue to defy them for six frustrating weeks. Some saw this as an ill-omen and begged Margaret to abandon the enterprise, but undaunted, she scornfully dismissed the portents as mere superstition.

So great was Margaret's determination to reach England and take her place at Henry's side, that three times she ignored the warnings of the seamen of Harfleur and put to sea with her fleet. Each time the ships were driven back, two sustaining serious damage and increasing the doubts of the more faint-hearted.

Sorcery, it was claimed, was responsible for the continuing opposition of the winds. Oblique references were made to Elizabeth Woodville, King Edward's queen, whose mother was believed to be a sorceress. Others saw it as a warning from God that no good would come of the venture – should she disregard the warning, they declared, great harm would befall her and hers.

Margaret paid no heed. She scoffed at the Jeremiahs – calling them faint-hearts, lily-livers. Only to her son did she reveal her apprehension.

'We cannot afford to dally,' she told him despairingly. 'I feel in my bones that it is now or never!'

'Never it will surely be, *maman* –' Edward said lightly, addressing her as he always did when they were alone. '– if you put to sea again now, with waves like precipices waiting to throw us into the clutches of Father Neptune!'

'You are like all the rest!' complained Margaret. 'Last year, this year, next year – it is all one to you!'

Edward made no reply. The accusation was too near the truth for comfort. Content in his marriage and his nocturnal encounters with his beloved lady, he was in no hurry to leave France for a possibly hostile England.

Whether in Paris, Angers, Rouen or Amboise, they were comfortably housed, shown every courtesy and kindness – and respected, honoured, even protected. In France, he and Anne could indulge their passion for each other – their delight in a relationship which, fed by the excitement of clandestinity, was sheer joy. Anne, as he was well aware, would have preferred the Paris idyll to continue for ever.

Edward Prince of Wales knew little of England – and even less of Wales. As with Anne and indeed all the English nobility, French was his first language; and English, French-accented, his second.

His father was all but a stranger to him. He knew him to be a man of peace – one who would rather parley or negotiate by peaceful means in the righting of wrongs or the settling of disputes. By no means a coward, having a sword-arm skilful enough to wreak havoc upon an opponent, Henry sought always the peaceful solution. A firm believer in the inherent goodness of Man – is not Man made in God's own image? he would ask mildly of those who questioned his views – Henry, as a king, had been a ready victim to the perils of his own philosophy.

Edward's mother was a force with which he must reckon. He loved her, he told himself firmly – of course he loved her. But she was strong-willed, dominating and indomitable, a woman whose powers of leadership enabled her to lead her husband's subjects in his stead.

Whilst Edward therefore was in no hurry to leave France, Margaret was all but consumed by impatience to reach England. She knew intuitively that a long delay would cost them dear. Warwick had restored Henry to his throne and, for the time being, the English people were on Henry's side.

Henry's side? To Margaret, Henry's side was in fact Edward's side – for in him, as Prince of Wales, lay the future. As soon as they reached England therefore and the House of Lancaster was once more firmly established, she would prevail upon Henry to abdicate in favour of his son.

His son? In the event, would Henry recognize Edward as his son? Margaret wondered. So unpredictable is he and so obdurate in his refusal to accept that Edward was of his begetting, I cannot be sure.

She had received a despatch from Warwick, informing her of the current situation. King Henry, he informed her, having been restored to his subjects in triumph, was on the crest of a wave of popularity.

The simile brought Margaret little joy. *The crest of a wave* suggested a passing triumph, a temporary ascendancy over others. Was Warwick then urging her to reach England with all speed, to lose no time in reinforcing and establishing more firmly Henry's triumph with the presence of herself and the Prince of Wales?

Warwick had further informed her that he had received intelligence that Edward of York was back in England. How, Margaret asked herself, could the usurper have crossed the seas when I and my entourage could not? She smiled to herself, as she gave thought to it – though the smile was a little crooked. There can be only one answer to that. Edward of York did not, as was supposed, flee from England – but simply had word passed that he had done so!

Warwick had made reference also to the Duke of Clarence – a veiled reference, as Margaret told herself with a frown. Clarence disapproved, it seemed, of Henry's restoration. But how could that be? she wondered. Henry's restoration was the sole purpose of the enterprise. The matter is not plain, Warwick goes on to say, but one must none the less be on one's guard!

Once in England, I shall be able to enquire into the matter of Clarence. As it is, I am helpless, frustrated – I must needs remain here, cooling my heels, whilst I yearn, heart, mind and body to be across the seas in England.

Do I trust Warwick? she asked herself, by no means for the first time. I must trust him, came the plain answer – whom else might I trust? He is an able commander, the greatest soldier this century perchance – and he is at present firm in his support of Henry. Yet I ask myself – flinching at the remembrance – whether this could be the same wretch who first escorted Henry to the Tower, calling to the populace as he did so, 'Treason, treason! Behold the traitor!'

For long years after that, I was Warwick's most bitter enemy – and in my heart, still I regard him as such! Was not he largely responsible for the rumours concerning my son's birth – a woman does not forget such a slander!

I shall be vigilant. This time I hold the trump card. Clarence, it is true, is husband to Warwick's elder daughter – but Warwick's other daughter is bride to the Prince of Wales! Either way, one of Warwick's daughters would be queen of England – but 'tis certain Warwick would not crown Clarence, the turncoat Yorkist, in preference to the Prince of Wales.

The lady Anne is a pretty child, thought Margaret – her expression softening as she gave thought to her daughter-in-law. Serene and biddable, she has a virginal quality that appeals greatly to the opposite sex – and not least methinks to my own dear boy! A little shy as yet, unsure of herself, is my lady Anne – I observe Edward watching her at times as if he has not quite made up his mind about her yet!

Ah me! That will be my first task when we reach the palace of Westminster and are reunited with my lord. The Prince and Princess of Wales must be given their own household and thereafter will become fully man and wife.

Once the marriage has been perfected – and there would then be no point in delaying it further – all will be well. Content in the knowledge that his daughter's son, his own grandson, would be the future king of England, Warwick could be relied upon to support the Lancastrian cause with all his might and main. But first, to get to England ...

# *Seven*

Margaret's well-armed fleet finally put to sea in the fourth week of March and, after a long and hazardous journey, sailed into Weymouth on Easter Saturday.

Before disembarking, Margaret sent a despatch to Warwick whom she understood then to be north of London, informing him of her arrival. It being the eve of Easter, she told him, she and her company would repair to Cerne Abbey, there to keep Easter and rest from the rigours of the journey.

King Edward meanwhile, having taken refuge in Friesland, had indeed managed to return to England, landing at Ravenspur on the fourteenth of March – whilst Margaret had been still waiting impatiently at Harfleur. He had been aided by the Duke of Burgundy who, discovering that Warwick was siding with the French against him, supplied him with ships, gold and a thousand German mercenaries.

From York, where his following was assured, he marched south, men flocking to the standard of the white rose in their thousands. By the time he reached Nottingham, having circumvented the Lancastrian force, he had a following of several thousand men and felt strong enough to resume the royal title.

Unopposed, he marched on towards London where he again took prisoner the unsuspecting Henry, who once more became a pawn in a game of which he had not begun to understand the rules. Then, he headed south until, at Barnet, the forces of Lancaster and York, similar in numbers, came face to face.

Warwick and Clarence had meanwhile advanced towards London, encamping near Barnet on the thirteenth of April – only to discover that the town was filled with Yorkist troops.

'Edward of York appears mighty confident!' remarked Warwick to Clarence. 'I sent men into the town to mingle with the enemy. They report the Yorkists in fine fettle and declaring openly that they are here to give battle.'

'Bravado, my lord,' chuckled Clarence. 'Bravado, no more. My brother knows his force is insufficient to vanquish us in the field – so he uses such tactics to intimidate us!'

Warwick watched him consideringly. He is lying, he thought. I'll eat my boots if he is not! Never trusted the fellow, though he be my son-in-law – so often has he changed his coat, that he looks uneasy, as if trying to recall which one he's wearing!

'Is that all?' he asked lightly. 'Intimidation, you say? Ah well, time will give us the truth of that, son-in-law – we shall just have to wait and see!'

\* \* \*

The Yorkist troops had indeed come thither to do battle. Their leader was acting on a promise he had received from Clarence that he would desert with his force to him at the auspicious moment.

That night, Richard of Gloucester made his way openly to Clarence's tent, where the brothers embraced and seemed in fine fettle.

'How many men have you?' coolly enquired Gloucester.

'Some six thousand,' came the laconic reply.

Gloucester looked disappointed. 'Edward is relying on rather more – ten thousand at least. I told him it was ludicrous to expect support from you – either he'll turn his coat again and unleash his troops upon you, I said, or he'll drop you like a burning coal and offer his services to the King of Scotland!'

George of Clarence looked hurt. 'You do me an injustice, brother,' he said petulantly.

'You are doing Warwick a greater injustice!'

'Warwick is a time-serving knave.'

'Fie, brother!' mocked Gloucester. 'You speak so of your

lady's father! Such disrespect!'

'Richard, if you have come here solely to make trouble ...'

'To make war,' corrected Gloucester. 'We are encamped out there for the purpose of making war – not trouble!'

'Well then, yea or nay – which is it to be?' demanded Clarence. 'Stop all this beating about the bush – do you want my twelve thousand men or do you not?'

Not by so much as the flicker of an eyelid did Gloucester give away his surprise – and relief. He knew Clarence as only a brother may know a brother; he knew him to be treacherous, acquisitive and self-centred. He had known from the first that Clarence had something up his sleeve – just as Warwick a few hours earlier had known he was lying! That he had an extra six thousand men up his sleeve was good to know, but ...

'We do indeed,' he said evenly. 'When will you deliver them?'

'That is twice as many, you know.'

'I said *when*, brother – not how many.'

Clarence shrugged. What was the use? Richard, his baby brother, had seen through his little game. Had refused to play. Richard was always like that, he thought. I hate Richard when he plays these silly games – tries to spoil people's fun! I hate Edward too – but Edward's old, seven years older than I, and keeps out of my way.

He sighed. 'Shall we leave now?' he asked meekly.

Gloucester nodded. 'At once. Edward is waiting to greet you. So you give the order and I shall mount up and await you outside. Edward will welcome you with open arms, brother – an extra six thousand men will make all the difference.'

'Twelve thousand,' said Clarence as he made to leave the tent.

'Methought you said six thousand.'

'I did, but ...'

'Well then –' said Gloucester impatiently. 'Let us not dally – time and battle wait for no man, as Edward would say!'

\* \* \*

Warwick received a despatch from Clarence that same

evening, apologizing for his conduct and saying that he had made his peace with Edward his brother ...

Infuriated by the message and the knowledge that his army had in a matter of hours been reduced by twelve thousand men – and without a blow being struck! – Warwick brusquely rejected it, handing it back to the messenger.

'By God's blood,' he said incisively, 'I would rather be myself than a false and perjured duke! I am determined not to put up my sword until I have either gained my point or lost my life!'

A fierce battle took place soon after. Warwick's troops, though inferior to the enemy in numbers, fought valiantly and desperately – unhappily aware that, if they were vanquished and taken prisoner, King Edward having now reaffirmed his sovereignty, would have them executed as rebels.

Convinced that, if taken, he too would be executed, Warwick was determined to conquer or die in the attempt. For a time the battle raged fiercely, neither side making any headway.

King Edward then threw in his reserves – Clarence's troops for the most part – and charged the enemy on the flank. Confusion arose as a thick fog suddenly descended on the field. The Earl of Oxford wheeled about to recover his station but due to a similarity of standards – Oxford's displaying a star with rays and King Edward's a sun with rays – the Lancastrians mistook the former for the latter, and fell upon Oxford's men.

In the ensuing confusion, as Lancastrian fought Lancastrian, King Edward resumed his charge ...

# Eight

Margaret was with the Prince and Princess of Wales when the news was brought to her at Cerne Abbey.

Waiting to hear from Warwick before deciding on her next move, she had caught the sounds of a fast-moving horse approaching the abbey gates and assumed it was carrying Warwick's eagerly awaited despatch ...

The messenger had ridden hard, changing horses every ten miles to maintain speed. Having left Barnet under cover of darkness on the Saturday night, he was weary to the point of exhaustion when he reached the abbey.

Impatient and brusque, he demanded immediate admittance to Queen Margaret and, his credentials approved by the guards at the gates, was conducted to her presence.

Strangely, it was Anne who realized first. She turned ashen pale as she registered the newcomer's expression – recognizing the exhausted, mud-spattered Lancastrian as one of her father's most trusted henchmen.

'Could it be so?' she murmured under her breath. 'Could it truly be so!'

But Margaret and her son were waiting for the messenger to speak. He had fallen on one knee and seemed to be having difficulty in getting his breath.

'You are from Barnet, I believe,' said Margaret, not understanding. 'You bring us news of the battle I dare say.'

'Madam, the earl my master is slain,' the man said hoarsely. 'He fell in battle, fighting to the last for the Lancastrian cause.'

Margaret said nothing – but stared at him without expression. Has not she heard me? he wondered. Does not she understand how it was, how it is – does it mean nothing to her that my master is dead!

'My lord Montagu, the earl's brother, endeavouring to support him at the last, was likewise slain,' he added for good measure. 'The Duke of Clarence ...'

Margaret heard no more. Before anyone could save her, she had fallen to the floor in a swoon – and for a moment Edward feared she was dead.

'Anne –' he said, as he went to his mother's aid. '– ring for servants, my lady.'

He tried to raise the insensible woman, rubbing her hands, alarmed by her pallor.

He turned to look for Anne. She was no longer there. But why, he wondered, if she has summoned my mother's ladies, is there no sound of hurrying footsteps? Why ...?

The messenger who, facing Anne, had caught her expression as, white to the lips, she had slipped away, got to his feet and, going to the open doorway, bellowed loudly for the waiting-women.

When Margaret recovered consciousness, she quickly regained her composure, insisting on questioning the messenger on every detail of the disastrous battle and the rapid turn of events which had led up to it.

'My lord, following his custom, sent his charger to the rear when the battle was fiercest and thereafter fought on foot beside his men,' the man told her, his emotion plain. 'From the first the weather was against us, fog in patches and a mud-soaked field. The battle was still in the balance when someone called "treachery!" Lord Oxford was seen riding off the field with his men and it was believed that all was lost – it was not so, but the alarm was raised and there was much panic. It was then that the enemy resumed its charge – to great effect. So great was the confusion, that beleaguered by fog and panic – indeed I suspect the cries of "treachery" were a ploy on the part of the enemy – many a Lancastrian was slain by his own men.'

'God in heaven!' said Margaret, white-lipped. 'Is treachery ever to be the watchword of our cause!'

'Our troops were utterly demoralized – their companions fled or slain and confusion everywhere.'

'And my lord of Warwick?' asked Margaret quietly.

'Indomitable as ever, madam. His standard bearer slain, he himself raised the banner of the Bear and Ragged Staff and called upon his men to follow. Few answered the call – but turned aside and fled the field. I took the standard from my lord and, his visor raised, he met my gaze and shook his head. My lord was in his forty-second year and looked weary unto death – he had been twice wounded. He had fought valiantly, you must understand that, madam, but even my lord of Warwick could not single-handedly withstand an army of some sixteen thousand men!'

The man shrugged – as if the rest would better remain untold.

'And then, sir?' prompted Margaret.

'My lord turned away, I following, and moved in the direction of his charger –' The messenger paused, gathering his composure. 'God have pity, it was too late! His armour impeding his progress over the muddy field, he was an easy target – I was knocked senseless in the charge that followed, coming to myself again later still gripping my lord's standard ...'

'Pray continue, sir,' urged Margaret quietly. 'Continue if you will.'

'My lord of Warwick was dead – his head and helm lying some distance from him. Near that place they call High Stone, it was.'

# Nine

'By sweet St. George, I had forgotten!' declared Edward when he went to Anne's apartment a while later. 'I had forgotten he was your father.'

Anne lay on her bed, not weeping but pale as death. She made no reply but gazed up unseeingly at the canopy high above the bed.

Disregarding the convention which required that, as they were man and wife only in name, Anne must always be chaperoned in his presence, Edward dismissed the waiting-women and seated himself on the bed.

'By God's mercy, only say you can forgive me –' he said abjectly. '– that you have forgiven me!'

'It matters not,' she said slowly. 'You and the queen your mother always saw him as a tyrant – latterly a benevolent tyrant perchance – but never was he a real person to you.'

'A real person?'

'To me, he was the dearest, kindest, most lovable person in the whole world.'

Resisting the urge to enquire where that left himself, Edward sought for words of comfort.

'I respected my lord Warwick greatly, my lady,' he said with truth. 'He was a valiant soldier, gallant and courageous, eminently respected ...'

'There is no need to recite an obituary! He was *my* father,' interposed Anne passionately. 'Cannot you understand that, my lord?'

Edward looked hurt.

'Pray forgive my clumsiness,' he said. 'I do understand, sweeting, really I do.'

'How could you understand?' she demanded. 'You have not just lost *your* father.'

'Not yet,' he said quietly. 'There is still time.'

'Papa was the most wonderful man in the whole world – and now he is dead and I shall never, ever, see him again.'

'Not in this life,' Edward agreed, and then, telling himself he was sounding like his mother – this reminding him of Anne's mother, he asked, 'Shall I send the countess your mother to you?'

'Mama?' She stared at him aghast. 'Merciful heavens, I had forgotten mama ...'

She stopped short, refusing to look at him.

'Then that evens the score,' Edward said with a brave attempt at a smile. 'I forgot about Warwick being your father, and you forgot about ...'

'There is no need to look so pleased about it,' Anne put in, tears filling her eyes. 'And 'tis not the same thing, not at all – papa is dead and mama is alive!'

'The queen my mother is with her now,' Edward told her, trying to change the subject just a little. 'My mother is distracted by Warwick's death.'

'She would be!' came the retort. 'She has lost her ally, after all. But what is losing an ally – compared with losing your father!'

'Hearken to me, sweeting. I love you dearly – you have had proof enough of that methinks.'

'Speak not so, I pray you. Maybe it was my permitting you to seduce me that brought down God's wrath upon my family and ...'

'Stop it! Stop this nonsense!'

She fell into a fit of weeping at that and flung her arms around him.

'You are all I have now!' she cried. 'All I have – oh Edward, never leave me. Tell me you will never leave me.'

'Foolish child! How I love you!' he said with a kiss. 'And why should I leave you – who are my love and whole life?'

'Edward, when I was lying here just now, before you came in, I recalled my childhood and how papa was always my hero – the pivot of my existence and mama's also, I doubt not. Alas, alas, poor dear mama, I thought to myself – how will she bear it if I cannot? And I recalled my childhood, my growing-up years.'

'You are not exactly an ancient even now!' remarked

Edward lightly – but his words seemingly fell on deaf ears.

'You see, Isabel and I as children spent much of our time in the company of King Edward and his family – both at Middleham and Fotheringhay,' Anne said. 'Our families were close-linked by ties of blood and loyalty.'

'Loyalty?' mused Edward, thinking of Clarence whose treachery had been the prime cause of the Lancastrian defeat – but Anne did not hear him.

'Richard of Gloucester is but two years older than I – indeed, as children we had a great fondness each for the other, as a brother and sister. George of Clarence could be charming enough when he chose, though a mite peevish at times – and I believe 'twas then that he and Isabel conceived a regard for each other. Alack-a-day that one of those companions of my childhood might have struck the fatal blow that slew my father! Always I shall ask myself if it was Clarence, my sister's husband – or Gloucester with whom I shared a childhood infatuation!'

'Dear heart, try not to dwell on it,' Edward urged her. 'It matters not whose hand struck the blow. War is war, and ofttimes in the heat of battle, one knows not whose face is behind that closed visor. Dwell not upon the past – give thought only to us and our love, to our future.'

'But what of the future?' she asked tearfully. 'What hope is there now that the king your father will regain his kingdom – and that you, my very dear, will one day wear the crown of England?'

'Does my wearing a crown mean so much to you?' he asked with sudden tenseness.

She shook her head. 'To myself, nay. But to you – and the queen your mother – it means everything.'

'Not everything,' he insisted. 'To my mother perchance – but not to myself. Certes, lady, I know for truth that to live and love, and be with you for ever and ever – that is everything!'

'Would that we could see an end to war, my sweet lord,' she sighed. 'Would that we could walk away, hand in hand, at this very moment – to Paris perchance, where first we set eyes on each other and were happy. What bliss to make our abode there, rear our children and live quietly away from the press of courts and intrigue.'

'Naught would please me better,' Edward said.

He spoke lightly – yet he knew in his innermost being that such a life would not long satisfy him. He was grandson to Henry the Fifth; great-great-grandson to John of Gaunt and great-great-great-grandson to Edward the Third and Queen Philippa. Thus there was that in his blood which would not allow him to rest content and leave others – lesser men than Henry the Fifth, John of Gaunt and Edward the Third – to make free with what was his by right. For his posterity's sake, he must find a means of overcoming his enemies and restoring the king his father to the throne. Then one day, if his father truly desired it and abdicated of his own free will, he would take his place …

His posterity's sake? He looked at Anne. They had been lovers now for some eight months. It was surely possible then …

'Love me, my lord,' she murmured, her eyes bright with tears. 'Take me in your arms and make me forget that papa is dead, that the friends of my childhood have become my enemies, that my sister whom I love is married to a traitor – and that very soon I must go to poor mama and comfort her and hide my tears, when it is I who need comfort.'

He drew her close and rained kisses on her.

'We have each other. Nothing else matters,' he told her tenderly.

'Not at this moment – but later perchance.'

'Later is like the morrow – later and the morrow never come. There is only now, and love and kisses – you and me till eternity.'

She sighed and lay still, as if giving thought to his last words.

Then on a sob she drew him closer, clutching him frenziedly to her – as if of a sudden she feared that even their love, their future, their life together, were in jeopardy.

'Hold me,' she breathed. 'Hold me close, closer – closer than that …'

# Ten

'You realize what this means, my son, do you not?' Margaret asked Edward. 'We must negotiate another alliance for you – one which will gain us a strong ally.'

Two days had elapsed since she had received the dread tidings of Warwick's defeat. Throughout those days she had mourned, not for the great man's demise, deserted by his troops on a battlefield – but for her own lost hopes.

Hot on the heels of the first messenger had come a second – he too had ridden from Barnet, but from the Yorkist encampment. The letter he brought Margaret purported to come from Clarence, and informed her that he had changed sides solely because he had seen the Lancastrian cause as hopeless – and believed he could better serve her future interests by placing himself in a position whereby he could act as an intermediary for peace. 'In the light of this crushing Lancastrian defeat, as one who yearns for an end to the conflict, I beseech you to follow my example,' he had finished obscurely.

Follow his example? Margaret had asked herself. Defect to the enemy – is that his meaning? Would he have me turn traitor to my lord and king? Should I marry my son to the daughter of ...?

It was at that point she had recognized Clarence's meaning. She recalled how, when King Louis had first raised the question of a marriage alliance between her son and Warwick's daughter, King Edward had likewise proposed an alliance – between her son and his elder daughter, Elizabeth of York. The latter alliance, as she had recognized at the time, would have rendered Edward and Elizabeth the future king and queen, and thus united the warring houses of York and Lancaster, bringing lasting peace to the realm. An alliance with her enemies, her husband's enemies, had been unthinkable at that time, but now ...

'Another alliance?' Edward was asking. 'With whom could we form an alliance now, madam, since the Earl of Warwick, my esteemed father-in-law, is dead?'

'Ah, but Warwick was not your father-in-law!' exclaimed Margaret, with the air of one discovering a strawberry in a dish of plums. 'Not really and truly, my son.'

'Really and truly enough for myself – and for my beloved lady,' Edward insisted, having realized where his mother's thoughts were leading. 'Warwick died in a noble cause – fighting, almost alone at the end, to retrieve my father's crown.'

'May he rest in peace!' said Margaret dutifully, crossing herself. 'But many good men and true fell that day – you could as well marry one of their daughters!'

Edward nodded. 'I could, as you suggest, commit bigamy – but what, madam my mother, would grandfather René and cousin Louis, not to mention the Duke of Somerset, do then?'

'Why refer you in such a context to Somerset?' demanded Margaret suspiciously, her cheeks flushing with anger. But was it anger? Edward asked himself. 'What pray has your marriage alliance to do with that gentleman?'

Could it be, she wondered, that my son himself has heard the slanders regarding his paternity? God forbid it be so!

'Naught,' said Edward firmly. 'It has naught to do with Somerset or anyone else – save ourselves.'

'Then you will abide by my decision?' It was a statement of fact rather than a question. 'What would you say to Elizabeth of York?'

Much as I love my son, Margaret thought, I find him most aggravating at times. Doubtless he is as eager for a new, more politically valuable, alliance as I – he is ambitious, determined, his mother's child through and through. But he is young, bless his heart, and likes to have his own way – or to be seen to have his own way.

'Very little, I dare say,' came the cryptic reply.

'She is Edward of York's eldest daughter – and enchantingly pretty by all accounts.'

'I am not sure that I find the prospect of being enchanted by a six-year-old particularly edifying!'

'A six-year-old, you say?' Margaret's eyebrows suggested surprise. 'Are you certain of that?'

'Nay.'

'There you are then, Edward – you are merely making difficulties!'

'She could well be only five.'

'Dear me! Dear me!' exclaimed Margaret, since her son had hit on the correct age this time. 'But children grow up – we all were children once, remember!'

It is curious, Edward thought, but I am quite unable to imagine *maman* as a child – still, I shall take her word for it!

'I suppose so,' he said non-committally.

'Childhood betrothals are by no means rare – as you surely know.'

'Rare for me.'

'Children grow up, my son – and from all accounts, the lady Elizabeth gives promise of great beauty.'

Edward sighed ostentatiously. 'Every princess is said to be beautiful, it seems to me – how refreshing it would be to find one not so labelled!'

'Somerset would favour such an alliance.'

'Then let Somerset marry her – he is your chief minister, after all! I would not stand in his way.'

'That, my son, as you well know, was not my meaning. As daughter to Edward of York …'

'The usurper,' put in Edward. 'My father's enemy.'

'Edward, my son, pray be reasonable. You would be marrying the daughter of …'

'*Maman*, hearken to me. I could not marry Edward of York's daughter, or anyone else's daughter for that matter – since I am lawfully wedded to the lady Anne.'

'Dear Edward!' Margaret's smile was patronizing. 'At such times as this, I observe a likeness to your royal father. Always he over-simplifies such matters – seeing them as white or black, right or wrong, good or evil. Life is not like that, alas – one must learn to compromise!'

'Then you, madam, must teach me how so to do,'

Edward said coldly. 'But I see not what that has to do with my marriage.'

'Your so-called marriage,' corrected Margaret.

'Madam my mother, the lady Anne is my life and my bride – she is my wife and spouse by the law of God and Man.'

'Alas, alas, that you are so unworldly-wise, my son!' declared Margaret. 'Hearken and I shall explain how it is. You were contracted to the lady Anne – but in accordance with an agreement betwixt Warwick and myself, an agreement witnessed by King Louis and King René, the marriage would be perfected only when Warwick's mission was accomplished and your father's kingship restored.'

'But Warwick's mission in that respect was accomplished, madam. The king my father's kingship was restored – or so I am told.' There was a bitterness in Edward's voice which was not lost on his doting mother. 'And this agreement regarding completion of the marriage was not of my making – neither my lady nor I gave our consent.'

'Edward, my son, you are being very childish.' Margaret was plainly exasperated. 'All that is in the past. Warwick is dead …'

'Alas, alas!' put in Edward infuriatingly, guessing what she had been about to say, and saying it for her.

She looked suspiciously at him and then continued. '… and therefore an alliance with his daughter has naught to offer you. Your both being of an age at that time to complete the marriage, God be thanked my advisers urged me to insist on a clause postponing completion.'

'Madam, I love the lady Anne with all my heart,' Edward told her.

Margaret sighed. 'You believe you do, no doubt. Anne is a pretty lass and, naturally enough in the circumstances, you have given thought to – er – bedding her. But you are a prince, indeed a very handsome prince, and there are lasses a-plenty for your pleasure, my son. You must put Anne of Warwick from your mind – she is not for you.'

'Madam, hearken to me,' said Edward incisively. 'The lady Anne is fully my wife. We companied together on the third night after the bridal.'

'But ...' Margaret's face turned white and then red. This was something she had not envisaged. Always Edward had been obedient to her will – and dedicated, she had believed, as much as she to the Lancastrian cause. He is still a boy, she had told herself, still a boy – one hopes, of course, that he does not too closely resemble his father in certain aspects! Now, in the light of this revelation, it was as if she had been talking to a stranger – a tall, handsome, defiant stranger. 'My son, is this true?'

'As God is my witness,' said Edward soberly, knowing a passing uneasiness at the thought of the Almighty's witnessing their love-making. 'So you see, madam ...'

'Well, no real harm has been done,' interposed Margaret, recovering her equilibrium and determined to make the best of a bad job. 'None but ourselves need know. The lady Anne is in no position to demur should the marriage contract be revoked.'

'Anne of Warwick is my wife –' insisted Edward. '– and my wife she will remain. We share a deep regard.'

'Edward, fair son, you are so gallant, so loyal. But you do not deceive me with such talk.' Margaret wagged an admonitory finger at him. 'You see it as a matter of principle – just as would your poor dear papa in like case! But I cannot permit you to waste yourself on a useless match – when a new alliance, as for instance with Elizabeth of York, would secure the crown for you.'

Alas, alas – and again alas! thought Edward. It seems to me that my mother is as unscrupulous as Clarence – and with less excuse I dare say. In Clarence's case it was an accident of birth – in my mother's it is a way of life! *Par Dieu*! Clarence merely changed his coat and returned whence he came – *maman* would have me change my coat *and* my wife, and marry the daughter of my royal father's enemy into the bargain!

'Madam, it grieves me that you would have me follow so dishonourable a path,' he said coldly. 'But you waste your breath. The fact is ...'

How beautiful my Edward is when he is angry! Margaret thought, watching his face more attentively than she was taking in his words. He is enamoured of Anne of Warwick, has bedded her – and wishes to do the right thing by her. He is, God be praised, a true prince amongst men!

'... the lady Anne is my wife – and is carrying my child.'

It was the word *child* that caught Margaret's attention.

'What was that you were saying, Edward?' she asked. 'I fear I am a little weary today. Ever since ...'

'The lady Anne is carrying my child,' Edward repeated succinctly.

'Saints preserve us! That is not possible.'

'Believe that if you will,' shrugged Edward nonchalantly. 'Now, with your permission, madam, my mother, I will away.'

'Since when have you known about the child?' demanded Margaret. 'Could the lady Anne be mistaken? Perchance 'tis a false alarm.'

'A false alarm?' Edward's raised eyebrows spoke volumes. 'Who, pray, is alarmed – certainly not myself nor my lady!'

'How many moon-times has your lady missed?'

Edward noted the 'your lady' with some satisfaction – it seems to me she is half-way to accepting the situation, he thought.

'Madam my mother,' he said, 'questions of so delicate a nature are for my lady to answer.'

'Then I shall go at once to her apartments and question her.'

'Only in my presence, *maman*.'

'You do not trust me?' asked Margaret in a hurt tone. 'Alas, my prince, that it should have come to this!'

'I want not my lady troubled needlessly – made over anxious at this time,' explained Edward. 'Forget not, I pray you, that she has recently suffered the loss of a beloved father.'

'Then she shall attend us here,' decided Margaret on a note of resignation. 'I shall then question her in your presence – since that be your desire, my son.'

# *Eleven*

Anne, her face pale with grief, entered the chamber that had been allotted to Margaret at the Benedictine abbey, and curtsied to her and Edward.

At once she sensed a tenseness in the atmosphere, and asked herself what further disaster was about to be revealed to her.

'You sent for me, madam,' she said to Margaret, avoiding the prince's gaze.

'Be seated, my lady.' Margaret's manner was gracious enough, although Anne registered a small edge to her voice. 'May the Holy Spirit have charge of you and bring you solace during these days of mourning! The earl your father's death is a sorrowful loss to all of us.'

Anne's eyes filled with tears and she glanced at Edward. My lord looks stern and remote, she thought – as if, after all, he is not mine.

'You are looking over-pale,' remarked Margaret. 'Are you in good health?'

'Thank you, my lady – I am well enough.'

'I am glad to hear it, Lady Anne –' Margaret glanced at Edward '– in view of the circumstances. The Prince of Wales has informed me of your interesting condition.'

The Prince of Wales? thought Anne. Usually in my company she refers to him as 'my son' or 'your lord husband.' Why the sudden formality – as if she wishes to tell me something and is preparing the ground!

'Of my condition?' There was the smallest of frowns on Anne's smooth brow. 'My grief – is that your meaning, my lady?'

Edward spoke next – and his voice certainly had an edge to it. It seemed to be trying to convey a message to her – or a warning maybe?

'I have informed madam my mother of the child, my lady,' he said plainly. 'Her Grace was referring to that in enquiring as to your health.'

Anne's heart gave a great leap and for a few moments, shock and grief having robbed her of sleep, she was beset by dizziness.

'The child?' she asked. What child? she thought. Whose child? My lord is speaking in riddles – and still I sense that he is seeking to convey a tacit message to me. 'Of what child do you speak, my lord?'

'Our child.'

'You mean …'

'I revealed our secret.'

'What secret is that, my lord?'

'I informed her Grace that our marriage was completed many moons since – and that, God willing, you are to bear me a child.'

At last Anne understood. So that is it! she thought. But why has Edward fabricated such a tale? He knows, as well as I, and regrets it as much as I, that I am not yet with child. So there is something amiss – something which has prompted Edward, the most truthful of men, to concoct this story. I must tread warily, watch my step …

'Our dearest wish,' she managed to say, though plainly flustered. 'You see, madam, we both desired a child above all – indeed, we thought of little else!'

'Of little else?' asked Margaret coldly. 'Dear me – dear, dear me!'

'Madam, my lady means …'

Margaret ignored her son.

'And what of the marriage, Lady Anne?' she asked, her voice hard. 'Did you give yourself to the Prince of Wales of your own free will?'

'Of my own free will, my lady –' Anne said quietly and then, resentful of a sudden of having to share their secret with another, on a plainly defiant note '– most freely and willingly, in fact.'

'And the child you carry was sired by the Prince of Wales?' asked Margaret.

Anne hesitated and looked at Edward.

'By the Prince of Wales,' she said, her cheeks flaming.

'Can you be certain of that, Lady Anne?' Margaret enquired.

Anne recoiled at the insult – the words, like a jug of cold water flung in the face, taking her breath away. The shock was the greater for being delivered by one who, though a trifle overbearing, had always shown her the courtesy due to her high rank.

It was in those moments that Anne recognized for the first time that her father really was dead – that, without his protection or that of another of high rank, she must endure such insults.

Another of high rank? she asked herself. But my lord is Prince of Wales and, as such, ranks second only to the sovereign. As my lord's wife ...

It was then that she came face to face with the truth. In the twenty-five seconds it had taken her to reach that point and Edward to control his fury sufficiently to address his mother, Anne saw that her marriage too was in jeopardy and it was of that Edward had been trying to warn her ...

'Be silent, madam!' She heard Edward address his mother and registered his white-hot fury. 'You go too far. None shall insult my lady and escape my wrath!'

'Edward, fair son ...' Margaret's smile was all bravado. 'Be at peace – remember you speak to her who bore you!'

Edward turned to Anne. 'Pray leave us, my lady. I shall be with you anon. I would speak with the queen my mother alone.'

As soon as Anne had curtsied and retired, Edward turned coldly to his mother.

'I doubt I could forgive such an insult,' he said icily. 'That you, who know so keenly the misery of being falsely accused of carrying a bastard, could lightly visit such misery upon another, appals me!'

'Edward, my son, believe me, I long since cast from my mind the slanders which surrounded your birth. I, Margaret, am a woman of steel – life and misfortune have forged me thus!'

'Then you are to be pitied – if you can no longer feel for the joys and griefs of others!'

'Only you matter to me, my prince.' There were

unaccustomed tears in Margaret's eyes. 'Not for your father, but for you, have I striven, battled, schemed, begged and connived, all these years. Now I see your marriage alliance with the House of York as the only means left of reaching our goal.'

'*Our* goal? Nay.' Edward's tone was brutal. '*Your* goal, madam my mother – not mine.'

'You are cruel, my son.'

'You were cruel, my mother – to her I love.'

'And have you no love for your mother – who bore you and has striven endlessly for you?' Tears were streaming unheeded down Margaret's face.

'I know not, madam,' Edward was making towards the door. 'I know not. Perchance when I have talked with my lady and comforted her, I could the better answer your question. Anne is all in all to me – never again try to come between us!'

# Twelve

'Edward – how could you!'

Her eyes red with weeping, Anne gazed reproachfully at him.

'Tell my mother an untruth, do you mean?' Edward asked lightly. 'In fact, it was quite easy – with a mite more practice, I could perfect the art!'

'It is no matter for levity, my lord.'

'I agree, my lady,' Edward said whole-heartedly. 'Had the king my father perfected the art, I wager he would be in different case today – truth and honesty, piety and plain-speaking are chiefly encumbrances to a sovereign, alas!'

'My lord, if I seemed to reproach you just then, it was because you failed to warn me of your intention.'

'My intention?'

'To tell the queen your mother everything.'

'Be assured, sweeting, that tell her everything I did not – most certainly not,' insisted Edward, seating himself beside her on the fireside couch. 'I did not tell her what a shameless hussy you are at times – how when we lie together, be it by candlelight or firelight ...'

Anne smiled suddenly, as if for a time sorrow had abated. 'And both of us naked as the day we were born. And I touch your lips, gently, just as I am touching them now. Alas, I wonder why!'

'Why you are touching my lips, do you mean?'

'Nay, my lord.' Anne's sigh suggested she thought he was being deliberately obtuse. 'Nay, why your mother is displeased about the child.'

'I expect she wanted to marry me off to someone else,' Edward said carelessly. 'To Edward of York's baby

66

daughter or his widowed mother perchance!'

'Now you are being silly, my lord!' She turned to look at him as if, despite her words, she would read the truth in his expression. 'You are being silly, are you not? She did not really and truly wish you to marry another?'

'Only when I told her about the child – and that, needless to say, was why I told her.'

'You are trying to confuse me,' she pouted. 'I believe none of it.'

'No more do I – so not another word. The subject is closed, beloved.'

'But when she learns I am not with child ...'

'You could be with child at this very moment – or would you give the lie to that? You led the queen my mother to believe you were.'

'My lord, it was you led her into such a belief – for some reason known only to yourself. How could I, not knowing his mind, contradict my lord?'

'How indeed!' nodded Edward complacently.

'When time passes and it becomes obvious ...'

'When it becomes obvious,' interposed Edward, 'then my mother will know you were telling the truth!'

'Obvious I am not with child, was my meaning.'

'But how do you know you are not?'

'As far as I know, I am not.'

'And how far is that, pray?'

'You are confusing me again, my lord – and, as you yourself said a while back, the subject is closed.'

'Good. There is, after all, some unfinished business to attend to!'

'Nay, my lord, not now – I am in mourning, remember!'

'Would you have mama discover her son is given to half-truths, my lady?'

'It has naught to do with me ...'

'It has everything to do with you.'

'Of course, if you insist on taking me against my will.'

'I most certainly do!'

' 'Twould be unseemly at such a time.'

'You sound like the queen my mother.'

'And you sound like the king your father!'

'What mean you?'

Looking up at him, Anne thought he looked displeased of a sudden.

'They say the king your father took her only the once. In the dark, it was, and ... ouch! That really hurt, Edward – you are a cruel beast! It really hurt.'

'Good. That was for casting aspersions upon my parentage! And now to remedy the omission of which we spoke.'

'Nay, my lord, not so soon after ...'

'The sooner the better.'

'But I am in mourning – and it *is* the middle of the afternoon ...'

'Morning or afternoon –' he put in, pretending to misunderstand '– there is still such a thing as duty, my lady.'

'But ...'

'I shall not leave here, dear heart, till I have had my wicked way with you!'

'Nay, nay, pray let me go – please Edward!'

'No need to say please, my love – it is always a pleasure to oblige you!'

'Stop – oh, do stop! Wait ...'

'When I have done with you, you may dress up in your finery and go to Her Grace with a clear conscience!'

'Only the once, they say it was, but he took her many times – in the dark, of course ...'

'Provocation will get you anywhere, 'tis said ...'

'I love you, my lord,' she said softly and he was surprised to see tears in her eyes. 'I love you – and want you. But with papa dead and my heart full of woe ...'

For a moment he hesitated, touched by her tears. But then he recalled the interview with his mother.

'And I love you, and want you,' he told her. 'But whilst my love cannot, alas, give your papa new life – by God's grace, it could give life to another.'

'Pray release me, my lord. As you know full well, it is not meet that we company together at this time of mourning.'

'Release you? Nay, fair lady – not till you've a babe under your girdle and we can look the queen my mother in the eye!'

'Let me go ...'

Anne was astonished by the effect those three small words had on him.

'Never in this life!' he said with passion.

# Thirteen

When the news was at last brought to Margaret that Henry, recaptured by King Edward prior to the battle of Barnet, had once again been incarcerated in the Tower of London, she fell into a deep melancholy.

Warwick was dead. Henry was a wretched prisoner. René, her father, had all but beggared himself to aid her enterprise. The Lancastrian cause was lost. They were without a leader. And, above all, her son cared more for a sixteen-year-old lass than the crown of England! All, as Margaret saw it then, was woe, misery and hopelessness. She betook herself to her bed, refusing to see anyone save one waiting-woman. Exhausted, she eventually fell into a deep, troubled sleep ...

When she awoke many hours later, it was to find Edward, an anxious contrite Edward, sitting by her bed.

'Woe is me,' were her first words, delivered in a weak voice quite unlike her usual brisk tones. 'Woe is me that I did not take the veil in my thirteenth year!'

'*Maman*, pray do not fret,' pleaded Edward. 'All is not lost. 'Tis no more than a setback.'

If Margaret heard him, she gave no sign.

'Woe is me —' she said again. '— that all my efforts for my poor dear lord have been to no avail! I fear that Our Lord has turned his face from me, since he has not blessed and aided my enterprise. I know not how that may be — I know only that I should rather die than live longer in this state of infelicity.'

'Madam, pray do not blame yourself for what has befallen — but rather those whose wickedness and treachery have brought my lord father to such a pass. What of Clarence, who played us false — and those wretches who deserted Warwick in the field and left him to the swords of the enemy! Cast blame where it is deserved – but never reproach yourself, who have laboured untiringly and for so long in my father's cause.'

'Alas that it was not wholly in his cause, my son!' Margaret lamented. 'It is your cause in truth that has exercised my mind these many years past. You are very dear to me – and of such gallant and princely bearing as would make a fine king.'

'*Maman*, methinks I am not worthy of such esteem.' Edward was a trifle shamefaced. 'I expressed myself in a disagreeable and unmannerly fashion, and for that I beg forgiveness. In regard to my marriage, if it would please you and revive your spirits, I would reconsider the ...'

'Nay, Edward, say no more,' interposed Margaret, patting his hand caressingly. 'Since the lady Anne is to bear you a child, the marriage must now be deemed a true and complete marriage. There is no more to be said.'

Edward hesitated, torn by conflicting loyalties.

'*Maman*, I have a confession to make,' he said at length – but he sounded troubled, Margaret noticed. 'That the marriage is true and complete, and has been so these eight months past, is certain, yet ...'

Margaret's gaze met his and held it for a moment. 'I know how it is, my son. I knew even that day. I have not lived so many years without having knowledge of such things. Time will remedy the matter, I doubt not.'

'*Maman*, can you find it in your heart to forgive me the deception? As God is my witness, I have never lied to you before.'

But this latest revelation had given Margaret fresh heart. God be thanked Edward does not take after his father! she thought. No waiting eight years for his bride – he saw what he wanted and took it, thus flouting the will of two monarchs and the most powerful nobleman in England ...

She clasped Edward's hand and this time her voice was stronger. 'You are forgiven, my prince,' she said. 'A thousand times over you are forgiven. Even the other day ...'

Her voice trembled and for a moment she looked away –

and when she spoke it was as if she had put the past, particularly the recent past, behind her and looked to a brighter future.

'We must look to our next move, my son – plan our final confrontation with the enemy, a victorious confrontation!' she said. 'But first, I must find a new resting-place – I fear that already word of my sojourn here will have reached the ears of our enemies.'

'Madam, fearing to remain here any longer, the Countess of Warwick accompanied by my lady Anne, departed in haste yesterday. She was bound for sanctuary at Beaulieu Abbey. She requested that, when sufficiently recovered, you join her there.'

'That I shall do, my son,' said Margaret. 'And without delay. By the morrow, I shall be strong enough to travel – though in a litter perchance – and shall make all haste, with yourself and all my company, fleeing through the New Forest to Beaulieu. Once there, in the great sanctuary, I shall register myself and all with me as privileged persons.'

# Fourteen

'As soon as we received information of Your Grace's whereabouts, we resolved at once to journey here to Beaulieu in a body and assure you of our continuing hope and support for the Lancastrian cause.'

The Duke of Somerset, accompanied by his brother, Sir John Beaufort, and a group of other Lancastrian nobles, had been admitted to the large but austere chamber, part of the sanctuary building, which Margaret shared with her ladies.

Edmund, fourth Duke of Somerset, was in fact brother to Henry, the third duke, who had been implicated in the scandal over the Prince of Wales's paternity. Edmund had succeeded to the dukedom following his brother's capture and execution by King Edward in the year following the prince's birth.

Sons of Edmund, second Duke of Somerset, who had been killed at the battle of St. Albans, the three brothers, Henry, Edmund and John, shared the same flamboyant temperament and an almost fanatical loyalty to the Lancastrian cause.

Idealistic and courageous, notorious for his fiery temper, outside his own admiring circle, Edmund of Somerset inevitably had many enemies – not all of them of Yorkist persuasion.

Standing before Margaret now, he gave the impression of a man triumphant in a victorious cause, rather than one cast down by defeat. The shining fanaticism in his dark eyes, his confident manner and speech, as well as the trust he inspired in his peers, revived Margaret's flagging spirits and put fresh heart into her.

'We are now without a strong leader, my lord,' she

reminded him. 'Since the death of Warwick, who is renowned and experienced enough to rally our people in sufficient numbers?'

'Madam,' said Somerset, 'we already have a good puissance in the field, and trust, with the encouragement of Your Grace's presence and that of the Prince of Wales, swiftly to draw all the northern and western counties to the banner of the red rose.'

'My lords,' said Margaret, addressing the company, 'I hold myself to blame in the most part for our defeat at Barnet, in that the winds for so long being contrary ere we sailed from France, I arrived too late with my company to rally overwhelming support for the cause.'

'Madam, such a situation could not again arise,' pointed out Somerset. 'There would be no treacherous seas betwixt us and the enemy – but solid English soil! Once you are recognized, and the Prince of Wales beside you, I doubt not England will rise as a man.'

'My chief concern now is for the Prince of Wales, on whom depends the future of the red rose,' replied Margaret. 'For his precious safety, my lord, I passionately beseech you to provide.'

'The prince shall be well guarded, madam – you may be assured on that. As our future sovereign, and the hope of every Lancastrian in the land, there will be no shortage of men to guard him!'

Margaret was silent for a moment as she gave thought to what had been said. Somerset was mighty persuasive but his fanatical devotion to the cause prompted him to rashness at times. An able warrior, loyal and trustworthy, he sometimes needed a restraining hand.

Is he right about the safety of my son? she wondered. The restoration of the Lancastrian monarchy depends solely on Edward. Henry, whether restored or deposed, is a broken reed, alas! Edward is his father's only child and, should he die without issue, the Lancastrian royal line would then be extinct. I have protected him thus far – and shall continue so to do till his future and the future of the Lancastrian dynasty is assured.

'My lords,' she said then, 'it is my considered opinion that no good will be done in the field at this time – it is too soon. Confusion has arisen, fanned by the sequence of events which first plucked the crown from the usurper and returned it to King Henry, only to again depose King Henry shortly after in favour of the usurper. To the commonalty, Yorkist or Lancastrian, it will all seem to have taken place in the blinking of an eyelid – indeed I would hazard a guess that the majority of ordinary English people would be unable to tell us at this moment whether Henry of Lancaster or Edward of York was their sovereign!'

'Madam, the commonalty has a short memory, as is well known – our defeat at Barnet will be forgotten once Your Grace and the Prince of Wales are seen raising your standards.'

'Barnet will soon be forgotten, you say, my lord?' Margaret shook her head. 'I fear you are over optimistic there. The loss of Warwick will have caused much despondency among our subjects. Warwick ever had the confidence and respect of the English people: to them he was not merely the Kingmaker – but to all intents and purposes the king. His death, I fear, has dealt our cause a mortal blow.'

'It could well be as your Grace says,' agreed John Beaufort. 'And it is for that reason we should not dally. It should be seen, and seen promptly, that our cause did not die with Warwick – that his death on the field of battle, though calamitous, was not death to our cause. We lost a battle – we have still to win the war!'

'My lords, your enterprise has my blessing – pray be assured of that,' said Margaret. 'However, for the safe-keeping of the Prince of Wales, on whom rest all our hopes, I deem it expedient for myself and the prince, and any who elect to share our fortunes, to return to France – there to tarry till it pleases God to show us better favour.'

Edward could remain silent no longer. Not yet eighteen, he had no voice in such debates and must leave it to his mother to speak for him. Am I, he asked himself, to stand here like a spare adjutant whilst my mother announces her intention of leading me back by her apron-strings to France! We have been a seven-night in England – shall we then slink back to France with our tails between our legs!

'Madam,' he said trenchantly, 'there can be no question of my returning with Your Grace to France. That you should return forthwith, I heartily endorse – but our enterprise, so long planned and so soon halted, must continue without more ado. This time, I shall ride at the head of the army, the standard of the Prince of Wales plain for all to see – and neither Your Grace nor any other, save the rightful king of this realm, shall say me nay!'

'Bravo, young prince ...' Somerset started to say – but Margaret, frowning with displeasure, interposed.

'My son, you are but a stripling – a headstrong, inexperienced youth,' she said – and many a man there, misliking her delivery, knew a sudden partisanship for the prince. 'As rightful queen of this realm, I command your obedience in this.'

Edward was unabashed, it seemed.

'My allegiance, madam,' he said, 'is to the king my father. He alone has the right to command my obedience. Forgive me, I pray you – but my mind is made up.'

For several moments there was an awkward and pregnant silence. Overbearing as Margaret was, every one of the assembled nobles knew that without her untiring efforts and indomitable will, the Lancastrian cause would long since have perished. They waited uneasily, their hearts and spirits with the defiant young prince; but their loyalty – albeit in some cases an unwilling loyalty – with the queen.

She nodded briefly – as if assent were a mere formality, an acknowledgement of defeat.

'It shall be as you say, my prince,' she said, and there were audible sighs of relief from the assembly. 'Youth will have its fling – regardless of commonsense and the advice and experience of its elders!'

Edward looked coldly at her, stifling a retort. It was Somerset who answered for him – he whose fiery temper was a byword.

'The matter then is settled,' he said belligerently. 'There is no occasion to waste more words. We of this deputation are determined to a man, while our lives shall last, still to keep war against the enemy.'

Margaret sighed. If only I were not so weary, she

thought – if only I felt as they do, could still muster energy for the fight! Warwick is dead, and strangely – since he ofttimes showed himself my enemy and I mistrusted him to the end – my hopes died with him! All of them are against me, she thought. At times like this, it seems to me that they are no less my enemies than the Yorkists. Even Edward is looking at me now with disdain, as if …

'Well, be it so,' she said – and only Edward registered the small tremor in her voice. 'Be it so.'

# Fifteen

Having abandoned her intention of returning to France, Margaret left Beaulieu and sanctuary on the following day, and proceeded with the Prince of Wales and the Lancastrian nobles to Bath.

In one respect at least she had her way. During all her campaigns, she had kept secret her destination. This was to be no exception. Not even to Edward did she divulge the information. A quirk maybe of one who had learned to her cost that few in this world could in the final analysis be trusted, or feminine satisfaction at the sense of power the unshared knowledge gave her, a woman much put about by the intrigues and weaknesses of men: whatever the reason for Margaret's secrecy, it was to do her good service in the days that followed. Men of the western counties were flocking to her standard in their thousands and, whilst King Edward remained ignorant of her actual location, she was mustering a formidable army.

King Edward had advanced to Marlborough but, whilst his scouts were doing their utmost to discover the whereabouts of the Lancastrians, Margaret, her army still inferior in numbers to that of the enemy, took advantage of the opportunity to divert to Bristol to obtain much-needed supplies and reinforcements. Thence to Gloucester where, if all went according to plan, she would lead her troops across the River Severn and join up with Jasper Tudor's army in Wales.

All went well until the bridge was reached. By order of Richard of Gloucester, it had been strongly fortified and was well guarded — and no force, however large, could storm a narrow, fortified bridge to any purpose.

The officer detailed to guard the bridge was sent for

but, in reply to Somerset's demand that the way be opened, refused to give passage.

'Would you defy the queen of this realm by refusing her free passage in her own dominions?' demanded Margaret.

'My lady, I am in the service of Richard of Gloucester – he who is brother to Edward, king of this realm,' came the reply. 'My orders are that you and your followers be refused passage across the bridge.'

'Richard of Gloucester, you say – why, he is but a lad!' said Margaret scathingly. 'Out of our way, sirrah ...'

Edward and Anne had been riding only a few paces behind Margaret – and they sat their mounts now, watching and waiting as an altercation took place between the officer, Margaret and the now irate Somerset.

Edward sensed Anne's quickened interest as Richard of Gloucester was mentioned. He recalled her telling him, following her father's death, how as a child she and her sister had been much in the company of Richard of York's children. *Alack-a-day,* she had said, *that one of those companions of my childhood may have struck the fatal blow that slew my father! Always I shall ask myself if it was Clarence, my sister's husband – or Richard with whom I shared a childhood infatuation.* Was she thinking of that now? he wondered.

In fact, Anne had not quite reached that point in her train of thought. He is but a lad, mother-in-law says, as if Richard were a boy playing at soldiers! was what she was thinking. But Richard must be in his nineteenth summer – one year older than my own beloved lord. Dismissive as mother-in-law is, it seems to me, of anyone under the age of thirty – even I find it hard to accept that he who is responsible for halting the entire Lancastrian force, is none other than him with whom I shared many happy times at Fotheringhay. *Alack-a-day that one of those companions ...*

'That's as maybe,' the officer was saying doggedly. 'The king's brother the duke is, and lord of this fair city. My men are in his service and, if need be, will take up arms to defend the bridge in obedience to his command.'

A halt was called, giving the troops the opportunity for a much-needed rest, and Margaret conferred with her nobles. She decided on another ploy. Having a number of influential supporters in the town, she sent Somerset with a request that these intervene for her with the officer, offering him a substantial bribe to allow passage across the bridge to herself and her followers. But bribes, threats, nothing had any effect – the officer either would not or dared not acquiesce.

Thus had Margaret no choice than to turn aside and lead her supporters on to Tewkesbury and the next bridge, hoping against hope that King Edward was still ignorant of her actual position.

The twenty-four mile march that followed was gruelling in the extreme. The road consisted for the most part of uneven, stony tracks through woodland and, since Margaret was still relying on the element of surprise to secure her an advantage against the enemy, little time was taken for rest and refreshment. The army consisted mainly of foot soldiers; and although the horsemen went ahead, leaving the infantry to follow as best it could, the horses too were in need of rest by the time the bridge at Tewkesbury came into sight.

Despite this, Margaret knew a sense of urgency not to dally. She had received intelligence that King Edward, having now been informed by Richard of Gloucester of their movements, was encamped with his army one mile distant on the other side of the town. Exhausted and travel-sore, she was none the less determined to permit no respite until the bridge was crossed and she could join up with her allies in Wales.

Somerset took a different view.

'Madam, I am weary,' he said. 'What is more, my men are weary and the horses are weary! Therefore I for one mean to tarry here and take such fortune as God shall send.'

Margaret summoned the other nobles and put the matter to them. With few exceptions, one of them Somerset's brother, all shared her opinion that they should not dally until they had joined their allies. Somerset being still vociferous in his determination to make camp there and then, Margaret next summoned her most experienced captains and invited their opinions; each one supported her view, and said so – but still Somerset gave no heed.

'It is Friday, the third day of May,' he said belligerently, 'and for sixteen hours of this day, I and my men and horses have journeyed twenty-four miles! I shall pitch my tent in yonder field – and the rest of you shall do as you please, *par Dieu!*'

Margaret was in a quandary. Twice her plans had been overruled – firstly by the prince her son's refusal to return with her to France, and now by Somerset's determination to remain at least overnight at Tewkesbury. On that first occasion she had given in – for her son's sake. Now too she must give in – for expedience's sake. Was not Somerset her most powerful ally? she asked herself. Was not he her most able captain?

The grumbles and disapproving stares which greeted her decision suggested that some there did not share her high opinion of Somerset.

As the assembly left Margaret's pavilion, it was observed that already Somerset had pitched his tent in a nearby field and was there entrenched with his followers for the night.

# *Sixteen*

The Yorkist army, having cooled its heels for two days outside Tewkesbury whilst its scouts sought to discover the precise whereabouts of the enemy, was raring to go.

King Edward, no less eager to do battle – the decisive battle, as he told himself it would be – recognizing that the enemy would be weary from much marching, saw and seized the advantage. He led his troops into Tewkesbury and, whilst the Lancastrians were enjoying a much-needed rest, occupied the vantage points and prepared for battle next day.

The Lancastrians, alerted after a few hours' rest, quickly assembled in battle formation under cover of darkness, there to lie low until daybreak when the location and strength of the enemy waiting out there in the darkness could be accurately assessed.

During the hours that elapsed before the start of the battle, Margaret and her ladies, together with Anne, Lady Katherine Vaux and the Countess of Devonshire, were accommodated at a nearby priory. They settled down to wait, to pass as best they might, in prayer or silent thought, those nervous, introspective, closed-in hours before the dawn.

\* \* \*

Some two hours before dawn, Margaret sent for Edward who, along with all the Lancastrian nobles and their men, had pitched tent on the field with a view to snatching an hour or so's rest.

She spoke first of her hopes for the coming battle, of her belief that this would be the decisive conflict. But she seemed ill-at-ease, Edward noticed, as if her words were not entirely in accord with her thoughts.

'It is regrettable that we could not first join up with our Welsh allies,' she said. 'Thus would we have commanded a formidable force. But it was not to be, alas! God will surely be on our side this time – he will make plain his judgement by bringing us victory.'

'*Maman* –' Edward said, sacrificing formality to affection '– you look weary unto death! Is not it high time that you abandoned the field, henceforth leaving myself in right of the king my father to lead our supporters?'

'An hour or so's rest will work wonders for me, my son,' Margaret assured him. 'Have no fear – am not I a woman of steel, as I told you!'

In truth, he has the right of it! she thought. Edward and I are very close – he sees that which others do not. I am afflicted as much by spiritual frailty as bodily frailty – my spirit is weary, oh so weary, of the whole wretched business! Were it not for Edward, I would retire forthwith to my native Anjou and forbid those around me ever to speak in my hearing of England, its kings or wars. She gave a rare smile and Edward, watching her, was surprised by the sudden transformation. And I would banish all red and white roses throughout my father's kingdoms of Provence, Lorraine and Anjou ...

'*Maman*, why do you smile?'

'Why do I smile, you ask?' The smile broadened and of a sudden she looked younger, less formidable. 'Edward, fair son, God has seen fit to deprive me of many blessings – but he made up for it by giving me yourself. That is why I smile.'

'*Maman*, I would speak alone with my lady,' he said gravely, broaching the matter closest to his heart. 'I would ask her blessing, as well as yours, ere battle commences.'

'Were I to permit you to go to her chamber now, I should be abusing the laws of hospitality, my son – you see, a cell was vacated by one of the nuns for the lady Anne's use!' Margaret was no longer smiling. 'Gentlemen are rarely admitted to the nunnery.'

'But since I am here, madam ...'

'You are Prince of Wales – and my son,' Margaret

reminded him – a little sharply, he thought. 'My attendants wait by the door within earshot – such is the rule! If you wish it, the lady Anne shall attend us here.'

'Alone, *maman*,' Edward's manner brooked no refusal. 'Alone – if you please.'

Margaret hesitated. Ofttimes a man on the eve of battle lies with the damsel of his heart, be she wed or unwed – she not wishing to have his death on her conscience! she thought to herself. The thinking behind such is naught but supersitition and lechery – or, as I have heard said, a ploy of the opposition to diminish a fighting man's strength before the contest! All the same, were I to refuse Edward's request and he ...

'There is a small outhouse beyond the nuns' kitchen-garden,' she said. 'Go now and await your lady there – there is no moon but the stars will be sufficient, I dare say, to light your path whilst you yet remain invisible! I shall send your lady to you.'

# Seventeen

The outhouse, a small timber building used to store fruit, apples and pears from the convent garden, was clean and dry – and in total darkness when Edward arrived.

Anne arrived shortly afterwards and was carrying a lantern – thus bringing light as well as joy to the scene.

'Only ten minutes, Her Grace said,' she told him, after a joyous greeting. 'I had not slept a wink when her lady-in-waiting brought the message – so concerned was I as to your whereabouts and so filled with yearning for your presence.'

'The morrow methinks will see an end to all our ills,' Edward told her cheerfully as, having already made them a rustic seat by piling empty sacks on an ancient bench, he drew her down beside him. 'Thereafter the privations of past weeks will be at an end. It will be a feather bed and silken sheets for you, my lady – and the Wars of the Roses will be merely a tale of romance, glory and heroic deeds, with which to mislead our grandchildren!'

'God keep you from harm, my sweet lord!' said Anne fervently. 'By madam your mother's command, I am to remain here at the priory during the conflict – she will watch the course of the battle from beside her chariot on a small hill. I would I could be there with her!'

'I utterly forbid it,' he said. 'It is bad enough having a mother who, in her thirst for victory, resembles naught so much as a present-day Boadicea!'

'O Edward, I wish we could run away – go hand-in-hand from this place and never be separated again!'

Edward raised his eyebrows. 'And leave madam my mother and her supporters to win my future crown for me?' he demanded in a shocked tone.

Is he truly vexed with me for speaking thus? Anne wondered. I am never *quite* sure of Edward – I love him dearly, much much more than one should love anyone, save God! Yet at times such as these I suspect that war and all it entails – danger and heroism, defeat and triumph, death and glory – are in his blood, that proud Plantagenet blood which I in some measure share!

'Does the crown mean so much to you, my lord?' she asked plaintively.

'*You* mean much to me,' he said evasively, kissing her.

'More than your hopes of a crown?' she persisted.

'The crown would be mine in right of my father. To become king and rule this divided country of ours – bringing peace and plenty such as few living today have known – that whether I like it or not, is my God-given duty!'

'And do you like it?'

He hesitated, torn for an instant between what she wanted him to say – and what he saw of a sudden to be the truth.

'I like it,' he said quietly. 'Duty aside, to win the crown of England, I would fight to my last drop of blood!'

'Then what of us, my lord?' Anne asked tremulously. Why must he express himself so? she wondered – in the language of war, as if he is eager to be out there on the field dealing death and destruction with sword and battle-axe! 'What of us, pray?'

'Us?'

'You and me. Where do we, you and I, come into all this – this crown-seeking?'

'Are you asking me to equate the one with the other?' His voice was more than a little stern. 'I love you dearly, as I love and esteem no other – and I confess I can see no conflict between love and duty.'

'Yet your duty would prevent your coming away with me now – prevent us from escaping under cover of darkness.'

'Escaping? From what, my lady, would we be escaping?'

'From all this.'

'This?' he asked, indicating the out-house. 'It is somewhat primitive as a rendezvous, it must be admitted – but what matter as long as we can be together!'

She suspected he was being deliberately evasive – making

pretence of not understanding her.

'By this, my lord, I was referring to the campaign, all that riding through every kind of weather – why, only yesterday we covered twenty-four miles in sixteen hours!'

'As one believed to be with child, you could have been drawn in a litter – as well you know, sweeting!'

'Have you, my lord, ever travelled in a horse-drawn litter – bumped over stones and ruts till you are black and blue! Nay, horseback is far, far preferable!'

'Well, then …' he said vaguely. 'If campaigning is unacceptable to you, why did not you remain comfortably in France, my lady?'

'With you, my lord, I would have liked nothing better.'

'Would the earl your father, given the choice, have given up soldiering – to follow the pursuits of a retired nobleman!'

Reminded of her father, Anne burst into tears. But the tears were for herself also – for the knowledge that, as the Prince of Wales's lady, she must travel with fear and uncertainty till the end of her days. She had loved her father deeply: in the prime of life he had been slain in battle – just as had so many others she had known in her sixteen summers. Never would she know peace – always at the back of her mind would be the dread that one day, be it near or far, the sword of an enemy would deal her prince a death blow.

The question had been rhetorical and needed no answer. They both knew that.

'Be watchful on the morrow,' she said through her tears. 'In the mêlée, have every care, I pray you – for my sake.'

'What a strange child you are!' laughed Edward. 'Have every care, my lady says – would she then have me keep my feet dry, my hands clean, shy from the battle and run from the enemy?'

'I would that you could, my sweet lord – I would that you could!'

'Even if I could – I would not. Dear heart, that is what you fail to understand, alas – and you your father's daughter! *Par Dieu*, that ten minutes you spoke of is long past …'

'Nay, nay,' she interposed. 'It matters not – we have wasted time speaking of war, disagreeing a little …'

'My time is up, beloved.'

'You should not say that!' exclaimed Anne superstitiously. 'You should never speak thus – 'tis tempting fate!'

'My time is up,' repeated Edward, smiling wickedly and refusing to take her seriously. 'I must return to the encampment – already my squires will be waiting to put on my armour.'

'And then, my Lord?' she asked tremulously.

'By this time on the morrow, the battle will be well and truly over,' he told her lightly, holding her close. 'Victory will be ours. And I shall come to you as soon as I may, and laugh and mock your fears – and you will see then how foolish you have been!'

She shook her head. 'Not foolish, my prince – just loving.'

'Yea, foolish,' he insisted – but his voice was warm and loving none the less. 'And when I have teased you and made you angry – and I see those tiny sparks in your eyes that bid me beware – I shall carry you off to some secret arbour and give you such a rollicking as will make you beg for mercy!'

She smiled. 'Then I shall indeed look to the morrow – and to my prayers, beseeching God to keep you safe for me.'

'Amen to that.' He kissed her then and held her very close – and for a few moments she clung to him, willing him to stay. 'You are my delight and joy – the happiness you have given me these many months past is beyond my deserving.'

' 'Tis nine whole months since our bridal day –' she said dreamily. '– yet it will seem but a drop in the ocean in years to come.'

'In years to come indeed,' he said, and Anne registered the sudden coldness in his voice and wondered at it. 'Always you are, will be, mine – never forget it, my very dear.'

'Never could I forget –' she said softly, her eyes as they gazed up at him catching the light and shining with love – or could it be tears, Edward asked himself. '– never for a single moment, my sweet lord.'

'Now,' he said, 'I must say *adieu*. Nay, come not with me

– even a little way. Close your eyes and count slowly to ten – and then open your eyes and return at once to the convent. That way there will be no need to say farewell.'

She did as he said and closed her eyes – and he kissed her lips and she heard his retreating footsteps. She counted to eight – but then was assailed by an almost uncontrollable urge to see, touch, speak to him once more before he was out of reach.

'Wait!' she cried and opened her eyes.

But already he had gone. She listened, hoping to catch the sound of his footfalls – but they were lost in the sounds of the night, the sounds of men making ready for battle and the light of a new day.

She felt of a sudden bereft; as if he whom she loved had walked from her life, never to return …

Trembling uncontrollably, she picked up the lantern and made her way slowly back to the nunnery.

# *Eighteen*

Somerset assembled the army in three lines within the entrenchments; he commanding the advance guard, the Prince of Wales – under the direction of Lord Wenlock and the legendary warrior monk, the prior of St. John – commanding the van, and the Earl of Devonshire the rearward.

As soon as the battle lines were drawn up, Margaret, accompanied by the Prince of Wales, rode along the ranks inspecting the troops, offering encouragement and promising large rewards once victory was assured.

Day dawned bright and fair on that fateful fourth of May; but the battle that followed was clouded by murder and treachery.

Battle commenced at first full light, the Lancastrians getting off to a bad start. Richard of Gloucester led the Yorkist attack, and at once King Edward observed that Somerset had left openings in his front line through which he intended to sally. Well acquainted with the latter's fiery temper, he gave orders to Gloucester to draw Somerset from his entrenchments by retreating rapidly until he observed the duke and his line in open plain – and then to wheel and renew the charge, at which time he could rely on further support.

Gloucester carried out the manoeuvre with considerable success, ordering his men to halt and reform, after which he led them back to the charge. The Lancastrians fled back to their entrenchments in some confusion.

Somerset, observing at this time that Lord Wenlock had not moved to sustain the front line, was greatly incensed, believing that such lack of support had lost the Lancastrians the advantage.

Wenlock was in fact as easy-going as Somerset was fiery-tempered. Indeed, the Lancastrians had little cause to trust him, for he had changed sides more often even than Clarence and was notorious for double-dealing. Somerset had therefore resolved to keep a watchful eye on him.

With a furious oath, he spurred his horse and rode up to Wenlock.

'What do you here?' he demanded. 'Is the battle too hot for you – or are you waiting to fall in with the victor!'

'I decided to tarry a little, my lord,' Wenlock said evenly, stung by the other's taunt but refusing to show it. 'Methinks 'twill be a long contest – I shall therefore give my support wheresoever the need is greatest.'

'A likely tale!' scoffed Somerset. 'And what of the Prince of Wales who is under your protection – I see him not!'

'The prince was raring to go, and rode off to the charge, the prior of St. John and his henchmen with him!'

'And what if the mad monk too, in his zeal to lop Yorkist heads, should desert the prince?'

'Too? Desert the prince? How dare you, sir – you go too far!'

'Then where is the prince, for God's sake? By the living Christ, Wenlock ...'

Wenlock's smile was mocking, his voice laconic.

'Be a good lad, Somerset – get back to your game of soldiers!' he said.

Somerset raised his battle-axe in a manner seen by Wenlock and his men as threatening – no more.

'Traitor!'

The blow fell even as the accusation left Somerset's lips. It cleft Wenlock's skull and he fell, already dead, from his charger.

His fury still upon him, Somerset led his men into the mêlée and was soon to be found in the thick of the fighting.

King Edward had meanwhile issued a proclamation. 'Whosoever shall bring Edward, called prince, to Edward the King, shall receive one hundred pounds a year for life, and the prince's life be spared,' it said.

This gave fresh impetus to the conflict, for in the

furious charge that followed, Edward the prince became the prize for which every Yorkist fought.

Margaret, watching from a small incline, was alarmed at the course the battle was taking; and having learned of King Edward's proclamation, even more alarmed for the safety of her son. I am concerning myself needlessly, she told herself sternly – I am permitting mother-love to outweigh commonsense. Wenlock has charge of him, my son being a minor – and despite Somerset's poor opinion of that nobleman, he has ever shown himself a stalwart in the field ...

King Edward meanwhile, following with the second line, was completing the overthrow of the Lancastrian army, which was routed soon after with great slaughter.

The Earl of Devonshire and Sir John Beaufort were among the slain which numbered some three thousand. Somerset, the prior of St. John and more than twenty gentlemen, retired to the abbey church for sanctuary.

And the Prince of Wales? He too had been taken prisoner. Sir Richard Crofts, an impecunious knight, lured by gold and King Edward's proclamation, had gone in search of him. Finding the prince ill-supported, he had surrounded him with his men and led him off to the Yorkist encampment.

Thus was the prince brought before the victorious King Edward. The latter was immediately struck by the noble presence of the youth, by his handsome appearance and fair-haired blue-eyed Plantagenet features.

This one is no bastard! he thought. Despite the rumours and the tittle-tattling – this one is true Plantagenet, a chip off the old block if ever there was one! He was reminded then of his own son, his long-awaited heir, that other Edward who, God willing, would one day wear the English crown – this could well be his own Edward, his infant son, seventeen years hence! A pity, he thought, it has to be so – already Gloucester and Clarence know what's to be done. They stand there now, awaiting the signal! A pity indeed – but there is no room for two princes named Edward, two heirs to the throne. A king must look to his posterity, leave the way clear for those who come after ...

'How durst you so presumptuously enter our realms,

young sir, with banners displayed against us?' he demanded of the fettered youth.

The king and his brothers still wore their armour, but their helms had been removed.

Edward looked the older Edward boldly in the eye. So this is the enemy! he thought. At last I am face to face with the usurper, he who long coveted and seized my father's crown, who yet keeps his lawful sovereign captive in a miserable prison.

'My lord,' he said, 'I came here to recover the king my father's crown and mine own inheritance!'

There was a stir amongst the company at this defiant reply – and then silence as all waited to see how Edward the King would respond to the provocation.

Edward the King hesitated – but only for a moment.

Then, with a suddenness that was a measure of his fury, he struck the fettered prince in the face with his gauntlet.

It was at once apparent that the dastardly action had been a pre-arranged signal. For four of the company closed in on the prince.

Manacled and with blood streaming down the side of his face, the prince looked from one to another in shocked disbelief. Thomas Gray, Marquess of Dorset, son of Queen Elizabeth Woodville by her first marriage; Lord William Hastings, lord chamberlain and a devoted loyalist – these were unknown to him. He recognized Richard of Gloucester – but George of Clarence, Edward the King's other brother, was his lady's brother-in-law and well known to him.

Clarence? he thought. What in God's name is he doing here? He is husband to my lady's sister and swore fealty to the king my father when in France. Did not he sail to England with Warwick ...? Nay, Clarence cannot be my enemy. Even at this moment, he is smiling at me ...

'Clarence, my brother ...' he started to say.

He got no further.

'Death to the Lancastrian!' cried Clarence.

Three of the four seized him at that – and manhandled him from the royal tent. Then, unsheathing their daggers, they buried the blades in the prince's heart.

# *Nineteen*

Margaret had witnessed from her vantage point the alarming course of the battle and had registered the comparative isolation of her son.

Where in God's name is Wenlock? she asked herself. I can see the Prince of Wales's standard and the banner of St. John – but of Wenlock there is no sign. Edward is with his own henchmen, all good men and true, but insufficient to withstand a concerted Yorkist attempt to take him hostage.

'O holy Mother,' she prayed silently, 'thou who knowest the love of a mother for her only son, intercede for me that my son shall not be taken from me. Let him be spared, I beseech you – yea, even in the midst of his enemies!'

She saw a group of Yorkist horsemen approaching the prince then and the lively skirmish that ensued. Lancastrian knights were stricken from their chargers, some to lie still, others to struggle to their feet and grapple with the enemy.

The Lancastrians surrounding the prince were hopelessly outnumbered. They fought skilfully and heroically – but were overtaken by the uneven odds. Even as she watched, four Yorkist knights closed in around the prince, hemming him in, keeping his battered henchmen at bay. She identified one of the four from his banner and saw him point with his mailed fist in the direction of the Yorkist encampment ...

She saw the Yorkist horsemen turn to look at her as they led the prince from the field. Outlined against the sky, she was an impressive, formidable figure – in truth she was a woman, a lonely woman, with a terrible dread in her heart.

She knew even then. She had heard not a word that was

spoken, not a command that was given, and could identify none save by standard or banner – yet she knew with a mother's instinct that her son, the pivot of her existence, was in dire peril.

It was over. All was lost. The battle had gone against them and the Prince of Wales, for some inexplicable reason, had been ill-supported on the field and taken prisoner.

For the time being, she must ignore the pain in her heart – a pain that defied consciousness. There was a task to be done, she told herself, and done there and then.

Drawing her sword, her richly ornamented queen's sword, she held it aloft.

'Take me to the field!' she ordered her charioteer. 'The day has gone against us and I would take my place there amongst the slain.'

'Madam,' said the charioteer, 'should aught happen to Your Grace, the Lancastrian cause would be abandoned, lost for ever. I beg you ...'

'Where then is the prince my son?' she asked, blinded by tears. The pain now was becoming too much to be borne – she wanted an end to it. 'The prince my son? Where in mercy's name is he hiding?'

'My lord Somerset is riding fast in this direction, madam.' There was relief in the charioteer's voice. 'I doubt not he brings word as to the prince's whereabouts.'

'I want none of Somerset's words!' exclaimed Margaret, beside herself with anguish. 'Sirrah, take me at once to ...'

'Madam, I bear tidings,' cried Somerset, leaping from his charger despite his armour and making towards her, his visor raised. 'Grievous tidings, alas, alas!'

'Then it is so,' Margaret said softly as to herself. 'It is as I feared.'

'How shall I tell Your Grace ...?' Somerset appeared uncharacteristically lost for words. 'How shall I ...'

He was given a respite.

So suddenly that none was prepared, Margaret lost consciousness and fell heavily, striking her head a resounding blow against the side of the chariot.

Her attendants, hastening to her aid, made her as comfortable as possible and then bade the charioteer convey her, themselves following on horseback, to the priory where Anne, with two other noblewomen, had remained throughout the calamitous day.

\* \* \*

Having hitherto remained in ignorance as to the progress of the battle, Anne and her companions watched in alarm as the still-unconscious Margaret was carried into the nunnery by her devoted attendants and put to bed.

They exchanged glances, she and Lady Katherine Vaux and the other Anne, Countess of Devonshire – and each thought she knew what the other was thinking. The day has gone badly for the Lancastrians, they were telling themselves. The red rose has been defeated yet again and the queen, as is natural, has taken it badly.

But a terrible fear, an icy coldness, had pervaded Anne's being. Could it be that ...? She put the dread thought from her, seating herself beside Margaret's bed and trying to concentrate her attention on the afflicted woman.

The rigours of the day have been too much for madam my mother-in-law, she thought – she is in her forty-second year, and women of that age are prone to sudden attacks of faintness. There is talk of a fall – she struck her head, someone said, against the side of her chariot.

'What of the battle?' Anne asked the queen's attendants, for already she had seen from the window embrasure that fighting had ceased out there on the distant battlefield. Men were moving about on the field, casually, without fuss or haste – as at the finish of a rather disappointing tourney. 'Is the battle over?'

'It is over, my lady,' replied one of the women evasively. 'We know not the outcome – we were waiting on Her Grace, you see! Someone will be here anon I dare say – they'll tell us then.'

The women's voices were hushed as they went about their tasks – and they gave all their attention to the queen, as if they were uncomfortable in the presence of the young Princess of Wales and would rather she kept her distance.

*Ask no questions and ye'll be told no lies!* Why does that come into my mind now? Anne wondered. It was my nurse's favourite maxim when I was a small child – but why now?

'Where is the Prince of Wales?' she asked the women – and she heard the defiant note in her own voice and wondered at it.

'Out there on the battlefield, I dare say, my lady,' the woman who had spoken before told her, glancing meaningfully at her companion. 'Now, let's get Her Grace settled – and then we'll have them summon a physician.'

Averting their gaze from Anne, they completed their task and left the chamber – saying nothing further to Anne and seeming to walk on tiptoe.

'Why are they creeping about like that? Anne wondered curiously. 'Tis not as if the queen can hear them and ... Yea, that is it – it is because of me they are walking on tiptoe and speaking in hushed tones. Even my questions made them uneasy – they shied from them as if they had something to hide!

Alone then with her thoughts, Anne's fear was suddenly the greater – it refused to be quelled, ignored. The icy coldness was everywhere, her hands, her head, her whole body – but most of all around her heart ...

With a tiny sob, she got up and fled the chamber. Making unseeingly for the nun's cell vacated for her, she went in and closed and bolted the door.

She flung herself down on the narrow bed and, giving her tears a free rein, unleashed her thoughts.

She knew with a great certainty that Edward, her sweet lord, was dead and lost to her for ever. Never, ever, she told herself, if I live to be a hundred and one, shall I see him again – hear his voice, feel his caresses and the warmth of his body close to mine. I might, I just might, if God be kind, even yet bear his child – his heir.

She was some two weeks past her moon-time. Edward had been aware of that – but not Margaret, for already Margaret understood her daughter-in-law to be with child. A lie it had been – a lie to keep them together.

And now we are not together, thought Anne, and the lie is no longer a lie – what a topsy-turvy world it is! Or perchance I am a little mad – distracted by grief and uncertainty! By not knowing, not really knowing – whilst recognizing beyond all doubt that I shall never see my beloved lord again!

'Edward is dead.' She said it aloud to the empty cell. The stone walls echoed the words, throwing them back to her, mocking her grief – confirming her fears. 'Edward is dead. Edward is dead. Edward …'

I am carrying his child – I must draw comfort from that. 'Tis all that is left – of love and joy and a summer's idyll. I am but in my seventeenth summer – how then shall I pass the empty years? Never again shall I love anyone as I love – yea, love – my gallant prince: never again shall I know the ecstasy I shared with him. He was my life, a part of me – and part of me has died with him!

She must have fallen asleep then because she woke to find early morning sunlight streaming in through the narrow window. She had been vaguely aware over the past hours of voices and people knocking at the door – but the sounds had not properly entered her consciousness, seeming to be half dream, half reality.

Now as she lay inert, telling herself she must rise and go to the queen, there came a knocking on the door which somehow carried a note of urgency …

'My lady,' called one of the queen's waiting-women, 'The Duke of Somerset is here and desires speech with you.'

'I shall be with him anon,' Anne said, unbolting the door but standing well back in the shadows to conceal her dishevelled appearance.

'His Grace is awaiting you in Reverend Mother's parlour, my lady.'

'Pray send for my maid – I shall be with His Grace shortly.'

\* \* \*

Many noblemen and knights had been slain on the field of battle, or captured, like the Prince of Wales, in the rout that followed. However, the Duke of Somerset together with Sir Thomas Tresham, Sir John Longstrother and a number of other knights had turned away from the town during the rout and made for sanctuary at Tewkesbury Abbey.

On learning however that the queen had not yet

regained consciousness and that none at the priory was in a position to inform the Princess of Wales of her lord's murder, Somerset broke sanctuary a few hours later. At great risk to himself and by a circuitous route to avoid detection, he had made his way to the priory. Margaret's whereabouts had so far been kept secret and it was hoped would remain so until she was well enough to be moved a safe distance from Tewkesbury, prior to taking ship for France.

'He died bravely, my lady,' Somerset said, following his formal announcement of the prince's death. 'Every Lancastrian shares your sorrow – that gallant springing young Plantagenet was loved by us all.'

'Then it is all over,' Anne said forlornly. 'The Lancastrian cause is lost – the red rose is dead, its blood-soaked petals strewn on Tewkesbury field!'

'The cause is not dead, my lady,' Somerset assured her. 'It is not dead – but sleeping. One day, in God's good time, the red rose will rise from the dust. Even yet it will bloom in triumph – you will see!'

'Maybe I shall,' Anne said softly. 'Maybe I shall, my lord. But the Prince of Wales will not, alas, alas!'

# Twenty

Margaret recovered consciousness on the day following the battle, but for three more days her life hung in the balance. She was unable to speak and it seemed as if the prince's murderers had dealt her also a mortal wound.

When she finally recovered consciousness, though restored in mind and speech, she looked drawn and frail, a shadow of her former self.

Her devoted attendants did all they could to make her comfortable, but Margaret spoke little and wept much, refusing all but a minimum of food. Her spirit, it seemed to those around her, had finally been broken. With the death of her son, her beloved prince, the gallant youth who had given meaning to an otherwise wasted life, her inner resources had given way.

When a deputation purporting to come from King Edward and headed by Earl Rivers, presented itself at the priory and demanded to see Margaret, there was considerable alarm. So Edward of York has discovered the whereabouts of herself and the lady Anne! her attendants said to themselves. She was too ill, they told Earl Rivers, far too ill to see anyone.

'We are informed that the lady Anne, lately termed Princess of Wales, is here also,' said Rivers. 'We would see her, that we might entrust her with a message for the lady Margaret.'

Anne had passed much of her time at the bedside of her sorrowing mother-in-law, her own grief well hidden so that some among the queen's ladies wondered if, after all, her seeming devotion to the Prince of Wales had been superficial. She at once agreed to see the deputation.

Buoyed up by the hope that she was with child, she

looked serene and elegant as she entered the priory's great hall and formally greeted the deputation. She was dressed entirely in black, the low neckline of her long fur-trimmed gown emphasizing the whiteness of her throat. The hennin, the steeple head-dress she wore after the current fashion, was two feet high and enveloped by a transparent veil which hung in folds almost to the ground.

Anthony, Earl Rivers, was brother to King Edward's queen, personable and a champion of the joust. He had fought for the Lancastrians at Towton but had changed his allegiance and now held high office under King Edward. To Anne, he was just such another as Clarence, her brother-in-law – a time-serving traitor of the ilk that had brought about the deaths of her father and husband.

'My lady,' he said now, 'we are here by order of King Edward, who tenders his condolences to the lady Margaret, former queen of this realm, on the death of the noble prince Edward.'

'On the lady Margaret's behalf, I thank His Grace for his courtesy,' responded Anne coolly. 'And is that the extent of the message entrusted to you, sir? Others were slain also on Tewkesbury field: the Earl of Devonshire, Sir John Beaufort, Lord Wenlock ...

'Lord Wenlock indeed!' put in another member of the deputation, as if he too were aware as to how that gentleman had met his death. 'A sorry business!'

'... Sir Thomas Tresham, Sir Robert Whittingham –' coolly continued Anne, '– and with these noblemen, many of their followers, brave men all!'

'My lady, you will be happy to learn that Tresham is not in fact among the slain, but was taken prisoner, together with Sir Hugh Courtenay, Sir John Langstrother ...'

Anne was not in truth listening to the list of those taken prisoner. What were they to her? She was glad, she supposed, for somebody's sake that they had escaped with their lives – but Edward was dead, and Edward was him she loved, the father of her unborn child.

'... and the Duke of Somerset,' continued Rivers.

'Somerset?' asked Anne, called to attention by the name of him who had temporarily left sanctuary to inform her of Edward's murder. 'But how could that be? – Somerset, I understood, sir, was in sanctuary.'

'That is so, my lady – Somerset and the aforementioned gentlemen all sought sanctuary at the abbey.'

'But if that be so, my lord, how is it they are now King Edward's prisoners?'

'Alas, my lady, the abbey does not at this time possess a franchise as a sanctuary – not for those who have committed high treason!'

'High treason!' exclaimed Anne. 'Is it treason now to fight for the restoration of one's rightful sovereign!'

'King Edward himself entered the abbey and ordered his men to kill many Lancastrian troops who had sought shelter there – Somerset and the other aforementioned gentlemen were taken prisoner and sent for trial yesterday!'

'So Edward of York violated sanctuary,' said Anne. 'I doubt God will pardon him so heinous a crime!'

'Times change, my lady!'

'What of the verdict?' asked Anne quietly. 'You tell me Somerset and the others were sent for trial – what judgment was passed on them?'

'They were judged guilty – and condemned to be executed at Tewkesbury upon the morrow, my lady.'

For a long time Anne remained silent. She appeared calm, accepting – yet devoid of speech. The deputation watched her curiously, uneasily – awaiting a storm of protest that never came.

Anne was in fact shocked to the depths of her being. Sanctuary had been violated and, as a consequence, men who had given all in defence of their lawful sovereign were condemned to die. Shocked she was – and dead to all feeling. Her beloved lord was dead – murdered in cold blood by order of the monster who called himself king and who had set his brothers on a fettered youth of seventeen. Now Somerset and those others ... Alas, I have no words to express what I feel, she thought – I must rediscover my feelings ere I seek for words!

'You would have me convey such tidings as these to Her Grace?' she asked slowly. 'To her who has recently suffered the loss of her only son?'

'It is needful that Her Grace is fully cognisant of the

situation,' came the answer. 'She must understand that the House of Lancaster is no more and that Edward of York is now sovereign of the realm.'

'And why, pray, must the lady Margaret understand as much?' demanded Anne. 'Could it be, sir, that Edward of York fears that his claim will be misunderstood?'

'King Edward fears naught, my lady – be assured on that. It is His Grace's will that the lady Margaret surrender her person to us, his representatives.'

Anne's heart missed a beat. 'You mean to take the lady Margaret prisoner?' she asked.

'For her own sake, Her Grace must be placed in safe keeping,' was the dissembling reply. 'Needless to say there is no question of imprisonment!'

'And what of Henry of Lancaster, her husband, sir?'

'He is in the Tower of London, my lady – he is in good heart and amiable as always!'

'But London, I understand, is yet held by the Lancastrians,' said Anne. 'Him they call *The Bastard of Fauconberg* took London several weeks since ...'

'It has fallen, my lady – London has fallen to our troops, God be thanked! The Bastard's assault on London gained the Lancastrians the advantage for only a few days – his Kentishmen have since surrendered to Richard of Gloucester.'

God have pity! said Anne to herself. Is there no end to it? My husband, my father, my uncle, all are slain. Richard of Gloucester, it seems, overcame the Kentishmen ...

What visions of childhood that name conjures up! The Richard I knew then was a gentle youth – of medium stature, not overly handsome. Yet I recall how, as we played chess or dominoes, he would make some whimsical remark that made me laugh – and his eyes, large and deep blue, would light up then, as if he took pleasure from my pleasure.

How impossible it is to equate that Richard, *my* Richard, with him who, as Somerset informed me, was among those who murdered my sweet lord – he being fettered and unarmed!

She registered of a sudden that Rivers and his companions were looking curiously at her – and she made

an effort to collect herself. If only they would go away, all
of them, and leave me to my thoughts, my grief ...

'They have surrendered to Richard of Gloucester, you
say, my lord?' she asked coldly of Rivers. 'What pray is that
to myself – and the lady Margaret?'

'King Edward proposes to enter the capital two weeks
hence – on the twenty-first day of May,' Rivers told her.
'There is little time therefore and the king my master
commands the lady Margaret's surrender forthwith –
together with that of yourself, my lady.'

'Myself?'

'A formality only, my lady.'

'I see.' Anne did indeed see and did not like what she
saw. Were she to bear a child within the nine months
following, it would be deemed the child of the murdered
Prince of Wales – as grandchild to the deposed King
Henry, it would be seen as a threat, a new scion of the
House of Lancaster. 'I see, sir.'

'As soon as possible, my lady,' urged Rivers. 'Today has
been suggested ...'

'Today is out of the question, sir,' interposed Anne.
'Were the lady Margaret in sufficiently good health to
undertake a journey to London – I assume it is to London
– would I be deputizing for her? Her Grace has been at
death's gate, sir. Such grievous tidings, you understand ...'

Rivers's manner was brusque. 'Then we shall bide till the
morrow, my lady. The former queen must surrender to
myself, as the king's representative, on the morrow.
Thereafter she will be escorted to London to await the
entry of the king. Should the lady Margaret's health be
such as to preclude horseback-riding, she shall be borne in
a litter.'

'As to a litter, sir ...'

She felt the eyes of the deputation upon her, as if their
spokesman's next words were pre-arranged and of deep
significance.

'My lady, you too shall be borne in a litter, needless to
say – should you be in – er – delicate health!' he said
pointedly.

There was no escaping Rivers's meaning, nor the
knowing stares of his companions. Anne flushed under

their scrutiny, thus revealing to her own annoyance that she knew what they had in mind. She felt suddenly uneasy, menaced ...

'I shall ride on horseback, sir,' she said firmly. 'It is the lady Margaret, not myself, who is in delicate health – as to Her Grace's mode of travel, you will be informed of her decision in due time.'

'My lady, have no fear ...' one of the others started to say.

'Fear?' demanded Anne. 'Am not I the Kingmaker's daughter? Was not I bride to the gallant Prince of Wales – him they so foully murdered? What on God's earth is there to fear now?'

# Twenty-One

King Edward made his triumphal entry into London on the morning of Tuesday, the twenty-first of May. By the end of that day, the deposed King Henry, a prisoner in the Tower for the better part of five years, had breathed his last.

And on that same fateful twenty-first of May, Margaret of Anjou, Henry's Queen, was taken captive to the Tower in the train of the victorious Edward, and placed in one of the more gloomy apartments only a short distance from that of her husband.

Margaret was separated from Anne on their arrival in the city, and had no idea where her daughter-in-law had been taken. She assumed Anne would be placed only under house arrest in one or other of the royal residences. Even by Edward of York's harsh standards, Anne has committed no crime, she told herself. She supported the Lancastrian cause only passively, it might be said, out of deference to her father and her husband.

Margaret had her own servants to wait on her, and a small fire burnt in the hearth to lessen the chill that pervaded the Tower's thick walls even in springtime.

In truth, she thought to herself as she warmed her hands by the fire, it is a relief to be here after the rigours of the journey from Tewkesbury – here I have my servants, my own bed and such clothing and belongings as I brought with me. Here I have peace and solitude – time in which to recover my strength and composure, time to rebuild and make plans for the future. The Lancastrian cause will rise again from the ashes – if not soon, then at some time in the future. Jasper Tudor, Earl of Pembroke, that loyal and courageous Welshman, waits patiently in

Wales with his nephews – he waits for a sign, for a new leader, for the day when the tyrant will be overthrown. That day will dawn, as surely as there is a God in heaven!

On the morrow, I shall ask to see Henry. 'Tis five years since last we met, and then only briefly and in the company of others. I wish to assure myself that he is in good health and tell him of our son's death – how he died bravely on the field of battle, a youth not yet eighteen, defending his father's crown. I shall beg him not to despair – God is on our side, I shall say, and right will yet prevail. At this moment, I long to see Henry, the father of my beloved prince, more than anything else in the world. Surely my request will not be refused!

\* \* \*

Henry had suffered five years of solitary confinement. In all that time, apart from a brief spell of freedom prior to the battle of Barnet, and a daily walk on the ramparts in fine weather, the upper chamber of the Wakefield Tower had been the extent of his world. A few learned manuscripts and books of meditation had helped to pass the time – and a singing-bird in a cage which, frequently released to fly round the room, was a much-loved companion. A priest visited him daily to administer the sacraments, but this was the extent of outside contact.

He had been informed of the outcome of the latest Lancastrian stand at Tewkesbury, and knew in his heart that for him it was the final battle – his sovereignty was at an end. Cast at first into the depths of gloom and despair at this, he had prayed for acceptance. Why has Our Lord forsaken me? he asked himself. In what manner have I offended him that he turns his face from me?

Then came other thoughts, other questions. He was told nothing of his family, of their health, their whereabouts, their plans for the future. Where is my lady Margaret? he wondered. And where is the Prince of Wales? Even to himself, Henry never acknowledged Edward as his son – but he was God's gift, a miraculous birth, and he loved him dearly.

What then of the future? he asked himself. Am I to

remain here, alone and useless, for the rest of my days? I am the rightful king of England, as was my father and my grandfather before me. I love my people, and ask nothing more of life than to rule my kingdom wisely and for the common good. But always there has been war and dissension, both at home and abroad, whilst I sought only for peace in the land. God knows I have never knowingly given hurt to any man. Am I not the Lord's anointed? What displeasure the actions of the usurper must have caused him. But I bear my enemies no malice. God will act – will show them his will in his own good time. I must be patient ...

Even as he made to rise from his prie-dieu, the chamber door burst open. He turned, surprised – someone is in a hurry, he thought. Have they further news for me? Of the queen perchance? Of the Prince of Wales?

Richard of Gloucester, it was, who strode into the chamber, his henchmen following. It was approaching midnight and the candles had burned low – and for a moment in the flickering light Henry failed to recognize his Yorkist kinsman.

He concealed his surprise.

'We bid you welcome, my lord of Gloucester,' he said courteously. 'Methinks you bear news of some import.'

'You are about to rejoin your son, cousin,' Gloucester told him, his expression inscrutable. 'You and he are shortly to be reunited.'

There was no mistaking Henry's pleasure.

'You are taking me to the Prince of Wales?' he asked joyfully.

'In a manner of speaking,' said Gloucester, turning furiously on a guffawing henchman. 'Be silent, sirrah – remember where you are!'

'Then pray let us lose no time –' Henry started to say.

'Enough of play-acting!' Gloucester brusquely interposed. 'You are a dead man, Henry of Lancaster!'

Henry stared uncomprehendingly at him. First I am to join the Prince of Wales – and now I am a dead man. By the Mass, Gloucester is possessed of a very strange wit!

'You speak in riddles, my lord,' he said. 'We are well enough in health – though a little weary perchance.'

'Then you will surely welcome a long rest.'

Registering the menace in Gloucester's voice, Henry understood. For a few moments he held the other's gaze in silence, as if resolving some inner conflict. When he spoke, it was in a voice so lacking in malice or bitterness that it laid emphasis on the quiet conviction of his words.

'So the Prince of Wales is dead,' he said. 'Murdered.'

Gloucester made no reply, but watched his gentle adversary warily.

'God will avenge him,' continued the mild voice of the Lancastrian. 'His murderer, whosoever he be, will lose his son also ere he attains his majority. Beware, Richard of Gloucester! God will set brother against brother, uncle against nephew, kinsman against kinsman – until the House of York is no more!'

Gloucester, more shaken than he would have admitted by the prophetic words – and the gentle manner in which they were delivered – drew his dagger.

Henry raised a staying hand.

'Permit me first to make my confession, my lord,' he said. 'Summon a priest, that I may repent me of my sins.'

'Your sins?' Gloucester laughed mirthlessly. 'And what sins might they be? Gluttony? Vanity? Lust? Covetousness maybe? Nay, Henry of Lancaster, you are too good a man by far to live …'

With these words he raised his dagger and his henchmen encircled the unarmed man. His hesitation was momentary. But then – for some reason he could not have explained, avoiding the gaze of his erstwhile sovereign – he plunged the blade into his victim's heart.

Even as Henry fell, his life-blood streaming out across the stone-paved floor, Gloucester and his henchmen were leaving the chamber.

# Twenty-Two

'May God give him time for repentance, whoever he was, who laid his sacrilegious hands on the Lord's anointed!' remarked a Lancastrian chronicler upon hearing of the murder of King Henry.

The sentiments thus expressed were echoed throughout England – and nowhere more vociferously than in London, where the citizens watched in awed disbelief as the corpse of him they had long revered and held in their hearts to be their true king, its face uncovered, was borne on a bier from the Tower of London, through Cheapside to St. Paul's.

Most watched in a chilled silence which owed nothing to the weather; others fell to their knees as the hearse passed by, praying for the dead monarch and asking him to intercede for them. But there were those, usually of feminine gender, who expressed to each other in low tones – or what seemed to themselves if not to others as low tones – their sense of outrage at what had been done to the last Lancastrian king!

'I can't bear to look, Lettice – tell me when it gets here and I'll take a peek from atween me fingers!'

'I'll remember that when it's your turn, Kate – and I'll see to it as none of 'em looks till you've gone past!'

'Nearly here, is it?'

'Is what nearly here?'

'The bier, of course.'

'They don't dole out beer at funerals – leastways not *state* funerals – only at weddings and coronations.'

'*State* funerals, you say – well I'm in a state right enough, thinking about poor old King Henry living all those years in the Tower, and then bein' done to death by ...'

'Shush, Kate – someone will hear you!'

'Don't care if they do! Poor King Henry never hurt a fly – all he wanted in life was a bit of peace and quiet and the chance to wear 'is crown now and then. Not much to ask, was it!'

'I can see the hearse now – it's getting quite close. It's growing dark though – looks like we're in for a storm. Like it was when Jesus was crucified – the darkness was over all the earth, it says!'

'They say King Edward and *'im-as-did-it,* left London at daybreak, riding as if the devil was after 'em!'

'Off to *you-know-who's* castle at Middleham, I 'spect – afraid you'd tell 'em what you thought if you saw 'em, Kate.'

'I might at that, the murdering ...'

'Kate, it's almost here! It's hard to see the king, 'cos he's surrounded by men with halberds and bills.'

'Bill's? Bill's what?'

'If you take a proper look, you'll see what I mean. Look, it's almost level with us now – oh, get out of the way, you great Yorkist ox!'

'You talking to me, Lettice? I'll 'ave you know ...'

'Nay, that fellow there beside the bier – he's blocking my view ... Christ save us! Look there – just look there, Kate!'

A sudden unisonal cry had gone up at that point from the hitherto silent spectators, a mixture of horror, awe – and satisfaction!

'Then he's not dead after all, Lettice – dead people don't bleed, you know!'

'He's dead all right – you can see that from 'is face!'

'God save us, did you see that? Fresh blood is welling up from his chest and soaking the drapes, and now 'tis running down and falling on to the roadway! God have mercy, Christ have mercy – he's trying to tell us something!'

'And I can tell you what it is – he's telling us as 'e was murdered, foully murdered by *we-know-who* and ...'

'Sh! Lettice, have a care for God's sake!'

'Look, the blood's leaving a trail and people are dipping their fingers in it – and crossing themselves like it was holy water.'

'As it is, Lettice – as it is. See, there it is – I've got some on me own hands! I'll wipe them on me neckerchief and I'll keep me neckerchief for ever and ever – a relic of King Henry who was murdered by ...'

'Sh!'

'*You-know-who*, I shall say to me grandchildren. And if they don't know who, *Doctor Foster*, I shall tell 'em, *went to Gloucester, in a shower of rain. He stepped in a puddle, up to his Middleham, and could never wash the blood out again!*'

'They've stopped for a few moments, Kate – the men with bills looked a bit queasy when they got a sight of the blood!'

'With Bill's, you say? Bill's what?'

'You asked that before – look, they're moving off now. Let's give 'im a cheer, Kate.'

'Who? Bill, you mean?'

'Nay, silly – poor King Henry of course. Come on, Kate ...'

'But it is a ...'

'Hooray! Hooray! Bravo! Good for you, Henry of Lancaster – bless you, bless you! God keep you, Henry of Lancaster – bless us, bless us! O sweetest heart of Jesus, have mercy on us all!'

# Twenty-Three

At midnight of the day that the bleeding body of King Henry had been paraded through the London streets for public view, the coffin of the last Lancastrian king was buried secretly in an unmarked grave.

Placed on a torch-lit barge, guarded by soldiers from Calais, the hearse was conveyed quietly and without ceremonial up the Thames to Chertsey. There, at the abbey, attended by only two priests, was interred the remains of him who had been son to the great Henry the Fifth.

Margaret was grief-stricken by the manner of her lord's demise and, it following so soon on the murder of her son, there were fears for a time for her reason. But Margaret was a woman of strength, one born to riches and high estate who had none the less suffered hardships and tragedies such as few are called upon to bear.

Her family too suffered a number of bereavements at this time. When informed of these in letters from King René, Margaret's melancholy increased. Having lost her husband and son so tragically, she must come to terms also with the death of her eldest brother, John of Calabria, King René's heir; and her sister, Blanche of Anjou.

King René, deeply distressed by these bereavements, was himself plunged into despair on being informed of Margaret's misfortunes. He none the less wrote to her, a tender loving letter in which his own misfortunes were given second place to hers.

'My child,' he wrote at one point, 'may God help thee with his counsels! for rarely is the aid of man tendered in such reverse of fortune. When you are able to spare a thought from your own sufferings, think of mine; they are great, my daughter, yet would I console thee.'

Thanks to the intervention of Elizabeth Woodville, Edward the Fourth's queen, Margaret was removed from the Tower in the July following to more congenial surroundings at Windsor – and from there a few months later to Wallingford Castle.

During the months and years that followed, René worked ceaselessly for the release of his daughter. Eventually, more than four years after the disastrous defeat at Tewkesbury, she was ransomed by Louis of France for the sum of fifty thousand crowns – but only through the sacrifice of René who for half its true value ceded Provence to Louis to provide the wherewithal for his long-suffering daughter's release.

Conducted from Wallingford to Sandwich in the November of that year, Margaret thereafter began the long journey to her homeland and freedom.

She reached Dieppe in the January following, and on the twenty-ninth day of that month was required at Rouen to formally renounce all her English rights. She had nothing to lose. Henry and Edward were dead, murdered by orders of him who had usurped the English crown. God would avenge them: she could do no more.

'I, Margaret,' she wrote a little shakily, 'formerly in England married, solemnly renounce all that I could pretend to in England by the condition of my marriage, with all other things there, to Edward, now king of England.'

She reached her homeland a few weeks later. After an emotional reunion with her father, she was conducted by René to the castle of Reculée, his favourite residence. The wheel had turned full circle, for it was in the great hall at Reculée that Margaret, then aged fourteen, beautiful and gifted, had received the English ambassadors who had come to sue for her hand on behalf of their royal master.

For the next six years, Margaret lived at Reculée in deep seclusion until, afflicted both in mind and body, she died in her fifty-first year.

From that moment when she and Anne had reached London, at the end of the long, exhausting journey from Tewkesbury, they had not set eyes on each other again. After a brief but emotional farewell, sharing a common grief, the older woman and the younger had been separated – Margaret to captivity in the Tower and Anne to none knew where.

At first Margaret had asked about her daughter-in-law, how she was, where she was. She had written letters to her but had received no reply. She had longed to see her, to talk with her of the golden youth, the gallant springing Plantagenet, they both had loved. But none could – or maybe dared – tell her of Anne, and after a while Margaret ceased to ask. She tried, not always successfully, to put her from her mind ...

# PART TWO

## *Anne, Duchess of Gloucester*

# Twenty-Four

Anne stepped from the barge which had brought her and Margaret, with their custodians, from Richmond on the last lap of the several days' journey from Tewkesbury to the Tower of London.

Shivering with cold, oppressed by a sense of disbelief, as if all that had happened in the past week were no more than a dream, she stood helplessly beside Margaret, asking herself what further miseries fate had in store for her.

Earl Rivers addressed Margaret.

'You will come with me, my lady,' he said. 'You are to be held here under house arrest only, with your own servants to attend you and such comforts as the Tower can provide.'

'I am ready, sir,' said Margaret. 'But first I would bid farewell to the lady Anne.'

'The lady Anne, being also under attainder, is likewise being committed to the Tower,' Rivers explained. 'You, madam, are to be held in the Beauchamp Tower and the lady Anne in the Garden Tower. I shall therefore first escort Your Grace with your servants to your apartment and will return very shortly for the lady Anne.'

Margaret embraced Anne – and the latter, sensing intuitively that they would never see each other again, could not contain her tears.

'Would that I could be with you, madam my mother-in-law,' she said. 'Wherefore are they holding me – and for what reason?'

'Be of good cheer, child.' Margaret's smile gave the lie to her own dismal spirits. 'Youth is on your side – fortune, please God, will yet smile on you!'

'But what of yourself, *maman*?' Anne asked, using her

lord's mode of address and thereby bringing tears to Margaret's eyes. 'What of yourself? I would that we might remain together – and share our sorrows.'

'We shall be together again very shortly. King Edward cannot hold us prisoner for ever – be patient, my child!'

'O grief of heart!' cried Anne, clinging to Margaret as if to life itself. 'O grief of heart.'

'We must not tarry, child,' Margaret told her with a briskness that did her credit. 'The wind from the river blows chill. Farewell, daughter-in-law, farewell – our Lord have you in his keeping.'

And then she was gone. Anne wept copiously – watching through a mist of tears as the woman with whom she shared a common grief, walked from her life for ever. She was reminded, and the reminder seemed to pierce her very soul, of that other farewell, and of the other walking away …

'Go with God, *maman*,' she called after her, not caring who heard. 'Go with God!'

She looked around, feeling doubly bereft. She was alone, isolated in a strange place. The broad quay between moat and river which was the Tower wharf, suggested a region of forgotten things, a limbo.

Her servants had been pensioned off by Earl Rivers and during the journey from Tewkesbury she had shared Margaret's waiting-women. Now only two of the Yorkist guards who had accompanied them from Tewkesbury, stood close by – detached, surly, talking to each other in monosyllables, anxious to see the end of a thankless task.

A gentleman approached from within the Tower. Crossing the moat by a narrow bridge, he bowed and addressed Anne.

'The lady Anne of Warwick?' he enquired.

Anne inclined her head. Why, she thought, does everything, everyone, remind me – while I must nod and look meek, instead of shouting to the roof-tops that, nay, I am the Princess of Wales!

'Have the goodness to come with me, my lady,' said the newcomer, in a tone more than a little officious. 'I shall conduct you to your new abode.'

As Anne stepped forward and the two guards fell in

behind her, the newcomer spoke authoritatively.

'You are dismissed,' he told them. 'You are to await the return of Earl Rivers who has further orders for you.'

The men nodded, glad to be rid of so onerous a task; and the newcomer conducted Anne across the narrow bridge by the Byward Tower.

They continued on over a causeway, passing the Middle Tower and crossing a shorter causeway. Skirting the Lion Tower which held the royal menagerie, they came to the stone causeway that crossed the outer moat and was the only gateway to the Tower by land. Here, to Anne's surprise, men with horses were awaiting them.

Her custodian assisted her to mount before mounting his own horse and leading the way, his men following, at a smart pace across the causeway and out on to Tower Hill ...

'I regret the necessity to prolong your journey,' her custodian said.

'Am I not then to be held in the Tower, sir?' asked Anne.

'Nay, not in the Tower, my lady.' That he was unwilling to reveal her destination was plain. 'We have but a short distance to go – less than half a mile.'

The discovery that she was not, after all, to be imprisoned in the Tower, did not altogether please Anne. Margaret was at the Tower, and Margaret of a sudden seemed her only friend in an alien world.

'Whither am I bound, sir? It is nearing dusk and methought ...'

'Have no fear, my lady. Someone is waiting to greet you when you reach your destination – then all will be made plain.'

But Anne *was* fearful. She suspected that the king, not knowing whether or not she was with child since she had refused to answer any questions on the subject, had decided to have her done away with. Since she might well be carrying the Lancastrian heir, the rightful heir to the English throne, it was expedient to destroy her and a possible child with her ...

But already her custodian was calling a halt. They were in a narrow city street, a back street. Glancing upward,

Anne saw tall, faceless buildings on either side of her, and built so close together that persons leaning out of upper windows could have shaken hands across the street – had there been any windows!

This is likely the rear of some nobleman's residence, she thought. Clearly it is not a prison – or a royal palace.

'I do not understand,' she said nervously – telling herself she understood only too well.

'You very soon will, my lady. Look! A servant is coming forth from yonder door – she will take charge of you.'

'But ...'

Already her custodian was helping her dismount. The serving-woman came forward then and indicated that Anne was to go with her.

Having little choice, Anne accompanied the silent woman into the dark building and through a labyrinth of dimly-lit corridors, until they reached what she judged to be the front of the building. Then, darting forward of a sudden, the woman opened a door at the end of a gallery.

'Enter, my lady,' she said with a small bob curtsey. 'Pray enter.'

'But ...'

Even as Anne hesitated, the woman turned away and was gone. Knowing not what to expect and having no idea where she was, Anne nervously went forward into the room.

The chamber was ablaze with light from many candles, and for a few moments she was dazzled by the sudden brilliance. But as she waited uncertainly, expecting every moment to be her last, a figure moved towards her and enfolded her in a warm, perfumed embrace.

'Welcome, Anne dear!' said the figure. 'Alas, my sister, it has been so long!'

'Isabel!' exclaimed Anne – and dissolved into tears. 'Is it really you? Methought I was in deadly danger – that I was about to lose my life!'

'So did we, my dear,' sighed Isabel, helping her off with her cloak and leading her over to the fire. 'That is why we evolved the plan, you see – it was the only way.'

'But they will surely find me, my sister. You cannot keep me hidden for ever!'

'And why not, pray?' smiled Isabel. 'If need be, we shall do just that!'

'But what of your lord husband? As the king's brother, he would surely not permit it.'

'Oh, it was my lord's idea in the first place,' Isabel said airily. 'And of course I was overjoyed when he told me of it. Why, I said, I have not seen my little sister for ages and ages – not since I left Beaulieu in fact!'

'How long ago that seems,' sighed Anne. 'In truth, it is little more than six weeks.'

'Poor dear Anne! I wept and wept for you when I heard about the prince your husband, and I pestered my lord for news of you.'

'Alas, Isabel, it has all been so dreadful. But let us not speak of it now – some other time perchance.'

'Not another word, my dear. You look dreadfully pale and tired – but a good night's sleep will work wonders, I am sure. Could it be that you are with child?'

Such a question was natural enough between sisters not long wed, yet for some reason she could not have explained, Anne shied from it. She knew instinctively that the child within her was something of which she must not speak.

'Alas that it is not so!' she said softly. 'Would I have ridden so far on horseback had it been so! Now tell me, Isabel, of your plan.'

'Not now – but later on. You need rest, and you shall go to my chamber now and sleep for a while. Then, when you are rested, my maid Hortense, who has been sworn to secrecy, will bathe and dress you – and when you are ready, you will come and sup with me here in my solar – just the two of us. Later on, my lord will join us, and then we shall tell you of the plan – and you will see, Anne, that you have naught, naught in this world, to be concerned about!'

* * *

Anne's baggage, containing a sizeable wardrobe of clothes and jewels, like Margaret's, had been in the barge that had followed behind theirs from Richmond to the Tower. Now

Anne had nothing save what she was wearing and gratefully accepted her sister's invitation to select whatsoever she needed from her own well-filled closet.

When she presently returned to Isabel's solar, Anne was attired most becomingly in a gown of black silk altered to fit her slender figure by the nimble-fingered Hortense.

There was a strong likeness between the sisters, both having an abundance of fair hair and a flawless complexion; though Isabel had a pleasing roundness of figure that contrasted strikingly with Anne's now fragile appearance – a legacy of the woes and privations of recent weeks.

'You look beautiful, my sister,' Isabel enthused as Anne entered the chamber – though whether the compliment was inspired by Anne herself or her own borrowed gown was debatable.

Isabel's affection for her sister took second place to her love for her husband – and third place to love of self.

'Hortense is a treasure!' smiled Anne.

The remark seemed to trouble Isabel – for she looked sharply, almost suspiciously, at Anne.

'I should warn you ...' she started to say, but then, as if thinking better of it, she smiled and said, 'Now as I said, we shall sup alone – the two of us together like the old days!'

Anne winced. *Why must she remind me of former days?* she thought – *of the years of childhood and innocence when we were protected from intrigue and the harsh realities of life. Does not she understand how it is with me now?*

'None knows of your being here, save Hortense who is devoted to myself and even more devoted, I suspect, to my lord –' continued Isabel in her cheerful bubbly manner. 'the gentleman who brought you here – one of my lord's most trusted henchmen – and needless to say my lord and myself!'

'But what of the other servants?' asked Anne.

'Ostensibly I have retired to my chamber with a migraine – a not unknown occurrence – and unable at such times to abide sound or light, I will have none but Hortense attend me. So, my dear, let us partake – and in a very little while, my lord will be here and will tell you all.'

'But what of ...?'

'Ah, here comes Hortense with the repast! I ordered all your favourite dishes: venison, beef, pork – everything to please you. And afterwards, your very favourite sweet-meats. Indeed, I find I have quite an appetite myself – for a lady with a migraine!'

# Twenty-Five

George Duke of Clarence was a composite of his elder and younger brothers. Fair and blue-eyed after the Plantagenet mould, he was taller than Richard but of a slighter build than Edward the king. An able warrior, he was more devious than the flamboyant Edward but more extroverted than the inscrutable Richard. Edward was a womaniser and made no bones about it; George was a womaniser and enjoyed adulterous affairs and secret rendezvous; Richard was rumoured to have sired a bastard or two, but none gave proof of it. In that, as in everything else, Richard was an enigma.

Clarence looked handsome and debonair as he came forward to greet his sister-in-law.

He bowed, kissed her hand and then embraced her, kissing her warmly on both cheeks – before standing back to gaze consideringly at her.

'How alike you are, you sisters!' he said lightly. 'And how close the bond between you – I declare I have not seen my lady smile so happily for many a long day!'

'It is good to see you, cousin,' said Anne, using the mode of address customary between herself and the children of her great-aunt Cecily.

'It saddens me that it is your adversity that has brought us together – many and undeserved are the trials and tribulations heaped upon you of late! Why, when I left France, departing with the earl your father for England, methought you in line for a roseate future!'

'I am grief-stricken by my lord's demise,' Anne told him, lest there be doubt on it – and stung by his refusal to make direct reference to the prince's death. 'At heart, I am a sorrowing widow still – and shall ever remain so!'

'Come, my dear, time heals all things, it is said! There are more fish in the sea – and not all of them tadpoles –'

'My lord, I ...'

'– waiting to get their hands on your fortune!'

'I shall remain a widow till the day I die!' Anne declared coldly.

'I know of one, cousin, who would make you his bride.'

'Pray speak not so, my lord.' Anne was clearly distressed. 'I would hear none of it.'

'My lord, let us be seated comfortably by the fireside, that we may talk together, all of us,' put in Isabel lightly. 'I told Anne that, when we had supped, you would reveal your plan to her.'

'Yea, the plan,' nodded Clarence. 'I have indeed formulated a plan and trust that you, cousin Anne, will find it agreeable.'

Seated by the fire, the three of them exchanged pleasantries for a while – until it seemed to Anne that the other two were loth to reveal what they had in mind.

'Pray tell me of your plan, my lord,' she said at length to Clarence. 'There is much I do not understand – as for instance, how and why you contrived to have me brought here.'

The response was unexpected, brief and to the point.

'As to why, my lady –' said Clarence '– the short answer is that Richard my brother desires to marry you.'

'To marry me?' repeated Anne in horror. 'You would have me believe that he who murdered my beloved prince, rightful heir to the kingdom, desires to marry his victim's lady!'

Clarence watched her for a few moments in silence.

'I would not say the prince was murdered,' he said then. 'Nay, he was slain on Tewkesbury field along with many other good men and true. By Richard's hand, it cannot be denied – I was there and saw it all, though I stayed my hand, not drawing my sword out of respect for you, my cousin. I saw it all, as I say, dear lady, and though 'twas Richard dealt the first blow, Hastings and Dorset swiftly followed. I would I could have prevented it – but it all happened so quickly, you must understand. Battle-fever was in our blood.'

'You say that Richard desires to marry me – even though you know him to be my lord's murderer?'

'I said he slew him – not that he murdered him!'

At the back of Anne's mind was the remembrance of Richard as she had last seen him – even then, as a youth of fourteen, he had been a difficult person to know, one who kept his own counsel. And yet always had there been a warmth in his voice when he had addressed her ...

'Hearken to me, my lady,' continued Clarence, and there was a new determination in his voice. 'Richard my brother desires to wed you – he also desires your inheritance!'

'My inheritance?' asked Anne. 'Grief and loneliness, do you mean?'

'You are, with my lady, co-heir to the vast inheritance of the families of both your parents,' Clarence reminded her. 'You and Isabel have expectations which will make you eventually the richest in the land, with very few exceptions.'

'And that is why Richard wishes to marry me?' There was a catch in Anne's voice.

'Alas that I cannot say otherwise! My brother, as you may recall, was ever a law unto himself. He is loyal to the king and myself, but even so –' Clarence sighed '– there are times when I look at Richard and wonder!'

'And what, pray, do you wonder?'

'I wonder what he has in mind. Does he, I ask myself, regret being the youngest brother – the one who has little hope of inheriting crown and fortune? When he is supporting the king, winning his wars for him, playing the part of the young ingenuous brother with the interests of his sovereign very much at heart, loyal, true, ready to die in his brother's cause – does he never ask himself why? Does he never consider his own position and how many stand between himself and the crown? Or does he say to himself, "The Prince of Wales no longer stands in my way – but still there is Edward my brother and his infant son, and George of Clarence as well as any sons of Edward and George yet unborn!" What goes on behind that enigmatic exterior – does he plot and plan and bide his time?'

'If what you tell me is true ... That is to say –' Anne

added hastily '– if you, my lord, are not mistaken in believing that Richard of Gloucester wishes to make me his bride, then the answer is nay, very much nay! I shall, as I said, remain unwed.'

'I told my lord that would be your answer,' put in Isabel who had so far remained silent. 'I know you so well, my sister, better methinks than I know myself – and I saw how greatly you loved the prince, how idyllically happy you were together.'

'We were indeed,' agreed Anne tearfully, 'and there can be no question of my marrying another. Should Richard sue for my hand or send you, brother-in-law, to sue on his behalf, the answer would be nay.'

'What if you did not see him as one who slew the prince?' asked Clarence curiously.

'As my lord's murderer, you mean?' asked Anne pointedly. 'It would make no difference in respect of my marrying him. A mere three weeks have elapsed since my lord died – it would be a heartless one indeed who could contemplate remarriage so soon! But with Richard it can never be!'

'Then we were not mistaken, my dear,' Clarence said, turning to Isabel. 'We have acted in accordance with your sister's wishes.'

'Then already you have refused Richard on my behalf? Without consulting me, without so much as …'

'Nay, such was not my meaning,' put in Clarence, registering her indignation with some interest. 'And if you believe that my brother is one who takes nay for an answer – from anyone, let alone a lady on whom he has set his heart – then you know him not!'

'His heart, you say?' Anne's voice was cold. 'Has Richard of Gloucester a heart?'

But even as she posed the question, she was aware of the answer. Why do I speak thus, she wondered, and confuse myself as well as my hearers? I know full well that Richard has a heart – or had one when last I saw him. He was gentle, kind and generous towards myself – never did I receive so much as a sharp word when in his company. And it is commonly held that the boy is father to the man …

'Hearken to me, my lady.' Clarence spoke briskly, as if he had reached a decision and would tell her of it without more ado. 'Richard is determined to marry you – aye, determined! He seeks, as a youngest son, to enrich himself by acquiring a wealthy bride. But since I hold you, as my lady's sister, in deep affection and reverence, I mean to prevent his marrying you.'

'But had I remained at the Tower ...'

'Richard would have persuaded the king to release you – to himself, as his future bride!' interposed Clarence.

'I would not have agreed.'

'There are ways of forcing a lady to change her mind,' came the chilling reply. 'Or of making life extremely unpleasant for her if she remains obdurate. Richard has set his mind on the match – there is therefore no other way.'

'No other way, you say? What mean you, my lord?'

'None, save my servants, knows you are here,' Clarence reminded her. 'You were snatched from the Tower – none knows by whom or for what reason. You will remain here till such time as the hue and cry has died down – and Richard has put the matter from his mind.'

'Which, from what you say, could well be never!'

'Anne dear, we must look on the bright side,' Isabel told her. 'There is no point in meeting trouble half way!'

'And if Richard does not put the matter from his mind?' persisted Anne. 'After all, any who call here, my lord, be they friends or relations – maybe Richard himself – would at once recognize me. I cannot remain hidden for ever!'

Clarence's gaze was cold and there was that in his voice which riveted Anne's attention.

'I fail to see why not,' he said evenly. 'Anyway, that is more or less how it will be.'

'I must hide, do you mean?'

'It is the only way, Anne,' put in Isabel. 'Truly it is. We have talked and talked, my lord and I, and because we love you and wish to protect you, we want you to remain here with us.'

'You would have me remain in my chamber – that is what you are saying, is it not?' demanded Anne. 'You want to treat me as a prisoner. I would have been better off in the Tower, God help me!'

'Anne, my dear, hearken to me,' Isabel said in the manner of one pouring oil on troubled waters. 'There is no need to look so alarmed. You will not be locked up, I promise you – but simply placed in a situation where none would think of looking for you.'

'How so, pray?'

Isabel appeared to hesitate and looked uneasily at her husband.

'Pray continue,' Clarence urged her. 'There is no point in our beating about the bush!'

'We require a new cook-maid,' Isabel said. 'No experience is necessary – the under-cook is responsible for the training of underlings. The work is not arduous, needless to say – and the master cook, I am told, acts fairly and reasonably towards those in his charge.'

'Why are you telling me this, Isabel?' asked Anne. 'What pray have your domestic arrangements to do with myself? As for the little homily about your head cook acting reasonably and the work not being arduous – we both know that neither of us has ever seen the inside of a kitchen in our lives! Why else would we employ chamberlains, stewards and housekeepers!'

'There is an empty attic on the upper floor,' Isabel told her. 'Small it is, but it would give you privacy.'

Anne looked at her sister aghast. 'You are actually suggesting that I – that I ...'

'Clothing is provided – two of everything. Starched aprons, fustian kirtles, linen caps and clogs are the order of the day, I understand.'

'You surely cannot be serious!'

'Never more so,' said Clarence.

'You are actually suggesting that I make pretence of being a cook-maid?' asked Anne, white to the lips. 'I refuse, of course – the idea is preposterous! I insist on being conducted back to the Tower forthwith.'

'Garbed as a cook-maid, you would not get past the hall-porter of a gentleman's residence –' Clarence told her '– let alone the chamberlain of Clarence House!'

Realizing at last that this was no bizarre jest; that she had in fact been snatched from the portals of a known prison to be deposited in one as yet unknown but distinctly sinister,

Anne was suddenly very much afraid.

'Since I am not yet garbed as a cook-maid,' she managed to say incisively, 'I shall at once betake myself to the Tower on foot.'

Clarence smiled at that. 'You imagine they would lower the drawbridge for a mere woman?' he asked scornfully.

'You can forget about your cook-maid, brother-in-law,' Anne said defiantly, making for the door. 'I am taking my leave of you ...'

But Clarence too had turned towards the door.

'Hortense!' he called.

The door opened instantly to admit Hortense, making it plain that the maid had been waiting within earshot.

'Come with me, if you please,' she said to Anne, dispensing with the customary mode of address. 'I will show you to your chamber.'

'It is for your own good,' said Clarence. 'Believe me, my lady and I have given much thought to this – it is the only way.'

'You will come to no harm, my sister, I promise you.' Isabel was close to tears. 'Only for a few days – till we can send you away to the country and safety. Bear with us, my sister.'

'Come,' said Hortense in a peremptory tone. 'I will show you to your chamber and there you can remain till the morrow – your duties do not commence till then.'

'But I am ...' Anne tried to push her away as Hortense seized her arm. 'Nay, I shall not go with you. This is a trick, a cruel trick – I know not what you are up to, any of you, but you have not my welfare at heart, God help me!'

'Anne, pray be reasonable!' sobbed Isabel. 'I was so longing to see you, to have you visit us here in London – and now you have spoilt it all! How could you be so tiresome – so selfish!'

'Nay, nay –' Anne cried, struggling as Hortense propelled her towards the doorway. 'You have no right – no right. Remove your hands from me this instant ...'

But it was no use. Even as she struggled, a man strode into the solar – the one who had snatched her from the Tower a few hours earlier.

This time he showed her no courtesy – seeming not even

to recognize her. Gripping her other arm, he and Hortense marched her unceremoniously from the chamber.

'Isabel, how could you!' Anne called from the doorway. 'You have been influenced by that turncoat husband of yours – how could you be party to such duplicity!'

'I had no choice.' Isabel's sobs followed her still-struggling sister down the corridor. 'Believe me, my sister, I had no choice!'

# Twenty-Six

'A lazy good-for-nothing, is that one!' declared the under-cook to her superior. 'You've only to take a look at 'er hands to know she's been dodging it all 'er life!'

'Give 'er a chance, Meg!' said the master cook, a cheerful-looking man who, dedicated to his work, preferred to leave the training and disciplining of underlings to his assistant. 'She's not overly strong by the looks of 'er. Just got over the small-pox, Hortense said, when she brought 'er in – told us to go easy on 'er for a bit!'

'Go easy on *her* and you'll be piling more work on the rest of us,' grumbled Meg. 'Anyway, what's 'er ladyship's maid got to do with the kitchen?'

'Took pity on 'er, it seems. Found 'er wand'ring in the street.'

'A likely tale – that Hortense is a hard one, for all she's a dab hand with the curling tongs!'

'They say 'er ladyship thinks the world of 'er.'

Meg snorted knowingly. ' 'Er ladyship hates 'er guts, I dare say – what woman wouldn't, when 'er maid is having it off with 'er bloke!'

'Enough of that, Meg! I'll not 'ave tittle-tattle in my kitchen – as well ye know.'

'I dare say 'er ladyship would as soon not 'ave 'is lordship carryin' on with 'er maid – but there's naught she can do about it!' With an air of put-that-in-your-pot-and-stew-it, Meg turned away.

At once her gaze alighted on Anne.

'You're supposed to be scrubbing that there table, girl – not soothing its feelings! Put a bit of beef into it, do!'

'Beef?'

'Nay, leave that beef alone – it's naught to do with you.

134

The table's your task at the moment – so no changing the
subject unless you want to feel the back o' me hand!'
'I am doing my best.'
'You are indeed – doing your best to ruin that there table!
Nay, not like that, girl – where 'ave you been all yer life? In a
pigsty – or don't they 'ave tables where you come from?'
'Where I come from ...'
'No back-answers – or you'll get the housekeeper's birch-
rod across your rump! We don't stand for back-answers in
this establishment.'
'The housekeeper had better keep her hands off me ...'
'Mend your ways, girl – and you can start by doing a bit
more than your best with that there table. Anyone'd think
you hadn't seen a scrubbing-brush afore! Scrub the way o'
the grain – look, I'll show you! See, like that, the way o' the
grain – that gets the grease out o' the ruts and saves the table
getting criss-crossed with brush marks. Here, try again!'
'It looks clean enough to me already.'
'Then get on with the others. There's five more to do –
and then you can 'ave a go at the ovens.'
Conscious of a sudden silence in the great kitchen as Meg
moved away, Anne looked up to see the gaze of the greater
part of the kitchen staff centred on her. She was not one of
them – they knew it as well as she did; had recognized it
from the moment she first set foot in the kitchen. Her
French-accented English seemed incongruous in a kitchen-
maid, and her fellow-servants could no more easily follow
what they termed her la-di-da accent, than she could theirs.
'Poor thing!' exclaimed another of the cook-maids to her
companion as they resumed work. 'Hey, Meg, you're being
a bit hard on 'er, ain't yer?'
Meg shrugged. 'Not as hard as the housekeeper would be
if I gave her the nod!'
'She looks a bit frail to me, Meg – give 'er a chance.'
'I'm giving 'er a chance, ain't I? Didn't I show 'er nice and
friendly-like how to scrub down a trestle! Beats me where
the girl comes from.'

\* \* \*

'Have you 'eard the latest?' Jackie – the cook-maid who had

spoken up for Anne – asked of her fellow-worker a week or
so later. 'Anne of Warwick, 'er as was Princess of Wales, 'as
disappeared. Snatched from the guards, she was, as she
stepped off at the Tower and she's not been seen since.'

'Been done away with, I 'spect,' said the other girl. ' 'Twas
rumoured she was carrying – and none o' this lot wants the
Prince of Wales's brat turning up at the last moment, do
they? Stands to reason. Aye, 'tis clear as mud – she's been
done away with and that's an end of it!'

'They do say as Richard of Gloucester fancied 'er.
Wanted to marry 'er, but this one 'ere –' Jackie nodded
towards the ceiling. '– would 'ave none of it!'

'What's it to 'im?' Lil, the other girl, likewise indicated the
ceiling. 'He can't marry the lass, when all's said an' done.'

'He didn't approve, did he!'

'Why not?'

'Obvious, ain't it? He didn't want 'er ladyship's inheritance split atween the two of 'em.'

'Atween 'er ladyship and 'er sister, d'yer mean?'

'Aye. Him upstairs –' Again the ceiling seemed to have
taken on a human, and decidedly masculine, identity. '–
wanted to make sure as Richard of Gloucester didn't get a
look in. Wanted it all for 'imself, didn't he?'

'So you're saying it's 'im upstairs as 'as done away with ...'

'Sh! For Christ's sake sh, Lil! D'yer want to get us all
hanged!'

\* \* \*

'See we've a new turnspit this morning, Lil!' remarked
Jackie to her friend several weeks later.

Lil nodded. 'The other's gone to 'is lordship's Yorkshire
place. Going with the family, he told me 'e was. He said it all
proud-like – as if the duke and duchess couldn't do without
'im! A spit's a spit, no matter who turns it, I said to 'im when
'e told me, and he boxed me ears – for me sauce, he said!'

'Handsome, ain't he?'

'Bit long in the tooth for me – and too handy with 'is
hands!'

'Nay, I was meaning the new fellow – he's not above
twenty-five, I'd say. Gorgeous, ain't he – don't seem cut out

for a turnspit somehow. Oh, there you are, Annie,' said Jackie with a smile – catching sight of Anne. 'Feeling all right, are you, love?'

'Thank you, I am well enough,' replied Anne.

'Then take this over to the turnspit, Annie love – he'll need it for basting the ox.'

'Funny one, ain't she?' remarked Lil when Anne was out of earshot. 'Never speaks unless you speak to 'er – and she sounds real la-di-da, don't she?'

'I 'spect that's why Meg's got 'er knife into 'er. Gives 'er all the roughest tasks – I feel quite sorry for the lass. She's that skinny too – and you know, Lil, no-one could say as cook himself keeps us underlings short of food! Her hands is raw, poor thing, from all that scrubbing. Meg made 'er do one o' them tables three times over the other day – said she was shirking, but I couldn't see nothing wrong with it.'

'Caused quite a rumpus though, our Annie – didn't she!'

'I'll say. What with Meg shouting and Annie standing 'er ground – and Meg calling the housekeeper to give 'er what-for!'

'Didn't cry out or anything though, when they carted her off to the outhouse!'

'More fool her! I told 'er afterwards – I said, if it 'appens again, cry out fit to bring the ceiling down and you'll likely get off lightly. But I doubt she knew what I was on about.'

'It was 'er not making a fuss as made Hetty Housekeeper lay it on so hard. You know how she is, that one! A bit twisted, if you ask me!'

'Afterwards when I spoke to Annie, she was pale as ashes. "That's it" she said, "now 'er ladyship shall hear how I'm being treated!" I didn't know what she meant at first – and of course Meg 'ad overheard! Before I got a chance to ask her, Meg poked her nose in again. "I'm responsible for seeing you do yer work proper, so you'll do as you're told and like it – or take the consequences!" But Annie 'ad got the bit atween her teeth by then. "I shall go to the duchess," she said, "she can have no idea what goes on here or she would have done something about it long since".'

Lil chuckled. 'That's just 'ow Annie speaks – that's exactly it!' she said admiringly. 'What did Meg say to that?'

' "The duchess?" she said. "You'll not get near enough to 'er to tell 'er anything – none of us ever sees her. Thomas Burdet, the steward, is the power behind the throne, if you get me meaning, in this place! Besides, the duchess isn't 'ere – went off with 'is lordship yesterday to Yorkshire. They'll not be back for weeks, maybe months – so if you know what's good for you, you'll watch your tongue, do as you're told and show proper respect for your betters!" '

'So that's what made her take on so!' said Lil. 'She didn't speak to any of us for ages after that.'

'But she put her back into the scrubbing, and that in turn got 'er on the wrong side of cook 'imself. Her hands got that raw, they started to bleed and cook said she wasn't to handle the food – so they put 'er on dry jobs instead, like filling the coal-hods and running to and fro 'twixt oven and spit.'

'The turnspit's taken quite a fancy to 'er, if you ask me!' remarked Lil.

'To Annie?'

Lil nodded. 'A bit thin for the likes of most men, I'd say – too pale and bloodless looking! *And* she don't talk like the rest of us!'

'Nor does he – the turnspit, I mean. Haven't you noticed, Lil?'

'Can't say I had – still, *now* you mention it! Birds of a feather then, I s'pose! To tell the truth, Jackie, all I noticed was 'ow handsome 'e was – and I asked meself which of us would tickle 'is fancy!'

\* \* \*

Anne felt tired and listless. It was the fifth consignment of melted dripping, and the earthenware basin was boiling hot and stung her chapped hands.

Over-full this time, the basin tilted and slopped some of its contents on the stone floor. Anne slithered on the slippery surface, lost her footing and fell, basin and all, to the ground – spraying the rest of the hot liquid on to whatever happened to be within range.

Pandemonium followed. The master cook ordered the

maids to take buckets and mops and clean up the mess –
while Meg turned on Anne who was lying, as if stunned, her
apron sodden with melted fat and one hand twisted awk-
wardly beneath her.

'Get up, you lazy good-for-nothing!' she cried. 'Up on
your feet at once and give a hand with this mess – then
betake yourself to the outhouse while I go for the
housekeeper!'

The turnspit, having mopped his fat-bespattered jerkin,
turned to Anne.

'Are you hurt?' he asked, ignoring the fuming Meg. 'That
fat was nigh on boiling!'

'Only my wrist,' Anne said tremulously. 'I seem to have
twisted it.'

'Stop your moaning, girl ...' Meg started to say.

But the turnspit interrupted – seeming of a sudden to
take charge of the situation.

'Annie must go to her closet and change her apron,' he
said calmly to Meg. 'Then, upon her return, I shall examine
and bandage her hand. I worked for a horse-dealer before,
you see, and have a fair knowledge of such matters.'

'The girl's a fool!' declared Meg scathingly. 'And if you,
sirrah, encourage her laziness, she'll go from bad to worse.'

A turnspit worked independently of the rest of the
kitchen, having boys to assist him and calling on menials as
necessary – answerable only to chamberlain or steward.
Roasting the ox was the focal point of the preparation of
food for a large household and a good turnspit was the
pride of any nobleman's kitchen.

'Go, lass,' this one said to Anne, giving no heed to Meg.
'Take your time, return when you are ready – and then we
shall take a look at that wrist.'

\* \* \*

'Does that feel more comfortable?' the turnspit asked
presently.

'It does indeed.'

'Thanked be fortune, no bones are broken – though you
must undertake only the lightest tasks for a few days.'

'The lightest tasks?' Anne smiled wanly. 'I know not what

they would be!'

'Come over to the light and let me take a look at your other hand,' he said, leading her over to the window. 'Now, whilst I make pretence of examining it – pray you, my lady, hearken carefully to what I have to say!'

'You call me "my lady"?'

'I know who you are,' he said in a low tone, all the while scrutinizing her uninjured hand. 'Richard of Gloucester, my master, had me fill the post of turnspit here – thus gaining, as it were, a foot in the door!'

'Richard of Gloucester knows?' Anne asked. 'You mean he knows I am here?'

'Ever since your disappearance, my lord has left no stone unturned to discover your whereabouts, my lady. Believing you to be in great danger, he was loath to force the issue when he discovered you were here. Now, with the departure of his brother, he sees his opportunity. I can say no more just now, for I see Meg bustling towards us – but pray be ready to act as I shall indicate, at a moment's notice if need be!' His voice continuing on an even keel, only the content of his words changed. 'There, lass, that'll do well enough – but the next time you feel like throwing a bowl of dripping at me, tip me the wink first!'

'What a fuss!' declared Meg, having noted the bandage – as well as the new turnspit's interest in one of her underlings. 'Serves the girl right, master turnspit, I say.'

'An accident, no more,' said he, turning his attention to the spit. 'I suggest she be let off with a caution this time!'

Light-hearted as the remark was, it suggested to the jealous woman a partisanship for the girl that was not to be stomached. Been making sheep's eyes at 'im, I suppose, she thought. Running after 'im, playing the strumpet, I shouldn't wonder – and 'im too good by far for the likes of 'er!

'Let 'er off? I'll let her off all right – off to the outhouse!' She turned to Anne. 'Go on, girl, don't stand there gawking. The floor a-wash, good dripping wasted – whatever next! It's high time she was taught a lesson. The girl's 'ad it coming to her these many weeks past – let 'er off indeed! It's me that's off – to fetch the housekeeper.'

'This lesson you speak of –' said the turnspit amiably, his

eyes on his task as the now-weeping Anne disappeared. 'Of what does it consist pray – jam or sauce making, soup or broth making, butter-churning, marinating?'

The cook laughed raucously. 'Rump reddening, I'd call it! She's a useless hussy, that one – but Hetty can be relied upon to teach her a thing or two!'

'Hetty?'

'The housekeeper.'

'But 'twas at myself the girl threw the dripping!'

'Then you're accusing 'er of doing it on purpose? That, sirrah, is a very serious charge.' Meg's eyes gleamed. So the fellow's not as taken with Annie as I thought, she said to herself, and in truth, I'm not surprised! All skin and bone she is, and a fellow like 'im, tall and well-made – an 'andsome devil if ever I saw one – wants a real woman, that's for sure ! 'But you could be right, turnspit – in fact, now I come to think of it, I'm sure you're right.'

'And since I'm right –' He spoke casually, his attention still on the spit. '– it surely gives me the right to administer the lesson!'

'Since you put it like that,' She shrugged – though inwardly gleeful. '– I've no objection. The girl's in the outhouse – she's all yours!'

'And since *you* put it like that ...' he said with a lascivious grin, parodying her words, 'I say the outhouse is too public a place for my choosing! Nay, I'll take her up to her closet – the boys can tend the spit while I'm gone. It will not take long to do what has to be done, and the wench can make as much fuss as she likes up there – none will hear her at this time of day!'

\* \* \*

'My lady, forgive me this little charade,' said the turnspit, closing the attic door. 'But I saw the chance of both saving you a beating – and talking to you in private.'

'At first methought you meant it,' said Anne tearfully. 'Methought ...'

'My lady, were I to lay so much as a finger on you, Richard of Gloucester would have me flayed alive!' her companion interposed and Anne had no doubt he meant it. 'You may be sure of that – even were I tempted to outrage the rules of chivalry!'

'You are a knight, sir?'

'To my lord of Gloucester,' he acknowledged, adding with a bow, 'Armand of Poitiers at your service, my lady.'

'I know not if my lord of Gloucester can help me. You see, sir …' Anne looked troubled, chary of telling her new-found champion that she believed Richard of Gloucester to be her first and foremost enemy. '… I have been here many weeks, maybe months – I know not how long in truth, since I lost count of time and had not the means of keeping a record.'

'You were snatched from the Tower during the last week of May – it is now late September,' Armand of Poitiers told her.

'Four months?' asked Anne, watching his expression closely. 'You say I have been here four months?'

'Almost to the day, my lady – does that surprise you?'

She nodded. 'So short a time in reality – yet to me it seems like four years! It is as unreal as a nightmare, yet my roughened hands and aching limbs are real enough! The countess my sister surely cannot know …'

'You have seen the Duchess of Clarence?' interposed Armand of Poitiers in surprise.

'Yea, when I was first brought here. She was kind, receiving me most amiably – and later, she and the duke together revealed their plan. At first I was amenable to the plan.'

'Pray tell me of it, my lady.'

'I was to remain in hiding for a short while, until a safe, more rural, refuge was found for me. I demurred, misliking the plan when the details were more fully revealed to me and decided then and there to return to the Tower – on foot if necessary. It was then that I found myself a prisoner – a prisoner who, a few hours later, was also a skivvy in her brother-in-law's kitchen.'

'Could not you have approached your sister?'

'How so, sir? As you know, kitchen staff are not permitted entry to the main house – and from the street, garbed as a cook-maid since I have no other attire, I am barred from admittance save by the servants' door at the rear.'

'You say you were amenable to the plan at first. Why so, my lady? Why did not you insist on joining the countess your mother at Beaulieu for instance?'

To Armand of Poitiers's consternation, she dissolved into tears at that. 'At Beaulieu, you say? Then poor mama must still be in sanctuary!'

'She is indeed – and I could think of worse places to be!' he said pointedly, before swiftly changing the subject. 'Forgive me if I seem to ask too many questions, my lady – but I judge we have but half an hour to ourselves, if we are not to raise doubts of my *dishonest* motives! I shall report to the duke my master this very evening, so it is necessary that I am fully cognisant of the facts. Indeed, from every aspect, time is of the essence!'

'Why do you say that, sir?'

'My lord has it on good authority that his brother will be returning here within the week – indeed, why else would Clarence House remain fully staffed during a long absence of himself and his lady, even to the extent of a new –' he smiled, '– and highly recommended turnspit!'

'As a matter of interest, sir, who did recommend you?'

'Why, my lord of Gloucester – who else, my lady?'

'And you are saying in fact that my brother-in-law is not in truth bound for Yorkshire?'

'He intends to journey only part of the way with his lady and then, on some pretext, will double back here. My master reasons that it is then that you would be in grave danger.'

'If that be so, then ...' She fell silent and he saw that she was trembling.

'Be not afraid – forewarned is forearmed, and be assured my lord of Gloucester has the matter well in hand. But the facts, my lady – the full facts, if you please.'

'You ask, sir, why at first I was amenable to the plan,' said Anne, making a valiant attempt at composure. 'I shall speak openly – trusting, sir, in your good nature to assist my escape from the situation in which I now find myself.'

'Lady, you have my word on it – as a knight,' he assured her. 'Pray continue.'

'George of Clarence claimed that Richard of Gloucester desired to wed me – with a view to gaining control of my inheritance.'

'*Par Dieu!*' exclaimed Armand of Poitiers. 'That you should have been so deceived! Whether or not my master desires to marry you, is beside the point. That he esteems you greatly cannot be denied – that he is concerned for your welfare is beyond debate! Of such, you may one day judge for yourself, my lady – and answer for yourself. I am charged solely with the task of gaining you your freedom and placing you under my master's protection.'

'Then my lord of Gloucester would not force me to marry him – for the sake of my inheritance?'

Armand of Poitiers's voice was a little brusque, Anne thought – as if, in his opinion, it went without saying.

'My lady, the truth is as follows: the Duke of Clarence, not wishing to divide his lady's inheritance with any gentleman Your Ladyship might in the future decide to marry, hid you away – though whether with or without his lady's knowledge of his true motive, is not known!'

'Nay, nay, my sister would not have been party to such a plan!' declared Anne. 'Such a cruel plan, it was – in truth sir, I know not how I have endured these past months.'

'Rest assured you will not be here much longer, my lady,' Armand of Poitiers told her gravely. 'Once I have informed my master of the situation, and the degradation and humiliation to which you are being subjected, I doubt not he will move heaven and earth to release you!'

'Could not you take me with you now?' she asked plaintively.

'Should I, a humble turnspit as it is believed, attempt to smuggle a kitchen-maid from the household of the Duke of Clarence, it just might arouse suspicion!' he said ironically. 'The aforesaid duke retains a sizeable body of men-at-arms who are under orders to attack first and ask questions afterwards!'

'I would be willing to take that risk.'

'As would I – for myself. And whilst I would give my ears to see my master's expression as I presented him with a somewhat dishevelled cook-maid, complete with starched apron, clogs and all –' Armand of Poitiers smiled wryly '– it is my desire, my lady, to present you to my lord Richard in one piece!'

'Then I must practise patience,' Anne said wistfully.

'For a short space only, I promise you. Now we must return whence we came. I trust you feel equal to enduring the interested stares that will doubtless greet our return.'

Anne blushed. 'You mean they will think that – that you ...'

Armand of Poitiers's voice was cold and carefully dispassionate. 'If it be any comfort to you, my lady, the role of a brutal ravisher is not at all to my taste! But since one might as well be hanged for a sheep as a lamb – and as your freedom and perchance your life could well depend on it – I shall play the part of a satiated lecher and you of an ill-used skivvy!'

'I am not sure if ...'

'Tell yourself 'tis naught but a game – a game in a good cause! That, my lady, is what we tell new recruits on the eve of battle – the Kingmaker could have vouched for that.'

The mention of her father was a masterly stroke. It did the trick, he noticed. She wore a look of determination that had not been there before.

'I am ready,' she said quietly.

'Just one thing more,' he said, taking a small diamond brooch from his jerkin and passing it to her. 'Keep this concealed always upon your person.'

Without asking the obvious question, Anne pinned the brooch to the inner lining of her bodice. Already Armand of Poitiers was holding the door open for her.

'Into battle!' he said smiling. 'Cry God for England, Edward – but not methinks for cousin George!'

# Twenty-Seven

Armand of Poitiers, alias Peter the turnspit, swaggered into the kitchen and, cuffing the lads who had been combining a game of tiddley-winks with their allotted tasks, took over the roasting of the ox.

The kitchen had suddenly fallen silent, as work was temporarily halted and all eyes turned first to the turnspit – and then to the dishevelled cook-maid who followed.

'Giving the ox a basting now, are you, Pete?' asked Meg, with a knowing glance at Anne. 'A right dab-hand you are at the basting – by the looks of 'er!'

'Teach her a lesson was what you said – well, she's a good deal wiser than she was a while ago, I can tell you,' said the turnspit with truth, winking at Lil. 'I'd wager her own ma wouldn't know her now!'

'Poor kid!' said Jackie in a low voice to Lil. 'She can 'ardly walk by the looks of 'er – 'e must 'ave given 'er a right larruping! And even now Meg's not satisfied – putting 'er to wash the dishes and she with an injured hand into the bargain!'

'Funny, Jackie, but I thought Pete had taken a fancy to Annie – he seemed all on 'er side at first!'

'Hm, he did – but 'e wants to keep in with Meg, don't he – Lord knows why! I'm going to lend Annie a hand.'

'You'd better not, Jackie. You know what'll happen if you do – you'll get on the wrong side of Meg and ...'

'Give Annie a rest?'

'Well, don't say I didn't warn you! If Meg thinks you're taking Annie's part, she might set 'im as is over there on you next.'

'Let 'er try!'

'She's gone to talk to him now – just look at 'er, Jackie!

146

Simpering and patting 'er hair, she is – fancies her luck, she does, the bitch! Better watch out – you could likely find yourself in hot water if she gets 'er knife into you.'

'Sooner find meself in hot water than hot dripping – like some I could mention!'

'All the same ...'

'I can take care of meself, Lil, as we both knows. There's naught any of 'em could do to me as hasn't been done afore!'

'You're alive, ain't you?'

'That's more than you could say for poor Annie at the moment – just look at 'er, Lil. Makes me heart bleed, it do – she'll not see next Christmas if one of us don't give 'er a hand!'

'Jackie, where are you off to? You're surely not serious ...'

'I've finished the pickling in record time – cripes though, them onions don't half make your eyes run! I'm off to lend a hand, as I said.'

'What about me?'

'You can stay here, moaning and groaning and doing nothing for no-one!'

'I'll give 'er a hand as well if you like.'

'That's up to you, Lil – give 'er a foot as well if you want to!'

'Watch out, Jackie – Meg's looking at you!'

'A cat may look at a king.'

'Watch out just the same – for 'er and randy rascals and basins of hot dripping!'

'Suffered 'em all in me time. But our Annie, poor love – she's no match for a great hulking brute like him. Meg'll have me to reckon with from now on!'

'Wait, Jackie – wait for me!'

# Twenty-Eight

Armand of Poitiers, his men-at-arms following, rode into the courtyard of Clarence House two days later, dismounted and strode into the great hall.

'His Grace is from home, sir,' said the surprised Thomas Burdet, the steward. 'He departed for Yorkshire three days since.'

'I am aware of that,' said Armand of Poitiers evenly. 'Richard of Gloucester, my master, was informed of his brother's movements, needless to say, and was charged furthermore with the administration of a certain family matter during his lordship's absence. I am come hither then as my master's representative in the aforementioned matter.'

'Then you will wish to use the library, sir,' said Thomas Burdet urbanely. 'The duke my master's papers are kept there. Allow me to show you the ...'

'You misunderstand me. My reference to a family matter pertained to a theft believed to have been committed by one, a servant in this household.'

The steward was smooth, suave – yet there was that in his manner that suggested to the perceptive knight that here was a man with more than one guilty secret.

'Theft?' he was asking. 'I assure you, sir, that the menials are most carefully selected – by myself.'

'Permit me to explain. Since her departure, the Duchess of Clarence has discovered the loss of a diamond brooch. She questioned Hortense, her maid, who after much persuasion, admitted the theft. It seems that, unable to dispose of the article without arousing suspicion prior to departure from London, Hortense deposited it with a kitchen-maid, one known to have connection with robbers

148

and others of ill-repute in the city.'

'A kitchen-maid, you say?'

'A cook-maid who goes by the name of Annie – not her real name, needless to say!'

'Annie?' The steward frowned thoughtfully. 'I seem to recall a wench of that name – yea, I have it! In fact, she was not engaged by myself or the head cook – she was brought to us by Hortense!'

'Ah, the culprit herself!' nodded the knight in a satisfied tone. 'They are partners in crime I doubt not!'

'Sir, I find this matter deeply distressing,' declared the steward. 'To think that on the one occasion I relied on another's judgment ...'

'The duchess also, I understand, is deeply distressed at her loss. The cook-maid must be questioned – closely questioned, as I doubt 'tis the first time she has been party to a crime. She may then be charged and taken before the justices.'

'I shall see to it, sir.'

'Nay, at the duchess's request, my lord of Gloucester will attend to the matter. There is, you see, the question of the brooch – if the wench is alerted, she could well dispose of it before we have a chance to search her – and could thus implicate another! Therefore, Master Burdet, I must ask you to have the creature brought here, that I myself may interrogate her before conducting her to my master.'

\* \* \*

Anne recognized Armand of Poitiers at once – and was surprised that the steward had not.

But then she realized why. To a man such as Thomas Burdet, servants were seen, not as individuals, but collectively as menials. They went about their tasks, quietly and unobtrusively if they were wise, and it was therefore doubtful whether the steward, faced with a turnspit recommended by his lordly master's brother, would have noted his appearance.

Thinking back to her own privileged childhood, Anne recognized with a disconcerting sense of guilt that it had always been so. One knew one's personal maid and those that supervised at table – but the menials who did the greater part of the work behind the scenes were as faceless and unknown in truth as a nestful of worker-ants going about their business.

On the orders of the steward, she herself had been bundled unceremoniously from the kitchen by two of the Clarence House men-at-arms, and stood now, flanked by the two men, waiting uneasily for Armand of Poitiers to speak.

He does look different, she thought. Stern, unbending, his eyes are cold, so cold as he meets my gaze. Is he then not who he claimed to be the other day? Was it merely a ruse to put me off my guard and plant a diamond brooch on me? Is he in truth in Clarence's employ ...?

'It was from close by the Tower that you came here, was it not?' asked the erstwhile turnspit.

'Yea, sir,' she replied – ah, she thought, so he is on my side after all. He is about to reveal my true identity. 'That is so.'

'And shortly after your arrival, you were placed in the charge of one Hortense – lady's maid to Isabel Duchess of Clarence.'

'I was indeed, sir – though not until ...'

'Answer yea or nay, wench – we want no maunderings,' said the knight sternly. 'Hortense, I am told, found you a place here in the kitchens – is that correct?'

'Yea. But you see ...'

'And she gave into your keeping a diamond brooch, I understand.'

'Hortense?' Anne looked at him in bewilderment. 'Nay, not Hortense ...'

'You deny receiving the brooch?'

'Nay, not the brooch. It was Hortense I was ...'

'Search her!' ordered Armand of Poitiers, his voice like the crack of a whip. 'Search the creature and be sharp about it. I have not got all day!'

Meg, the under-cook, who had followed Anne from the kitchen, being the only female present, went to the task with a will.

At last, groping inside Anne's bodice, her fingers closed round the diamond brooch.

'Here it is!' she cried triumphantly, breaking the pin in her enthusiasm and tearing her victim's bodice. 'Fixed to 'er bodice, it was!'

The retrieved brooch caught the light, the diamonds seeming to wink at the stern-faced knight.

'What have you to say for yourself, wench?' he asked tersely. 'You are a thief, as well as a known pickpocket – the scourge of this fair city!'

'I knew it, sir,' Meg told him. 'I knew from the first she was wicked through an' through. God knows I did my best by way of correction, as did the housekeeper – and the turnspit, bless 'im, 'e did his utmost! But 'twas all in vain – too far gone, she were, ah me! ah me!'

Armand of Poitiers turned to one of his men.

'Take her into the courtyard and mount her up,' he ordered. 'Then chain her ankles under the horse's belly.'

'Best not take any chances with 'er!' Anne heard Meg saying as she was led away. 'Thieving and whoring, and deceiving decent folk – let 'er be whipped at the cart's-tail, I say!'

Anne burst into tears. It was as she had feared. And that dreadful, vindictive woman had had the last word! There was no hope for her now. She was being taken away – in Clarence's absence but by his design, no doubt – to be charged before the justices with theft and any and every other crime that could be foisted on her. The knight, the diamond brooch, Hortense: it had all been part of a carefully laid plan. She would be convicted and sentenced – then taken out, if not to be hanged, then to be pilloried or whipped at the cart's tail and left, bleeding and helpless, to beg her bread till she lay down in a ditch and died.

'Nay, not like that!' Armand of Poitiers was saying to his man-at-arms. 'No point in crippling the wench *before* her trial! That way, she'd be bandy ere she'd gone half a mile and that would spoil somebody's fun later on!'

As he bent to loosen the chain that joined her ankles, he caught her eye and winked – and she registered the hint of a smile in his eyes. Relief flooded over her. Everything was all right. Armand of Poitiers was merely playing a part. He was on her side, after all.

And then they were moving off, riding out of the

courtyard and into the narrow city street beyond. They moved at a smart trot for about a quarter of a mile, when the knight called a halt.

'Here you are, wench!' he said, dismounting to wrap a warm cloak around her and unchain her ankles. 'She'll not escape us – but we bear her no malice, do we, lads!' he said cheerfully to his men.

Anne realized then that they were unaware of her true identity, seeing her as the cook-maid she looked to be, and that her rescuer was compromising between guarding her secret and making her as comfortable as possible.

'Thank you, sir,' she said quietly. 'I am grateful.'

'We shall soon be there – once we reach the end of Newgate Street, we shall be in sight of our destination.'

'Whither are we bound?'

'St. Martin's-le-Grand.'

'But that is surely a college of secular canons, associated with Westminster Abbey.'

'It is indeed – it also possesses rights as a sanctuary!'

'Then ...'

'A certain person, who shall be nameless, entered you in the sanctuary yesterday,' the knight told her as they came to a halt. 'There you will remain till other arrangements can be made.'

Anne sensed the other men watching her as the knight spoke. It must have become obvious to them by then that the matter was not as it had seemed at Clarence House, but they would not dare their master's wrath by making comment.

She looked towards the sanctuary and then turned to her rescuer in dismay.

'But I cannot go in there – like this!' she exclaimed, mindful of her ripped bodice, menial's garb and generally dishevelled appearance. 'I cannot – I should die of shame should anyone recognize me!'

'None will recognize you,' was the curiously chilling reply. 'And remember that those who seek sanctuary are more often than not fleeing from danger or some other adversity – arriving in a variety of conditions and states of dress and undress. None cares, none asks, none tells – that is the rule, as I am sure you are aware. My lord entered you simply as "Anne of Warwick" and unless you should elect to divulge your full identity – as could be unwise at present – it will remain inviolate. After all, there must be hundreds of Annes who were born in Warwick and share your name!'

'You are right of course, sir. But ...'

'Come,' he said, seeing her hesitation. 'Come, I shall accompany you.'

He helped her dismount. She was light as a feather, he noticed, and was alarmed by her frailty. It seems to me, he thought, that we found her not a day too soon!

'I shall take you first to the dean – he, incidentally, is the only one here in our confidence,' he told her as they entered the great cloistered building. 'We deposited baggage for you at the sanctuary – clothing and such toiletries as were deemed necessary for your transformation!'

She smiled then and Armand of Poitiers was well satisfied. My lady smiles, he thought – the sun has come out from behind a cloud!

'You say *we* deposited the baggage, sir?'

'My lord of Gloucester's housekeeper and myself.'

Her face then was suddenly grave.

'How long am I to remain here, sir?' she asked.

'Until my lord has made other arrangements for you, my lady. Such things take time – although it must be admitted that my lord, when informed of your plight, was only with difficulty restrained from riding full tilt for Clarence House and rescuing you himself. I have rarely seen him so incensed – as when I told him all.'

Anne blushed. 'You told him all, you say?'

'All,' he repeated. 'Now, my lady, you have entered sanctuary. You will be safe here and will have time methinks to recover your strength – and look to the future. St. Martin's methinks will enable you to make the transition from low estate to high estate.'

\* \* \*

Four weeks later, attired now as befitted her station, Anne was conducted by Armand of Poitiers to the house of her uncle, George Archbishop of York.

Received with great kindness by her uncle, she had difficulty in containing her tears – it was so long since she had seen any of her family, save Isabel, and she was not sure that she wanted to see Isabel ...

The earl her father and her uncle John Neville, Marquis of Montagu, had both been slain at Barnet, their bodies exposed for two days at St. Paul's before burial. The prince her husband, whom she had loved – and, she told herself, still did love – best in the whole world, was dead also. Margaret of Anjou, her respected mother-in-law, was now at Windsor and beyond Anne's reach; while the countess her mother was still, as far as she knew, in sanctuary at Beaulieu and similarly beyond her reach.

The Countess of Warwick, wholly unable to protect or aid her daughter in any way, had made several unsuccessful attempts to leave sanctuary. King Edward's men, armed and vigilant, guarded every exit, leaving the countess in no doubt that, should they take her, she would be imprisoned for life or worse. She had written many letters, to relatives, friends and ecclesiastics, begging for news of Anne and asking that a search be mounted to discover her whereabouts, ascertain whether or not she was alive or dead – but all to no avail. Even Richard of Gloucester's plea to the king his brother for the release of his former guardian's widow, met with no response.

George Neville, Archbishop of York, had received his weeping niece with open arms. He had noted without comment her frail appearance. She has suffered much, he told himself, both through bereavement and ill-usage. Please God her sorrows are at an end and her life henceforth will be one of joy and contentment!

It was there at York House a few months later that, fully restored to health, Anne came face to face for the first time in five years with Richard of Gloucester.

# Twenty-Nine

Richard of Gloucester, now nineteen, had not seen Anne of Warwick for some five years.

Of medium height and having dark brown hair, he was not cast in the Plantagenet mould. He had a strong physique and a powerful sword-arm; the latter despite an injury sustained during the Battle of Barnet, which had left his right shoulder permanently a little higher than the other – a fact which Richard's enemies, the which there were many, were wont to exaggerate.

Already renowned as a soldier and strategist, he was courageous and resolute, though lacking the flamboyance of his eldest brother. By nature reserved, he kept his own counsel, dreamed his dreams and was content to wait for the tide of fortune to turn in his favour – at which time he would not hesitate to give fortune a helping hand!

His eyes were his most arresting feature. Large and wide, deep blue in colour, they gave hint that he was, after all, a Plantagenet. They suggested warmth, passion, even a little of sadness; yet at times they held a brooding look, as if he were gazing into a far-off future – and would, if he could, have averted his eyes from what he saw!

He planned, plotted, bided his time. He looked to a golden future, and Anne of Warwick was part and parcel of that golden future ...

He loved Anne. She was his second cousin, great-niece to his mother, the lady Cecily, whose favourite son he was. Anne had married another, had become the bride of Edward Prince of Wales. But Richard could wait ...

Edward Prince of Wales had been slain by command of Edward the king. Richard had himself borne no malice towards the youth who had been as near as made no difference his own age, but the prince had stood in his way ...

155

After Tewkesbury, the way had been clear for Richard. But then George of Clarence, his own turncoat brother, had kidnapped Anne, hidden her in his London Mansion and subjected her to all manner of indignities. His hands clenched with fury whenever he gave thought to how she whom he loved and who would one day be his had been treated. One day Clarence would pay, and pay dearly, for his treatment of Anne, but first had come the need to rescue her, to have the attainder against her revoked and her restored to her rightful position. The rest could wait ...

He had asked to see Anne alone – and the archbishop had acquiesced to the extent of remaining in the next chamber, but with the dividing door open.

Anne had smiled ruefully to herself when her uncle had informed her of the arrangement, but had refrained from comment. After the abuse and indignities I suffered at Clarence House, she thought, this show of chaperonage is ludicrous in the extreme. Alas, dear uncle, he knows little of what I suffered then – and far be it from me to enlighten him! As for Richard himself, I know not how much Armand of Poitiers told him. He said he had told him everything, but in truth not even he himself knew everything ...

As she entered the chamber where Richard was awaiting her, there followed a breath-taking few moments when both were devoid of words – each of them yearning to roll back the years and resume their former uncluttered relationship, yet conforming with the rules of etiquette.

Anne curtseyed and gave him her hand to kiss, and Richard, taking her hand, bowed deeply and waited correctly for her to speak first.

Anne was wearing a gown of deep blue with white fur trimming – its high waist-line emphasized by a four-inch wide girdle – worn over a pale grey undergown; and a gold chain necklace. Her hair, braided and piled high on her head, was concealed under a gold hennin with a butterfly veil.

There were now no outward signs of the sorrows and privations visited upon her following the defeat at Tewkesbury, a fact Richard noted with no small relief. She looked pale, composed, very much the snow maiden of his dreams.

Richard was no less richly and becomingly attired than she. He was wearing the newly-fashionable short tunic over an embroidered under-tunic, the former of brown velvet embroidered with gold thread, exaggeratedly padded and trimmed with fur; together with waist-to-toe hose. Clean-shaven, his dark hair was shoulder-length and worn in the page-boy style. A number of jewelled and signet rings ornamented the fingers and thumb of his right hand thus indicating – since one's sword-arm must of necessity be free of adornment – that he was left-handed. In fact, following the injury to his right shoulder – though it affected him no longer and he was, like all warriors, ambidextrous – his left had become and remained his sword-arm.

'It is good to see you, my lord,' Anne said.

'It has been a long time, cousin,' he said. 'And yet, over the years, you have been ofttimes in my thoughts.'

'Indeed, my lord?' Anne told herself: I must try to forget, at least for the time being! I must put from my mind that it was he who stands elegant and quiet-spoken before me now, who slew my beloved prince in cold blood. She seated herself, arranging the folds of her gown unhurriedly, gaining composure. 'Time changes many things – and us mortals most of all.'

There was a silence then, during which each was remembering something they would sooner have forgotten: Richard was remembering that she was not as virginal as she looked, that she had been the bride of one she was said to have held in deep regard – and Anne was remembering that which she had told herself she must forget.

'Methinks you know why I am here, my lady – why I have remained in the background these several months past, leaving Armand of Poitiers to do that which was needful. But now that you are, as I understand, fully restored to health, I shall no longer remain silent.' He was watching her closely, fearing what her answer would be and wishing to judge in the event whether or not she spoke from the heart. 'My lady, I ask that you do me the honour of becoming my bride.'

'I cannot,' she said – and he heard the tremor in her voice.

'I cannot, my lord. You do me much honour by the asking – but methinks we both know that the answer must be nay.'

'You have been a widow nigh on a year, my lady,' he reminded her. 'You would not dishonour your late lord's memory by promising now to wed myself one year hence – and thus placing yourself under my protection.'

'I cannot,' she said, close to tears. 'It cannot be – and you, Richard of Gloucester, surely know as well as I why it cannot be!'

'Tell me,' he said quietly.

'You were of those who murdered my lord – he whom I loved so dearly.'

'Murdered, you say?' Richard shook his head and spoke mildly. 'Edward of Lancaster was slain on the field of battle – as were many of his supporters, alas! War is war, as every man knows – and most of us, I suppose, when attempting the impossible, expect to find death on the field!'

'The prince was not a man, my lord – he was but a youth.'

Richard's expression was inscrutable. 'Think you he would applaud you for speaking thus, my lady? Man or boy, he died as a man, I assure you – how one dies, that one gives a good account of oneself, is what matters to a warrior.'

'I know not if it be so.'

'You, the daughter of a warrior, the most brilliant and courageous warrior of his time, must know it is so. Warwick was at one time my guardian, as you know – I respected him and knew his worth. We Yorkists vanquished and slew him on Barnet field – would you then reproach us for that?'

'I know not. I know not. I know only that I cannot agree to marry him who, in contest fair or foul, drove his blade into my precious lord's heart!'

Richard sighed. 'It is too soon, I dare say. I should have waited longer – eagerness got the better of me, alas! My lady, I shall accept your answer for the time being – but only for the time being. I shall not take nay for an answer, believe me – I have waited too long for you for that!'

'Time will not alter the case, my lord,' she said firmly –

though her thoughts were less firmly disposed. I must ignore the fact that this is Richard, he for whom I once had a great fondness, who was kind and gentle towards me – for Richard has surely changed. It must be so. And yet, seeing the sorrow in his eyes, hearing the warm timbre of his voice, I know that this is indeed the old Richard, the companion of my childhood ... 'If your regard for me is real and true, and if as recent events suggest you have my welfare at heart – then, my lord, you will not ask me again, ever.'

'You would wed another?'

'Nay, I wish to live out my days in prayer and mourning – remembering the beautiful times, the joyous hours that are gone.'

Richard knew a stab of jealousy – but, as always, his feelings were carefully hidden.

'You are so beautiful –' he said '– so remote and serene – indeed your very remoteness increases my regard for you, my desire to attain the unattainable. I respect your loyalty and devotion to your late lord – how could I not! – and yet somehow I shall find a means of weaning you from your wish to live in solitude. Some day, Anne of Warwick, I shall make you mine!'

# *Thirty*

Richard paid many visits to York House during the months that followed, conversing with Anne either in her uncle's presence or out of it. But always he received the same reply to that same question: always he went away a spurned lover. Richard could wait, as has been said, though maybe he was getting a little tired of waiting ...

George Neville, Archbishop of York, was younger brother to Anne's father. Now in his fortieth year, he had been chancellor of England in King Henry's reign. When, two years earlier, the victorious King Edward had entered London, the archbishop had surrendered Henry and himself to the new king. Imprisoned for two months only, he had then been fully restored to favour.

Anne, being still under attainder, was virtually under house arrest at York House, the archbishop being held responsible for her safe custody. She was allowed out occasionally at her uncle's discretion and was on the point of seeking permission to visit Margaret of Anjou, then at Wallingford, when disaster struck again.

York House was rudely awakened one midnight by armed men hammering on the great door and demanding admittance. On entering, they were found to be under orders of the Privy Council to arrest the archbishop. Taken completely by surprise, the archbishop was ordered to dress hastily and speak to none, after which he was seized and bundled unceremoniously from the house.

Anne was distraught when she learned what had happened. Her uncle was a kindly, God-fearing gentleman who, in latter years, had distanced himself from political intrigues and had given every appearance of acceptance of the Yorkist regime. Puzzled and fearful, she remained indoors all next day, hoping against hope that it was a false alarm, that her uncle would walk in the door unharmed and that life for them both would continue as before.

Towards early evening a servant announced, not as Anne hoped, the return of her uncle – but the arrival of Richard of Gloucester.

'Show him in,' she said uneasily, telling herself she had no real choice but wishing more than ever for her uncle's presence.

Richard entered the chamber and greeted her courteously as always – if he registered the archbishop's absence, he made no reference to it.

He spoke instead of Anne's mother as soon as they were seated – as if, Anne thought, it were the sole reason for his visit.

'My mother?' she asked in surprise. 'Has some ill befallen her? Pray tell me, my lord …'

'Be at peace, my lady,' he told her quietly. 'All is well with the countess your mother – indeed her situation is much improved. She has now left the sanctuary.'

'God be praised, she is free at last!'

'Not quite free. As with yourself, my lady, the countess is still under attainder for making war in the kingdom against our sovereign lord King Edward …'

'But …'

'… She fled sanctuary, eluding the king's men and hastened from Beaulieu to London whence she appealed to her future son-in-law for protection!'

Anne frowned. 'Her future son-in-law, you say, my lord? You surely refer to George of Clarence but …'

'Her future son-in-law,' repeated Richard. 'She had heard a rumour, it transpired, that her younger daughter had consented to become my bride – and she therefore fled to myself for protection.'

'Mama is well?' asked Anne, since that was her first concern and was the least complicated of replies. 'She is in good health?'

'Alas she suffers much from the ague!' Richard said evenly, surprised by her non-reaction to the son-in-law statement – but not showing it. 'She looks wasted and coughs much – indeed she looks to have aged beyond her years!'

'The life of a sanctuary person is little better, I dare say, than that of a cook-maid,' said Anne sadly. 'Poor dear mama – what did she do to deserve such treatment!'

'The countess is under my protection – for the time being ...' Richard paused significantly – to let the words sink in, Anne supposed. 'As with yourself, my lady, she is under house arrest only. She has agreed to renounce everything she possesses, her entire wealth and property, in favour of yourself and your sister.'

'And in return, my lord?'

'She will be granted a measure of freedom – following parliamentary partition of the Neville estates.'

'But, for myself, I have no desire for mama's possessions.'

'You are content to remain as you are – a pauper?' Richard spoke dispassionately, his voice carefully modulated – but the sting was none the less there.

Anne paled. 'The archbishop my uncle has promised me a home with him as long as I will. Here I am content.'

'Content?' Richard looked rueful. 'Alas that your contentment must be short-lived – and that I am the one who must be its destroyer!'

'You have news of my uncle,' she said then in alarm. 'Tell me, I pray you – I feared greatly for him.'

'He is well enough in health, I believe,' he told her. 'But the king is displeased with him. He has consequently been banished to Rouen and will remain a prisoner there at His Grace's pleasure – his possessions and his see, needless to say, being forfeit to the crown.'

'Needless to say,' agreed Anne, close to tears. 'So that is it – solely because he gave his penniless, widowed niece a roof over her head and offered her protection from her enemies, my uncle is being penalised – he now is landless, penniless and lacks his own freedom!'

'Alas, you paint a mighty gloomy picture!' Richard sighed ostentatiously. 'Let us not forget that the archbishop's widowed niece is penniless only because she wills it so – his widowed niece's mother furthermore is a fugitive only because her widowed daughter is stubborn and unrelenting!'

'You play with words, my lord!' Anne said angrily. 'My uncle is ruined, my mother is an ailing fugitive, and you have the gall to suggest that I am to blame for their misfortunes – I, who love them both dearly and would give my all to spare them suffering!'

For a few moments there was silence in the chamber.

'Would you so do, my lady?' Richard asked then. 'Would you, as you say, give your all for their sakes?'

Pale as death, she gazed at him. She was trapped, ensnared by her own words, by her love for the two she held most dear – those loved ones still remaining to her. She said nothing – having nothing to say. Should she say, *Nay, I meant it not – I would not give my all for them, or for anyone else. They could go to prison, sanctuary, be held in irons, starved, neglected – they could go to hell and I would do naught to aid them, since that which I could do is unpleasing to me!*

'Marry me, Anne,' Richard said, as if he had read her thoughts – his voice caressing, using her name for the first time since childhood. 'Become my bride. Give me the right to love and protect you – I swear you would want for nothing for the rest of your days. And those for whom you would, as you say, give your all, would be restored forthwith to their former station.'

'Has Richard of Gloucester then the ear of Parliament, that he could make such a promise in respect of the archbishop my uncle?'

'Nay, not of parliament – but of the king his brother,' Richard said coolly. 'The king his brother, you see, depends much on his support – does not Richard of Gloucester lead his armies in the north and in Scotland, whilst his other brother whiles away his time by transforming princesses into kitchen-maids!'

'You are displeased with Clarence?'

'One could say that. The court is alive with gossip – which, it must be admitted, is not unusual! Word is around that Clarence is the one displeased. As one courtier wrote to me in a letter, "The court seems queasy, for all those about the king's person have sent for their armour, on account of the quarrel regarding the inheritance of the lady Anne!" '

'So it was as he said – Clarence was seeking to protect me from yourself, my lord.'

'How so protect you? Clarence's so-called protection came close to costing you your health, your virtue – even your life! Nay, Clarence sought merely to protect your *inheritance* from myself. Once you were dead ...'

'Dead?' she asked tremulously. 'Then you ...'

'... or had disappeared for ever –' continued Richard, '– his lady, your sister, would have inherited the countess your mother's entire fortune – which, the law being what it is, would be tantamount to brother Clarence inheriting that same fortune!'

'As it is, my lord, were I to agree to become your bride, it would be tantamount to your inheriting that same fortune!'

'Anne, believe me, it is you I want, have always wanted –' Richard said earnestly '– ever since childhood, long before Edward of Lancaster set eyes on you.'

'Speak not so!' she said tearfully. 'Speak not of him – the wound is yet unhealed!'

'Forgive me,' he said tenderly. 'I wanted you to understand how it is with me, that is all. Needless to say your inheritance would please me greatly – I do not deny it. Who does not dream of inheriting a fortune! It would be a bonus – and I rather imagine that, should I not benefit from it through marriage with yourself, it is unlikely that the Neville family, your mother, uncle, sister or yourself, would benefit from it either. I suspect that my kingly brother would see to that. So what, fair lady, is your answer?'

Anne remained silent for a few moments, faced with a question that was at once simple and complex.

'What choice have I?' she asked at length.

His smile was boyish, and struck a chord in her memory. 'If the truth be told, very little – may fortune be thanked!' he said.

'And you would understand?' she asked plaintively.

'Understand? About what, my lady?'

'About the prince my husband – that I loved him in a way that I could never love another.'

'I understand that you believe that now,' he said quietly. 'I also understand that Time is a great healer.'

'And you would be kind to me?' she asked softly, not meeting his gaze. 'Always?'

He drew her to her feet and then, her hands in his, stood

looking down at her. Anne was reminded of their aloneness – of the absence of her uncle.

'Always and for ever shall I cherish you if you consent to be my bride,' he said steadily. 'Once under my protection, you would be safe and free from care – I would take on the whole world for your sake. I, Richard of Gloucester, swear it!'

'For their sake then – the answer is yea,' she said slowly, and he registered her reluctance to commit herself. 'For my loved ones.'

'God grant that one day Richard of Gloucester will be numbered amongst those loved ones,' he said ruefully. 'For them, you say, you would give your all – then so be it!'

# Thirty-One

Richard and Anne were married at Westminster Abbey in the following July, the bride and bridegroom setting forth soon after with their retinue on the first lap of the journey to Middleham, where the honeymoon would be spent. Middleham Castle, Richard's stronghold, was to be the young couple's chief abode, it being convenient for Richard as governor of the northern counties.

The days that had preceded the wedding had seemed to Anne like a dream. Forced, as she told herself, for her family's sake into a marriage which was anathema to her, it was only as she stood at the altar in her finery that she emerged from the dream long enough to realize with a sense of horror what was taking place.

How has it come about? she asked herself. Richard of Gloucester was among those who murdered my beloved prince, and afterwards King Henry my father-in-law; who connived at my uncle's banishment and, for his own gain, reduced to penury my mother when in distress she fled to him for protection ... He tells me he loves me, and indeed his conduct towards me has been exemplary: but for him, it must be admitted, I should still be a servant in his brother's kitchen – assuming I had not succumbed. Is he then as bad as he is painted? When I was ten, I would have laughed to scorn the suggestion that Richard of Gloucester was a villain ...

Neither her mother nor her uncle had been present at the wedding, the former being already at Middleham, having been conducted there several months earlier on Richard's orders by Sir James Tyrrel. Anne had wept, but secretly, after Richard had told her on the evening prior to the wedding that her mother's frail health made it impossible for her to undertake the long journey to London. Is it as he says? she had asked herself. Or does he suspect that I shall change my mind about marrying him – and therefore is holding mama as a surety for my keeping my word?

'It is not so,' Richard had said then – as if he had read her mind. 'The countess will make her abode at Middleham – where else than with her beloved daughter!'

Where else indeed, Anne had thought – since by the partition of the Neville and Beauchamp fortunes, mama is now destitute!

'My lord –' she had asked, being then still at York House where she had been permitted to remain until the wedding '– you will be patient with me, will you not?'

Richard had watched her, held by the magical power she possessed to stir his blood. The dreamy look in her eyes – those Plantagenet eyes that were much like his own though of a lighter blue – suggested one as yet unawakened. Her delicate air, virginal, untouched, accorded with the Anne he had long remembered. She was to him, as she had always been, beyond compare.

At this moment, he thought, she is a winter rose caught 'twixt the thorns of the Red Rose and the White – uncertain which way to turn to reach the light! She looks to be inviolate ... By sweet St. George! Could it be so? Was it no true marriage? There was no issue. Maybe the prince, like his sire, was of celibate inclination.

'Anne –' he said at length, treating her question as rhetorical '– out of my deep regard for you, I have made provision for the future by the insertion of a clause in our marriage contract which would enable you, should you ever so wish it, to gain an annulment.'

Anne had at once been reminded of her former marriage and the provisions in regard to its completion. Well, she and Edward had circumvented that small difficulty, defying two kings and a queen in the so doing. But the alliance with Richard was a different matter in that, as she told herself, she was undesirous of the match. Thus an escape clause was surely in her best interests.

'You show me much kindness, my lord,' she said, slightly shamefaced. 'I trust I shall be an exemplary wife.'

'As an exemplary bridegroom-to-be, I am determined that you shall marry me only of your own free will – without any form of material or moral coercion. The King has given his consent to a parliamentary act whereby I am empowered, and I quote, *to continue the full possession and enjoyment of the lady Anne's property, even were she to divorce the aforementioned duke, provided he did his best to be reconciled and re-married to her.*'

'In the event, my lord, I as well as my mother and uncle, would be rendered penniless,' Anne pointed out.

'Not at all, my lady,' Richard assured her. 'Not at all. On the contrary, in fact. By such a provision, your future interests are safeguarded. Clarence my brother, as you have cause to know, is of a somewhat unscrupulous nature and would pass by no opportunity of seizing the Neville fortunes for himself.'

'My lord, you spoke of annulment,' Anne said then. 'Holy Church does not countenance such between persons lawfully wedded.'

'It is as you say,' he agreed. 'And the matter has therefore been made plain. Be the marriage not to your liking or it be incomplete after a reasonable lapse of time, then you are enabled to seek an annulment without impediment.'

Anne was touched by his solicitude.

'My lord,' she said, her eyes downcast, avoiding his gaze, 'I shall be a true and faithful wife to you, I swear it. You have shown me much kindness – indeed I suspect I owe my life to your intervention. In the matter of my mother and my uncle, I told you that for their sakes I would give my all – I meant no less, my lord. My inheritance will become yours upon the morrow – I likewise shall become yours.'

Richard watched her for a moment in silence.

'Then you have forgiven me my transgressions?' he asked quietly.

She looked him full in the face. 'Did I say as much, my lord! In childhood, I held you in some affection. Always you treated me with kindness and gentleness.'

'And yet?' he asked ruefully. 'There is an *and yet* methinks!'

'And yet such tales have I heard of you as make me fearful,' she said tremulously.

'Fearful? Believe me, dear lady, never would Anne of Warwick have cause to fear Richard of Gloucester! Very shortly you will be mine own – my very own. Despite the aforementioned provisions, I truly believe I can make you happy – and yearn that it shall be so.'

'But the prince ...' Her voice was low. No more than a whisper it was, a sigh – but it conveyed a need of reassurance.

'Was my enemy, alas!' Richard said. 'The King his father also was my enemy. That was their misfortune – and mine, since it merited your anger and caused you hurt. A man learns early in life to know his enemies – 'tis likely else that he discovers his enemy only with his last breath!'

'It occurs to me, my lord, that Richard of Gloucester has many enemies.'

'Richard of Gloucester is ambitious. An ambitious man always has enemies – tales are told, be they true or false. But the ambitious man, be he also wise, knows his enemies and counts his friends on the fingers of one hand!'

'Five friends?' Anne smiled. 'Who are the five so favoured, my lord?'

The reply came swiftly, without hesitation.

'Ratcliffe, Catesby, Kendal and Lovel,' he told her.

'And the fifth, my lord?'

'The fifth? But I, my lady, have but four fingers on that one hand!'

'And what of Armand of Poitiers – is not he your friend?'

'Methinks Armand of Poitiers is more friend to Anne of Warwick than to Richard of Gloucester,' Richard said with a smile. 'He is none the less a true and loyal knight – more a thumb perchance than a finger, the odd one out!'

'And what of the King your brother?'

'Edward is my liege-lord – as such, I could never regard him as an enemy.'

'And George of Clarence?' Anne asked quietly, unable to resist the question.

This time there was hesitation – but only for a fraction of a minute.

'Could the one who treats so ill her whom the other loves best in all the world, be aught but an enemy?' he asked quietly. 'Brother George has yet to feel the weight of my wrath. But I can wait, bide my time – always Richard of Gloucester can wait ...'

'Do not you forgive your enemies, my lord – as Holy Church bids us?'

He looked rueful. 'A contradiction in terms is that! A forgiven enemy must be called friend – *ergo* Richard of Gloucester does not forgive his enemies.'

'I understand not your meaning.'

'Turn the other cheek, Holy Scripture bids us – yet, by turning the other cheek, does not one avert one's gaze from the death-blow!'

Anne sighed. 'My lord, when you express yourself thus, with such cool dispassion and logic, I believe what you say is so. But then, later, I give thought to the prince ...'

'And then you are back where you started?' he asked knowingly.

'Never shall I understand, alas! I doubt not that papa would have followed your reasoning and approved it, but not I – not in a month of Sundays!'

Richard had taken her hand and kissed it then.

'Lady, that is because you are not a warrior – thanks be to God!' he said.

\* \* \*

And so the wedding had taken place. Richard's five friends had been there, four fingers and a thumb – as well as an enemy in the person of George of Clarence. It was the first time Anne had seen her sister Isabel since that calamitous day at Clarence House. Isabel's manner was cool and formal, and she studiously avoided Anne's gaze. Anne wondered what she was thinking, whether she had since been informed as to the manner in which she had been held to all intents and purposes a prisoner under Isabel's roof.

She had known an urge to go to Isabel, to embrace her and assure her she was not to blame – you too were misled, she would have told her, and have long since been forgiven. But have I in truth forgiven her? she asked herself. But for Isabel's siding with her lord against myself, would I be in this unenviable situation now? Would I still be marrying him who murdered my beloved prince ...

# Thirty-Two

The journey to Yorkshire was long and arduous, with stops overnight at the residences of various members of the nobility where the newly-weds occupied separate apartments. There was no question of the marriage being completed until they reached Middleham and a degree of privacy and repose – such as was unattainable on a journey of hundreds of miles on horseback over rough roads.

Richard rode by Anne's side for most of the way; always courteous, solicitous for her comfort, sometimes coupling her horse to his with a leading rein to give her rest – calling a halt if he saw signs of fatigue in her.

He himself seemed never fatigued – he rode straight and tall in the saddle of his magnificent and richly caparisoned white steed. Not once throughout the wearisome journey, in rain or shine, did he display ill-temper; patient and courtly with Anne at all times, he was very much the Richard she had known and loved in childhood.

The weather was cold and wet for the latter part of the journey, and at one point Richard enquired as to whether she would prefer to be drawn in a litter.

'Might one enquire whether you, my lord, have ever travelled in a litter?' she asked, parrying one question with another.

'Not of late,' was the enigmatic answer.

'You mean you have?' asked Anne in surprise. 'You truly have?'

'A long time ago, it was – some nineteen years ago in fact,' replied the nearly twenty-one year old duke. 'The duchess my mother would not take nay for an answer, it seems – I was ever her favourite son!'

'Were you so, my lord?' For a few moments Anne was burdened by sorrow – recalling how dearly she had wanted a son, Edward of Lancaster's son. 'How fortunate is the duchess Cecily in having had eight strong sons – when some, like myself, have not the one!'

Richard looked at her then and met her gaze, and she blushed and turning, cast her eyes on the road ahead. Alas that I spoke thus! she said to herself. Whatever will my lord think of me?

'There is yet time, fair lady,' he said in a low voice. 'God be praised that we share one ambition at least!'

At last the massive walls of Middleham Castle came into view and at once the travellers' spirits lifted. The cavalcade stepped up its pace, the horses whinnied as if in sight of home and their riders talked and jested with each other.

Only Middleham's lord and lady seemed unaffected by the prospect of journey's end. It was as if both were occupied with their own thoughts, wrestling with doubts; as if each were wondering about the other.

The castle with its magnificent keep had been built in the year 1170 by Robert Fitz Randolph. The favourite residence of the Earl of Warwick, it was therefore already well known and well loved by Anne. Latterly, it had become Richard of Gloucester's favourite residence also and was therefore the place to which he had chosen to bring his bride.

\* \* \*

The newly-weds and their train rode into the castle's great courtyard in mid-afternoon, and soon after retired, each to their separate apartments, to rest and prepare for the evening's banquet.

Anne was overjoyed to find her mother awaiting her in her apartments. Thereafter followed a tender, joyful scene of reunion when each asked questions without giving the other a chance to reply – and when tears and smiles followed each other in rapid succession.

'Mama, dearest mama!' cried Anne. 'Methought never to see you again. It is all of two years and I declare that you have not changed a bit!'

'Oh, I've changed, daughter,' insisted the indefatigable countess. 'I have changed, both inside and out – but thank the Lord you recognized me none the less!'

'Mama, what of your health? My lord told me of your frailty.'

'My only frailty, child, is in respect of my daughters. I would have remained in sanctuary for ever – and very nearly did – but always I feared what they would do to you and Isabel if I failed to put in an appearance. So I escaped.'

'How, mama – how?'

'In a laundry-basket – if you must know!'

'Mama, how exciting! And what then?'

'I rode with just a groom and one servant all the way to London. It took us many days and … well, your lord was right then in thinking I looked frail! But they fattened me up like an old hen and packed me off to Middleham – and here I am, dearest child, ready for action, as your papa was wont to say!'

'Papa? Alas, mama, how often I think of papa – was it truly only two years ago? Already he seems part of another lifetime.'

'I know, I know.' Tears glistened in the countess's eyes. 'And what of yourself? Richard told me a little of your adventures at Clarence House – but I suspect he kept the worst bits from me!'

'Richard, you say? Mama, you speak as if you bear my lord no grudge – yet is not it he who deprived you of your possessions?'

'I went to Richard for protection. I knew he wished to marry you – solely for yourself, was and is my belief – and I knew also that he and George of Clarence coveted my fortune. Well, much good my fortune was to my daughters whilst I remained at Beaulieu! So I cut my losses, besought Richard's protection and here I am – and, what is more to my joy, here are you. Richard, I believe, takes good care of his own – though few are thus privileged.'

'And what of now, mama?'

'Now?' The countess smiled. 'I believe we are celebrating a wedding. I believe – or have been led to believe by one who shall be nameless – that tonight is the night!'

Anne blushed. 'Alas, mama, I am more than a little fearful!'

'Of marriage – of bedding, you mean? But were not you fully the wife of Prince Edward? Methought ...'

'Yea, mama, I was fully the prince's wife – and our coupling was a deep joy to us both. And that is it – how can I who loved Edward so dearly, give myself to his murderer?'

The countess sighed. 'Life is hard, daughter – we have to learn to compromise. Ofttimes we must concede our principles, our loyalties, even our love – though never our faith, for that is our mainstay. I loved my lord dearly and will so love him till the day I die – but he was not always right in his decisions and judgements. He was a man, heroic and brave, a leader of men – a maker of kings and decisions. But in the end, it seems to me, he threw away his life in a hopeless and ill-supported cause. Do you follow my meaning, child?'

'You are saying that I must learn to compromise my principles and loyalties – even my love?' Anne asked slowly. 'You loved papa dearly, though you believed him not always right in his decisions and judgements – and you would have me love Richard likewise, whilst abhorring certain of his decisions and judgements. Is not that so, mama?'

The countess nodded. 'You are Richard's bride, his lady and his duchess. Richard, as I said, looks after his own – you have nothing to fear, daughter, save your own emotions!'

'Oh mama, dear mama, how wonderful it is to have you here with us!' exclaimed Anne happily. 'I trust you will remain here for ages and ages.'

The countess looked rueful. 'In truth, daughter, there is little choice. By decree of the king, I am under house arrest here at Middleham. Oh, I have my own well-furnished apartments, an amplitude of servants, and may entertain and wander in the gardens at will. I have everything in the world – except my freedom!'

'And you expect me to honour and obey Richard – for exacting such a price for your protection?'

'I expect you to honour and obey Richard,' came the answer, '... and to love him, if it please God!'

# Thirty-Three

Anne lay in the great bed, revelling in its feathered warmth and the comfortable seclusion of the bedcurtains. Of royal blue embroidered with gold thread to match the drapes, the bedcover, like the bed itself, was brand-new, having been made to Richard's requirements. 'A new bed for a new bride!' he had said when he had taken her round the main rooms of the castle a few hours earlier.

The castle's refurbished interior had delighted her. Memories were everywhere: of childhood, of her father, of joy, happiness and laughter – even of Richard himself who, when under her father's guardianship, had seemed part of the family. The castle's new look had been designed with taste and artistry. Exquisite tapestries and wall carpets abounded, together with handsomely carved furniture, comfortable couches, austere bench-seats and embroidered cushions – wherever one looked there was beauty and colour.

'The kitchens?' she had asked Richard at length – but diffidently as if half expecting the enquiry to be treated with scorn. 'I would some day take a look at the kitchens, my lord.'

Richard smiled, and the smile as always transformed his face – making him look boyish, more approachable.

'Methought you would ask that question,' he said lightly. 'On the morrow, if you will, you shall betake yourself to the kitchens and dig and delve to your heart's content!'

'You knew?'

'Naturally. My lady would wish to assure herself that the kitchens in her home are well-run – as unlike those at Clarence House as could be!'

Anne watched him thoughtfully, surprised by his

perception.

'I wished to assure myself that the servants are happy in their employment,' she said on an apologetic note. 'That they are not treated as in some kitchens!'

'You would have a kitchen full of happy, smiling servants – menials who go about their tasks with a will, never shirking or taking advantage of a lenient supervisor?'

'I believe you are laughing at me, my lord!'

'Nay. In truth, I love you for your desire to spare others that which you yourself were subjected to – whilst I accept that the world is a harsh place, alas, for many!'

'You seem to understand, whilst at the same time shrugging, as if to say, "Forget it, it is none of our business!" '

'Maybe I do – maybe I do,' he said carelessly. 'Armand of Poitiers in reporting to me on your situation at Clarence house, made mention of a certain kitchen-maid who befriended you.'

'Jackie, you mean?'

'I know not her name.'

'Her name is really Jacquetta, my lord. I owe her much – indeed methinks I would not have survived those last days without her help.'

'You owe her much, you say, my lady – then why not discharge your debt?'

'How so, my lord?'

'You said a while back that you would be requiring a new personal maid.'

'You mean ...?' Anne smiled delightedly. 'But that is a wonderful idea – why did not I think of it! Of course, I know not how she is placed now, or whether ...'

'Armand of Poitiers will be setting out for Westminster in a day or so,' Richard interposed. 'Whilst there, he shall make a few enquiries. Now, my lady, I will leave you to your own devices whilst I have a word with my steward about tonight's banquet.'

After he had gone, Anne remained at her chamber window, gazing out at the delightful view she remembered so well; at green lawns, formal arrangements of herb and rose gardens, a splashing waterfall – and the small shrine

to Our Lady of Walsingham which was new to her and stood
centrally placed to her chamber window.

How lovely it all is! she thought. I could be happy here –
were it not for my remembrance of Edward and the knowledge that my new-wedded lord was one of those responsible for his death. Richard's choice of Middleham as our
first home was dictated by the belief that I would be happy
in the place that was papa's favourite abode. Indeed I shall
be happy here, no matter what. As mama says, I must learn
to compromise. Richard will of necessity be much away
from home, at Gloucester, Warwick or Westminster for
days, sometimes months at a time. But when we are
together as now, I must needs try to set aside my feelings,
remit my loathing of the crime committed against me and
mine ...

Now, the banquet over, Anne was lying in her new bed,
one curtain as yet undrawn, waiting for her bridegroom to
come to her. The chamber looked different by candlelight,
appearing to bear little resemblance to that which Richard
had shown her earlier. It was shadowy and a trifle menacing
and she felt sure that the coat of arms, Richard's coat of
arms, engraved on the bedhead, had not been there before.

She was more than a little fearful. She felt alone, isolated,
trapped – and she wished of a sudden, and surprised
herself in the wishing, that Richard would come to her ...

As if the thought had been father to the deed, the door
opened to admit Richard. Clad in a robe of sapphire velvet
open to the waist and loosely girded, he came and stood by
the bed, looking down at her for a moment without speaking, his eyes reflecting the candlelight.

'I am come to claim my bride –' he said then in a low voice
'– her for whom I have waited these many years.'

Unaccountably, tears filled Anne's eyes. But she was not,
as he assumed, giving thought to her dead husband – and
indeed could not at that time have explained the curious
mixture of feelings within herself. But the bed was warm
and the outside world had become all at once a hostile
place ...

'Your bride is here, my lord,' she said softly. 'The waiting
methinks is over.'

He made no reply but, without haste, removed the four

rings he wore on his right hand and placed them on a nearby table. Then, leaning over her, he kissed her on the mouth for the first time – gently and dispassionately as if sealing a pact.

As he drew away, she held his gaze and was surprised by her own reaction, by her need of him, her desire for him; by an overwhelming urge to be loved by this enigmatic being who was as much a mystery to her now – and indeed to the vast majority of his countrymen – as in childhood.

He removed his robe and, with a single movement, was in the bed and looking down at her.

'You have a rare beauty,' he said wonderingly. 'Ofttimes I have asked myself if 'twas an ice maiden, an enchantress, who long ago cast her spell on me!'

'Love me, my lord,' she said, and there was fire rather than ice in her voice. 'Love me well – and make me forget!'

He ran his fingers lightly and caressingly over her body, tracing the contours of her face and lips, throat and breasts – and then, of a sudden, with new intent, he kissed her passionately on the mouth and drew her close.

'Love you I do – and love you I shall!' he said fervently. 'As to forgetting, I know not – but give me a child, a son, and looking at him, please God we should both forget.'

Her eyes shining with tears, she drew him fiercely to her and, in so doing, banished coherent thought – and with it, for a space, anger and sorrow ...

# Thirty-Four

When Anne awoke next morning from a sound and dreamless sleep, it was to discover that Richard was no longer with her. Surprised then by a sense of disappointment, she lay there for a while, giving thought to the night that was gone.

Matilda her maid, who was shortly leaving her service to be married, came in presently and drew the curtains.

' 'Tis a fine morning, my lady,' she said cheerfully. 'My lord went off early, hunting – he said to tell you when you awoke that he'd be back ere midday.'

'Thank you, Matilda.'

'I've brought your breakfast,' the maid said, placing the breakfast-tray in front of her mistress. 'Will there be anything else, my lady?'

'Not at this moment, Matilda – I shall ring for you when I have given thought to the day.'

'Oh, there is one more thing, my lady –' Matilda paused in the doorway '– The countess said to tell you she'd be with you anon.'

'Anon?' frowned Anne, not sure if she wanted to receive a visitor at once.

'You being a new bride and all that.'

Why, Anne wondered, as her maid left the chamber, is mama behaving as if I were a virgin bride – and she therefore had a duty to do?

She was soon to find out.

Anne's arrival at Middleham had done much to raise the countess's spirits. She was determined to get on with her son-in-law and any resentment she had of Richard was carefully and expediently hidden. In truth, she believed that Richard bore far less responsibility for her present situation than did his two brothers. He had not been among those, she understood, who had slain her husband at Barnet and it was not Richard's men who had waited, ready to pounce whenever she had tried to leave sanctuary. Clarence she held chiefly responsible for Warwick's death – Clarence who with his troops had deserted to the enemy at the eleventh hour and thereby influenced the outcome of the battle. He, however, was her son-in-law, her other son-in-law, so she would tread warily for Isabel's sake ...

As she entered Anne's chamber now, the countess kissed her daughter on the forehead and seated herself beside the bed.

'Did you do your duty, daughter?' she enquired without preamble.

'I did, mama.'

'I am glad to hear it. And your linen? Proof, as you know, is onerous upon the bride's mother or mother-in-law – lest doubt later be cast on the legality of the marriage.'

'Mama, have you forgotten, pray?' asked Anne, puzzled by what she saw as her mother's interference. 'I am a widow.'

'You *were* a widow – you are now a wife.'

'I was a virgin when Edward of Lancaster first took me. How then could I give proof this time?'

'Were there witnesses then to the loss of your maidenhead? In other words, since I know naught of the matter, was another responsible matron charged at that time with the duty of inspecting your bed linen?'

'Nay, mama.'

'And why not, pray?'

'None knew of it.'

'You and the prince did not, by prior agreement, company together immediately following the marriage, daughter – one must assume then that Queen Margaret later countenanced completion of the alliance.'

Oh, why must she go on about it! thought Anne. This talk of my former marriage turns a knife in the wound – reminding me of things I want to forget.

'Not exactly,' she said.

'You are telling me she did not? But how could that be – on the one hand you insist that the marriage was completed, and on the other that Queen Margaret …'

'Hearken to me, mama. By the terms of the contract, the marriage was not to be perfected until King Henry had regained his crown. Thus, if papa had failed to achieve a decisive Lancastrian victory, a more advantageous match would have been sought for Edward.'

'That is so.'

'But you see, mama, Edward and I were much in love and refused to obey the terms of an agreement over which we had not been consulted.'

'Since when have …'

'Listen to me, mama, if you please. The marriage was perfected on the third night after the wedding – but it was several months before Queen Margaret discovered the fact.'

'I see,' said the countess. 'I see. Dear, dear me! And what am I to tell Richard?'

'So that is it!' said Anne coldly. 'Richard suspected that my former marriage was not perfected – that my lord and I remained apart despite our obvious affection for each other.'

'It has been known, daughter. You must not blame Richard. He needed to know.'

'He knows now – and if he has anything further to say on the subject, he may say it to myself. In truth, it is highly improbable that he still harbours a doubt!'

'I am glad, my child, that all is well.'

'And I also, mama.' Anne was very much on her mettle. 'Always shall I mourn Edward – and yet, despite everything, I confess to some small liking for my new lord – he did, after all, say I might betake myself to the kitchens today.'

'To the kitchens!' exclaimed the countess – looking anxiously at Anne as if wondering whether, having previously taken leave of her maidenhead, she had this time taken leave of her wits. 'Did you say, to the kitchens?'

'I did, mama. I most certainly did. Perchance you would like to come with me.'

The countess was plainly amazed. 'Never in all my days

have I set foot in a kitchen, daughter. One employs a chamberlain, steward and housekeeper to oversee such matters – to say nothing of a head cook!'

'A head cook – yea, I doubt not there is a head cook – and an under-cook, a turnspit and dozens of cook-maids!'

'I fail to understand your meaning, daughter. And as for your entering the kitchens, the servants would not like it at all I dare say! Anne, I have something to ask you …'

'Indeed, mama?' Anne was a little on the defensive.

'… Could it be that you are already with child?'

' 'Tis a little too soon to say!' Anne said coolly, guessing where her mother's thoughts were leading. 'The morning after, you know …'

The countess was determined to discover what lay behind her daughter's strange caprice. To visit the kitchens indeed! she said to herself.

'Rumour has it that Richard forced you to his will several weeks since,' she said to Anne. 'Could it be that there is truth in the tale – and that you are now enceinte?'

'No truth at all, mama,' Anne said lightly. 'No truth at all. As to my inspecting the kitchens, it will not be the great adventure you seem to think it – as if I were an explorer sailing uncharted seas and about to fall off the edge of the world into an abyss! I was, as you know, a cook-maid for a time in my sister's kitchen.'

'For your own protection, I believe. Richard, as I said before, told me something of your adventures – but left it to you methinks to furnish me with the details.'

'Mama, it was far from being an adventure!'

'Of course, child – it must have been quite tedious for you, so pray let us not speak of it!'

'I shall spare you the grim details of my sojourn at Clarence House – you have suffered grievously in the past two years and I would save you further distress. Suffice it to say that I was not well treated. But for Richard's intervention, I doubt I should be here with you now!'

At that, tears filled the countess's eyes.

'Alas, that the Nevilles have come to this – your papa, your uncle George, and now yourself! That you should have been forced to serve one who helped to depose and murder his lawful sovereign …' She stopped in mid-sentence. 'What of Isabel – where was your sister when you were playing the menial in her kitchen! What of her?'

Anne shook her head. 'I know not, mama – and that is for truth. 'Tis hard to believe that my sister would be party to such wrongdoing – perchance she was misled or simply closed her eyes to what was going on.'

'Clarence is a turncoat, as all know – that he is a womaniser is also commonly held! Perchance he treats Isabel harshly – and she fears to displease him. Certainly she has done naught, as far as I know, to aid her mother and her sister in their adversity. Anyway, enough of such talk – what a way to greet a newly-bedded bride! Tell me of yourself and Richard, daughter – can you find happiness with him?'

Anne flushed, thinking of the night that was gone. 'I ...'

'I have your answer – the note in your voice and the roses in your cheeks have spoken for you!' smiled the countess. 'You can find happiness with Richard – you can and you will! May God grant you a child soon – and then there will be no more talk of annulments and marriage settlements! My lord Richard, unless I am much mistaken, looks to found a new dynasty.'

'A new dynasty?' asked Anne in surprise. 'But, dearest mama, how could that be? Only the sovereign or the heir to the sovereign could dream such dreams.'

'We shall see, my daughter,' said the countess complacently. 'Henry of Lancaster and his heir no longer stand in your lord's path.'

'You surely are forgetting that Richard is the youngest brother. Even if King Edward should die – and by all accounts he is in robust health – he has two sons to succeed him. And Clarence is closer to the succession than Richard – and he too may yet have a son.'

'Richard has a deep grudge against Clarence, chiefly on account of the lengths to which Clarence went to prevent your marrying him – and to gain entire control, through Isabel, of my inheritance.'

'Clarence would have had to kill me ere he could have made claim on Isabel's behalf ...' Anne paused, looked stricken – and dissolved into tears. 'So that was his plan! He really did intend me to die ...'

'There, there, child!' said the countess, fondly patting her hand. 'You must not dwell on it. All is now well, thanks be to God!'

'To God indeed, mama — but to Richard also!' cried Anne. 'Who else could or would have come to my rescue? If it was as I now believe, I owe my life to Richard and his knight-errant.'

'There you are then!' declared the countess in the manner of one solving a jolly puzzle. 'In his own good time, Richard will exact payment from Clarence for his treatment of yourself — a payment that has naught to do with anyone's inheritance! Thus, if King Edward should die, the way would be clear ...

'Mama, you speak treason!'

'This is between you and me, daughter — 'twill get no further than these four walls. Should King Edward die, suddenly, as I was about to say ...'

'And as I *did* say, King Edward is in robust health.'

'Stranger things have happened than a robust king departing this world suddenly! He is a womaniser, that one, and makes no secret of it — why, his infidelity is a byword! He declares openly that he has many concubines, among whom are three, one of whom, he says, is the merriest, the second the wittiest, and the third the holiest in the world — she being always in a church when he sends for her!'

'Is that really so, mama?' Anne asked, her tinkling laughter making the countess smile. 'How came you to hear it?'

'Ah-ha! How and from whom is a secret — and you will not worm that out of me, child! The plain fact is that the King lives life to the full.'

'But, as I said, he has two sons to succeed him — not to mention his daughters.'

'Not to mention his daughters, indeed,' nodded the countess. 'The English have ever been opposed to gynocracy — and Queen Margaret but strengthened their opposition.'

'Mama, that is unfair!' protested Anne, loyal still to her unhappy mother-in-law. 'That poor lady ventured much for the King her husband — and suffers still for a lost cause.'

'Unfair it is, child — but life is unfair,' declared the countess. 'I dare say you and I are of one mind there!

Margaret of Anjou fought her husband's battles from the best of motives – yet the commonalty sees her only as the author of its misfortunes; the cause of some twenty years of civil war.'

'Poor dear Margaret!' Anne sighed. 'When next we are in the vicinity of Wallingford, I shall beseech my lord to ask the king's permission for my visiting her. I have several times sent letters to her but have received no reply, alas!'

'I dare say she herself could say as much!'

Anne looked startled. 'You are suggesting that our letters have been intercepted – but how dreadful! Mama, do you truly b ...'

'As I was about to say –' interposed the countess pointedly '– none of King Edward's daughters will ever be queen in her own right and his sons are but babes. Should the king's reign be a long one, one of his sons could well succeed him. But should he die whilst they are yet minors ...'

The countess shrugged, leaving the prognosis in mid-sentence.

'You believe there would be hope then for the Lancastrian cause?' asked Anne.

'Nay, such was not my meaning. The Lancastrians will yet have their day, but not for a while methinks. Had you borne Prince Edward a son, it would be a different story. As it is, it will take time for another leader to emerge – though the time will come, have no fear! Richard meanwhile ...'

'Pray continue, mama,' urged Anne, intrigued by her uncharacteristic hesitancy.

'Methinks I have said enough, daughter.'

'What of Richard?' persisted Anne. 'Pray tell me what you have in mind, since it concerns my lord and therefore myself.'

'Richard watches and waits – I doubt he will have scruples when the time comes!'

'Mama, you make me fearful when you speak thus! You refer to my lord as if he were a schemer of the worst order – one who would seek the crown for himself!'

'Oh, Richard would seek the crown for himself – I doubt it not! But also for those he loves – namely yourself, daughter, and any offspring of the marriage.'

Anne watched her mother for a few moments in silence,

wondering if she were serious. Could she be right? she asked herself. But, of course, it is all speculation. King Henry and his heir have, alas, been removed from Richard's path! But the possibility that my lord's two brothers – as well as King Edward's two sons and any sons Clarence might sire – would also be removed from Richard's path, is utterly ludicrous. Richard's path? Why do I think thus? Could it be that I too ...?

'Mama, this will not do!' she said brightly. 'I shall shoo you away and summon Matilda to dress me without more ado. Whatever would my lord think, were he to return and find me still abed!'

'Doubtless he would draw the obvious conclusion, daughter – but you have no need of your mama to tell you that!'

# Thirty-Five

Anne was seated at her *toilette* some three weeks later, brushing her long hair and telling herself she must put her mind to engaging a maid to replace the now departed Matilda. She was temporarily sharing the services of her mother's maid Florence, but she having been many years in the countess's service was rather set in her ways.

There was a knock at the door and Anne, thinking it was Florence, called to her to enter. She continued absently brushing her hair, her thoughts far away, until it struck her that someone other than Florence had entered the chamber and was awaiting her attention.

She looked in the mirror at the newcomer's reflection – and, in a flash, had crossed the room and was embracing her.

'Jackie!' she cried. 'Oh, Jackie – I could not believe my eyes! How good it is to see you!'

'And I you, Annie – er m'lady.'

'I just cannot believe you are real – come and sit down and tell me everything! Peter the turnspit, I suppose, paid another visit to Clarence House.'

'He did indeed!' smiled Jackie. 'I thought I was seeing things when he came in the kitchen, bold as brass – he'd disappeared, you see, about the same time as you left us, and none knew aught about him – but there he was again, large as life and twice as handsome!'

'Did he speak to you directly?'

'He spoke to the head cook – told him he wanted to 'ave a word with me and gave him a gold coin. The cook looked at me, winked at 'im and pocketed the coin – and that was that! The turnspit asked me then if I'd go with 'im – and I said nay, not likely! And I could see Lil was green with envy, hoping he'd ask 'er next – to you-know-what! Well, our turnspit said as how 'e didn't mean *that* – said he was really a knight-errant in disguise and that he'd come to carry me away on his white charger! Of course, I didn't believe a word of it at first – but then he told me about you, who you was and 'ow you'd married his master, Richard of Gloucester – and of course all of us 'ad heard about the wedding, it being at Westminster. My cousin, Kate, was there to watch the procession – but of course she don't know you, m'lady!'

'But surely you did not believe it – that I am who I am!'

'Oh, I believed it all right.' Jackie smiled. 'Annie, me love, d'yer think I didn't know you wasn't one of us – no disrespect, mind, but facts is facts! Those white 'ands of yours – not so white when our Meg 'ad done 'er worst – but nay, you can always tell a lady! The turnspit said how about me coming up to Yorkshire to be your lady's maid – but I told him I couldn't, and gave him dozens of excuses why I couldn't. Dead scared, you see – never been away from London to foreign parts afore – but then 'e said as how you needed me ...'

'I do, Jackie. I do indeed!'

'... and then what do you think? Our turnspit gives me a letter from the duke 'imself. I couldn't read it, of course, but I got the housekeeper to read it to me. 'Er eyes nearly popped out of 'er head when she saw the duke's seal – but she said it was genuine and as 'ow I'd be a fool to turn down the offer.'

'What did my lord say that persuaded you?' asked Anne curiously.

'Naught much. Just, "The lady Anne, Duchess of Gloucester, is pleased to offer the post of lady's maid to one, Jacquetta." Summat like that, it was.'

'And was it that convinced you?'

'Not exactly. Not the words nor the seal – what know I about them things? Nay, 'twas 'im saying "Jacquetta" as got me. You see, me lady, none but you and me ma – and me cousin Kate, of course – knows me name is that. Ma died the other week and that's another reason why there wasn't nothing to keep me in London.'

'I am sorry to hear about your mother, Jackie!'

Jackie shrugged. 'Yea, well, so am I in a way – but that's another story, me lady. You got out just in time, you know – things in that there kitchen went from bad to worse after you and the turnspit went. Meg thought he'd run off with you, you see, both of you disappearing about the same time, and she took out 'er spite on the rest of us. I was black and blue all over – then Meg took up with the steward, Thomas Burdet. Crafty old devil, 'e is – says he's a sorcerer, would you believe it, witchcraft and all that, making spells!'

'That is all finished with now, Jackie,' Anne told her. 'Things will be very different here, I promise you. I just cannot tell you how happy I am to have you here at Middleham. Your closet adjoins my bedchamber – 'tis small but cosy and will be all your own, and you can take your meals there or downstairs in the servants' room as you please. You will be answerable only to myself.'

'I'm quite good at dressing hair, me lady – the girls used to get me to do theirs, as you know – I did yours for you once, didn't I? And I'm quite handy with me needle, though I say it meself – so I'll be all right with the sewing and mending and making-over, and all that lark – and most of the rest's commonsense I dare say. But it's the fal-di-lals I'm not sure about!'

'Frippery, you mean – frills and furbelows, that kind of thing?'

'Nay, you know, Annie me love, me lady – how you speak to 'em is what I'm meaning.'

'Modes of address?'

'I'm all right with the modes – I shall enjoy all that. Nay, 'tis the "address" bit that bothers me. You see, I'd not want to make an exhibition of meself. I'm a great one, as you know, for scrubbing down tables – but I'd not be much good at sucking up to gentry!'

'Hearken to me, Jackie. To have you here is my pleasure – to give you a happy home will be my joy. Should you wish to improve your knowledge, I would teach you most willingly. But as I said, as my personal maid, you will be answerable only to myself.'

Jackie burst into tears at that. 'Oh, Annie me love, you've made me so happy – so happy!'

'So it would seem!' laughed Anne, blinking away her own tears.

'I'll try ever so hard to please you. 'Twill be like I'm in heaven living here in this great castle, and working for you, Annie me love. Oh, and what do yer want me to call you?'

'Hm, I was asking myself that!' Anne admitted. ' "My lady" is usual.'

'Not Lady Annie?'

'When we are alone, Lady Annie it shall be – but in company, "my lady" would be better understood. Methinks I should call you Jacquetta.'

'As you will, my lady – as you will. Always seemed a bit of a mouthful to me, a bit high-falutin', if you knows what I mean!'

'My lord remarked upon your name – and reminded me that the queen's mother is so named – so you, Jacquetta, are in good company!'

'I am that,' smiled Jacquetta happily. 'I'm in Lady Annie's company – and that's the best company of all!'

'You must be tired, after that long journey,' Anne said. 'I will summon the housekeeper to show you round and take you to your closet and then you shall, if you wish, take a rest.'

'I quite enjoyed the journey, my lady. The turnspit ...'

'Armand of Poitiers, knight.'

'Yea, him! He kept asking me if I was all right – if I was tired, hungry or wanted to quench me thirst. I was beginning to think I was a lady as well!'

'Except on special days, we dine at midday here and sup in the evening – just as at Clarence House.'

Jacquetta gave an exaggerated shudder. 'Oh, don't remind me! You know, my lady, I 'ave to keep pinching meself to make sure as I'm not dreaming!'

# Thirty-Six

Thenceforth a tender and loving relationship grew up between Anne and her new lord. As much as his service to the King and his stewardship of the northern counties permitted, Richard remained at Middleham. Each night he went to his lady's chamber. He was a vigorous but considerate lover, and Anne thrilled to his caresses and endearments.

Yet still Richard was an enigma. Passionate, courteous and generous, he lavished gifts on Anne, sometimes expensive flamboyant gifts, at others, small thoughtful gifts he knew would please her.

'Richard –' Anne said when he went to her solar one evening after a day's boar hunting, and presented her with an enamelled gold reliquary on a gold chain. '– you are good to me beyond my deserving.'

'Then you must be more deserving,' he said lightly, 'if that is indeed the case!'

'How so? How can I please you better?' Anne asked smilingly. 'Am not I yours to command – did not we make a pact when I promised to give you my all!'

'Give me a child, Anne,' he said soberly. 'Give me a son, is all I ask!'

'When God wills it, my lord,' she said demurely. 'Man proposes and God disposes, it is commonly said!'

'It is no subject for levity!'

'I agree, my lord – it most certainly is not,' Anne said – but she thought, how prim Richard can be at times, as if he, the great Richard of Gloucester, really does fear the Almighty!

'Tonight I shall come to your chamber.'

'And I, my lord, shall welcome you with open arms – as

always.'

'Perchance this very night ...'

Anne pretended not to understand. 'Yea, tonight, as you said.'

'I but referred to our making a child.'

*But* he says, Anne thought – as if it were a mere nothing, as if it were naught, when we both know it means more to him than anything else in the world.

'That is out of the question, my lord,' she said ruefully.

'My coming to your chamber, mean you?'

'Nay, our making a child – though needless to say, my lord, if it be to your pleasure to ...' She modestly lowered her gaze.

'Why speak you thus?' he demanded and there was a hint of anger in his voice. 'Why would our making a child be out of the question? Could it be you are barren – one cannot ignore the fact that despite some nine months of wedlock with Edward of Lancaster, you bore no child!'

What had started as coquetry on Anne's part, had somehow got out of hand. She was close to tears. Richard rarely makes reference to my beloved prince, she thought – he knows how it saddens me and he therefore avoids the subject. Yet now he raises the question in respect of that most delicate and heart-rending of matters. It is, I suppose, the measure of his desire for a son.

'My lord, pray be seated here beside me,' she said, and he heard the tremor in her voice and wondered at it. She took his hand and drew him down on the couch beside her. 'I had resolved never to speak of this to anyone – for indeed I cannot do so but tears overwhelm me! But now you shall hear it, so that never again will there be need to speak of it. You shall hear that first.'

'First?' he asked. 'Why say you first?'

If she heard the question, she ignored it. 'After the prince my husband was slain, I found myself to be with child. I told none, for I believed that if it were discovered that I was carrying the heir to the House of Lancaster, my life and that of my unborn child would be in jeopardy.'

'The Plantagenets wage not war on women and infants!' declared Richard incisively. 'You surely were aware of that.'

'Maybe it is so, my lord, but I could not take the risk – if the child be a boy, I said to myself, he will be taken from me as soon as he is born and kept in captivity, finally perchance sharing the fate of his royal grandfather.'

For a few moments, struggling for composure, she was unable to speak further.

'Take your time,' Richard said gently.

'When we reached Richmond, at the end of a horseback journey of such length as is not wisely undertaken by a woman in that condition, I was deeply concerned for my child.'

'You could have travelled by litter.'

'And thus revealed my secret? Nay, my lord, I prayed to God and Our Lady to aid me and I disembarked at the Tower of London with no small relief at finding my secret still intact. Well, you know what happened after that – how I was snatched from the Tower wharf and taken to Clarence House. Tired and dispirited, a widow of two weeks, I welcomed Clarence House as a refuge – and took rest for a few blissful hours in a soft feather bed! Then I discovered the truth – I had been stolen from the Tower only to be placed in a harsher, more damaging, prison than that great fortress. You see, my lord, I was worse treated than the other menials and God knows there was little kindness shown to them! But I was not one of them – I spoke differently, I ate daintily. Could I, in a few days, change the ways of a lifetime! For the first week, all was well in respect of the child, but then as I reached what I judged to be the end of the second month of my pregnancy ...

She dissolved into a paroxysm of weeping at that point. Richard made no move to comfort her this time, but waited in silence for her to continue.

'... I miscarried the child,' she said on a sob. ' 'Twas at night after I had retired – and I besought God to let me die. It was not the pain, you understand, and not so much the loss of the child – as the belief that somehow I had let Edward down! Well, they never found the child. I managed to conceal it – pray ask me not how, my lord – but for several days after, I was unable to carry out my tasks properly and was punished accordingly.'

'By God's blood, I knew not how it was!' exclaimed Richard, beside himself with fury. 'Believe me, I knew not!'

'None knew till now – though, from something she said to me at the time, methinks Jackie suspected. If such be the case, I doubt not she will continue to keep her suspicions to herself.'

'What of the lady Isabel? Did not you confide your condition to your sister when first you arrived at Clarence House?'

'Nay, it is hard to say why. At first, you see, I had no notion of what was planned for me. I imagined I was to be held under house arrest – as indeed it was, of a sort! Also, methinks in my heart I did not trust Isabel even then – there was something in her manner. She had changed. I cannot explain, my lord, but that is how it was, alas!'

'By my faith, I swear that he who subjected you to such misery, shall pay dearly for his evil-doing! The duke my brother has much to answer for. I should have acted long since – when he first changed camps and threw in his lot with the Lancastrians! But Richard of Gloucester can wait – and, by sweet St. George, the prince's child shall yet be avenged!'

'Glad am I that you said that, my lord – about the prince's child,' Anne told him tremulously, looking up at him through her tears. 'I love you for that – and it augurs well for what I am about to tell you.'

'That *first* you spoke of?'

She smiled a little through her tears. 'Methought you had forgotten – about the *first*, I mean. The signs suggest that seven months hence, I shall bear you a child. That was why, when you spoke of our making a child tonight ...'

He drew her into his arms, but gently, and kissed her.

'What joy you bring me with *those* words!' he said. 'But oh, what wretchedness with the others!'

' 'Twas you yourself prompted the first revelation – and yet in truth I wanted you to know how it was. The joy I see in you now is the joy I once longed to see in Edward – somehow I felt I owed it to him to tell you how it was with his child. Now, my lord, I must try to bury the past – and look to the future.'

'Have you told the countess your mother of the child?' Richard enquired then.

'Before I told yourself?' asked Anne in surprise. 'Indeed I have not, my lord!'

'Then pray permit me to convey the good tidings,' he said. 'She too will be overjoyed – and I shall bid her keep a close eye on you.'

'That you and mama are on such amicable terms surprises me, my lord,' observed Anne. 'I gather that your reception of her when she fled to you for protection was hardly conducive to good relations!'

'I would not say that exactly. The countess looked exhausted, not surprisingly, from the rigours of travel and from living for many months with anxiety. "Here I am, my lord of Gloucester –" was her greeting, "– come to you for protection! So pray tell me here and now, if you please, what you propose to do with me." "Do with you, madam?" I asked. "Why, offer you the hospitality of my house – what else!" She gave me a long hard stare and then, taking my hand, kissed it. "I thank you, kind sir," she said.'

'And that was all?' Anne asked.

'That was all – more or less. We looked not back after that, it seems to me.'

Anne smiled. 'Mama speaks her mind, does she not?'

'She certainly does – the countess speaks her mind and Richard of Gloucester, it is commonly held, does not – which gives us methinks an excellent working relationship!' Richard said, with one of those rare, beautiful smiles reserved for his nearest and dearest. 'We came to terms on – er – a certain subject – and since the countess is your mother and I value her opinion on some matters, particularly on the proper conduct of duchesses who are with child, a bond of trust has grown up between us. One day perchance, it might be bruited about the court that the countess and her much-maligned Gloucester son-in-law are good friends!'

'Then all is well, my lord.'

'Well indeed!' agreed Richard, kissing her. 'Dear God, how I love you! You must take no chances – get plenty of rest and avoid horseback riding like the plague.'

Anne pouted. 'Just now and then maybe. A little exercise, after all ...'

'I should be deeply vexed – horseback riding during the coming months is strictly forbidden!'

'You mean you would beat me if I disobeyed?' she asked coquettishly.

But Richard's eyes were stern, unsmiling. 'Speak not so – still am I appalled by your revelation of the treatment you received at Clarence House. Never have I laid a hand on you save in love – and never shall!'

# Thirty-Seven

Anne Duchess of Gloucester gave birth to a son in the following May, just ten months after her marriage. From the moment of his birth, the child was his parents' pride and joy.

Anne saw the likeness that very first day. Exhausted by a long and difficult labour, she slept afterwards for several hours, oblivious to what was going on around her; to the swaddled infant being placed in the cradle beside her bed, and the happy father stepping quietly into the lying-in chamber to take a look at the new arrival.

When Anne awoke, she took the infant and cradled him in her arms.

'How beautiful you are, little one!' she said softly, gazing down at him. 'You are so very like your ...'

She paused. She was still drowsy, and her eyes felt strained and bruised from labour. Nay, she thought, it cannot be so – I am a little confused.

With the baby asleep in her arms, she lay back on the pillows and gave thought to the matter. It could be, I suppose, that I am imagining the likeness, she told herself – that by wishing it so, I have made it so. The connection is there – but is so tenuous as to defy belief. The common ancestors of Edward, Richard and myself are Edward the Third and Queen Philippa; Edward and myself through the Lancastrian line of John of Gaunt and Richard through the Yorkist line of Lionel, Duke of Clarence. Thus whilst Edward was great-great-great grandson to Edward and Philippa and I great-great-great granddaughter, Richard is their great-great-great-great grandson. A tenuous connection indeed – and yet looking at my infant now, 'tis as if the years and generations have rolled

back and the warring houses of Lancaster and York are
united in him.

Has my lord noticed the likeness? If so, will he comment
upon it – or keep his thoughts to himself? Certainly I myself
shall make no reference to it.

In truth, this little fellow's likeness to my dead lord brings
me joy and no small satisfaction. Edward was denied the son
he should have had – but each time I look at my infant, I
shall be reminded of Edward and the happiness we shared.

'He takes after his mother – I see it now!' Richard said
when he came to see her later. 'When I first saw him, he
reminded me of someone but I could not place who it was,
would you believe it!'

Yea, I would believe it! Anne said to herself. The last
person you would want your son to resemble, is the one
whose enemy you were – whose lady is now yours!

'I would not say he took after me,' said Anne, careless of
the fact that she was treading on dangerous ground. 'He *is*
like someone – but I just cannot place who. He is certainly
not like his papa, alas, alas!'

'He is like his mama,' insisted Richard. 'Everyone will
agree, I am sure, that our little Edward takes after you.'

'Edward?' asked Anne in wide-eyed astonishment. 'You
would have him named Edward, my lord?'

'Naturally.'

'Then you do see ...' Anne paused. Was he making
pretence that the infant is like myself – to see how I would
react? she wondered. Does he really see the likeness to
Edward? If not, then why does he say *naturally*?

'Edward – after the king my brother,' he told her.

Anne breathed a sigh of relief. She realized then that she
wished none to share her secret – and certainly not Richard.
She could not have said why: she only knew that it was so.

The countess entered the lying-in chamber a few minutes
later, bound for a sight of her new grandchild.

'Saints preserve us!' she exclaimed in the manner of one
peeping into a crib and discovering a changeling. 'Is it
possible! Why, the little fellow is the living image of ...'

She paused, recovered her composure and turned to
Anne.

'... well done, daughter, well done!' she said approvingly.

'So you see it too, madam,' Richard said complacently, with an I-told-you-so glance at Anne.

'See it, my lord?' asked the countess coolly. 'My new grandson, do you mean? A fine lad he is, bonny, good lungs – you have done well, son-in-law.'

As soon as her visitors had departed, talking amicably together as they went out of the door, Anne lifted the infant from his cradle again and rocked him gently in her arms.

'How beautiful you are,' she murmured. 'But whom you are like, is our secret, my son – our secret and God's methinks!'

\* \* \*

In the months that followed, Richard was much away from home, his official duties as governor of the northern counties becoming ever more onerous. Furthermore, England was then at war with Scotland, and Richard led the king's armies across the Border, winning a number of battles and taking Edinburgh in the course of his campaigns.

Anne and her mother remained at Middleham during Richard's absence. Anne was happy with her baby son, her little Edward, occupying herself with him for much of each day and making him the pivot of her existence.

The next two years passed happily and uneventfully – and Anne began to look and pray for another child. To have a brood of strong sons was Richard's dearest wish, as she was well aware – in an age of almost continuous warring, a man needed more than the one son to safeguard his posterity.

In the November of the second year, Anne learned with joy of her archbishop uncle's release from captivity in France. George Neville returned to England, but his possessions and his see remained forfeited to the Crown. But captivity and anxiety had done their worst, affecting his health to the extent that seven months later, in June of the year 1476, he died.

Anne and Richard were at Baynard's Castle, their London residence – having left two-year-old Edward in the care of his grandmother and his nurses at Middleham whilst they attended the archbishop's requiem Mass – when they learned that her sister Isabel was gravely ill.

Isabel, it seemed, having given birth to a son, also named Edward, in the preceding year, had afterwards contracted childbed fever. Though the fever had abated, she had never fully recovered her strength and was thought to be close to death. On being informed of this by Richard, having not seen her sister since her fateful arrival at Clarence House five years earlier, Anne at once resolved to pay her a visit.

As she entered the great house that had been the scene of so much distress and heartache, despite her resolve, Anne knew a sudden trembling in her limbs and would have fallen but for Richard's steadying hand. His announcing his intention of accompanying her, had come as a surprise – visiting the sick being generally regarded as a female prerogative or duty. It was one of those silent but perceptive gestures that endeared Richard to her: he had recognized how she would feel on entering the place she had sworn never to enter again – and recognizing it, without explanation, was there by her side.

As Anne entered her sister's bedchamber, she was shocked by her appearance. Emaciated, her eyes dark-rimmed and sunken, her once-beautiful hair sparse and lifeless, Isabel looked a shadow of her former self. At first, she failed to recognize Anne, seeming lost in fever and listlessness – but then, as Anne spoke her name, she stared hard at her until, recognizing her, she started to weep.

'Anne, you should not have come – you should not have come!' she cried – and Anne was glad that Richard had remained downstairs in the great hall with his brother. 'I am so ashamed – always I was so ashamed. I told myself I had no choice, you see – but always there is a choice if one wills it so.'

'Be at peace, sister,' said Anne, taking her hand. 'You will overtax your strength with so much weeping – and all for naught!'

'All for naught, as you say,' wept Isabel, misunderstanding her. 'We started out with such high hopes, you and I – and here we are, I at twenty-four already at death's gate, and you wedded to one you hate!'

'To one I hate?' asked Anne quietly. So that is what is said! she thought. But no matter – this is no time for recriminations. 'I am well enough, my sister. Believe me, I am well enough. Our little Edward grows apace – I would you could see him.'

'Anne, I knew not how it was with you here in this house – truly I did not,' Isabel told her. 'Alas, I was party to the plan to keep you hidden – for I could not bear the thought of your being held in prison maybe for years and years, as is Queen Margaret!'

'Queen Margaret's troubles are over,' said Anne, trying to change the subject.

'Mean you she is dead?' asked Isabel, her tears flowing anew. 'Alas, poor dear Queen Margaret ...'

'Nay, nay – I meant that she was ransomed by King Louis and returned to Anjou at the beginning of this year, God be thanked!'

'Then she is more fortunate than you and me,' said Isabel dismissively. She placed a fevered hand on Anne's arm. 'Anne, I must tell you how it was ...'

'Nay, there is no need.'

'... Methought you were safe, hidden in the servant's quarters, but having a comfortable room and everything you needed save your freedom. I accepted my lord's word on that – and stayed away from you at his bidding because, as he said, none must discover our relationship. I judged it better, you see, that you were a prisoner here, than in the Tower – and so, God forgive me, failed to realize what was going on.'

'It was an unhappy time,' admitted Anne, in a laudable attempt at understatement. 'In truth, I would have been more honourably treated in the Tower.'

'I know that now – a while ago I overheard a bitter quarrel betwixt my lord and yours,' Isabel said wearily. 'So fierce were the accusations and so threatening was Richard of Gloucester, that I feared a mischief would be done! The latter told my lord how it had been with you then – and I trembled so at his furious rage and was so ashamed at what I heard had been done to you, that I had afterwards to take to my bed. It has affected me greatly, Anne – and I earnestly beseech you to forgive me ere I go.'

'Go? Go where, my sister?' asked Anne with an attempt at lightness. ' 'Twill be a week or two yet ere you are up and about again!'

'Only say I am forgiven.'

'You are forgiven, my sister,' Anne said, still on a light note and kissing her on the forehead. 'There, I trust you are feeling better already!'

'Anne, my son is a bonny little lad – is not it pleasing that each of us has a two-year-old son named Edward! When I am gone, keep a watchful eye on him, I pray you. Should aught happen to my lord in these uncertain times, Margaret of Burgundy, his sister, would I know care for my little Margaret, her namesake – but 'twould be needful that my son remained in England to make claim in due time to that which is his.'

'You have my word on it, my sister. In the event, it would be as you wish, I promise you,' Anne assured her. 'But you will yet recover – you will see! You are feverish and low-spirited at present – but forget not that you were ever the robust one. You were one of the lilies of the field and I a fragile snowdrop!'

'Anne, 'tis no use – my strength is ebbing even as we talk ...'

'Then rest, my sister. Rest and grow strong again.'

'I had to speak – about my son and that other matter that had long troubled my conscience.' Isabel sighed. 'I have but twenty-four hours at the most, the physician informed my lord – I have received the last rites. And in truth – though I would not explain it even if I had breath – I wish not for longer life except for my little one's sake. My marriage has not been a bed of roses, alas!'

'Pray speak no more – you must conserve your strength,' Anne told her. 'I shall go now, that you may get some sleep. I shall return on the morrow, and each morrow following ere I depart with my lord for Middleham – and by that time, I doubt not you will be a picture of health!'

'Anne, dearest Anne, in a few days you will be attending my funeral,' Isabel told her. 'Nay, weep not for me – I myself have wept a veritable river of tears these five years past. God keep you, my sister – pray for me.'

'I shall pray for you – and I shall return as I said,' Anne promised, blinking away her own tears. 'In a very little while, we shall be laughing together at your fears, just as we did in the old days.'

Isabel Duchess of Clarence died early next morning, the twelfth day of December. Within a few months, Anne had lost two more close members of her family for whom she grieved deeply.

She and Richard attended Isabel's funeral and, afterwards, more than ever aware of the need to increase her immediate family, Anne prayed fervently for another child. A little more than a month later, she and Richard having remained in London to attend a royal wedding, Anne's prayers were answered – though not quite in the way she would have chosen.

\* \* \*

On the fifteenth day of January, Richard and Anne attended the wedding at St. Stephen's Chapel, Westminster, of Richard of York, the king's five-year-old younger son, to Anne Mowbray, the five-year-old daughter of the Duke of Norfolk.

An occasion of much splendour, the wedding was attended by the king and queen; three of their daughters, the princesses Elizabeth, Mary and Cecily; the Duke of Clarence; the bride's family and a large gathering of the nobility. A nuptial repast and entertainments followed in the Painted Chamber.

On the morning after this splendid occasion, the capital was startled by a rumour that George of Clarence had been arrested.

A difference had arisen between Clarence and the king, it transpired, due to Edward's refusal to permit his brother to marry Mary of Burgundy – an alliance actively encouraged by Mary's stepmother, Margaret Duchess of Burgundy, who had always regarded Clarence as her favourite brother.

Clarence thereafter had attended the court rarely, claiming that he was being poisoned and refusing to take food and drink there. He furthermore accused his deceased lady's maid, Hortense, of causing the death of her mistress by poison. 'A venomous drink of ale mixed with poison,' he claimed, 'was administered, causing my lady to die.'

As a result of Clarence's accusations, Hortense, together

with a John Thoresby, was taken before the justices and charged with poisoning the duchess, and attempting to poison her eighteen-month-old son. Found guilty as charged, both Hortense and her accomplice were hanged.

There followed further accusations by Clarence against members of his own household: Thomas Burdet, who had been steward at the time of Anne's imprisonment, together with a clerk of the household, John Stacey, was charged with necromancy and of attempting to compass the death of the king by black magic. Both were likewise found guilty and hanged.

Alarmed by these events and the doubts they inevitably raised about Clarence's part in the crimes, the king was further alerted to Clarence's duplicity by two happenings: Louis of France sent word to him of Clarence's boast of what he would do in England once he had acquired the Burgundian dominions; and a rising in Norfolk, led by an impostor claiming to be the Earl of Oxford, which was believed to have been instigated by Clarence.

His patience exhausted, the king took firm action. Clarence was sent to the Tower charged with 'committing acts violating the laws of the land and threatening the security of justices and jurors.'

On being informed of Clarence's arrest by Richard's chamberlain, Anne's thoughts turned at once to her small nephew and niece, and the promise she had made to Isabel.

Richard was at Westminster but was expected to return shortly, for he and Anne were planning to set out next morning on their long-deferred return to Middleham. They had come to London for a funeral, had stayed for a second funeral and then a royal wedding – when all the time both of them were longing to be back in Yorkshire with their son.

I shall speak to my lord of the matter as soon as he arrives, Anne said to herself. Once he has confirmed that his brother is indeed lodged in the Tower, I shall ask him of the children.

She was in her solar when Richard came in, quietly and unannounced. He looked weary, she noticed – and withdrawn, as if he had something on his mind.

So it is true! she thought. It is indeed true. But surely the matter is not too serious. Clarence has displeased the king. But Clarence is for ever displeasing the king in one way or another: one might almost say that Clarence is an adept at displeasing the king – and, at some time or other, everyone else who crosses his path! The king is wont to upbraid him or banish him from court for a few weeks – to teach him a lesson, one might suppose. And then it all blows over and Clarence is meek and contrite for a while – and then the displeasing begins all over again!

'My lord, what ails you?' she asked evenly. 'You look a mite weary – or troubled perchance.'

'The duke my brother has been arrested,' he said formally. 'He has caused much hurt and offence to the king. The matter is serious – he has been confined in the Tower.'

'I am sorry to hear that, my lord,' Anne said, feeling it was expected of her. 'Clarence methinks ofttimes acts without thought – doubtless this will be but a passing cloud!'

What am I saying? she thought. Why am I offering words of comfort to him who has sworn vengeance upon his brother?

'My lady, I acted as I thought best in the circumstances,' Richard said gravely. 'Since we are setting out for the north on the morrow, a swift decision was necessary.'

'A decision about what, my lord? Could it be that you have some dire news to impart!'

'It concerns my brother's children.'

'Then …'

'When I learned of my brother's arrest, I called to mind the promise you made to the duchess your sister. I rode hotfoot to Clarence House and then proceeded to Westminster to consult the king's wishes in the matter.'

'And, my lord?'

'He is outside in the corridor.'

Anne looked startled. 'The king, you say, is outside in the corridor?'

'Nay, nay … Wait and you shall see.' Richard opened the door to admit a young woman with a child in her arms. 'With the king's permission, I brought Edward of Warwick with me, my lady.'

Anne burst into tears.

'Methought something dreadful had happened,' she said

through her tears. 'I feared that some disaster had overtaken my sister's children!'

Is not it a disaster for a child to have its mother die, perchance from poison, and its father committed to prison on charges too many to enumerate! thought Richard – but he kept the thought to himself.

'Margaret, the elder child, is to remain for the time being with her nurse at Clarence House,' he said. 'My sister Margaret, the child's godmother, is sending envoys to conduct her to Burgundy.'

Anne had taken the little boy from his nurse and was smiling with joy.

'You are coming to stay with us for a little while – is not that nice!' she said. 'On the morrow, we are going home to a place called Middleham and you, little nephew, are going with us.'

'I am Edward,' the child lisped. 'And that's my nurse.'

'And your nurse is coming with us – of course she is. And shall I tell you something, Edward?'

'No, thank you.'

'My little boy is called Edward too – now what do you say to that?'

The child said nothing, but gazed unsmilingly at her.

'On the morrow, at daybreak, we shall all of us be setting out for Yorkshire, where *my* Edward will be waiting for us. What do you think of that?' Anne asked, sitting them both down.

'Am not I your Edward too?'

'Of course you are!' Anne said, kissing him. 'For just as long as you want to be.'

'Are you my mama?'

'Nay, nephew.'

'My name is Edward – not nephew!'

By criminy! Anne thought. My life has been ever bound up with Edwards: Edward the prince, Edward the king, Edward my son – and now this little fellow.

'I know it is,' she said gently, 'but how would you like to be called Ned? That then would be your very own name, just between uncle, yourself and myself – and then Edward your cousin, he who awaits us at Middleham, would be just plain Edward.'

The child hesitated, watching her thoughtfully as if suspecting there might be a catch in it. Then he nodded.

'I should like that.'

'And so should I, Ned.'

George of Clarence was not again referred to until later – not until the small hours of the next day in fact. There were other, happier things to occupy Richard and Anne. There was a long journey to make ready for, a toddler to accommodate, and best of all – a joyous reunion to look forward to at the end of the road ...

\*    \*    \*

In the event, Anne set out next morning from Baynard's Castle, with her nephew and her retinue – but without Richard.

Their sleep had been disturbed in the early hours by the arrival of a messenger wearing the king's livery.

Richard had assumed that, as had been the case on a number of previous occasions, his brother had imprisoned Clarence to teach him a much-needed lesson. Clarence had been implicated in the charges, but only to a minor degree – or so it was at first believed.

But the nocturnal messenger disabused Richard of that idea. The duke his brother was in serious trouble this time, as Edward's letter made clear.

Thus it was that Richard's return to Middleham had to be postponed: the king his brother had urgent need of his services and support. Regretfully – for it was only in Yorkshire with his beloved family that Richard felt truly at peace with himself and others – but without hesitation, at daybreak he turned his back on Middleham and rode instead to Westminster. Again, Richard must wait ...

# Thirty-Eight

Much discontent had arisen among King Edward's nobles, because of the preferment given to Queen Elizabeth Woodville's relatives. This had been the prime reason for Warwick the Kingmaker's change of allegiance in latterly supporting King Henry.

Richard, reserved by nature and always prepared to bide his time, concealed his anger and resentment in order to avoid an open confrontation with the government; but Clarence, self-seeking and rash, impervious to the consequences, refused to subdue his indignation and gave full rein to his fury.

Clarence hated the queen – and more particularly her Woodville relatives and the government which he openly blamed for depriving him of Tutbury and several other manors that he had enjoyed by virtue of the king's gift – and being Clarence, he made no effort to conceal his hatred.

Charles of Burgundy having died shortly after Isabel, Clarence had sought the assistance of his widowed sister Margaret, the Dowager-Duchess of Burgundy, to marry her stepdaughter Mary. Clarence was Margaret's favourite brother and, the alliance being beneficial to English interests, she enthusiastically espoused his cause. The matter had been almost accomplished when King Edward was alerted by Louis of France as to Clarence's possible motives: in truth, Louis had his own axe to grind, in that an English alliance with Burgundy could well have constituted a threat to France. Edward was still weighing up the pros and cons of the alliance, when his queen spoke out firmly against it: she too had an axe to grind, in her case a nepotistic axe in that she wished to secure the match for her brother, Anthony Earl Rivers.

Not surprisingly, Clarence was outraged when he discovered that, influenced by his queen, Edward had come out firmly against the match. He railed furiously and publicly against the king, the queen and all her relatives – this afterwards being relayed by Richard to Edward with no detail spared. Richard, having waited a long time to even the score against his brother George, had seen his opportunity. Clarence was, after all, an obstacle to his own secret ambitions ...

Clarence's treasonable utterances added the last straw to the pile of grievances against him, and he had at once been arrested and committed to the Tower.

That then was the situation when Richard, receiving a summons from Edward, had deferred his departure for Middleham.

\* \* \*

Clarence was charged with treason and other crimes and sent for trial. Found guilty on all charges, he was to remain in the Tower at the king's pleasure.

Edward, loath to order his brother's execution but at the same time unable to pardon one who had openly and actively worked against his interests, was in a quandary. Of course, he told himself, should he sue for pardon ... He talked to Richard of his predicament.

'This is a grievous matter, my brother,' he said ruefully. 'A most grievous matter – as we both know to our cost, Clarence is impetuous, quick-tempered, and more than a little foolish at times! He has ever been his own worst enemy – you know it and I know it.'

Richard said nothing, but waited for his brother to continue.

'I would that he would sue for pardon, in which case clemency might be considered,' Edward continued. 'As it is, he has acted so wilfully against the Crown, the queen and her family, that in truth I know not how to resolve the matter.'

'Banishment?' suggested Richard, in such a tone as suggested he did not think much of the idea – but could offer no other.

'Whence should we banish him? To Burgundy?' asked Edward wearily – but then he grinned. 'Or perchance to France – to become a thorn in Louis's side as he is now a thorn in mine!'

'There is always Ireland, sir.'

'One might almost imagine, brother, that you were being vindictive!' Edward's tone was highly satirical.

Richard smiled. 'One might indeed, sir.'

Edward sighed. 'Our brother is already lieutenant of Ireland – not that the Emerald Isle sees him from one year's end to another. Having in mind Clarence's talent for sowing seeds of discontent, I doubt the wisdom of letting him loose amongst that wild and disaffected people!'

'Sir, with respect, you would seem to have little choice than to let the law take its course.'

'I'd not hesitate to pardon the rogue if he would make his submission. As it is, I can do naught to aid him – and that is God's truth!'

'One wonders if it might be unwise to pardon him, sir – would not it give *carte blanche* to any ambitious rascal to foment insurrection or worse? Your subjects howl for blood – there is much talk in the city, many disapproving of your leniency.'

'My subjects, my queen, my ministers – all howl for blood, alas! I recall Clarence as a lad – quarrelsome, fiery-tempered he was even then.' There was affection in Edward's voice. 'To me he is still that same quarrelsome lad – it seems to me he has just never grown up!'

'Sir, the queen shows wisdom in this matter as in all things,' said Richard, who had no great opinion of her and deplored her influence with his elder brother. 'It could be that her fears for the future of your heir are justified. Need I say more?'

'And if I say, "Nay, you need say no more," I rather suspect you would say it one way or another just the same! So?'

'Should aught happen to you ere your sons are of age – as God in his mercy forbid – Clarence could well become a force to be reckoned with, sir. Have you given thought to that, pray?'

'I know you are right, Richard,' sighed Edward. 'Leniency in this instance would be seen as weakness – as of a certainty it is! But, God have pity, he is our brother!'

'Sir, if I might make a suggestion,' said Richard quietly. 'The bill of attainder against him, brought forward by Your Grace, has already been discussed in the Lords and approved by the Commons. I therefore suggest that sentence be passed, not by yourself, but by some nobleman of your choosing.'

'Yourself, for instance?' asked Edward sardonically, well aware of the enmity between his brothers and its cause.

'Nay, that would be most unwise,' replied Richard coolly. 'The sentence, if severe, might be construed as arising from some personal animosity.'

'Which would not be the case, needless to say.'

'Needless to say,' agreed Richard with emphasis. 'Indeed, sir, my grudge against Clarence is personal and long-standing – I do not deny it. Justice must be done and be seen to be done, by the State – since it is the State against which our brother's crimes were committed. I therefore suggest that you delegate a peer of sound judgment to pronounce sentence.'

'Whom have you in mind, my brother – Hastings, perchance?'

'Hastings, if Your Grace so wishes – I confess I had Buckingham in mind.'

'Buckingham is one of your close supporters, is he not?'

'With respect, sir – one of *our* close supporters,' corrected Richard smoothly. 'He is utterly loyal to the Crown and its interests – are not we, after all, brother, of one mind?'

Edward's hesitation was momentary. 'I trust so, Richard – I trust so. The queen has sought more than once to persuade me otherwise, alas!'

'Indeed?' asked Richard, inwardly seething but outwardly calm. 'Ladies have strange fancies, as is ofttimes said, when they are enceinte.'

His queen having recently given birth to her ninth child, Edward chose to take this remark at its face value.

'They do indeed,' he said. 'And I soon disabused my beloved lady of that small fancy, I assure you. "How is it, my lady," I asked, "that you place loyalty to your relations before everything else, whilst showing suspicion of the family loyalties of others!" '

'Might one enquire as to her reply, sir?'

' "Before everything else?" she asked sweetly, in that winning way my lady has. "Certes not before you, my dear lord – surely not before you. Why, do not you recall how only yesternight ..." ' Edward's words ended in a great guffaw of laughter. 'I'll not weary you, brother, with my lady's soft nothings – suffice it to say she's a lady in a million!'

'Sir, since Buckingham is clearly unacceptable to you –' There was a small coldness in Richard's voice which Edward wrongly attributed to his seeming hesitation over Buckingham. '– would you be pleased to appoint another to pass sentence?'

'Buckingham will do well enough –' declared Edward, desirous only of having the matter settled '– since you yourself decline the duty.'

'Duty?' asked Richard. 'With respect, sir, do you see it as my duty? If so, you must surely imprison myself also – for dereliction of duty. To pass sentence on one's own brother would be inhuman – I could not bring myself so to do. However, I would *carry out* the sentence imposed, were it within my power – should you demand it of me, as please God you would not!'

'I shall bear it in mind,' said Edward sardonically. 'I shall bear it in mind. So hold yourself ready, brother, for the role of lord high executioner. As for myself, I should rather hear no more of it!'

\* \* \*

Sentence was duly pronounced by Buckingham on the seventh day of February, twenty-three days after the marriage of the child bride and bridegroom which seemed somehow to have acted as a catalyst to seal Clarence's fate.

A week passed and the execution, customarily effected within three days of the sentence, had not been carried out. Speculation was rife throughout London, the citizens believing that the king would once again pardon his treacherous brother. Had not he pardoned him, welcoming him back with open arms, when Clarence had defected to the Lancastrians in King Henry's time? they asked themselves.

Two more days passed and then another, and public interest began to wane. The king had pardoned his turncoat brother yet again, the commonalty told themselves, had forgiven his threats against himself and the royal family – and had thus condoned his fomenting insurrection in the realm …

*    *    *

News travelled slowly from Westminster to the northern counties; and Anne, happy with the two Edwards at her beloved Middleham, eager to be reunited with Richard but accustomed to long separations, gave little thought to the question of her brother-in-law's imprisonment, having already decided that the king would pardon his treacherous brother yet again.

On those rare occasions when Clarence did come to mind, it was not his predicament that concerned her – but the realization that once he was pardoned she would have to part with little Ned. She loved the child dearly. Having been born only eight months after Edward and cast in the same Plantagenet mould, he could have been taken for Edward's twin. The children themselves had become close – playing together, sharing a nursery, quarrelling now and then, and each demanding a share of Anne's affection. Watching them together, Anne dreaded the day when she would be required to relinquish her nephew to his father …

It was nearing the end of February when Richard, his arrival unannounced, rode with his retinue into the courtyard. Anne, hearing the sound of many horses' hooves on the cobbles, picked up Edward and ran to her solar window.

'Look!' she said. 'It is your papa come home – see, over there!'

Ned clamoured to be picked up.

'Me see – me see!' he cried, pulling at Anne's skirts. 'Ned wants to see the horses too!'

'Climb on to the window-seat,' Anne told him, depositing Edward beside him as he clambered up. 'Now look, both of you – what do you see?'

'Horses,' said Edward.

'Big horses,' said Ned, going one better.

'Look, there he is!' cried Anne. 'Look, over there – give him a big wave!'

'I am waving – but he's not waving back!'

'Horses don't wave, silly!' said Edward. 'They'd have to stand on three legs – and then they'd fall over!'

'I can stand on *one* leg,' bragged Ned.

'So can I – see!'

'I can stand on *no* legs – but only for a minute or I'd …'

Ned, demonstrating his legless pose, fell off the window-seat at that point, quickly followed by Edward who refused to be outdone. In the ensuing hullabaloo, Richard had disappeared from the courtyard and Anne, having summoned the children's nurses to take them back to the nursery, hastily made herself presentable to greet her returned lord.

In fact, it was some time before he set foot in the solar. Anne put this down to the fact that he would first wish to discard his riding boots and outer gear, and remove the more obvious signs of a very long ride in inclement weather.

Her first sight of him startled her. He looks weary unto death! was her first thought as he entered the chamber. What then is amiss? she asked herself. What catastrophe has there been at Westminster to give him that look of brooding melancholy?

'How good it is to see you, my lord,' she said.

He embraced her warmly but in silence – as if for the moment he did not trust himself to speak.

'It is good to be home,' he said then. 'Sometimes when I return from much journeying, I tell myself I shall never roam again – that I shall remain here at Middleham with you and our son for the rest of my days.'

'I would it could be so, my lord,' Anne said with sincerity. 'There is something amiss, is there not?'

'There was something amiss – but all is now well. Justice has been done.'

'You are saying the king has now released the duke your brother – that he has served a sentence of some five weeks and is once more restored to the king's favour?' Anne managed to say calmly, though inwardly far from calm. O God, she was praying, let it not be so – for then little Ned will have to leave us!

Richard did not answer the question directly – but Anne, occupied with her own thoughts, did not recognize the fact right away.

'The Warwickshire estates which went to my brother at the time of his marriage to your sister, are being granted by the king's will to the countess your mother,' was what he said.

'My father's estates?' asked Anne in surprise. 'But why would the king do that, my lord – indeed I suspect that, since they have been the subject of so much controversy and she already has all she wants here with us, mama will refuse them. But I fail to understand – how has this come about?'

'The duke my brother no longer has need of them.'

'You mean ...'

'George of Clarence is dead,' Richard said quietly.

'May he rest in peace!' said Anne, crossing herself – but gazing all the while at Richard. 'Then the king did not pardon him, after all.'

'The king did not pardon him – pardon was not sought and was therefore not granted. Sentence was pronounced but was not carried out right away – Clarence was executed one night last week.'

'One night, you say?'

'Friday, it was. But he was not found till next morning, drowned in a butt of malmsey.'

'Drowned? In a butt of ... Then surely, my lord, his death was an accident – he was imbibing wine to lift his spirits, I daresay, tripped and fell headlong into the butt, knocking himself senseless and drowning.'

'Many will say as much!' said Richard grimly. 'There was no blood, you see, to prove the matter one way or another. He struggled with his executioner – *par Dieu*, how he struggled! But his executioner is a determined fellow – the wretch deserved to die, had long deserved to die! "You?"

he said to his executioner. "But you cannot – you are my ..." But his executioner had had enough. He thrust his head into the butt – and that was the end of that.'

'The executioner told you of his last words? He reported to you ...' Anne fell silent – her expression changing to one of horror. 'Then it was – it was you! Nay, nay, say it was not so, my lord ...'

'Richard of Gloucester –' he said quietly, '– carried out the judicial execution – in so doing he avenged one dearly loved and woefully mistreated.'

Pale as ashes, clutching a chair for support, Anne gazed at him in silence. Numb with shock, thoughts, disconnected thoughts, flitted in and out of her mind. Richard did it for me, she said to herself. Clarence has at last paid the price ... all these years my lord has waited ... alas, my unborn child, the agony and the grief ... the confusion and disbelief of being at one moment Princess of Wales and the next a menial ... the humiliation, the hopelessness ... all over now, all over now ... my lord bided his time, waited and held his peace ... all for my sake ... my sister's child, my nephew, my own flesh and blood ... Edward and Ned, Edward and Ned.

She felt a little faint and thought Richard was watching her curiously.

'So Ned can remain with us, after all!' she said.

Richard made no reply. He turned on his heel and was gone, slamming the door behind him ...

# Thirty-Nine

Life went on happily and uneventfully for Anne and her little family at Middleham during the next six years. That she bore no more children was a deep regret to her and Richard, but the arrival of Ned in their household had to a great extent, for Anne at least, alleviated that sorrow. Anne believed that the treatment she had received at Clarence House, culminating in the loss in dire circumstances of her child, was the chief cause of her difficulty in producing more children.

Single-minded in his loyalty and affection towards those he loved best, namely, Anne, Edward his son, Edward his liege-lord, and the few he called friend, Richard was no less single-minded in his ruthlessness towards those who had caused hurt to his loved ones – or who stood between himself and his ultimate goal.

Only the king came into both categories, being liege-lord and obstacle. Some in the second category had by one means or another been removed from Richard's path already, as for instance King Henry, Edward Prince of Wales and George of Clarence. Richard regretted the prince. Some day, he thought, I shall tell Anne about the prince, how it was and why it was – that I myself did not draw my sword against him. But that can wait a little longer … There remained now only the king's two sons, Edward and Richard – and Edward Plantagenet, Earl of Warwick, otherwise known as Ned.

Ned was a special case in Richard's scheme of things. In years to come he might well claim his father's place in the succession – thus he was an obstacle. That he constituted a threat to Richard's ambitions was undeniable; that he was dearly loved by Anne and young Edward was likewise undeniable. Ned was therefore in a category all his own: he was unique. Richard, giving thought to the matter, told himself firmly that he must leave something to God and Time.

Edward the king was Richard's elder by ten years. He seemed latterly to be resting on his laurels in regard to statecraft and foreign policy – having given himself up to rich-living and a life of debauchery. God could be relied upon to remove Edward from his path, Richard decided – without the help of Time! He loved Edward and would mourn him – but, as he was the first to acknowledge, one could not quarrel with the acts of the Almighty.

Until then, Richard would be patient. He would continue loyally and tirelessly to lead Edward's armies, protecting the northern counties, holding Berwick against the invader, carrying out reprisals across the Border for Scottish raids on northern towns and villages; everywhere winning his brother's battles and destroying his brother's enemies.

During the course of these campaigns, journeying to every part of the realm and away from home for many months at a time, Richard frequently put up for the night at the castle of some nobleman. A welcome guest, he met many beautiful ladies who were nothing loath to offer their favours to the king's brother. He thus acquired two bastards at this time, John of Gloucester and Catherine, both of whom he maintained and publicly acknowledged.

Richard's enemies, and there were many, referred to him with odium; as a hunchback, small, ugly and born with teeth. Others spoke of him in glowing terms. Had not the Countess of Desmond, having danced with him, declared, 'Except for his brother the king, Richard of Gloucester is the handsomest man in the hall!' Slender and of medium height, the vigour and skill with which he exerted himself in battle was proof positive of his strong physique.

Whosoever knew Richard, whether Yorkist or Lancastrian, friend or foe, none could deny that he possessed a charisma which would be with him till the end of his days – and perhaps beyond.

# PART THREE

*Anne, Queen of England*

# Forty

King Edward died suddenly from natural causes on the
ninth of April 1483. Forty-one years of age at the time of
his death, he named his son, thirteen-year-old Edward, as
his heir. At the same time, unhappily aware of the
unpopularity of the queen and her acquisitive Woodville
relations, and realizing that their further assumption of
power would be likely to plunge the kingdom into conflict,
he nominated his brother, Richard of Gloucester, as lord
high protector of the realm during the new king's
minority.

When the king died, his heir was at Ludlow Castle
where, under the tutelage of Earl Rivers, his uncle, and
the guardianship of Sir Richard Vaughan, his chamberlain, he was being educated. In fact the Woodvilles held
all the vantage points. Sir Edward Woodville, the queen's
brother, was admiral of the fleet; the Marquis of Dorset,
the queen's eldest son by her first marriage, was constable
of the Tower of London which housed, amongst other
things, the late king's treasure and the vast store of
armaments he had been holding ready for an invasion of
France.

Richard was at Middleham when a fast-riding messenger brought him the news of his brother's death. He had
just returned from Berwick, having led a powerful force
there to take and occupy the fortress, thus nullifying the
Scottish king's threat of a full-scale invasion of England.

No limit had been placed on the number of troops
which were to escort the Woodville uncles and the boy
king to London, until Hastings, fearing the effect a display
of Woodville might would have on the commonalty,
threatened to leave the country unless a limit was imposed.

The queen gave way to the extent of limiting the Woodville force to the still considerable number of two thousand men, which would undoubtedly have overwhelmed the forces of Richard and Buckingham – limited to three hundred and two hundred men respectively – had not Hastings sent Richard a warning.

Richard acted swiftly. He set out at once with his three hundred men but left at York Sir Richard Ratcliffe, his knight of the body and one of his four friends, to raise a large force and follow him southwards with the reinforcements.

On reaching Northampton, Richard was joined by the Duke of Buckingham with his force. On learning from Buckingham that the young king's arrival was imminent, Richard resolved to assume the role of protector right away and himself escort his nephew to London.

It became thereafter a battle of wits, the queen's party seeking to get the better of Richard by being the first to reach London with the king. Recognizing to their chagrin that any attempt to prevent the protectorship would increase the resentment and suspicion of the commonalty, they sought instead to establish a regency council to which Richard would be answerable.

Aware that he must act quickly if he were to carry out his duties as protector without Woodville interference, and Ratcliffe with strong reinforcements from York having now caught up with him, Richard had Rivers, Vaughan and Grey arrested as they entered Nottingham. He next dismissed the boy king's two-thousand-strong Welsh escort and, with expressions of avuncular reassurance, himself escorted him the rest of the way to the capital.

The boy king entered London early in May, only to discover that his mother, together with his brother and sisters, on learning of Richard's actions at Nottingham, had gone into sanctuary at Westminster.

Twelve days later, the Woodvilles' worst fears were realized. Anthony Earl Rivers, the queen's favourite brother for whom she had sought the hand of Mary of Burgundy, Sir Richard Grey, the queen's second son by a former marriage, and Sir Richard Vaughan were executed at Pontefract for high treason.

In the weeks that followed, Richard acted decisively. He lodged his nephew in the old palace within the Tower, comfortably and with the boy's own servants to wait on him, and then set about separating the chaff from the wheat.

Buckingham was his main ally – but one who needed watching. As a lineal descendant of Edward the Third's son, Edmund, Buckingham had his own personal ambitions – but until the goal was in view, he was content to be a fellow-traveller. To this end, handsomely rewarded by Richard, he worked assiduously for the closer entrenchment of the protector and the annihilation of the queen's leading supporters.

\* \* \*

Anne, accompanied by Edward, Ned and a large entourage, journeyed from Middleham a few weeks later and took up residence at Baynard's Castle, her lord's London abode.

Built some fifty years before by Humphrey Duke of Gloucester on the ruins of the original castle built by the Conqueror and destroyed two centuries earlier by King John, Baynard's Castle stood in a delightfully rural part of the city, where two rivers, the Fleet and the Thames, joined. An idyllic place, the children loved it and Richard found it a welcome refuge from the pressures of statecraft.

Anne, like so many others, was bewildered by the rapid change of events which had set the country in a turmoil. Rumour and speculation were everywhere. Over the past weeks, her lord had become at one and the same time the most hated and applauded man in England.

Richard was seldom at home; and on those occasions when they were together, Anne found him uncommunicative and withdrawn. It was as if, finding it necessary to guard his thoughts from those around him at Westminster, he had forgotten how to lower his guard.

It was not until one afternoon in the third week of June that Anne learned of her lord's intentions. He dined with her at midday, having returned unexpectedly from Westminster, and afterwards retired with her to her solar.

It was obvious that he had something important to impart to her.

'To become king?' she asked uncertainly, thinking she had misheard.

'There is no help for it,' Richard told her, in the manner of one duty-bound to support an unpopular cause. 'To govern this divided land through a protectorate is impossible – always there would be some to challenge, foment rebellion, to cry dissent! The Woodvilles are for ever howling for blood – they rail against every bill that comes before parliament, so that naught is accomplished and we leave the council chamber in disarray.'

'Since the number of the queen's supporters has lately been reduced, their influence must surely have declined.' There was a small edge to Anne's voice. 'Rivers, Vaughan, Grey were executed – and yesterday I learned that Hastings, who had ever opposed the Woodvilles, had been beheaded.'

'Hastings, being even more bitterly opposed to Buckingham than to the Woodvilles, changed sides, alas!'

Anne was troubled by this revelation. She had no great opinion of Buckingham – and knew that Hastings had in the past made clear his loyalty to Richard.

'Is Buckingham entirely trustworthy, my lord?' she asked. 'I have ever had doubts of that nobleman – whereas Hastings ...'

'... was resentful of the rewards received by Buckingham in respect of his services in conducting the prince to London.'

The prince? Why does my lord not refer to him as the king, Anne wondered, since that is his title even under a protectorate?

'As to what you were saying, my lord, about becoming king –' she said uneasily. '– Mean you to assume the sovereignty, and thus rule in the new king's name until he attains his majority?'

'The prince's majority has naught to do with the case, alas!' Richard told her dolefully. 'An investigation has been made and has brought to light the fact that the aforementioned prince is in fact a bastard.'

'Sweet mother of Jesus! How could that be, my lord?'

'The king my brother's alliance with the lady Elizabeth Woodville was no true marriage, since he was pre-contracted to Lady Eleanor Butler.'

'The Earl of Shrewsbury's daughter?' asked Anne, as if there were half a dozen ladies of that name and she meant to establish to which he had referred.

Richard nodded. 'The issue of the marriage is therefore illegitimate.'

Anne was aghast. It seemed to her that, in a few simple words, the late king's progeny had been swept from the succession.

'What of Ned?' she asked then, her voice tense. 'With the princes removed from the succession and Clarence dead, is not he next in the succession?'

Richard sighed. 'There is an impediment there also, Ned being excluded under his father's attainder. It is unfortunate, but there it is!'

There was silence in the chamber for a few moments. Then my lord meant what he said, thought Anne. He means to become king, not as a kind of regent protecting the sovereignty till his nephew is of age, holding power and safeguarding his crown – but for himself.

'And you yourself being next in the succession, are the rightful heir to the House of York,' she said at length, feeling it was expected of her. 'Is not that so, my lord?'

Richard nodded. 'At this moment in time, strong leadership is essential if peace in the realm is to be preserved – after almost thirty years of civil war, the English people want a lasting peace. With the many opposing factions at court and in government at the present time, a conflagration is certain unless there be firm and decisive leadership. Worse than the enemies within our gates, are those without – chiefly of Lancastrian persuasion, they watch and plan, awaiting their oppor-tunity! In Brittany, France and Burgundy they stand ready – whilst in England, dog eats dog, opposing factions do their worst, fighting each other and weakening the sovereignty. Then, when the commonalty is thoroughly demoralized and confusion reigns throughout the realm, those silent watchers across the sea will take to their ships. They will come upon us by stealth – and so occupied will be our people with fighting each other instead of the enemy, they will be stabbed in the back ere they've got wind of the invaders!'

'And you would prevent that, my lord.' It was a statement rather than a question, for watching him as he spoke, Anne had no doubt of his sincerity.

'I would prevent it,' he said quietly. 'Given total control, I believe I could prevent it. As protector, my power is limited – the Woodvilles make sure of that – and strong government therefore is not possible.'

'And what now, my lord?'

'On the morrow, Buckingham is heading a deputation that will wait on me here at Baynard's Castle – he will swear allegiance to myself as King Richard the Third.'

Anne watched him, knowing not what to say. So it is settled, she thought. My lord is not merely testing the ground – he has made his plans and with Buckingham's assistance is about to put the plans into action.

'And then?' she asked.

'Events will move swiftly methinks in the days following – prepare yourself, I pray you, for what lies ahead! Once the crown is mine, it will become yours also. On the day I am crowned king, you, my very dear, will be crowned queen. It is what I have always wanted for you.'

She met his gaze, trying to discover what was in his mind – whether he genuinely saw the crown rather than protectorship as the only means of averting war, both from within and without. A boy king, as she knew, was vulnerable to the ambitions and persuasions of unscrupulous ministers. A protector was neither sovereign nor subject, but a little of both – and, if aught went wrong, the butt of all.

'Perchance you are right, my lord,' she said uneasily. 'Perchance you are right. But should the bastardy decision against your nephews be revoked, what then? Once the prince had attained his majority, would you relinquish your power lightly, accept the situation willingly?'

'I know not.' He did not meet her gaze, she noticed – but spoke brusquely, as if impatient of the question. 'Who can tell what the future holds? Much could happen in the next five years.'

'And what of the prince meanwhile, my lord? Will he reside in one of the royal palaces with his own household – at Richmond or Greenwich perchance?'

'For the time being he will remain lodged in the royal apartments within the Tower,' Richard told her. 'Until we know which way the wind blows, it is better thus. Should there be insurrection, he will be more safely held in that ancient fortress.'

'Such a bleak place, it is – it always makes me shudder when we pass by on the river,' Anne said uneasily. 'I give thought and murmur a prayer for all those who have lived out their lives there as wretched prisoners!'

'The royal apartments are comfortable enough – and indeed my nephews so far have made no complaint!'

'Your nephews, you say, my lord?' asked Anne in surprise. 'Methought only Prince Edward was lodged in the Tower – Prince Richard being in sanctuary with his mother and sisters.'

'Until yesterday, it was so,' agreed Richard. 'But then, at the Archbishop of Canterbury's request, the queen-dowager permitted him to leave sanctuary. His brother had asked for him, saying he missed his company, I am told – and the queen was therefore persuaded to let him go.'

'That is well, my lord,' smiled Anne. 'They will be good for each other. 'Tis said that the sanctuary at Westminster is an awesome place.'

'That was my reason for entering a certain lady of my acquaintance at St. Martin's-le-Grand instead! And with that small piece of information, my lady, I shall leave you awhile. The Council is meeting within the Tower this afternoon – and to some purpose methinks.'

'How strange is Fortune!'

'What mean you, pray?'

'Had the prince my former husband not been slain at Tewkesbury – following the death of King Henry, I would have been Queen of England. Now the wheel has turned full circle – as the wife of a Yorkist nobleman, I am like to be Queen of England just the same!'

Why is my lord looking at me thus? Anne wondered. As if he is on the point of telling me something – but cannot

quite make up his mind to it. Whatsoever it is, it concerns
him greatly methinks.

'Time changes many things, my lady,' he said. 'Have
patience, I pray you – all will come right in the end!'

'Patience?' Anne asked – telling herself these were mere
words and that still the something that concerned him was
unsaid. 'Patience over what, my lord?'

'The queen's crown,' he told her. 'Think you that once
you had tasted the power of queenship, you would lightly
relinquish it?'

'My lord, despite what you have told me, always I should
tell myself that we were holding the crown in trust for
Prince Edward your nephew,' Anne told him. 'And in truth,
should that time come, I doubt not I should depart from
Westminster for Middleham with an easy mind and a light
heart!'

Richard watched her for a few moments in silence, as if
giving thought to what she had said. But he made no
comment.

'I expect to return here this evening at not too ungodly an
hour,' he said at length. 'I shall then, if it please you, come to
your chamber.'

\* \* \*

'My lord, it is many nights since you have lain with me here
in my chamber,' Anne said. 'You look different tonight,
elated, as if you see your plans nearing fruition.'

'As is the case,' he said sombrely. 'As is the case.'

'Yet still methinks you have something on your mind.'

'That may be so.'

'Something which concerns myself, it seems to me,' she
persisted. 'Not just our companying together ...'

'*Just*, you say?'

'My lord, you are being a little tiresome.'

'It was when you spoke this afternoon of Edward of
Lancaster – I realized then that the matter could be shelved
no longer.'

'Of Edward?' She frowned. 'My Edward?'

'Yea – your Edward,' he said ruefully.

'And what is it that can be shelved no longer?' she asked

belligerently. 'Methought we did not discuss my ...'

'Your Edward,' put in Richard helpfully.

'My lord, if you have come here merely to taunt me ...'

'Hearken to me, my lady –' he said, raising himself on one elbow and looking down at her in the candlelight. His bantering tone had gone and he looked suddenly serious. '– it was not I.'

'To what are you referring, my lord?'

'I drew not my sword against Edward of Lancaster – recalling that he was lord to her who was close kin to my mother and whose affections I had always desired to possess.'

Wide-eyed, Anne watched him for a few moments in silence, before she lowered her gaze.

'But the duke your brother told me ...'

'That it was his sword that remained in its scabbard,' interposed Richard. 'That it was mine that delivered the final blow – the *fatal* blow by implication!'

'And you say it was not so?' Anne asked tremulously. 'Why then did not you tell me how it was – why have you taken the blame all these years, letting it come between us? Why, my lord – only tell me why!'

'Did it in truth come between us? I am not sure.'

'But why –' she persisted '– why only now do you tell me?'

'Would you have believed me – in the beginning? I think not. I always wanted to tell you – maybe I hoped someone else would tell you! The king my brother knew, and the Flemish chronicler close by him witnessed the deed. I looked for a suitable opportunity ...'

She looked up at him, meeting his gaze for some moments as if she thought to read the truth in his eyes. Why, she thought, why only now.

'I am glad,' she murmured then on a sob. 'I am so glad.'

She reached out and clasped him to her in a sudden access of joy. Folding him in close embrace, she abandoned herself to him – all of herself, wholly, utterly. As he took her, her enfolding arms tightened convulsively, her fingers raking his naked back. Tears welled from her eyes and she moaned softly, though whether from ecstasy, joy or some other emotion, neither of them could have said.

# Forty-One

Events moved swiftly that summer – so swiftly that, in the event, Anne had only three days in which to make ready for her coronation.

The order was sent out on the third day of July to one, Piers Curtis, to deliver four and a half yards of purple cloth of gold upon damask for the Duchess of Gloucester's use; and tirewomen and seamstresses worked unceasingly, making and fitting the robes until all was ready.

On Sunday the fifth day of July, having already been proclaimed Richard the Third, King of England, Richard conducted Anne and his son Edward – now a lively nine-year-old – in great state in the royal barge, from Baynard's Castle to the Tower. There they took up residence in the royal apartments, it being the age-old custom for the sovereign to spend the night before his coronation at the Tower, whence he would make the journey next morning to Westminster Abbey.

The rest of that day was entirely taken up with preparations for the next, Anne being closeted with her ladies whilst the finishing touches were put to her robes.

She and Richard were lodged in separate apartments within the Tower, Richard having likewise to be made ready for his crowning – details of dress which he, being Richard, regarded with no small impatience.

It was not until quite late that night, long after she had retired, her head full of questions and anxieties about the awesome day ahead, that of a sudden the disturbing thought came to Anne. Where, she wondered, are Prince Edward and his brother? Richard told me they were lodged in the royal apartments – but if that be so, why did not they come forward today to greet us? Indeed, since my lord is in fact deputising for Edward in regard to the sovereignty, it would seem appropriate that he be lodged here with us prior to the coronation.

Yet now I come to think of it, neither prince has been so much as mentioned – let alone seen! Foolish it may be, but the matter troubles me. I dare say there is a simple explanation – alas that I did not give thought to the princes before! Shall I summon one of my ladies and enquire as to their whereabouts? I doubt she would know any more than do I myself – all would assume, if they gave thought to it, that some other arrangement has been made for them ...

In sudden determination, she rose from her bed and drew on a fur-lined robe against the chill night air. I shall go to my lord and ask him of the princes, she told herself.

She opened the door and went through the ante-chamber to the corridor, refusing to have any of her waiting-women accompany her. She quickly made her way towards that part of the old palace known as the King's House. Her ladies, well-accustomed to the nocturnal habits of the nobility, went back to sleep – finding nothing unusual in the queen visiting the king's apartments.

On reaching the King's House, she saw that guards had been posted outside the entrance and, taken aback and apparently unrecognized by the guards, she came to an abrupt halt.

It seemed to her then, as she waited uncertainly at one hour past midnight betwixt her lord's apartments and her own, that she was standing on the boundary between the old life and the new. She had come from the silent nocturnal darkness of the Queen's House, passed through shadowy corridors lit at long intervals by flaming torches, into the dazzling light of many candles and the hustle and bustle of nobles, knights, envoys, prelates and servants all going about their business as if it were the middle of the day.

Henceforth, as she recognized then, her life would be lived amidst the dazzle of court life: open to public gaze, all that she did, said, was imagined to be thinking, would be noted, debated, criticized and frequently misunderstood.

The happy, protected life she had enjoyed for the past ten years, with her lord whensoever his duties had permitted it, and with those beloved children – her son and her foster-son – was on the brink of change. Henceforth, whether she would or nay, she must live with intrigue and doubt, with fear for her lord, for the two Edwards ...

More than a little daunted and conscious of her night-time attire, she was on the point of turning round and retracing her steps whence she had come, when she saw Buckingham striding along the corridor towards her.

Now Buckingham was not one of Anne's favourite people. Tall, handsome, courteous and chivalrous as he undeniably was, his presence always made her uneasy. His manner now was cheerful, debonair – but still Anne had the curious impression that he was merely playing a part.

If Buckingham was surprised at finding the Duchess of Gloucester standing outside the King's House in night attire, he gave no hint of it. He bowed and waited for her to speak.

'My lord the king?' she enquired.

'His Grace is in the chapel, my lady,' came the reply. 'It is customary for the sovereign to pass the greater part of the night before his coronation in the chapel.'

'I understand,' Anne said, telling herself she should have known. 'I desired to speak with my lord on a matter concerning the princes his nephews.'

'My lady, I am well acquainted with the coronation arrangements. Could I perchance be of service?'

'A small matter,' Anne told him vaguely, feeling a little foolish. 'The princes – are they accommodated here in the old palace?'

Buckingham looked curiously at her, she thought – and at once she felt more foolish.

'Not in the palace exactly,' he told her. 'Prior to the arrival of yourself and the king this day, the princes were moved to the Portcullis Tower.'

'The Portcullis Tower?' asked Anne in surprise. 'But that is some distance from the royal apartments and, being both gatehouse and guardhouse, and overlooking the river, is surely unsuitable.'

'It was deemed preferable to spare the princes a sight of the coronation procession, my lady – doubtless they will return to the palace afterwards.'

'A sight of ...? Then Prince Edward will not be present at the ceremony,' Anne said in surprise. 'I understood that a robe had been prepared for him by the court tailor.'

'Such was the case, my lady,' Buckingham told her. 'The robe was for the prince's coronation. Many preparations were made – needlessly as it turned out – both at palace and abbey. But when the unfortunate facts of the prince's birth were discovered – the plans were curtailed, alas!'

'I see,' said Anne who thought she did. 'Yea, of course, foolish of me – I am a little weary, you understand, but wished to assure myself as to the princes' welfare. I shall detain you no longer, my lord of Buckingham. I bid you a good night, sir.'

She returned to her chamber and, this time, fell asleep almost at once. But so frightening were her dreams, so powerful her premonition of evil unidentified, that she awoke to a sense of oppression and the conviction that she was quite unequal to the challenging day ahead.

She lay without moving for a while, telling herself that Jacquetta would be coming in shortly to draw back the curtains. She sighed. As soon as this day is over, she said to herself, wishing it away before it had properly begun, I shall make it my business to look into the matter of the princes. I shall pay them a visit, speak with them, take my own Edward to see them. But before I so do, I shall speak to my lord on the subject ...

\* \* \*

The morning of the sixth of July dawned bright and fair, auguring well for the historic day ahead – for a coronation that was a dazzling display of pageantry.

Having ridden through the city with their son, the newly proclaimed Prince of Wales, and attended by four thousand northern partisans, Richard and Anne went by way of the white hall into Westminster Abbey. Walking barefoot on striped cloth, they then made their way to the shrine of St. Edward the Confessor, the nobility preceding them. The Duke of Norfolk bore Richard's crown, whilst the Duke of Buckingham with a white staff bore Richard's train. Anne followed, the Earl of Huntingdon bearing her sceptre, Viscount Lisle the rod with the dove and the Earl of Wiltshire, her crown. Anne walked under a canopy with a gold bell at each corner, a circlet of gold sparkling with precious stones on her head, and her train carried by the Duchess of Richmond.

Leaving the shrine, Richard and Anne seated themselves on thrones by the altar, and choirs processed into the abbey singing anthems and pricksong.* The royal couple then descended from their thrones and removed their outer robes for the anointing; after which they donned robes of cloth of gold and were crowned by Cardinal Morton with great solemnity.

The choir next sung the *Te Deum*; the Offertory following, Anne sat with the bishop and nobles whilst Richard received the kiss of fealty from his peers.

The crowns having been offered at St. Edward's shrine, Richard proceeded out of the abbey, Anne following, bearing the sceptre in her right hand and the rod with the dove in her left.

At four o'clock that afternoon, the newly crowned couple went to the high dais at Westminster Hall where four long tables had been set out. Richard seated himself at the middle of the table, with Anne at his left hand.

After the company had dined, the champion of England rode into the hall and made his challenge – which was not disputed. The Lord Mayor then served Richard and Anne with hippocras, wafers and sweet wine, by which time darkness had fallen. Flaming torches and tall candles were carried into the hall, illuminating the colourful scene – and, at that, the assembled company went to Richard and made their obeisance. The banquet had lasted five hours.

The new king and queen then made their departure, and the company dispersed to go its separate ways.

---

* musical notes set in alternate parts.

# Forty-Two

Richard and Anne resided at the palace of Westminster for the two days following the coronation and then, accompanied by their son, moved with the court to Windsor Castle.

Only then, on their first night together in the queen's chamber at Windsor, did Anne find the opportunity of broaching the subject of the princes – but by that time, the Tower and the princes were many miles away.

'On the eve of the coronation, my lord, I became alarmed for the welfare of the princes your nephews,' she said conversationally, wishing to hide her concern at least for the time being. ' 'Twas foolish of me, was it not?'

'Alarmed, you say?' frowned Richard. 'Why alarmed?'

Anne sighed. 'I know not – unless it be that I expected Prince Edward, if not his brother, to be present at the coronation.'

'A document bastardizing the so-called princes was ratified prior to the coronation,' Richard told her. 'Thus it would have been unfitting for my nephews to have been present.'

'I understand they were removed from the royal apartments and lodged in the Portcullis Tower.'

'Only temporarily. They are no longer in the Portcullis Tower.'

'Then am I glad, my lord – the old palace is ...'

'They have been transferred to the Garden Tower which, having needless to say a garden close by, is better suited to their needs.'

'Are they being held as if in prison?'

'For their own safety only. Should the Woodvilles gain possession of them, and have the bastardy decree revoked and Edward crowned king, civil war would result. That must be avoided at any cost.'

'At any cost, my lord?' asked Anne indignantly. 'At the cost of the princes' freedom?'

'They are comfortable enough in the Garden Tower,' Richard said complacently. 'New servants have been appointed – the former ones were, I fear, tools of the Woodvilles. But these, vetted most carefully by Tyrrel and Brackenbury, constable of the Tower, are entirely trustworthy.'

'Sir James Tyrrel?' asked Anne in alarm. 'Many tales are told of him – and none of them likely to bring the hearer a good night's sleep!'

'Tyrrel was vice-constable of England in the king my brother's reign,' pointed out Richard.

'I have heard it said that King Edward employed him to carry out illegal executions!'

'Tyrrel will be accompanying me on my northern progress –' Richard told her, adding sardonically '– so you, fair lady, need have no fear for the princes' safety!'

'I am delighted that such a one is not to be left in charge of the princes, my lord.'

But she does not look delighted, Richard thought – and her voice is decidedly cold.

'You concern yourself needlessly.' His voice was stern – and Anne looked at him in surprise. 'The lads are well cared for – but their safe-keeping is vital to the peace of the nation. Were the queen-dowager's party to gain control of them, they would become pawns in a very dangerous game.'

Anne shrugged – annoyingly, Richard thought, as if she were implying that she was not entirely in agreement with him but would refrain from further comment.

'My lord, when you set forth on the northern progress, I shall repair to Warwick Castle –' she said, changing the subject '– if it be to your approval.'

Richard registered the afterthought. Ah, he thought, so my lady is a mite displeased with me – but doubtless that will be remedied ere morning!

'I have a great fondness for Warwick, it being the earl my father's seat as well as the place of my nativity,' she told him. 'If you have no objection, my lord, I shall have Ned brought thither from Middleham to join myself and Edward.'

'I favour the idea,' said Richard absently, as if his mind were elsewhere. 'The boys get on well together and it is good for our son to have companionship. I shall engage new tutors, that the boys may share their lessons.'

'There is one other thing, my lord.' Anne sounded hesitant, as if expecting to be refused. 'It has to do with the princes your nephews.'

'Methought that subject exhausted,' remarked Richard. 'Or perchance the wish was father to the thought!'

'Since Ned is to remain in the royal household, could not the princes your nephews be part of the household also?' Anne asked and then, as if she must get the words out before her courage failed, continued quickly, 'I think ofttimes of the early days and the good times we had at Warwick, all of us – you and your brothers and sisters, myself and Isabel. By comparison, Edward and Ned are singularly unblessed. They derive much benefit from each other's company, it is true – but would not they benefit still more if the princes were part of the royal household?'

'There is a considerable difference in their ages,' pointed out Richard. 'Prince Edward so-called is four years older than our son, remember!'

'But the king your brother was ten years your senior, my lord,' pointed out Anne. 'And Margaret too was considerably older – but did that trouble us? Did not we see ourselves then as one big happy family?'

'The answer is nay,' Richard said firmly. 'For the reasons already given. At Warwick or Middleham, as part of a family or riding in your retinue, there would always be a grave risk of their being seized – not to mention the risk to yourself in my absence!'

'How long then must the princes remain in that bleak fortress, my lord?'

'For as long as I judge it needful.' Richard's voice was cold, Anne noticed – and wondered at it. 'Once my rule is firmly established and my subjects have had time to discover the impartiality of my justice, as well as my care for their interests, then shall my nephews be transferred to more congenial surroundings.'

'Then I look to the future, my lord – and the princes joining us later on.'

'Such would still be out of the question,' Richard said sternly. 'Our son being Prince of Wales, he and his cousins must needs have separate households – there is no help for it.'

'But why, my lord?'

'As you are aware, parliament declared the princes illegitimate. Shocking as was the revelation which led to the declaration, it was substantiated by records of the so-called marriage which further showed that no banns were called prior to the wedding – the marriage taking place privately in the house of Jacquetta, the lady Elizabeth's mother.'

'And so a petition for formal annulment of the marriage was presented to parliament. By whom, my lord?'

'By Buckingham.'

Yea, Buckingham, Anne thought – it would be Buckingham

'And that is how it came about that Buckingham led a deputation to Baynard's Castle –' she said '– and swore fealty to you as King Richard the Third – having deposed the boy king your nephew!'

'So that is how my lady sees the matter!' Richard said icily. 'Even though she had heard the truth from her lord's own lips, she implies that his nephew was wrongfully deposed!'

'Would you have me make pretence, my lord?' asked Anne quietly. 'Is your sovereignty to be an end of truth and plain speaking between us?'

'Indeed not, my lady. Indeed not. Such plain speaking has a value beyond price – for it shows what must be done to preserve my throne and thereby the peace for which my subjects crave!'

'What mean you, my lord?' asked Anne, white-faced.

'No more nor less than I have said. I am no dissembler, as well you know.'

'You would hold captive the princes for ever?'

'I shall give thought to it.' Richard sighed. 'I shall indeed give thought to it. But not now – now there are better things to do!'

'My lord, what if …'

He put a finger to her lips. '... the sky should fall? Or donkeys talk and men bray – or what if Anne of Warwick should be tumbled by the King of England?'

She made a determined effort to banish her uneasy thoughts. The bed-curtains were drawn, the bed was warm – and the world outside seemed of a sudden remote, part of another life. She was lying with her lord for the first time in many days, the first time in fact since the coronation – and he, when he set his mind to it, as now, was mighty persuasive!

'Give me another child,' he was saying urgently. 'Now, more than ever, is there the need!'

'Then make it so, my lord,' she said. 'A son perchance to be named Richard after his sire. Edward and Rich ...'

She bit her tongue on the names – recalling others similarly named. Others who were even at that very moment prisoners in a bleak fortress ...

But Richard appeared not to have noticed. He was removing the rings from his right hand, heavy jewelled rings which might cause her hurt.

She watched, fascinated as always by the ritual. He was a warrior of renown, one who acquitted himself in battle with skill and vigour, who wielded sword and battle-axe to no small effect – yet his hands were long and slender, with filbert nails always well-kept, an artist's hands ...

He turned then and met her gaze.

'Why the pensive look, sweeting?' he asked gently.

'I was thinking how little I know you,' she said. 'Always have you been an enigma!'

'Which is surely no bad thing in a king!'

'Your hands methinks are those of an artist or an ascetic – smooth and slender, they are untypical of a warrior's hands.'

'They do me good service – in battle.'

'And in boudoir?'

There also – my rings are removed for both!'

'Is battle then close kin to coupling?'

'It is indeed,' he said, his eyes inscrutable, meeting her gaze.

'Richard, did you love me a little – even in the early days?'

'You know I did.'

'How do I know?'

'That is a foolish question – a very foolish question!'

'What did you say to yourself then – about myself?'

He looked thoughtful. 'Oh, many things – many many things! And most of them unmentionable – particularly to ladies who ask foolish questions!'

'Tell me just one, pray.'

' "By sweet St. George!" I said to myself. "Let me live long enough to have my hands beneath her kirtle!" '

'Fie, my lord! And what else?'

' "I shall surely die of longing –" I told myself "– if that damsel does not bed with me soon and make me a necklace of her arms." '

'Like this, my lord?'

'Mm – "and press against me her white, smooth body." '

'Like this?'

'Nay, closer than that.'

'Like this then?'

'Mm – "and let me use her body as a pillow …" '

'A pillow? How … oh, like that, you mean!'

'Mm. "… and tumble her over and over again, till she cries out for mercy." '

'And then?'

' "… and give her a child, I suppose – since, by then, there'd be naught else to do!" '

'Richard,' she breathed, 'when you speak thus, fondle me thus, pleasure me thus, I can refuse you naught. Take me, my very dear lord – I am all yours.'

He looked down at her.

'You are all I have,' he said, his voice vibrant with passion – and she thought he spoke more to himself than to her. 'In truth, God help me, you and the boy are all I have!'

'All …?' she started to say – but the rest was lost in the tumult that followed.

# Forty-Three

Richard and Anne left Windsor Castle to go their separate ways, Richard on a progress which took in amongst other places Reading, Oxford, Woodstock, Worcester and Gloucester. Richard was attended by Buckingham and a large following of nobles and prelates. Buckingham's own secret ambitions were beginning to get the better of him: insolent where before he had been subservient, he so far offended his sovereign that Richard decided to humble his pride by banishing him temporarily to his castle at Brecknock.

Richard's progress continued with considerable success, and did much to win him the support and loyalty of his subjects. It became apparent to all who talked with him that he intended to govern well and to the benefit of his subjects as a whole, and this did much to eradicate doubts regarding the legality and rightness of his accession.

From Gloucester, he repaired to York, where he received Geoffrey de Safiola, the Spanish ambassador, whom Ferdinand and Isabella, the Spanish monarchs, had sent to renew the alliance between Castile and England, and to propose a match between their eldest daughter and the nine-year-old Prince of Wales. Encouraged by finding himself acknowledged by the Spanish sovereigns, Richard knighted the ambassador and sent courteous letters to his royal master and mistress.

Anne meanwhile had undertaken a splendid progress which was to end at Warwick. Everywhere she went, she won the hearts of the populace who compared her with Edward the Third's queen, Philippa of Hainault. Armand of Poitiers, looking handsomer than ever, rode immediately behind her and her son, having been appointed her personal bodyguard by Richard who, aware of the knight's devotion to his lady, trusted him implicitly.

Many petitions were handed to Anne *en route*, she receiving them graciously and promising to look into the grievance or request. Most were illiterate and could only voice their complaints, but Anne, mindful of the treatment she had received at Clarence House, listened sympathetically and, whenever possible, had the complaint investigated.

But Anne's good works were not confined solely to her lord's subjects. Approaching Warwick from Coventry towards the end of the progress, the cavalcade came up with a pitifully emaciated donkey which was so heavily laden as to seem to be sinking at the knees. A man was shouting at it and beating it with a stout stick to make it move, but it refused to budge, braying loudly as if for help.

'Mama, look there!' cried Edward, riding beside Anne and forgetting in his concern the formality due to her in public. 'That man's beating that poor old donkey to death!'

Anne herself had taken in the scene and turning to one of her entourage, told him to bring the donkey-man to her. The donkey-man refused at first but when a second man-at-arms appeared beside the first, he gave in with an obscene oath.

'That is no way to treat one of God's creatures, sirrah!' said Anne sternly. 'The beast is half-starved by the look of him, his back is covered with sores – and his load is too heavy!'

'He's lazy and good for nothing!' grumbled the man. 'It's all right for some to talk – but I'm a poor man and I paid good money for 'im. I'll get me money's worth out of 'im if it kills me!'

'It will kill him first,' said Anne. 'Now, if I give you money to compensate you, will you rest the animal for a few days and see that he is properly fed?'

'If it pleases you, ma'am – anything to please a lady!'

'But mama,' put in Edward urgently. 'He will not – he will not. I can see it in his face – he will take the money and go on treating the donkey the same till the poor thing is dead!'

Anne was very much afraid her son was right.

'Take no notice of 'im, me lady,' the man said, indicating the Prince of Wales. 'Just give me a coin or two and I can make a fresh start – I'll feed 'im proper and all that, 'ave no fear! The donkey's not the only one as is starving, you see – I've a wife and eight kids at home!'

'Mama –' pleaded Edward, turning tear-filled eyes on Anne '– could not we buy the donkey?'

'Buy him?' asked Anne in astonishment. 'What in mercy's name would we do with a donkey on a progress – a state journey? Nay, Edward ...'

'For Ned – as a present for Ned,' pleaded Edward. 'He is waiting for us at Warwick, as you told me – and the donkey could have his own little stable in the field behind the castle and Ned and I would visit him every day. Buy him, mama – if you please. He would be fat as butter in no time at all – if Ned had him.'

'Sirrah,' said Anne coldly to the donkey-man, 'would you be willing to sell the animal?'

'That all depends, me lady. He's me livelihood, you see ...'

Anne summoned a groom who was part of her entourage. 'What would be a fair price for yonder donkey?' she asked.

'I doubt any price would be fair, my lady,' came the answer. 'Wasted and verminous – why, the creature's naught but a bag of bones! He's not old though – 'tis a pity we didn't come upon 'im sooner. With respect, my lady, if the prince wants a donkey, he can do better than that!'

'He will die if we leave him!' cried Edward. 'Look, mama, see him watching you with his big brown eyes – and he's braying, asking you to save him. Please, madam my mother – please!'

'We shall have him,' said Anne, turning to her chamberlain. 'Pay his owner double whatever you and the groom judge to be a proper price – I would not want to save the donkey and then have starving children on my conscience!'

Edward had already leapt from his horse and was running over to the donkey.

'Best keep away from him, my lord,' advised the groom. 'He's alive with vermin and Lord knows what!'

But already Edward had hold of the animal's halter and was talking to it. The transaction completed, the donkey was relieved of its burden, fed and watered and tethered to the back of the last baggage wagon.

'Might I suggest we put up for the night at the next town, my lady?' asked Armand of Poitiers of Anne – as the Prince of Wales, refused permission to ride beside the donkey at the end of the cavalcade, reluctantly remounted and resumed his place beside his mother. 'I doubt the donkey will survive many more miles today!'

'We will indeed, sir,' agreed Anne. 'The head groom then shall check him over and, if he advises it, the animal will be put down.'

'Madam my mother, you surely mean it not!' exclaimed Edward, standing in his stirrups to gaze for the umpteenth time towards the back of the cavalcade – to be greeted by a loud bray. 'Did you hear that, mama? He saw me and was telling me he is all right. I just cannot wait to see Ned's face when he sees him!'

'And what of the king your father's face when he sees him?' smiled Anne. 'He will think we have taken leave of our senses. "Warwick Castle a sanctuary for donkeys" he will say. "Whatever next!" '

'I shall explain that the donkey is for Ned,' Edward told her. ' "Because Ned came not with us," I shall tell him. "He had to stay here, all on his own – so we brought him a gift!" And papa will smile and pat my head.'

'Papa?' asked Anne with an admonitory frown.

'The king my father will smile, with his eyes – papa always smiles with his eyes when he is pleased with me. And he'll say, "He can stay, my prince, since he's a gift for Ned – and we shall call him Neddy." '

'A mite confusing, would not it be, to have Edward, Ned and Neddy all in the one household?' enquired Anne lightly.

'You will soon become accustomed to it, mama –' Edward corrected himself hastily. '– madam my mother. I am so looking forward to reaching Warwick!'

He stood up in his stirrups again and looked back.

'I hope he is all right,' he said anxiously. 'He's not looking at me now!'

'The grooms will keep an eye on him, my prince,' said Armand of Poitiers, seeing the boy's concern. 'Donkeys are much the same as horses I dare say, when 'tis a case of knowing them!'

# Forty-Four

Richard joined Anne at Warwick Castle where they kept court with great splendour. Two weeks later the royal cavalcade set out again, with Richard and Anne riding this time side by side, reaching Coventry in the middle of August.

Moving on a few days later, they arrived at York, Richard's stronghold, on the thirty-first day of August, to scenes of great rejoicing. There, to the delight of Richard's subjects, he and Anne were again crowned with great pomp, he afterwards receiving oaths of allegiance.

Edward too was shown great honour and was re-invested as Prince of Wales, his father afterwards presenting him to his subjects on the steps of York Cathedral. Richard's paternal pride was plain to all.

'We present to you our son, Edward Prince of Wales –' he said, '– whose singular wits and endowments of nature wherewith – his young age considered – he is remarkably furnished, do portend, by the favour of God, that he will make an honest man.'

It was then, watching her son waving to the populace, smilingly acknowledging the acclamations, that Anne caught from near the front of the great concourse, the lone voice that made her blood run cold.

'And what of the other Edward?' demanded the voice, belligerent and male. 'What of the fifth Edward – him as is rightful sovereign of the realm? What of 'im as was done to death in the Tower?'

There was a sudden scurry in the foremost ranks of the crowd as Richard sent men to rout out the miscreant – but the people behind had separated a little and the man made his getaway like a rabbit in a thickly populated warren.

Then, from the side, came another cry – from a more youthful voice this time.

'May he rest in peace, the murdered young king – and long live his brother, Richard of York!'

Again there was a hustling and a scurrying – and again the miscreant seemed to vanish into thin air. Richard appeared unconcerned. He made no comment but continued as before, and presently the royal party retired and Richard attended a meeting of the city council.

Anne took the opportunity of accompanying her son on a walk in grand procession through the streets of York. Holding her hand, wearing the Prince of Wales's crown and jewels, Edward was a joy to behold. Smiling and gracious, golden haired, at nine years old having almost feminine beauty, he was the prototype of a Plantagenet. The aged, seeing him, recalled Richard the Second whose glorious coronation procession through the city some eighty years earlier – when they had been children and the king a lad of ten – had won him acclaim as 'a second Absalom.' Others were heard to remark on the new Prince of Wales's close resemblance to that other Edward Prince of Wales who had been slain at Tewkesbury – though none but Anne herself, it seemed, recalled that the other had been her husband.

A happy child, unspoilt by the doting affection of his parents, Edward enjoyed every minute of it. Only one thing, it seemed, marred an otherwise cloudless sky.

'I wish Ned were here with us,' he said to Anne. 'I see not why he had to remain at horrid old Warwick Castle!'

'Ned would have felt left out,' Anne told him. 'He could not have taken part in the coronation ceremonies.'

'But he could be here with us now, madam my mother,' persisted Edward – smiling disarmingly at a group of senior citizens and receiving a round of applause in return. 'We could have taken it in turns – I would not have minded at all.'

'Taken what in turns?'

'To wear my crown.'

Anne looked sharply at him.

'Speak not so, my son – and most particularly not in the king your father's hearing,' she said firmly. 'To wear your crown indeed!'

'But 'tis really quite a nice crown, mama – er – madam my mother,' said Edward, tilting it to a rakish angle for a moment and prompting a burst of laughter from the onlookers. 'On my faith, I'd not mind sharing it with Ned!'

'That may be so, Edward,' Anne told him quietly. 'But such a statement could well be misconstrued.'

'By papa – er – the king my father, mean you? You think he would be angry and beat me.'

'I did not say that, Edward.'

'By papa has never ever beaten me, mama.'

'I was not thinking of you, my son. I was thinking of Ned …'

'Papa has never beaten Ned either,' insisted Edward. 'He loves us both, Ned and me – just the same as one another. He would not mind a bit, I know he would not – if I let Ned wear my crown!'

'Come, my son, we must return now.' Anne moved away from the throng of people, anxious lest her son's innocent remarks were overheard.

'But, madam my mother …'

'Come.'

'You are vexed with me, are you not? Your face has gone all severe.'

'Vexed? Nay, my son, not vexed – sorrowful maybe and a little afeared.'

'Afeared – for me, mama?'

'Not for you, Edward.' She smiled fondly at him, seeking to ease his concern. ' 'Tis for Ned I fear.'

'I do not understand, mama.'

'That is well, my prince – please God you never will!'

# Forty-Five

Rumour was everywhere. The court was now at Pontefract and wheresoever Anne went, riding with her retinue through the city or on a visit to some abbey or shrine, whether with or without Richard and her son, she heard the dreadful accusations. From the midst of the crowd the incriminating words issued, faceless, anonymous – protected by the wall of people round about.

'What of the little princes?'

'What of Edward the Fifth – our rightful king?'

'Done to death, they be – murdered in their beds!'

'The Lord will avenge the innocents! For as much as ye do it unto the least of these, my little ones ...'

'It were better a millstone be placed around his neck than ...'

Anne tried to ignore them – as Richard himself did. Does he even hear what is said? she wondered. She stole a glance at him on one such occasion, but his face was impassive. Rumour and slander were the crosses of kings, the burdens they must bear without plaint: she was aware of that – but no less aware that in her innermost being, she too was posing questions and wanting answers.

It was her own unanswered questions that made her feel isolated from Richard; she felt disloyal in that she could, even for an instant, doubt the integrity of her wedded lord.

Her son looked at her sometimes, troubled and questioning, when an accusation was made loud and clear from the depths of a crowd. He too desired answers, wanted the dreadful incriminating words challenged – wanted her to hotly refute the slanders.

Only once did he speak of it – but it was that, and the

251

nightmare, which at last prompted Anne to broach the subject to Richard.

'Madam my mother, why do they call them *the little princes*?' Edward had asked. 'Are they dwarfs then?'

She had known it was his way of opening the subject; that quite unable to believe his father guilty of the crime the voices attributed to him, he none the less looked for reassurance whilst not wishing to seem disloyal.

'Of whom do you speak, my son?' she asked to gain time.

'Of the princes my cousins.'

'But you surely remember them, Edward — when Edward your uncle was King of England, you ofttimes saw the princes. You know therefore that they are not dwarfs!'

'I have not seen them since papa became king,' pointed out Edward. 'Prince Richard was nearer my age and I liked him because he used to make me laugh. I was seven last time I saw him and he said, "I was seven when I was your age!" and we both rolled about laughing!'

'The princes are in that part of the Tower of London known as the Garden Tower — 'tis close by the river and there is a fine garden in which they may take exercise.' Why, Anne wondered, am I making it sound so jolly — as if I had something to hide? 'It is by no means a prison, my son — if that is what you are asking!'

'Mama, why cannot they pay us a visit? Ned and I would be pleased to see them and, with all of us together, we could play all manner of games. And Ned would let them see Neddy, 'cos he said so — he only lets people he specially likes see Neddy!'

'One day, Edward — one day,' Anne said vaguely — having only then recognized just how troubled she was about the princes. 'The king your father considers it meet that they remain where they are for the time being.'

Edward was silent for a few moments and Anne assumed with relief that the subject was closed. But the words that followed struck a new chill into her.

'Then they are not dead?'

'Dead?' Anne's heart missed a beat. 'You foolish child — fancy asking such a question!'

'But people *say* they are dead.'

'People say many things that are untrue, Edward. As the

king your father's heir, you must learn to make your own judgements – judgements based on evidence and fact. Never must you be influenced by rumour – by the lies and accusations of your father's enemies, that is to say by your enemies and mine also.'

'I must do as papa does?'

Anne nodded. 'As you say, my son – you must do as papa does.'

'I have tried, mama. I have practised it in my chamber mirror.'

'Practised what?' frowned Anne.

'Looking as papa does – when people say wicked things like they do about the princes. I have watched papa then and his eyes change – they look cold and a little frightening.'

'That is because the king your father is a Plantagenet,' Anne told him. 'It has ever been so with the Plantagenet monarchs – when they are serene, it is said, their eyes have a remarkable sweetness; but when angry, they sparkle with indignant fire!'

'But you are a Plantagenet, mama, and your eyes are not like that.'

'I dare say Lord Plantagenets are different from Lady Plantagenets!'

'Maybe you have not practised it enough, as I did in my mirror – and besides you are pretty, prettier than papa!'

'I doubt the king your father would wish to be pretty, my son!'

'He said he did. He said, "I shall be pretty severe with you if you have not a better care for your manners!" '

\* \* \*

Whether it was prompted by her conversation with her son or her own dark fears, Anne had a terrifying dream that night.

She awoke to find her bed in total darkness: the fire had gone out and not a glimmer of light penetrated the hangings. The bedchamber seemed musty and airless, and the bedcurtains smelled inexplicably sooty and un-wholesome.

Reaching out for one of the curtains, she drew it back carefully, anxious not to disturb her sleeping lord. Bathed in perspiration, her heart thumping, she strained her ears for the slightest sound.

Her heart leapt anew as there came a spontaneous movement of the dying embers of the fire. Then, as if the heat had all at once gone from the hearth, the coldness spread out across the chamber, uniting with the darkness to convey a brooding sense of evil ...

What startled me into wakefulness? she wondered. I know not how long I have slept or what hour of the night it is. Richard fell asleep first and I lay awake for a while, troubled and fearful in a way I could not have explained – but which was with me from when Edward asked me of the princes. I believe he felt it too at the time, though we spoke not of it.

Something woke me, she thought then in a panic. I was dreaming – it was the early days, and summer, and we were together, all of us, in the gardens at Warwick ...

But then something wakened me and – and ... Why for mercy's sake is there no light? Are we still at Pontefract? Am I forgetting something, confused perchance by – by sleep ...?

She put out a hand tentatively. Ah, as I thought! I *was* confused. My lord the king is lying here beside me. I can hear his even breathing – though he is breathing faster than usual and, curiously, seems to be taking up less space ...

Her hand went instinctively to her bosom and again she knew the reassuring feel of the letter she had placed inside her bodice.* 'Tis still there, she thought, I am glad Edward agreed to my keeping it tonight – it gives me great comfort and persuades me that mama is here with me in spirit ...

Edward? Why Edward? My lord's name is Richard. Edward was my first husband's name – as well as my son's name. But it is also the name of another, one whom I cannot quite place – but who is very close to me at this moment ... This last, he whom I cannot, or perchance dare not, place at the moment – why should I have

* See *Prince of the White Rose* by the same author.

confused him with my lord?

Holy Mother, what was that! The sound came from the top of the stairs, just outside the door. The top of the ... How foolish I am! The nearest stairs are far off, at the end of the gallery that leads to the chapel.

I must keep still and silent, she told herself firmly. I must relax and then perchance I shall fall asleep again. I have no desire to disturb Richard, to trouble him with my fears. Fears? What fears? I am here in the royal apartments at Pontefract Castle – am I not?

There it is again! I heard it plainly that time – the sound of a booted footfall on the stairway. The stairway? Nay, nay ... Yet it was just such a sound that woke me – I recall it plainly. And there it is again, closer this time ...

God have pity, there is danger lurking out there in the darkness! I know it. I sense it. I must warn Richard. I must tell him of the danger that stalks in the darkness.

The presence is approaching the bed now; it is nearing the curtains. It approaches on the other side, Richard's side. I must wake him, warn him ...

Warn him of what? I am being foolish, very foolish. If I wake him, I shall be disturbing him needlessly. I must take a firm hold on myself ...

Sweet Saviour protect me! The curtain has been drawn aside and I can see a man with a lantern. He holds the lantern aloft, but its light is dim and I cannot see his face properly.

*I must warn Richard before it is too late.*

'E.....! E.....!'

The words will not come, alas! My mouth is dry and my throat constricted – my lips are moving wordlessly. I cannot speak, cannot even utter Edward's name.

Jesu have pity, I cannot even cry warning! Fear prevents my giving utterance to words which might, even at the eleventh hour, save Edward ... Edward? Why think I of Edward? I surely mean Richard – for 'tis my lord Richard who lies beside me. But nay, that cannot be. It is I myself who am Richard – Richard of York, brother to Edward, the boy king ...

Alas, I grow more confused! Why is my mind fixed on Edward, when I know full well that it is not Edward, but my lord the king who lies beside me ...

The man with the lantern is bending over him now. He is lifting up the bedclothes and wrapping them around Edward's head – and now he is removing the pillow and pressing it down over his face ...

I can feel Edward struggling. His arms are flailing and his limbs cavorting wildly, as he struggles for air. I am moving away from him in horror. I must get out of bed and hide myself before they turn their attention to me, before it is too late ...

Edward is silent now, and still. He is dead. I know he is dead, for one of his hands lies limp against mine and I can feel the cold sweat upon his body. Edward is no longer breathing ...

The man has removed the pillow and is surveying his handiwork. He grunts with satisfaction and beckons to another man, and now they are both looking down at Edward. They are straightening up and the first man is nodding his head in my direction.

The second man is moving round the bed towards me now. Holy Mother protect me! I fear my heart will burst from my chest with such wild thumping. I am rigid with terror as the man reaches me, looks down at me ... God in Heaven, I see now who it is ...!

He has taken hold of me and I am struggling desperately to free myself, kicking out at him and arching my back to escape his clutches. But he is holding me firmly and I cannot escape ...

'Be at peace, sweeting!' he says now in a low, warm voice that is vaguely familiar. 'Be at peace, fair lady – it is only I!'

'Richard?' she asked a little wildly. 'Richard? Then it was you all the time – God be thanked!'

'Who did you think it was?' he asked lightly. 'Louis of France or the Duke of Buckingham?'

It was the last three words that banished the nightmare and restored her equilibrium.

'The Duke of Buckingham?' she asked on a surprised note. 'What, my lord, would I be doing with the Duke of Buckingham?'

'You tell me, beloved,' smiled Richard. 'You were struggling so violently and your kick was so well judged – I doubt Richard of England will ever be the same man again!'

'You are teasing me, my lord,' she dimpled. 'You are surely teasing me.'

'Not altogether.'

'But why Buckingham? You surely cannot imagine ...'

'Oh, he would if he could – I doubt it not. Buckingham is my deadliest enemy.'

'You cannot be serious, my lord.'

'Serious enough to be leaving this very morning for Nottingham,' Richard told her. 'Assisted by Morton, the Bishop of Ely, Buckingham has raised an army against his liege-lord.'

'Why so, my lord?'

'His insolence had become insufferable of late, and I therefore banished him for a while to Brecknock to cool off – this is the result.'

'But he was ever one of your most loyal supporters.'

'He was ever one of my most *ambitious* supporters,' corrected Richard. 'He recalls his own high lineage. Now, sweeting, I must away to make ready for departure in two hours.'

'So soon, my lord?'

He kissed her. 'You sound regretful.'

'You said naught of this when you came to bed, my lord.'

'Ratcliffe came in a few minutes ago to inform me of the insurrection,' Richard told her. 'I heard the door open and, even as my hand reached for my dagger, I saw it was Ratcliffe carrying a lantern. You were sleeping fast and, wishing not to disturb you, Ratcliffe leaned over and in low tones told me what was afoot. As he left, I got out of bed and, preparatory to going to my robing chamber, moved round the bed with silent tread, as I thought, to see if you were still asleep. It was then that you did your impersonation of an all-in wrestler!'

Anne felt rather foolish. How much, she wondered, had been dream or nightmare – and how much the consequence of Ratcliffe's tactful silent-footed arrival?

'Richard, there is something which troubles me deeply.'

'So I gathered – just now.'

'Something about which you alone can reassure me.'

He watched her in silence for a few moments and then, kissing her again, moved away from the bed.

'When I return, dear heart,' he said firmly. 'When I return, I shall tell you all.'

'Is that a promise, my lord?' She was close to tears, he noticed – and he feared he knew what was troubling her.

'A promise it is,' he said as he drew on his dressing-robe. 'Meanwhile I am bound for Nottingham, where I shall muster my troops. I intend to go in quest of friend Buckingham and engage him ere he can gather reinforcements.'

Anne got out of her bed, her hair flowing freely around her shoulders and her long nightgown billowing out behind.

'Richard –' she said, clasping her long slender arms about his neck '– Godspeed, my very dear lord! I shall follow you with Edward and Ned to Nottingham in a few days.'

He shook his head. 'Till the commotion is past, it would be unwise to have our son as it were in the thick of things – a sovereign with but the one heir must be doubly careful of his safety. I doubt not that Buckingham would give much for the capture of the Prince of Wales.'

Anne watched his expression. 'The matter is that serious, my lord?' she asked with a catch in her voice.

His smile was brief – but warm and reassuring. 'As of now, yea – but it will not be so much longer, I promise you!'

# Forty-Six

And so Edward, accompanied by Ned and his own household, was sent, not without protest, to Middleham, whilst his father, and shortly afterwards his mother, repaired to Nottingham.

Buckingham, it seemed, had declared for Henry Earl of Richmond, the Lancastrian claimant to the throne. It had been agreed by both parties that Henry should seek an alliance with Edward the Fourth's eldest daughter, Elizabeth of York, to thus unite both Houses. The plan was communicated to the Countess of Richmond, Henry's mother, and the queen-dowager who was still in the sanctuary at Westminster. Both ladies approved the proposed alliance and, together with Buckingham, formulated a plan.

Richard mustered his troops and held them in readiness to move at a moment's notice. He then sent a message to Buckingham, giving him one last chance to come to terms and requiring his attendance at court.

Forced thereby to show his hand one way or another, Buckingham gathered his troops and retreated to the west, where he expected to be joined by his confederates. He advanced by forced marches to the banks of the Severn, intending to join his supporters in Devon and Dorset – but the river had overflowed its banks during a great storm, leaving the countryside flooded to such an extent that it was impossible for his men to make camp or find subsistence. The storm, spoken of ever afterwards as *The Great Water*, was of such severity as England had never before seen. The West Country was beset by a deluge – whole villages being swallowed up by the floods and ships sunk without trace in the ports.

Buckingham's rebel army, without food or pay, began to desert. Despite his new allegiance, Buckingham was not popular in Wales – few Welshmen being prepared to put their trust in a turncoat. The Welsh, it seemed, would rise only to the standard of their own Henry Tudor.

Deserted by all, save one servant, Buckingham fled disguised as a peasant to the house of a man called Bannister whom he had once befriended. But Bannister too was a turncoat, it seemed, for he promptly betrayed his erstwhile comrade to the sheriff of Shropshire. Conducted thereafter to Salisbury, Buckingham was beheaded without trial.

\* \* \*

Gossip abounded. Accusations and warnings of Divine vengeance filled the air whensoever the royal family rode through town or city. Always, whether at Nottingham, Coventry, Warwick or more particularly London, there was at least one man or woman in the street – Master or Mistress John Citizen – indistinguishable amongst a sea of faces, who spoke their mind or gave vent to their wrath.

'The little princes are dead, you know, Kate – smothered in their bed by their uncle!'

'Crouchback, do you mean, Lettice?'

'Crouchback, some call 'im – others call 'im murderer!'

'There's not much truth in any of it, I dare say.'

'He dotes so on his son, 'tis said – you'd think he'd have done right by 'is nephews.'

'You watch 'is eyes, Lettice, as 'e passes by – 'ave you ever noticed 'is eyes?'

'I'm always too busy looking for 'is humpback and his withered arm, Kate – they do say too as 'e was born with teeth!'

'Oh, that's a load of tripe. Someone …'

'Where Kate – where? 'Tis freezing cold standing here – I could just do with a load of tripe to warm the cockles of me heart!'

'… made it up – about his humpback, I mean. One o' them there Lancastrians, I shouldn't wonder! Nay, 'tis his eyes you want to watch!'

'You speak for yourself, Kate. What's wrong with 'em, anyway?'

'Naught. They're large and ever so blue, but they're cold as they look at you …'

'At me, you say – I'm just not his sort, I suppose!'

'… just a glance from 'im and I go all weak at me knees!'

'I don't see what all that's got to do with the little princes – or Queen Anne. 'Tis 'er and the Prince of Wales I've come to see – they say he's not much like his dad.'

'Makes you wonder, don't it? Like her first husband, they say – funny thing, the prince having the same name as him *and* being the spitting image of him! Of course, he was slain in battle – by Richard some say – years and years ago.'

'If it was years and years ago, I don't see how her son could be …'

'Chewksbry, it was – had a bit of a barney there, by all accounts!'

'Who did? Richard and Anne?'

'Really, Lettice, I do wish you'd try listenin', for a change.'

'Quiet, Kate. Here they come, Oo, ain't she pretty – a bit pale though! And just look at the prince – ain't he gorgeous? Looks like a lass, don't 'e?'

'He's smiling at us, Lettice. See! He's looking straight at us and waving – I'd like to give him a great big hug!'

'He heard you, Kate. You've made him blush – you are awful! He's still smiling though – and whispering to 'is ma. Look, she's turned to look at us now – wonder what 'e said!'

'Wonder what she thinks about people saying her hubby's done in his nephews. She knows 'tis a pack of lies, of course – same as I do!'

'I'm not so sure, Kate.'

'You wouldn't be – always thinking the worst of everybody. You'd better watch it, Lettice, or … Anyway, he can't 'ave done it – not really!'

'Folks think as 'e did. You listen and you'll hear them around us going on about it – cussing and swearing like troopers!'

'I calls it a right shame – mud sticks, you know! They say

'twas the Duke of Buckingham started it – after he'd fallen out with the king and wanted to get in with the Woodvilles. Gossip, just gossip – poor King Richard, I say!'

'And all because you like 'is eyes – really Kate! Listen to me for a minute and I'll tell you how I knows 'e did it.'

'He told you, I s'pose – admitted it!'

'Oh well, 'tis all one to me – if you don't want to hear the truth!'

'The truth? There with 'im, was you – handed 'im the pillow, I s'pose!'

'If I'd handed 'im a pillow, Kate, 'twould have been for other purpose than that!'

'There – I knew you was just making fun of it all!'

'And that, Kate, is where you're wrong – even if your cousin Jackie is the queen's maid, as you say!'

'I'll thank you to leave Jacquetta out of it, Lettice. Come on – you know you're dying to tell me how you know he did it!'

'Well, 'tis like this, Kate. There's been a deal of gossip and most believe King Richard's done away with the princes – and he can't help but know what they say, 'cos there's always some as yells it out when him or 'is missus rides by.'

'I don't see that proves anything.'

'Murdering kids don't win anybody any friends! And as what's said is making King Richard so unpopular, you can be sure he would, if he could, let us all know it's a pack of lies.'

'There's those as wouldn't believe 'im even then!'

'They'd believe it all right – if they had a sight of the princes!'

'But they can't, can they – if the princes ...'

'There you are, you see – you're not sure either! If them there princes are still alive, why for Christ's sake don't the king let them out – let 'em ride beside him through the streets of London and anywhere else as takes their fancy. Then we'd see for ourselves that they're alive and kicking – and that would be an end of it!'

# Forty-Seven

Anne, reunited with her lord at Nottingham, was relieved that the rebellion had ended without bloodshed. As soon as Richard judged it expedient, that no further threats to his sovereignty were in the offing, he disbanded his troops. After an absence of several months and with the Christmas of 1483 almost upon them, Richard and Anne thereafter journeyed with the court north to Middleham and a happy reunion with their son.

Shortly after their arrival at Middleham, Anne at last sought and found answers to some of her questions. It was a cold winter's evening and one of those precious and all too rare occasions when she and Richard were able to be alone together. Seated companionably before a blazing hearth in Anne's solar, they spoke little at first – Anne in fact seeking for words with which to open the subject she had long dreaded but could no longer ignore.

'My lord, what prompted Buckingham's betrayal?' she asked at length.

'A number of things,' came the answer. 'Ambition, for the most part.'

'I have heard it said that a disagreement with you in regard to the princes your nephews was the prime cause of his change of allegiance.'

'Much is said,' Richard replied carelessly as if Buckingham had long since ceased to concern him – as was indeed the case.

'And the truth, my lord?'

'About Buckingham?' Richard asked coldly. 'Buckingham was executed as a traitor. There is no point in our indulging in a *post mortem*.'

'I was not referring to Buckingham then, my lord –'

Anne said quietly '– but to the truth in regard to the princes. Wheresoever I go amongst your subjects, people cry out that the princes are dead, murdered in the Tower by their uncle's command.'

For a long time there was a pregnant silence between them.

So agitated was the beating of Anne's heart, that she thought it must outrun itself. She felt breathless, and her hands were shaking uncontrollably. She wanted the truth, she told herself – she must know the truth. Yet already in her heart she knew the truth, just as her lord's subjects knew the truth. Of a sudden she wanted to run from the solar, the castle, Middleham; from Richard, from the court and the populace and those anonymous voices – and disappear into oblivion before that which she knew was corroborated.

She had a childlike urge to close her eyes, cover her ears, hide away – that which could not be seen or heard, even oneself, did not exist!

Richard stood facing her now, his expression inscrutable – his eyes, guardians of a thousand secrets, seeming of a sudden dark and remote.

'You would have the truth?' he asked quietly then.

She nodded. 'Has not there always been truth between us, my lord – save in this one matter?'

'I would I could have spared you the knowledge,' he said as if to himself. 'Always have I loved and protected you.'

'You mean ...' Anne was watching him wide-eyed.

'Edward my nephew was quietly put to sleep,' he said slowly, evenly. 'His blood was not shed, the deed being done by one experienced in such matters.'

'Tyrrel?'

'Yea, Tyrrel had his orders. He carried them out in respect of my elder nephew – but apparently bungled it in respect of the younger, Richard of York.'

'How so, my lord?' breathed Anne.

'Richard of York escaped – word had got out of our intentions and someone, likely the servant who was to have carried out the execution, made a pact with a certain nobleman.'

'Buckingham?'

'I am not sure. Buckingham was in my confidence at that time, and could well have believed it to his ultimate advantage to inform our enemies – with hindsight, that would seem to have been the case. It consequently transpired that the corpse, assumed to be that of Richard of York, was in fact that of a waif found dead in the city streets.'

Anne shuddered. 'Where lie the remains, my lord?' she asked.

'In consecrated ground,' Richard told her. 'My conscience was troubled by the knowledge that the coffins containing the remains of my nephew and the waif, lay in unhallowed ground. I subsequently gave orders that they be exhumed from under the stairs of the Garden Tower and transferred to a place of Christian burial. The priest, as he informed me afterwards, secreted the coffins inside the entrance to his own chapel.'

'And Richard of York – what of him?'

'He was smuggled out of England and is at present alive and well as far as I know in Holland or Burgundy – my agents have been unable as yet to discover his precise whereabouts, though I doubt not that the Dowager-Duchess of Burgundy, my sister, is fully cognisant of the situation.'

'Dear Margaret!' Anne said softly. 'She was ever a gentle soul.'

'And now, my lady, you know the truth.'

'But why, my lord? How could you bring yourself to command so dreadful a deed!'

'In one word – prudence!'

'Prudence!'

'Wisdom applied to practice. For my son's sake – and for the peace and well-being of the realm. My nephew was heir to the House of York – though as a minor he was too young to rule. He was therefore a pawn in a game that boded ill for England and its people. During the next five years, wars and insurrections would have plagued my subjects – the wars of the roses, it seems to me, are not dead but sleeping! For thirty years past, bloody conflict wracked this fair land – and I am determined on peace in my time and a clear, uncontested succession to follow.'

'My lord, you are mistaken!' Anne cried, tears streaming down her cheeks. 'You are mistaken, alas! Think you God will allow such a deed to go unpunished – that he will not avenge the murder of an innocent!'

'But you surely love our son as much as I do, my lady – and desire all things of the best for him.'

'I love him, yea – and it is because I love him so dearly that my heart is filled with dread!'

'Dread? But there is no longer cause to fear for our son – my enemies and therefore his enemies, have been vanquished one by one,' Richard said patiently, as if to a confused child. 'Now, as never before, is there naught to fear – when I die, and please God my son will have attained manhood by then, I shall do so content in the knowledge that my son's future, my dynasty, is assured.'

Anne shook her head. 'My lord, do not you appreciate the enormity of what you have done? Do not you fear retribution?'

'Indeed I wrestled much with my conscience ere I made the decision,' admitted Richard. 'My personal doubts and weaknesses had to be overridden. Duty is paramount in a sovereign – and it was my duty to bring peace and prosperity to my subjects, to build for a glorious future.'

'But ...'

'Always have I worked to that end – even before our son was conceived. Always have I been single-minded in my ambitions and desires – in loving you right from the start and resolving to wed none but you; in vanquishing my enemies and yours, and removing from my path those who would have prevented my achieving those same ambitions and desires.'

'You mean those such as King Henry my father-in-law; Clarence ...'

'Henry of Lancaster was my hereditary enemy, the enemy of my House; Clarence comes not in the same category, having been sent for trial and judicially sentenced to death.'

'... Hastings, Rivers, Grey, Buckingham.'

'Each and every one had conspired against Richard Plantagenet when he was either protector or King of England.'

'And the little princes?'

'The little princes so-called were lads of thirteen and eleven – the younger, as far as I am aware, is unharmed.'

'But Edward your nephew had not conspired against you, my lord.'

'It was a matter of time!' declared Richard cynically. 'Then would it all have started again – the insurrections, the warring, the grinding down of the well-being and spirit of the English people!'

'And Ned?' asked Anne fearfully, voicing that which was close to her heart. 'What of him who is like a second son to me, a brother to our Edward? Does not he constitute a future threat to peace – to the safety of your kingdom and the succession?'

'That could well be,' acknowledged Richard. 'That could well be!'

'Oh Richard, Richard!' she cried, falling to her knees in front of him, her face wet with tears. 'Promise me you will not harm Ned – I could not forgive you if you caused him hurt.'

He bent down and tenderly drew her into his arms.

'Anne, still you do not understand, alas! Because of you, I abstained from dealing Edward Prince of Wales –' He smiled wryly. '– *your* Edward – his death-blow, though he stood in my path, both as to yourself and the crown.'

'In truth the king your brother bears the responsibility for my Edward's murder.'

'That is unquestionably so – the king my brother likewise had an eye to the future! Is not there rough justice in the fact that in ordering the assassination of Edward Prince of Wales, the Yorkist heir, I was but following the king my brother's example in ordering the assassination of Edward Prince of Wales, the Lancastrian heir and similarly a minor? The wheel of fortune, it might be said, has turned full circle!'

'But what of Ned?' persisted Anne. 'Why will not you answer me, my lord?'

'Have not I answered you, sweeting? Methought I had in referring to the Prince of Wales – your Edward! For the sake of yourself and my son, I would venture anything – move mountains, hold back the seas, even dare the wrath of God! Since Ned means much to you and my son, I would raise not a finger against him, whatever the provocation – indeed I myself hold the boy in no small affection.'

'You promise me?' Anne asked tremulously.

'I have given you my word – that shall suffice,' Richard said evenly. 'I shall tell you though that I have in mind to pronounce Ned second in the succession – does that please you?'

She gave a small rueful smile. 'It does indeed, my lord,' she replied.

'Yet still you are troubled as to the future – why so, my lady?'

'God methinks will avenge the prince your nephew –' she said on a sob, '– just as he has lately avenged the prince my late husband. I doubt he will allow the slaying of an innocent to go unpunished!'

# Forty-Eight

Except on those occasions when the Prince of Wales with his entourage was expected to occupy state apartments, he and Ned by their own wish shared a bedchamber.

At Middleham, they had come to regard the upper floor of the Turret Tower as very much their own. Tall narrow windows on three sides provided magnificent views of a large portion of Yorkshire; of Wensleydale, of Snape Castle which had been built by the Nevilles, and of Jervaulx Abbey – one of the great Cistercian monasteries of which Byland was the original.

The boys enjoyed a sense of splendid isolation in their turret chamber, though members of Edward's household were in fact close at hand – tutors, a priest and a scribe occupying the middle floor, and men-at-arms and servants the ground floor.

On wild nights, when the wind gusted across the dales like an army of invading banshees, creating chill draughts in every nook and cranny, the boys lay snug and protected in the great curtained bed. The bed was square and of exceptional size, and had once prompted Richard to remark tongue-in-cheek that it was twice the size of his bed and large enough for a game of croquet!

One cold, wet and windy night at the end of March, the boys lay in bed discussing the eagerly-awaited return of Richard and Anne from a state visit to Nottingham.

'The king my father said in his letter that they expected to arrive one week hence,' Edward was saying cheerfully. 'They seem to have been gone for ages and ages – but I expect 'tis only a few weeks.'

'I wish we could have gone with them,' said Ned lightly.

'I besought papa to let us go, but he said I was a big boy now and that a future king must be well-taught – well given to learning, methinks were his words!'

'You have the same name as him,' remarked Ned earnestly – his thoughts on a different tack.

'Papa's name is Richard, silly – fancy you not remembering that!'

'Nay, I was meaning the other Prince of Wales, the one who was it before you – Edward Prince of Wales.'

'I am Edward Prince of Wales.'

'All Edwards are princes of Wales, it seems to me,' remarked Ned a trifle dismissively. 'There is you for a start, and the one I said – then there's the Black Prince, as well as the one the queen your mother was married to and they say you are like.'

' 'Tis a good thing my name is Edward – otherwise I suppose I would have had to be prince of somewhere else. If I had been called Marmaduke, or Walter or Piers, I expect I'd have been proclaimed Marmaduke, Prince of Middleham, or Piers, Prince of Pontefract ...'

'Funny about them, is it not?'

'About whom – Piers of Pontefract?'

'Nay, the princes our cousins – they say they were murdered, you know!'

'Who is *they*?'

'People in the crowd – onlookers. They shout out as we pass by.'

'They say that papa did it.'

'Did what?'

'Murdered them, of course.'

'I know not why you say *of course* – he might *not* have murdered them ... Ouch! Why did you do that?'

'He did *not* murder them – not papa.'

'People do murder people, you know.'

'Not papa – not my papa. He is kind to you, is he not – and you are his nephew just the same as the others – and he has not murdered you, has he?'

'Not yet,' said Ned cheerfully. 'But ... ouch! If you are going to keep thumping me, I shall go to sleep and ignore you – I believe you are not the Prince of Wales at all, but a ruffian in disguise!'

'Well, you should not speak of the king my father like that.'

'Like what?' asked Ned innocently. 'Am I supposed then to say he *has* murdered me? I said he might *not* have murdered the princes, did not I? To hear you talk, Edward, anyone would think ...'

'Shut up. Go to sleep,' said Edward grumpily.

Ned made no reply.

'Are you asleep?' Edward asked meekly a few minutes later, neither a word nor a movement having issued from his companion.

'Yea.'

'You cannot be.'

'Well, I am – so there!'

' 'Tis a pity about the princes. I should not like to be murdered – it means you are dead and, if you are dead, you cannot be Prince of Wales and have everyone smiling and bowing at you.'

'Go to sleep.'

'I wonder what it is like to be ...' Edward's voice tailed off as if he were debating the possibilities.

He said nothing more and Ned assumed he had drifted off to sleep. It was hard to tell in the near-darkness, for only the one candle remained alight during the night and the fire had burned low.

Ned felt of a sudden uneasy, secretly wishing he had not spoken of murder. He had overheard the accusations – had wondered at and then dismissed them. But somehow, in the shadowy chamber with the wind howling eerily around the Turret Tower, it was hard to keep the distressing doubts at bay.

The princes Edward and Richard had been his cousins too: he had known them, played with them, and shared a bedchamber with them at Christmas-time when the king his uncle had been alive. Remembering them as boys only a few years older than Edward and himself, he had found it impossible to believe they were dead, murdered – and by ... But nay, he told himself firmly, it is naught but talk, gossip – wicked, wicked gossip! Uncle Richard would not hurt a mouse – unless it be a Lancastrian mouse, of course! I, Ned, should know. I am his nephew, just as the others are – as the others were, were, were ...

He must have fallen asleep then, for he woke with a start

some time later, gripped by a sense of fear …

The bed now was in total darkness, for the fire had gone out and not a glimmer of light penetrated the bedcurtains. Feeling for one of the curtains, he drew it back carefully, not wishing to disturb his sleeping cousin. Bathed in perspiration, his heart thumping, he strained his ears for the slightest sound.

A spontaneous movement of the dying embers of the fire, set his heart leaping anew – and then, as if the heat had all at once drained from the hearth, a coldness spread out across the chamber, uniting with the darkness to convey a brooding sense of evil …

What startled me into wakefulness? he wondered. I know not how long I have been asleep or what hour of the night it is. Edward fell asleep first and I lay sleepless for a while, troubled and fearful in a way I could not explain.

There it is again – the sound that woke me, that of a booted footfall on the staircase. 'Twas that which woke me – I recall it plainly now. And there it is again – a little closer this time …

I must keep still, perfectly still, so that none will know I am here. I must not disturb Edward, alarm him with my fears. Perchance it was what we talked about ere we fell asleep that made me fearful – yet Edward is sleeping fast, unaffected by wild imaginings …

Imagination – that is all it is. Edward will jeer, tease me unmercifully, when I tell him of it in the morning – which, on second thoughts, I shall not! I wish it were morning already …

There is naught to fear – it could have been a mouse in the wainscot I heard. Come to think of it though, there is no wainscot … Nay, it cannot be a mouse. Danger *is* lurking out there in the chamber. I know it. I sense it. I must tell Edward. I must warn him of the danger. It is coming closer now, approaching the bed on the other side, Edward's side. I must wake him, warn him …

But warn him of what? I am surely being foolish; very very foolish. If I wake Edward, he will make plaint at being disturbed – he will laugh when I tell him of my fears and call me his pretty baby cousin! He would be right, I suppose …

Sweet Saviour protect us! I can hear the curtain on Edward's side of the bed being drawn back. Yet still all is darkness – if one of our tutors or the priest had an urgent message for Edward from the king his father, as is unlikely, he would not enter by stealth and in total darkness: he would carry a lantern.

Whatever is out there is not human, for it moves without substance and sees without light. *I must warn Edward before it is too late.*

'E.....! E.....!'

The words will not come, alas! My mouth is dry, my throat feels tight and the words will not come. I cannot speak; cannot call out to Edward ...

He put out a clammy hand and, grasping that of his cousin, squeezed it agitatedly – hoping against hope that Edward would understand his silent warning.

Whether Edward understood, he could not tell. He heard him stir and start to form a question.

'Wherefore ...?' was all Edward said.

'Holy Mother protect us!' besought Ned, crossing himself. 'Protect us, I pray you!'

He could feel the bedclothes being pulled off Edward; could feel the cold air as the blankets were disturbed. He could feel Edward thrashing about, trying to fend off whatever was attacking him.

It must be a nightmare, he thought. Surely 'tis a nightmare – all will be well in the morning. There is no one here. How could there be. A heavy guard is posted always at the entrance to the Turret Tower. And none would walk through an unfamiliar place in total darkness – no human, that is! Then ...

'*From ghosties and ghoulies, and long-leggedy beasties, and things that go bump in the night, may the good Lord deliver us!*' he prayed silently, repeating the words of the ancient talisman with which he and Edward had ofttimes tried to frighten themselves. He crossed himself again for good measure and, his heart in his mouth, listened breathlessly ...

Someone is moving away from Edward's side of the bed, he thought then, his fingers clutching the crucifix which hung on a gold chain around his neck. They are moving away and making for the doorway – but still in darkness, total darkness. They have reached the outside landing now ...

By St. Crispin, what was that! I heard a loud bump from beyond the stairway. *And things that go bump in the night!*' he thought and dived for protection under the bedcovers.

Edward lies still now, and silent. He is dead, he told himself. I know he is. He and I are very close, like brothers we are – I need not put out a hand and touch him to know he is dead. I can feel inside myself that he is dead – lost to the world, as the priests say. No longer is there the sound of his breathing. Silence is all around us ...

I shall wait a short space and then, when I judge the coast is clear, I shall light a candle and, holding my crucifix in the palm of my hand, shall run to the stairs-head and call the guards ...

\* \* \*

Ned awoke some time later, how much later he never knew, to find the turret chamber seemingly full of people. Three men stood, stern and watchful, round the bed – men he recognized as John Nesfield, Edward's chamberlain; Michell Wharton, steward of the castle; and William Catesby, Speaker in parliament and esquire of the body to the king. The latter, on a mission to York for the king, had brought Richard's letter to Edward and had stayed overnight at Middleham Castle prior to setting out again next morning.

Armed guards stood on the threshold, both inside and outside the door. All looked solemn and ill-at-ease, and Ned was uncomfortably aware that the gaze of all, even covertly the men-at-arms, was focused on himself. His tutor was hastily drawing back the window-curtains – and Ned decided, with a small sense of resentment, that someone must have drawn back the bedcurtains also, noisily and waking him in the process.

As daylight flooded in, he narrowed his eyes against the strong light – only to open them again as he registered the fact that Edward was not there beside him. Then it is just me they are looking at, all frowning and angry, he

thought. I expect they cannot find Edward and they want to
see if I know where he is. I expect he's wandered off
somewhere – Edward likes wandering off and surprising
people. But why are they staring at me like that? Do they
imagine I am hiding him under the bedclothes? He felt
suddenly close to tears – though he could not have said why.

'He's not under the bedclothes,' he said helpfully, hoping
he would not start crying and they would think he was a
cry-baby.

'Him, my lord?' Catesby asked quite kindly. 'You mean
you have seen someone?'

They are still staring at me, Ned thought – as if they are
hanging on my words, eager for my reply. Of course – why
did not I realize it before? – this is all part of the nightmare.
That explains why they look so grim and staring – people
always stare at you in nightmares! My tutor's face is grey as
ashes and Edward's tutor seems to be weeping ...

'You are a nightmare!' he cried defiantly to the questioning faces. 'You are a nightmare and I shall not answer
your questions. I am going to sleep now – and when I wake
up, you will all be gone and Edward will be here!'

John Nesfield, Edward's chamberlain, spoke next.
Esquire of the body to the king also, he was held in such
high regard as to be entrusted with the protection of the
prince. But John Nesfield at that moment was visibly
shaken.

'The Prince of Wales, my lord?' he asked. 'What know
you of the Prince of Wales?'

'He was here with me when we went to sleep,' Ned told
him uneasily – aware of an undercurrent of tension in the
chamber that he had no means of understanding.

I shall answer their questions, he told himself, since it is
expected of me – but I shall give away no more than I must.
I wish Edward would hurry up – and then he could answer
the questions instead of I.

'And then, my lord?' prompted Nesfield.

'And then I woke up.'

'You woke up, you say? And what did you discover then,
pray?'

'That you were all here staring at me – and that the Prince
of Wales had gone.'

'Gone, you say?'

'Well, he is not here, my lord, is he?'

'That is indeed so, alas, alas! But have you any idea whither he was bound?'

'I expect he went to feed Neddy,' he said cheerfully – having decided he knew why they were there. It was a deputation – he and Edward were always playing at deputations – and this must surely be the real live thing! ' 'Twas my turn this week, you see – but I 'xpect the prince my cousin stole a march on me.'

At that, Catesby looked enquiringly at Nesfield – but the latter shook his head.

'No sign of mud on his feet, sir, and it is unlikely the prince would have ventured out in his nightshirt – even to feed the donkey!'

'Ofttimes he does,' volunteered Ned. 'He keeps a bundle of old clothes the stable-boys gave him in Neddy's stable – and he likes going barefoot, though I expect he'll thump me for telling you!'

Catesby turned to Nesfield. 'I shall set out forthwith to inform the king of the matter,' he said soberly.

'But the king knows already,' insisted Ned. 'He knows and does not mind a bit about Edward pretending he's a stable-boy!'

'What was that you said just now about a nightmare, my lord?' asked Catesby.

'I had a nightmare, that was all,' Ned said guardedly. 'Methought someone entered the room.'

'What exactly did you see, my lord?'

'Nothing. Nothing at all – that's why I knew it was a nightmare. It was quite dark, you see.'

Catesby did not see – and nor did anyone else apparently.

'Did you see the prince rise from his bed?'

'Nay, it was too dark to see aught.'

'Did he complain of feeling unwell?'

'Nay. He was asleep, you see. I was the one having the nightmare – not Edward.'

'Did you play about?'

'Play about?' Ned frowned. 'What mean you, my lord?'

'Did the two of you have a fight? Could you, accidentally needless to say, have …'

'My lord —' put in Edward's tutor gravely '— it might be unwise closely to question His Lordship at this stage. He has had a great shock.'

'Nay, it was not a fight I had — 'twas a nightmare, as I told you,' insisted Ned, his lower lip trembling. 'And if you cannot find Edward — then I shall have to go and see if poor Neddy has been fed!'

'My lord, bear with us for a moment, if you please,' said Catesby gently. 'It is my sorrowful duty to inform you that the Prince of Wales is dead, God rest his soul! He was found in his nightshirt at the stairs-foot this morning. How it happened and how he came to be at the foot of the stairs, is a mystery!'

Ned looked from Catesby to Nesfield — and back again. His expression was one of indescribable horror.

'You mean it was not a nightmare after all?' he asked then, his teeth chattering. 'You mean Edward is really and truly dead?'

'That is indeed the case, alas, alas!' nodded Catesby. 'The physician is examining the prince's body now, my lord, and will doubtless be able to tell us more in due course. The prince fell head-first, it would appear, and it seems likely that the fall and the impact of his head on the stone floor stopped his heart.'

'Nay, nay!' Tears streamed, unheeded now, down the boy's face. ' 'Tis all a nightmare, I tell you — 'tis not real, any of it. It is a nightmare and all of you are silly old nightmares too! Go away, *away*, I tell you … Shoo, shoo! Begone all of you and then I can wake up — and Edward will be here beside me and then we shall go together to feed poor Neddy …'

He jumped out of bed as if of a sudden Neddy was of paramount importance. Neddy represented reality, normality. Once he reached Neddy, he would be all right and — what was more to the point — Edward his cousin would be all right …

Catesby barred his way.

'Nay, my lord, it would be unwise — the physician is with the Prince of Wales, as I said,' he told him firmly but not unkindly. 'I shall ride to Nottingham forthwith to inform the king and queen of the grievous tidings — I doubt not they will set out for home immediately and, God willing, will be here within a few days. Meanwhile we must insist on your remaining here in this chamber – a guard will be placed on the door.'

'You mean I am to be held prisoner?' asked Ned fearfully. 'Then you think I ...'

'For your own safety, my lord – till we know what is afoot,' lied Nesfield, determined to make the best of a bad job. 'After that, it is up to the king.'

# Forty-Nine

Richard and Anne, sparing neither themselves nor their entourage, reached Middleham four days later.

They went at once to the chapel where the body of their son lay in state, with four tall candles around the bier and prayers being offered continuously for the prince's soul by monks from Byland Abbey. Nearing his tenth birthday at the time of his death, the dead prince looked waxen and doll-like – the sight of him but increasing his numbed parents' sense of disbelief and unreality.

Anne, by prior arrangement with Richard, then went straight to the queen's apartments, to remain for the time being in her chamber, seeing none but Jacquetta and those ladies-in-waiting who had attended her from Nottingham.

Richard talked briefly with Nesfield and Wharton, and even more briefly with the boy's tutors and the guards who had been on duty at the Turret Tower on that fateful night. He then made his way unaccompanied to the upper floor of the tower where Ned had remained throughout the intervening days ostensibly under house arrest.

Richard was closeted with his nephew for nearly an hour, the eyes of the one appearing afterwards as red-rimmed as those of the other. Anne's tearful pleas for her nephew, her insistence that he dealt leniently with the boy whether or not he were in any way to blame for the disaster, were very much in Richard's mind – the nine-year-old orphan was, after all, nephew to both of them, being offspring of her sister and his brother. He told himself he went to the interrogation with an open mind.

I shall remain calm, he told himself firmly, no matter the provocation. Ask questions. Hearken to what the boy has to say. Judge dispassionately. Act fairly.

By his own command unannounced, he ordered the guards to wait downstairs and opened the door of the turret chamber. Striding into the room, he met the frightened gaze of his nephew.

The boy reminded Richard agonizingly of his son, but he somehow looked smaller than hitherto – small and defenceless. Wearing tunic and hose of black velvet, having the fair curly hair and the almost girlish beauty of the youthful Plantagenets, he bowed and waited uneasily for Richard to speak.

But Richard, likewise garbed in mourning black, was finding it difficult to speak. He looked searchingly at the boy – as if he half expected to see the word *guilty* emblazoned on his forehead.

At length it was the boy that spoke.

'Methought it was a nightmare,' he said simply.

'It was a nightmare,' said Richard then. 'It is a nightmare – please God we shall wake from the nightmare soon, you and I.'

Ned ran to him then and Richard embraced the sobbing child, trying unsuccessfully to find words to reassure and comfort him.

'Let us be seated over there by the fire, nephew – there is a chill in the air today methinks,' he said, leading the boy by the hand and seating him beside himself on the long bench seat. 'When you feel able, take a deep breath and tell me exactly what happened that night – in your own words, taking your time.'

'But my tutor said …'

'This is between you and me – it has naught to do with anyone else. Fear not, nephew – I am clear in my mind as to what happened. But I desire to learn of Edward's frame of mind on the night in question – the small details of my son's last moments of life.'

'It was a nightmare, sir,' sobbed Ned., 'They will not hearken to me – they keep telling me over and over again that Edward is dead. He was dead, I knew he was dead – but it was only a nightmare. Why will not they permit me to see him?'

'It was both a nightmare and an accident,' said Richard

firmly. 'I suspect, from what your tutors have told me, that Edward suffered the nightmare too – and that when you fell asleep, caught betwixt nightmare and reality, Edward got out of bed and went to the stairs-head. Drowsy and confused, he missed his footing in the darkness and fell headlong down the stairs.'

'But they say he was not harmed, sir – that he just stopped breathing. They keep asking me who it was crept into the room – and I tell them it was a nightmare but, of course, they believe me not!'

'Why say you *of course*, nephew?'

'Well, if it was a nightmare that crept into the room, and then out again ...' Ned stopped, confused.

'Edward's heart stopped,' Richard told him firmly. 'The physicians say he landed on his head and the blow stopped his breathing, alas, alas!'

'Nay, someone came in, truly they did, and crept over to Edward. They removed the bedclothes. I could hear Edward struggling and then presently I heard whoever it was – the nightmare, I suppose – creep out again.'

'I believe it was Edward himself you heard,' Richard said thoughtfully. 'He was restless I dare say and threw off his bedclothes, struggling like yourself perchance in the throes of a nightmare – and then he got out of bed and, still asleep, crept out on to the landing.'

'But there was more than that – much much more.'

'Then tell me everything in your own words, nephew – and then perchance we can separate the reality from the nightmare.'

As Ned considered where to begin, watching him closely, Richard registered the horror that had beset him – and perhaps Edward also – that night.

'Something woke me with a start,' the boy began slowly, almost unwillingly. 'I knew not what it was but I was much afeared ...'

When he eventually reached the end of the account, there was silence for a while as Richard gave thought to it.

'Before you went to sleep –' he asked of a sudden then '– what had you and Edward been talking about?'

Ned gazed at him with troubled blue eyes. He had hoped against hope that his uncle would not ask him that.

'I would rather not say, sir,' he replied, white-faced. 'It was all silly nonsense anyway!'

'Then pray permit me to hear the silly nonsense, nephew.'

'We talked about people in the crowds, onlookers – and how they shout out things, silly things!'

'Like what, pray?'

Ned remained silent and Richard could feel him trembling.

'Go on,' he urged. 'I promise not to be angry.'

'About the princes my cousins – they call out that they have been murdered, you see. And Edward said ...' Ned paused.

'Continue, nephew.'

'Edward said, "They say that papa did it." '

'Did what?' enquired Richard.

'That is what I said to Edward. Edward replied, "Murdered them, of course." And I said, "He might not have murdered them." And then Edward thumped me. "He did *not* murder them – not papa!" he said. And I said, "People do murder people, you know!" '

Richard's voice was perfectly controlled, giving no hint of his feelings. 'And what pray did Edward say to that, nephew?'

'He said, "Not papa – not my papa. He is kind to you, is he not – and you are his nephew just the same as the others – and he has not murdered you, has he?" '

'And your reply?' asked Richard.

Ned hesitated, trying to think up some less truthful but more expedient reply.

'Go on, Ned,' urged Richard. 'The truth – only the truth, remember!'

'I said, "Not yet!" And I laughed, 'cos I was only teasing him, you see. But Edward thumped me again – and after that methinks we argued a bit and then we went to sleep.'

'And then you had a nightmare – and Edward had an accident.'

Ned nodded. 'If it was a nightmare – I am not sure any more,' he said with a catch in his voice.

'Well, I am,' said Richard with as much cheer as he could muster. 'You had a nightmare and I expect Edward had

one also – and all because you had been talking silly
nonsense and had frightened yourselves into one!'

'Uncle Richard?' For the first time that day, he used the
informal mode of address permitted in private.

'What is it, Ned?'

'What will happen to me now?'

Richard registered the tremor in the boy's voice and his
anxious expression – and was only too well aware of what
he had in mind.

'Now – at this moment, mean you?' he asked.

'Nay, not exactly.'

'Well, at some time in the future, I shall see to it that you
have your own household as befits your rank as Earl of
Warwick and your father's son,' Richard told him. 'Sheriff
Hutton is the place I have in mind – in Yorkshire, not far
from here.'

'But cannot I stay with you, sir – and the queen my
aunt?' the boy asked plaintively. 'Without Edward, you see,
I am all alone, and ...'

It had all been too much for him. He broke of a sudden
into a paroxysm of sobbing – and it was a while before
Richard could master his own emotions sufficiently to
comfort him.

'Be of good cheer, nephew!' he said then, his eyes
shining with anguish none the less. 'The queen and I also
are all alone, now that Edward is gone – very soon, if it be
to your liking, I shall have you proclaimed my heir.'

# *Fifty*

Edward Prince of Wales was interred at Sheriff Hutton church in a splendid tomb bearing his effigy; and Edward Earl of Warwick – otherwise known as Ned – was duly proclaimed heir presumptive to the English throne and, as such, took his place at the royal table. He was knighted by Richard in the same year.

Anne, despite her fondness for Ned and the happiness his continuing presence gave her and Richard, seemed quite unable to recover from the latest blow that life had inflicted on her. It was as if the tragic death of her only child had somehow severed the last link with that other one dearly loved and long departed – he whose name and title the former had borne and whom he closely resembled. The Kingmaker's daughter, she had been bride to one future king, consort to a reigning king and subsequently mother to another future king.

That Richard still loved her, Anne did not doubt. He had told her so and made plain his regard for her often enough. Whether she loved him was less easily answered. He treated her always with courtesy and consideration, and his ardour in lovemaking had roused her at times to such heights of ecstasy as had surprised herself.

Not once had he reproached her for her inability to give him further children, though now as never before he was desperately in need of another son. Anne had learned, though not from her lord himself, that certain advisers and so-called friends of Richard had issued dark reminders of the illegality of the marriage – the papal dispensation considered necessary to an alliance between even distant cousins having been dispensed with.

Further declining in health and spirits with each passing

day, Anne paid no heed to the talk; the ruffianly attempts by her lord's time-serving cronies to replace her with another – one who could give him strong sons and thus secure the succession.

Resting on the couch in her solar at Westminster Palace one afternoon three months after her son's death, Anne recalled the lampoon that had been found affixed to the great door of St. Paul's Cathedral that same morning:

'The Cat, the Rat, and Lovel our dog,
Ruleth all England under a Hog!'

This thinly-veiled reference to Richard – whose cognizance was a white boar – and his three favourites, Francis Viscount Lovel, Sir Richard Ratcliffe and William Catesby, was soon circulating all over England and was to cost William Collingbourne, its author, his life.

Richard's face had looked like thunder when he had told her of the lampoon.

'How dare the rascal refer so to my loyal friends and supporters!' he had said angrily. 'Is there no end to such impudence!'

'No end, my lord,' she had told him sadly. 'It is one of the crosses a monarch must bear – I doubt not that our forebears, the great Edward the Third for instance, were subjected to similar scurrilous nonsense!'

\*   \*   \*

'Sire, inasmuch as the parliament of the late king your brother, whose soul God pardon, considered there to be a loophole through which Your Grace could, if you so wished or it were to the benefit of the realm, put aside your marriage with the Lady Anne and take another bride –' said Thomas Rotherham, Archbishop of York '– I most earnestly beseech you to consider the matter.'

Richard sighed ostentatiously. He was tired of such suggestions – of the presumption that he would agree to the annulment of his marriage. Does not he comprehend? he asked himself. I love Anne. Always I have, and always I shall love Anne. *To the benefit of the realm*, he says – as if to put aside a wife one loves, who has been a good and faithful spouse for some twelve years and borne one a fair and well-loved son, were as readily done and as little considered as changing one's horse! Anne is unwell, alas! Her health and spirits have declined woefully since Edward's death – indeed my concern is not for how to be rid of her, but for how to ensure that I keep her!

'The queen is in frail health,' he said coldly. 'She is being attended by the physicians and has kept her chamber for several days. My chief concern is for her recovery – she pines for the Prince of Wales, whom God pardon, and is declining it seems to me by the hour.'

'I doubt not the matter is in Our Lord's keeping, sire,' replied the archbishop ambiguously. 'I shall order that prayers be said in all churches for the poor lady's return to health.'

'She is not at death's gate as yet, my lord!' declared Richard brusquely. 'She is unwell, as much in spirit as in body methinks – she was, as I intimated, greatly anguished by the death of our son.'

'Your *only* son, my lord,' said the archbishop – with both sympathy and emphasis. 'We must pray that the queen's ill-health does not long continue – you are still young, sire!'

'Leave me,' ordered Richard, his patience exhausted. 'Leave me. You offend me with your scheming, sir. You twist my words, you speak against my lady's interests – begone, I say, ere I summon guards and have you taken to the Tower.'

The archbishop disappeared with unusual rapidity and was soon to be found closeted with his cronies. To these he confided the matter of the queen's illness, the king's dilemma – and the pressing matter of the succession.

'The succession is assured,' pointed out one gentleman, 'in that the Earl of Warwick has been proclaimed heir presumptive.'

'Clarence's son?' asked another. 'There is bad blood there, alas – 'twere better the king should marry another and beget more sons.'

The archbishop looked roguish.

'If you gentlemen will swear to keep your mouths shut

upon the subject, I shall repeat what His Grace has just
told me.' He tapped his lips with his fingers, adjuring them
to secrecy – though well aware that none of his audience
would lose any time in passing on the information. 'Have I
your word, sirs?'

All nodded their assent and drew up their chairs – their
expressions eager, greedy for scandal and the chance to do
mischief.

'Knowing what I know and hearing what I have heard –'
the archbishop told them insinuatingly '– it behoves me to
warn you that the queen will likely depart of a sudden
from this troublous world!'

'You mean ...'

'Aye.'

'The King's Grace, you are saying, intends to ...?'

'Aye, and very shortly, I understand.'

'Poison?'

'That would seem to be the idea. But remember,
gentlemen, if you please – breathe not a word to a soul!'

\* \* \*

That was only the start – but it was a start that snowballed
until practically everyone at court except the two persons
most concerned had heard the tale and wondered at it.
One of the archbishop's confidants had conceived the
masterly idea of informing the occupants of the
guard-house – it was, after all, generally recognized as the
best place for releasing secrets for circulation! From the
guard-house, it spread through Westminster like wildfire,
reaching above and below stairs in no time at all.

Anne, who had been feeling a little better that day, was
seated in front of her long mirror, waiting for Jacquetta to
arrive with certain of her jewels. Richard, she had
ascertained, was alone in his library, writing letters. She
would go and surprise him. She knew he was anxious
about her and so, wearing a new gown of his favourite
blue, with her hair flowing free around her shoulders – as
he liked to see it – entwined at the crown with a rope of
pearls, she would go to him and make much of him. Poor
Richard! she thought – he has shown me much patience

during the past weeks – and I shall say as much to him, smilingly, lovingly ...

The door burst open and Jacquetta rushed in weeping. Then, her gaze falling on Anne, she gave a shrill cry – before putting her hand over her mouth to stifle the sound.

'O my lady – my lady ...' she cried incoherently. 'Methought – methought – oh, thank God, thank God!'

'Sweet Saviour protect us!' exclaimed Anne in astonishment. Cheerful and happy in her work, soon herself to be married to Middleham's head groom, Jacquetta had never before appeared in such a sorry state. 'What on earth is the matter?'

'Methought you was ... Nay, nay, don't ask me, my lady, don't ask me – I can't tell you!'

'You cannot tell me what?' demanded Anne, surprised by her distress. 'Compose yourself, Jacquetta, do – this is not like you at all!'

'Such a turn it gave me when I heard! You said as you didn't need me again till this evening, but as I was to come then with your jewels.'

'The jewels have disappeared – is that what you are saying?' asked Anne on a small sigh. 'Doubtless they will ...'

'Nay, 'twas not the jewels, my lady. I have 'em here. But such a turn it gave me when I heard ...'

'What did you hear, pray?' Thoroughly alarmed by then, Anne's voice was stern. 'Tell me at once, Jacquetta – I command it.'

'Don't make me, my lady – pray don't make me!'

'I insist that you tell me what has caused you such distress.'

'They said you was dead,' the weeping girl told her. 'Everyone's talking and gossiping, and I asked one of the maids what it was all about – and when she told me, I said it couldn't be, as I was with you only this morning. But she said it 'ad happened sudden-like – and I'd better go and see for myself!'

'Might I ask of what malady I am supposed to have died?' Anne's hands were trembling and she clasped them tightly together, trying to still them.

'Something you'd drunk, my lady.'

'Poison?'

Jacquetta nodded, the tears streaming down her face.

'But you're better today, my lady, aren't you?' she said quickly, as if Anne's question must not be dwelt upon. 'You looked much better and you wanted to dress up properly, so that, so that ...'

'I *was* indeed feeling better,' said Anne pointedly. 'I feel a little upset now – a trifle shaky. But there is something I have to do. Leave me now, Jacquetta – I shall send for you when I need you.'

'But the jewels, my lady – what ...?'

'I no longer have need of them – leave me. I wish to be alone.'

'My lady, let me brush and dress your hair – the pearls are already to hand,' pleaded Jacquetta. 'Then when you look at yourself in the blue gown – just the colour of your eyes, it is ...'

Anne said nothing more as Jacquetta started expertly to dress her hair. It was easier to acquiesce, to simply sit there quietly – whilst she gave thought to the dreadful revelation.

She saw it all now. Richard intended to kill her, poison her – to murder her as he had murdered all those others who had stood between him and his ambitions. She stood in his way now – in the way of his begetting children, sons to secure his dynasty. All these years he had striven, steadily and resolutely, for sovereignty – for power and kingship. Now, only she and her inability to produce another child, stood between him and the future of his line ...

Why did not I realize it before? she asked herself. I trusted Richard. But why did I trust him? I should have known better. His ruthlessness has, after all, been all too freely demonstrated – how he would stop at nothing to achieve his ambitions. For what reason other than vanity did I see myself as an exception, the only one who would be spared the fate of the others?

In truth, it matters not. Apart from Ned who has his own life to lead, his own future ambitions to achieve, I have none save Richard. Methought he loved me. He has said so ofttimes enough. But I failed him, alas! Love can dim with the passage of time and, once dimmed, is doomed to die ...

I shall go to Richard now and confront him. I shall tell him I know and that he has no need to resort to poison. Draw your sword, I shall say, and destroy me here and now, my lord – plead for mercy I shall not. In truth, he would be doing me a favour ...

'You look lovely, my lady,' Jacquetta told her, trying to cheer her – whilst concerned by her pallor and the restlessness of her gaze. 'Will you wear the pearl and gold necklace?'

Anne frowned. 'Nay, not in the morning – one never wears jewels in the morning, save on state occasions. You surely know better than that!'

'But 'tis evening, my lady – early evening.'

'Dear me! You are a little confused today, I fear – go and rest now, then you will feel better. I shall don my mantle – 'tis unusually cold today for March!'

'Begging your pardon, my lady – but 'tis the end of August!'

Jacquetta placed the mantle lightly around her mistress's shoulders and smoothed her hair.

'Nay, leave it,' Anne said.

' 'Tis a bit mussed by the mantle.'

'My lord likes it like that!' And so saying, Anne leaned forward, letting her long mane fall over her face – and then, with an air of abandonment, she threw her head back so that her hair fell around her in wild disarray. She stood up then and, without another word, ran barefooted from the chamber.

*   *   *

Richard was writing busily but wishing his task done. I shall go to see Anne, he told himself – she looked better this morning and quite gave me fresh heart. Still she pines for Edward, as I do myself – but cares of state in some measure keep grief and its many subtleties at bay. In some measure, in some measure ...

A knock on the door caused him momentary irritation.

He assumed it to be John Kendall, his secretary, and his tone was deliberately discouraging as he bade the caller enter.

He continued writing, vaguely registering the almost noiseless opening and closing of the door – and glanced up curiously.

'*Par Dieu!*' he said in astonishment, as he saw who it was. 'Anne – what is it? What ails you?'

She stood there before him, her hair dishevelled, her eyes streaming – gazing accusingly at him.

'What, my lord, have I done to deserve death?' she asked piteously. 'Tell me, only tell me, what I have done!'

In three strides he had reached her and had enfolded her in his arms.

'Dear heart,' he said, 'why speak you so? You are better, much better – I noticed it this morning and my heart was filled with joy. You have been unwell, debilitated by grief – and no wonder – but now you are on the mend, I promise you!'

She looked up at him and was surprised to see that his eyes too were bright with tears.

'You are weeping, my lord – why are you weeping?'

'I weep with joy that you are better –' he told her, kissing her '– and I thank God for answering my prayers.'

'Then you did not ...?' She eyed him uncertainly.

'What did not I do?'

'They thought I was dead already, you see,' she said on a sob, hiding her face against his shoulder.

'*They?* To whom do you refer, sweeting?'

'Everyone.' Like a child, she threw out her hands, palms upward, indicating the whole court – or the whole world, Richard thought grimly. 'And, you see, methought ...'

'What did you think?' he prompted sternly, holding her a little away from him so that he could see her expression. 'What did you think? – pray tell me, my lady.'

'Poison, they said ...' she sobbed. ' 'Tis all around the palace, Jacquetta says – that you are trying to poison me!'

'O grief of heart!' exclaimed Richard. 'O grief of heart! What will they think of next!'

'Then it is not true?' she asked softly, watching him as if she would read the truth in his eyes.

Picking her up then, he carried her over to the couch by the fire. Then, setting her down, he seated himself beside her and drew her head against his shoulder. He let several more moments elapse before he made reply.

'I am *trying* to poison you – is that what is said?' he asked then – and Anne was surprised to see the glimmer of a smile in his eyes. 'Could they believe, could you believe – indeed could anyone believe – that if Richard Plantagenet desired to poison someone, he would not accomplish it? *Trying* to poison you indeed!'

She smiled a little at that. 'Then you truly love me, my lord?' she asked plaintively.

'Do you know, sweeting, you have not asked that before – never once in all the years? The answer is yea, I truly love you and always will. Never again accuse me of ...' He paused and smiled that rare beautiful smile.

'Poisoning me.' she suggested.

'Oh, you can accuse me of that as often as you wish – but of *trying* to poison you suggests incompetence! Be of good cheer, sweeting – there is naught to fear!'

'Richard, I do love you,' she said.

He looked at her then, meeting her gaze, and she wondered, by no means for the first time, what he was thinking – and perhaps the wondering and the not discovering were part of his attraction for her.

'And you have never said that before.' His voice was deep with emotion. 'This is plainly an evening for revelations – I must remember to poison you more often!'

She laughed a little at that – the small tinkling laugh that pleased him – and said she must go and leave him to his task.

She paused before she reached the doorway.

'Should my lord desire this night to visit his lady's chamber ...' she said to him in a small voice as he opened the door for her.

She left the invitation in mid-sentence.

'Your lord does so desire,' he responded with mock gravity. 'The king will indeed visit the queen's chamber this night – and give his court something about which to gossip on the morrow!'

# Fifty-One

Richard and Anne had each received a warm letter of condolence on the death of their son from Richard's sister, Margaret Dowager-Duchess of Burgundy. There had always been a close bond of affection between Margaret and her family, although Clarence had been her favourite brother.

In her letter to Anne, Margaret had made particular reference to Ned, Clarence's son.

'I refer now to Edward Earl of Warwick, my nephew, who is, I understand, known to the family as Ned, to thus distinguish him from your very own angel-boy,' she had written. 'It warms my heart to know that you have taken Ned under your wing. His sister Margaret, my god-child, now in her fourteenth summer, is happy enough methinks though she pines still for her "baby brother," as she calls him.

'Ned writes to myself and to Margaret, as you are doubtless aware, and it is plain to me that he has a great fondness for his uncle and aunt. Every night I thank God on my knees for your loving kindness to that orphaned child.

'In recognition of my indebtedness to you, the Kingmaker's daughter, for the graciousness you have ever shown to me and to mine, I am sending you a gift. Soon after I, as a forlorn and homesick maid, arrived here in Burgundy, I conceived the idea out of the notion that, as the tapestry grew, more and more of my loved ones would be here with me. For many years, I and my ladies worked at it lovingly and painstakingly – for myself, it was truly a labour of love.

293

'But now it must return to England – the land of my birth and the home of the dear ones represented therein. People tell me it is a jewel beyond price – but to me it is simply a portrait of my family. May it give you pleasure, my dear – and help to ease the grief and the emptiness.

'Our Lord have you always in his blessed protection.

'By the hand of your affectionate sister and friend,

'MARGARET'

The tapestry had arrived one week later, brought over land and sea by an envoy from the court of Burgundy. Hung first in the privy chamber at Westminster Palace, it was soon after removed to Anne's solar where it covered the greater part of one wall.

It was a wonder of which Anne never tired. The work of many years and many diligent fingers, the tapestry showed Edward, George, Richard, Elizabeth, Mary – and Margaret herself. Below them were Anne and Isabel, hair and ribbons flying, holding hands in a ring-o'-roses; and below them, hand-in-hand, little lost Edward was standing between Ned and his sister Margaret. To the left of the main group, was the Earl of Warwick and his countess, Anne's parents; and to the right, Richard Duke of York and the lady Cecily, his duchess – Richard's parents and, in the case of Cecily, Anne's great-aunt.

Each of the characters was rivetingly recognizable, each one a portrait taken from life. The setting was a garden, an English garden with lavender and heliotrope – and roses white and red in equal numbers! Beyond the garden was a field of wild flowers, of poppies, buttercups and daisies: filled with sunshine, it was – and with Neddy. Ned, bless him, Anne thought, must have written of Neddy to Margaret!

Happiness radiated the whole scene. The colours were light and bright as a summer's day – the effect totally pleasing.

\* \* \*

Ever since the death of her son, the shock and distress attendant upon it and the fears it had raised – unfounded in the event – for Ned, Anne's health had steadily declined.

At first she had known a great weariness, a lethargy – 'tis as if, she told herself, I were an old old woman with one foot already in the grave! Despite his own deep distress, Richard had noted the change in her, and had gone out of his way to comfort and cheer her. And from time to time, she rallied, seeming to regain her former energy and spirits so that Richard was again moved to fresh hope that it was, after all, no more than a temporary malady.

The arrival of Margaret's gift had worked wonders and Anne's health had noticeably improved – suggesting to those who loved, watched and prayed for her recovery, that it was perhaps a malady more of the spirit than the body. It was as if, thought Richard, Margaret and her ladies, in bringing to life those depicted in the tapestry, whether long-dead or newly-mourned, had brought new life to Anne also.

One afternoon, being in low spirits, Richard having departed that morning for Winchester, Anne stood gazing at the tapestry – until her legs started trembling uncontrollably. Fearing they would give way under her, without removing her gaze, she sank down on to a strategically placed bench-seat. For a long time she remained thus, giving the tapestry all her attention, trying to lose herself, and her anguish, in the needlework picture before her.

It seems so long ago, she said to herself – so very long ago. And yet, as I look at the various scenes depicted, the years roll away and I am there, as I was then, a living part of the scene.

*The Duke of York's family*, Margaret has called it. She herself is there, with a massive piece of canvas draped all around her – I do believe she was starting to stitch this very tapestry! She has seated herself in the background – that too is symbolic, for dear kind Margaret who loved and was loved by us all, was soon after parted from us.

Edward, not then king, seemed old to me at the time. Methinks I was ever a mite afraid of Edward – of his rumbustious high spirits, his guffaws of laughter. He seemed always a little larger than life – and that explains why perchance, alone of the figures in the picture, the tapestry does not do him justice: it somehow fails to catch his likeness, as if his will was too strong to be contained in a few stitches ...

Let me see now: I must have been then in my tenth summer. Margaret, like Edward, seemed to Isabel and me to be quite grown up. The scene here is reminiscent of those Sunday afternoons we spent with our distant cousins at Warwick or Fotheringhay, in the great hall or the gardens, according to the weather ...

Even as she watched, the picture came alive, transporting her back through the years to when she had been a living part of it. Only Edward, dear Edward to whom I was first wed and whom I loved best in all the world, is missing from this scene of childhood, she thought. And yet somehow he is there – did Margaret, dear perceptive Margaret, intend it so? Elusive as a shadow, he is there in the guise of Edward my son – and even fleetingly in the face of Ned!

Sounds floated back from the past, epitomising the lively scene:

'I shall never marry!' twelve-year-old Richard was declaring. 'I shall be a soldier.'

'Soldiers marry,' pointed out Isabel. 'My father is a soldier and he is married – as was your father also!'

'But I shall be a *real* soldier,' Richard said carelessly.

'You are suggesting that our lord father was not?' demanded Edward, at twenty-two the eldest, overhearing the remark. 'Shame on you, brother!'

'But father was a duke –' demurred Richard, as if it were somehow relevant, '– as well as the king's lieutenant in France and Ireland!'

Edward chuckled. 'Ireland, you say? A convenient place for banishment is Ireland! Still, if you desire to be a soldier, little brother, and not wed – that is your affair!'

'I scarcely remember our father,' Richard said ruefully, as if to himself. 'It is all of four years since he was slain – and rarely was he at home.'

'I learnt a new song today,' put in fifteen-year-old George of Clarence, speaking for the first time.

'Then pray sing it to us,' said Isabel in her most winning

manner – already, it seemed to Anne, she was in love with Clarence. 'Please George – just for me!'

Pretending not to hear, Clarence ignored her. He turned to Edward.

'I overheard one of the stable-lads singing it,' he told his brother. 'And I struck him with my riding-crop for his pains – but not till I had heard it all!'

'Naughty George!' Isabel said coquettishly. 'Naughty George – and poor stable-lad!'

Still Clarence ignored her. 'It had to do with father,' he told Edward.

'Then will we hear it, brother –' said Edward cheerily. '– unless it be unfitting for female ears!'

George struck a pose, bowed exaggeratedly to the company and sang in an unusually good voice:

'O the grand old Duke of York
He had ten thousand men,
He marched them up to the top of the hill
And he marched them down again.
When they were up, they were up
And when they were down, they were down,
And when they were only half-way up,
They were neither up nor down!'

'A nonsense song, no more!' remarked Edward airily as he finished – making for the door, Anne thought, as if he feared a repetition! 'That way the troops would have been dropping with fatigue ere battle commenced!'

In fact, the ditty had become popular with them after that – and was amongst Anne's earliest memories. Sung rumbustiously by the three Yorkist brothers, it had many a time echoed and re-echoed through the halls of Fotheringhay Castle.

# *Fifty-Two*

The next thing that caused a stir at court was the arrival of Richard's niece, Elizabeth of York.

Elizabeth Woodville, the princess's mother, had been informed while still in sanctuary at Westminster of the fate of her sons the princes. The former queen's health and spirits had declined rapidly. In the space of a few months she had suffered the loss of her husband and, by beheading, of her brother Earl Rivers and her younger son by her first marriage, Lord Richard Grey. Faced then with the murder of her 'sweet babes' as she called them, she had come close to madness.

Cast down by anguish and despair, she had called on God to avenge her. She and her daughters would remain in sanctuary, she declared – for ever, if need be. Following Buckingham's insurrection and execution, the possibility of an alliance between her eldest daughter and Henry Tudor seemed remote in the extreme: she could look for no help from that quarter, she told herself. Her daughters must be never out of her sight – they would be taken from sanctuary only over her dead body ...

Richard had feared that his nieces would be secreted from the sanctuary and conveyed away by sea. Unwilling to follow his elder brother's example by violating sanctuary, he had resolved to place a guard round the abbey and thus cut off supplies. His method would take longer but Richard, as always, could wait ...

Refusing all entreaties and demands that they leave their retreat, Elizabeth Woodville and her daughters had found themselves in dire straits as the months passed and they were denied all contact with the outside world. The building was enclosed like a camp and guarded at all times by soldiers under one Nuffield, none being permitted to go in or out without a special warranty.

The situation had remained thus until the spring of the following year. Some six months had elapsed since the last sighting of the princes and their grieving mother seemed of a sudden to come to her senses. She looked around her, as if with fresh eyes, observing the frailty of her daughters and recognizing then that, if the situation continued, she would eventually lose them also. Pale and emaciated through insufficient food and fresh air, fearful of what their fate would be, they had seemed to be looking at their mother accusingly.

'Our Lord will yet avenge me!' she had said brokenly. 'I can do no more. But I doubt not He will remember it!'

'Then we are to leave sanctuary, mama?' had enquired Anne, her second daughter, her eyes bright with hope. 'Is that what you are saying?'

'All in good time, child – all in good time,' Elizabeth Woodville had told her distractedly, averting her face from the eager gaze of five pairs of eyes. 'First I shall require a solemn oath from my lord Richard guaranteeing the safety of my children – my remaining children!'

Elizabeth had looked troubled. 'But, mama, how could you be certain ...?'

Her mother had not been listening. Deep in thought, she was making her plans. She would take no chances. She would deliberate, move step by step. Perhaps all was not lost ...

At the end of March, having exacted a solemn oath from Richard in the presence of the lord mayor of London, aldermen and lords of the council, Elizabeth Woodville and her little family had finally returned to the world.

The terms of her surrender had been a bitter pill to swallow. On hearing them, she had told herself – and would go on telling herself till the day of her death – that but for her daughters, for those young innocent faces that gazed at her in mute appeal, she would have remained in sanctuary till the end of her life.

She and her daughters were reduced to the rank of gentlewomen and given humble apartments in the outer reaches of the palace of Westminster. Parliament had

allotted her an annuity of seven hundred marks for her
subsistence but, as a means of keeping her under personal
restraint, this was paid not to her, but to John Nesfield,
squire of the body to Richard. Furthermore – and this
perhaps was the most bitter pill of all – her marriage to
King Edward having been declared null and void, she was
required to revert to her former husband's name and must
be addressed as Dame Elizabeth Grey, with the
qualification 'late *calling herself* queen of England'
appended to any official document.

When, a few weeks after she emerged from sanctuary,
the former queen had learned of the sudden death of
Richard's only son, she had nodded.

'God has avenged my innocent babes!' she had said
softly, without surprise. 'In His own good time, He has
avenged them.'

Towards the end of that same year, not for the first
time, her daughters had been invited to attend Queen
Anne at court. She had declined such invitations
previously but this time, recognizing that she was doing
her daughters no service by keeping them shut away in an
obscure corner of the palace, she had reconsidered.

The Marquis of Dorset, her elder son by her first
marriage, was in Paris, renegotiating the final stages of a
secret treaty of marriage between the Lancastrian heir,
Henry Tudor, and her eldest daughter. She, Elizabeth
Woodville, must look to the future. She had nothing to
lose and everything to gain by encouraging Elizabeth to
ingratiate herself with her uncle Richard and his lady, to
keep her ear to the ground and use every means to lull the
former into a false sense of security.

Elizabeth is personable, she had said to herself, a damsel
of gentleness and grace. Some day, by one means or
another, she will be queen of this realm. I feel it in my
bones. Her attendance at court now would be but a
beginning ...

As a gesture of amity, it was said at court, Dame
Elizabeth Grey had sent her daughter Elizabeth, together
with her other daughters, Anne, Cecily and Katherine, to
attend Queen Anne during the Christmas festivities.

The former princesses were received very graciously by

Anne. Elizabeth, then eighteen, was only twelve years younger than Anne herself; and as the granddaughter of Anne's great-aunt, Cecily Neville, was distantly related to her. She and Anne soon became the best of friends – Anne, the court noticed, treating her like a sister.

It was with some surprise that, a few weeks after the Twelfth Night celebrations, Anne one morning discovered Elizabeth in tears. An amiable young woman with a sunny disposition, she had seemed to Anne rather unemotional.

'Whatever is the matter?' she asked in concern. 'Elizabeth, my dear, what ails you?'

'Naught – it is naught but foolishness!' Elizabeth wept. 'You have shown me much kindness – I cannot tell you! Pray do not command it.'

'But I do command it,' Anne told her. 'It is unlike you to give way to tears – so tell me, pray, what troubles you.'

'I overheard them talking, you see …'

'To whom do you refer?'

'Some courtiers … I believe they saw me and, in truth, intended that I should hear.'

'More than likely,' agreed Anne calmly, well accustomed to such ploys. 'Those who dwell in courts, alas, must accustom themselves to such irritations!'

'It was something more than an irritation, my lady – so appalled am I by what I heard that I cannot bring myself to speak of it – and least of all to Your Grace.'

'Tell me – I command it.'

'They said … they said –' Elizabeth composed herself and started again. 'Should some ill befall the queen and cause her demise, they said, the king my uncle would make me his bride!'

The shock this gave Anne was well concealed. Will I never become accustomed to the cruelties – to the lies and calumniations! she wondered. I must conceal my distress from Elizabeth.

'Oh, is that all?' she managed to say carelessly. 'Each new day, it seems, brings some fresh rumour or scandal!'

'Then there is no truth in it?' There was no mistaking Elizabeth's relief and, without waiting for an answer, she continued, 'God be praised! I was greatly afeared for you, my lady – and for myself!'

'For yourself?' asked Anne quietly.

Elizabeth looked apologetic. 'It is not that I do not honour the king – but to wed one's uncle would be a sin, a dreadful sin. And besides, though I respect his sovereignty and render obedience to him, as mama commanded me – it was he, they say, who ...'

She fell silent. Anne knew only too well what she had been about to say – and that she had forgotten in her anxiety to whom she was speaking.

'I know what is said,' she acknowledged coolly. 'My lord is accused of much – falsely for the most part!'

'Then you believe it was not Richard of Gloucester who ...'

'The king your father had every confidence in his younger brother,' interposed Anne – evading the unasked question. 'Was not he perchance better able to judge him than you or I?'

Elizabeth gave thought to that. 'Yea, that is so, my lady – papa trusted Uncle Richard above most men. Yet even as we speak, I am reminded of papa's firm belief in astrology – and that what he once told me touches both of those things of which we speak.'

'I would hear it,' said Anne.

'One day here in the palace of Westminster, surrounded by his nobles, papa was studying a book of magic,' Elizabeth told her. 'Of a sudden he became agitated, unlike himself, and was close to tears. The company was amazed but none durst ask him what troubled him, save I – being only a little child then and accustomed to basking in papa's smiles! I went and knelt before him for his blessing and he looked up and saw me – and at once threw his arms around me and carried me off to a high window-seat. When he had set me down, he gave me the horoscope he had drawn and bade me hide it away, letting none see it. "Why papa?" I asked for, at four years of age, it was naught but a pretty pattern to me. Again his eyes were over-bright as he answered me. "It plainly indicates that no son of mine will wear the crown after me. But you, queen of my heart, shall one day be queen and the crown will rest in your descendants!'

'That could well come to pass,' Anne told her quietly,

trying to ignore the anguish the prediction had caused her in respect of Richard and her dead son – England's heir. 'It could well be – none knows what the future holds. My lord has no heir apparent, alas – Ned of Warwick has, as you know, been proclaimed heir presumptive.'

'But you may yet be blessed with another child, my lady.' Elizabeth was appalled by her own tactlessness. 'I shall pray that you be so blessed – I shall pray every night!'

'Dear Elizabeth!' said Anne with a smile. 'Pray all you will – but pray hardest for yourself, that you may one day marry a man you love and give him many strong sons!'

\* \* \*

Anne's health declined further in the weeks that followed. Her time was short. She knew it and Richard knew it – but each went out of their way to hide the knowledge from the other.

Frail and emaciated, having an air of ethereality that belied her thirty-one years, it seemed to Richard that she was simply fading away. Her eyes were dark-rimmed and over-bright and she coughed frequently – yet still her hair, golden and abundant, lovingly dressed each day by Jacquetta's gentle hands, was her crowning glory.

She rose from her bed for a few hours each afternoon when, if in residence, Richard unfailingly went to see her. In his absence, she sat on a couch in her solar, a fur rug tucked around her, contemplating the tapestry. It somehow induced in her a sense of peace, of acceptance ...

Each time she looked at the tapestry now, the figures seemed to come to life. The echoes of childhood, of innocence and happy days, reached her insidiously, inexplicably, drawing her back so that for a short space, the past became the present – and the present a dream of the future, an unreality, a distant shore yet to be reached ...

Memories abounded: her father, Calais, Warwick Court, Barnet ... Edward – that gallant springing young Plantagenet – Paris, Amboise, Tewkesbury ... Margaret of Anjou, the Angevin princess who had married a king of England and ruined her life ... Edward – so like the other

Edward – who, nine years of age, had worn his crown and his jewels and made the people laugh, and had taken pity on a donkey ...

But with the last, the echoes of a sudden became louder, closer ... Too near the present they were, impinging on the dream of the future, on unreality, bringing too close too quickly the distant shore ...

\* \* \*

Enigmatical as ever, Richard by his very calmness soothed Anne's troubled spirit – and she looked forward to his visits to an extent she could not formerly have envisaged. He reminisced, speaking of past joys and happenings, of small pleasures they had shared – and, above all, of the lost child whose birth had first united them, and whose death had created an indissoluble bond between them.

Once only during these visits did Richard assure her she would get better; that it was merely a passing malady – though the physicians had told him otherwise. She had shaken her head.

'Nay, Richard – let there be no pretence between us,' she had said with tears in her eyes. 'Always we have been honest with each other – indeed I alone methinks of all the world know the truth of that which will baffle and divide men, long after we both are dead!'

As Anne grew weaker and rose from her bed less often, Richard gave thought to how, during his absences, he could ensure that she was properly cared for and protected.

Duty summoning him frequently from Westminster, aware that royalty had sometimes been badly served *in extremis*, he sought for a means of safeguarding Anne. He recalled how as a child he had wept secretly after hearing that his great ancestor, Edward the Third, had been deserted by all save a solitary priest as he lay dying – even the gold ring of sovereignty being torn from his finger.

Anne had no close relatives, the countess her mother having died the previous year; and his Woodville nieces constituted, in Richard's private opinion, a threat more than a blessing. He suspected that Elizabeth Woodville was behind the disturbing rumours that had so bedevilled the court in recent months and, but for Anne's pleas that they remain, he would have had his nieces leave.

He gave thought to Jacquetta whose commonsense and lively chatter had done much to cheer Anne during the darkest days. Of humble origin, she had held a much-coveted post throughout the twelve years of their marriage. Jacquetta was unchanged – loyal and practical, she could be trusted implicitly.

He sent for her.

Summoned to the king's privy chamber and interviewed by him with only Francis Lovel, his chamberlain, present, Jacquetta was shaking like a leaf. What have I done? she asked herself. Am I to be reprimanded – accused of some trumped-up misdemeanour?

Richard's first words did little to reassure her.

'I am much abroad about the countryside,' he said. 'I would ensure therefore that, in my absence, should the queen's health worsen, as God forbid, none will neglect their duty.'

'Speaking for myself, Your Grace –' Jacquetta said, a trifle on her mettle despite her trembling limbs '– none will neglect their duty if I know aught about it!'

'Should Her Grace suffer loss of speech, or become otherwise totally dependent on her servants, might I rely on yourself in my absence?'

'Of course you could, sir,' replied Jacquetta with un-courtlike emphasis. 'I'd stay by her side day and night – I'd see she came to no harm, I promise you!'

'Good. That is agreed then.' Richard's manner was practical, his eyes cold – giving no clue to the anguish within him. 'Henceforth you will be in charge in my lady's chamber – physicians, nurses, ladies-in-waiting, taking their instructions from yourself.'

'I dunno about that, sir.'

'What mean you?'

'Well, the physicians, ladies-in-waiting and all that – they'd not like it so! Not one little bit.'

'But I should like it, I doubt not that the queen would like it – and I dare say you yourself would not mind it too much!'

Jacquetta nodded. 'I'd be honoured, sir. She's a lovely lady – but, of course, you knows that! She's gentle and kind and – well, you see, sir, I likes to try and make her smile.'

'I shall issue the necessary instructions to my chamberlain here,' Richard told her. 'You will, in due course, be well rewarded.'

'Rewarded be bugg – blowed, sir! You go off, Your Grace, and do what you have to – and I'll take care of my lady. By my troth, the Mother of God herself would not be cared for better!'

Richard dismissed her and she gave a bob curtsy and bustled cheerfully from the privy chamber.

Richard stared at the door after she had gone, hearing her rapid footsteps receding down the corridor. His sight was of a sudden blurred ...

# Fifty-Three

Anne died at Westminster Palace on the sixteenth day of March in the year 1485.

She had rallied a little that morning – the result, it was believed, of the prayers that were being offered throughout the land for her recovery. Whatever the controversies that raged around her lord, Anne was much loved by his subjects. Most still remembered the Earl of Warwick, her father, with affection – the true King of England, many had dubbed him. They had honoured his daughter whensoever she had ridden abroad and had offered prayers, genuine prayers, as she had lain dying.

Soon after midday she had said she would get up for a while and sit in front of the tapestry. This had seemed to please her, for she had smiled and spoken softly to Jacquetta.

'How beautiful he is!' she said. 'He was not there the other day.'

Jacquetta looked at the tapestry. It looked the same to her.

'Who do you mean, my lady?' she asked curiously.

'Why, Edward – who else?' came the reply. 'He is waiting for me, you see. Alas, he has waited so long – fourteen years it is! Now he is smiling and beckoning to me.'

'But the prince your son was but ...' Jacquetta started to say, but then she realized. Her first husband, she thought – the other Edward Prince of Wales. But he's not there – I know he's not there, for Lady Annie and me have looked at the tapestry together many a time. She's told me of everyone there and how they were when they was children. But her first husband's not there ...

'Are you warm enough, my lady?' she asked cheerfully.

'Shall I send for them to replenish the fire – and bring you another wrap?'

Anne made no reply, but continued to gaze at the tapestry.

'My lady?' Jacquetta smiled. 'You'll wear that bit out if you keep staring at it like that – and then what would Her Grace of Burgundy say! She'd think we 'ad moths at Westminster – *and* she'd be right, of course ...'

She looked more closely at Anne. Had her mistress fallen asleep? But nay, her eyes were still open. She clasped her wrist in a soft practical hand – her pulse is still beating, she thought, but 'tis weak as water! I'd best get her back to bed quick sharp!

She rang the bell and summoned assistance and, under Jacquetta's direction, they got Anne into bed with a minimum of fuss. Still Anne's eyes were open, staring fixedly ahead – but she was still breathing and now and then she moistened her lips with the tip of her tongue. Jacquetta put salve on her mistress's lips and spoke briskly to one of the ladies-in-waiting.

'Best send for the king,' she said. 'God be thanked he's not gone off on his travels today – he was going but decided to put off his departure till the morrow, good for 'im! And summon the physician and a priest while you're about it – best be safe than sorry!'

\*   \*   \*

Thus, an hour later, Richard found himself kneeling at the bedside of his beloved queen. The physician had arrived and had pronounced his patient close to death.

'I doubt she will speak again, my lord,' he said sombrely. 'She is lost to the world already methinks.'

'Then leave us, sir,' said Richard by way of dismissal.

Priests had administered the last rites and were kneeling at prayer now in the shadows beyond the bed – and Jacquetta too, there in case she was needed, was trying to make herself invisible.

Richard said nothing further. He held one of Anne's hands – she knew he was there, he told himself, and that was what mattered. What was there to say? She knew he loved her, would mourn her and their son till the day of his own death – and he had never truly been one for words.

She stirred a little and he leaned forward and kissed her hand. She sighed then – a deep sigh and then seemed to have difficulty in drawing breath.

'Edward ...' she murmured.

'Our son,' he said as if to himself. 'She speaks of our son.'

But Jacquetta, on her knees praying silently in the shadows, knew differently.

Anne spoke no more. She gave another sigh, a small sigh – no more than the brush of an angel's wing – and was gone.

Richard offered a prayer for her soul and tenderly kissed her forehead. Then with a long slender hand denuded now of all but the one ring, he gently closed her eyes.

Bereft now of his lady as well as his son, those for whom he had cared more than for anything else in the world, he was to all intents and purposes alone ...

He straightened up and, after another long look at Anne, turned and with bowed head went quietly from the chamber.

Bosworth Field was five months away.

Richard himself had one hundred and fifty-nine days still to live.

# Author's Note

Richard the Third later named John de la Pole, Earl of Lincoln, as his heir in preference to Edward Earl of Warwick (Ned). He was mindful perhaps of the disasters and unrest which had invariably followed the accession of a boy king. Lincoln, similarly his nephew, being the eldest son of his sister Elizabeth, was already of age.

What became of Ned? Seized at Sheriff Hutton by order of Henry Tudor immediately after the Battle of Bosworth, the ten-year-old was imprisoned in the Tower of London for the rest of his life. He helped the so-called Perkin Warbeck to plan their escape, convinced perhaps that he was as he claimed his long-lost cousin Richard Duke of York – the younger of the princes believed murdered in the Tower. On the ludicrous pretext that he had conspired against Henry the Seventh, Ned was beheaded in his twenty-fourth year.

# Bibliography

*Battles in Britain*, vol. I: William Seymour
*Dictionary of National Biography*
*English Costume:* Doreen Yarwood
*English Social History:* G.M. Trevelyan
*History and Antiquities of the Castle and Town of Arundel:* M.A.
   Tierney
*Kings and Queens of Britain:* David Williamson
*Lives of the Queens of England*, vol. II: Agnes Strickland
*New, Complete and Authentic History of England:* Compiled
   (circa 1790) by Alexander Hogg
*Oxford History of England; The Fifteenth Century:* E.F. Jacob